T0042899

"This is a timely book for our times as we gra[...] race and justice, while at the same time we are shepherded more deeply into the heart of God. Expect to broaden your understanding and feel a deeper longing when you read this wonderful book."

James Bryan Smith, author of *The Good and Beautiful You*

"*Feathers of Hope* shows how forgiveness and daily spiritual practices anchor souls, taking us into the emotional and spiritual life where both pain and beauty exist. If you are looking for a realistic view of how anxiety and depression are part of the human experience, this is the book you want to read."

Diana Shiflett, author of *Spiritual Practices in Community*

"In her signature gentle style, Brown invites us once again into the lives of Kit and Wren. This is a story I sorely needed, and I suspect I'm not the only one. What a timely, powerful, revealing novel!"

Susie Finkbeiner, author of *The Nature of Small Birds*

"In *Feathers of Hope*, Brown has given us a story that can serve as mirror in which we see ourselves and others with more kindness and insight. I'm confident you'll find words of grace and truth as you read."

Alan Fadling, founder and president of Unhurried Living

"What a gift and a journey to dive into the lives of Katherine, Wren, and others. Meeting them again feels like a sweet reunion with a soul-expanding conversation. Prepare to be encouraged, stretched, and held in the hand of our loving God."

Amy Boucher Pye, author of *7 Ways to Pray*

"*Feathers of Hope* is a beautifully honest work. In Brown's fearless naming of these truths, we are reminded that we are not alone in our suffering. Returning to her characters and their healing journeys was like spending a rainy afternoon by the fire with a warm mug of tea and that one friend who truly gets you."

Autumn Lytle, author of *All That Fills Us*

"One of the things I love most about Brown's writing and her beautifully and transparently written cast of characters, is that I'm actually learning and changing as I read a gripping story. *Feathers of Hope*, like all her work, is edifying and entertaining. Brown has found the perfect balance of these elements in her spiritual fiction."

Karen Stiller, author of *The Minister's Wife*

"Because people of all ages have experienced suffering, loss, fear, and transition recently, I am grateful for *Feathers of Hope*. I found great beauty in this book's authenticity—the people, struggles, hard conversations, and faith. Brown's exquisite and tender writing may evoke tears, especially in realizing how much a faithful, quiet, and often hidden life of service can be used by God to change others forever."

Lucinda Secrest McDowell, author of *Soul Strong* and *Life-Giving Choices*

"*Feathers of Hope* tells a story of shedding the old to bring forth the new, giving hope to all of us who are confronted with our deep humanity and sinfulness after days or decades of our own sacred journey. A poignant, deeply personal, and relevant story for such a time as this."

Elizabeth Musser, author of *The Swan House* and *The Dwelling Place*

"Through the power of story Brown gently ushers us into deeper conversations about faith, pain, grief, and hope. We see ourselves in these characters and in this story, and that allows us to find ourselves in the bigger story and draw near to the Writer himself. *Feathers of Hope* is another gift to all who seek an honest relationship with others and with God."

Mary S. Hulst, University Pastor at Calvin University

"Sharon Garlough Brown does an exceptional job, once again, by portraying a cast of familiar characters as they navigate their very human lives and learn how to walk with God through them. Treat yourself to a strong dose of real hope by reading *Feathers of Hope!*"

Beth A. Booram, cofounder and director of Fall Creek Abbey

"As I walked with Kit and Wren in their own healing journeys, I was reminded to look for hope budding in its earliest and unlikeliest of forms. These 'companions in sorrow' once again left me encouraged to be a better companion myself and to consider how I might more faithfully steward my affliction for the sake of God's people."

Diana Gruver, author of *Companions in the Darkness*

"As with all Brown's novels, *Feathers of Hope* carries much-needed encouragement: while redemption is a long road, it does not have to be a lonely one when we travel close to God and each other."

Debra Rienstra, professor of English, Calvin University, author, *Refugia Faith*

SHARON GARLOUGH BROWN

Feathers of Hope

A Novel

ivp

An imprint of InterVarsity Press
Downers Grove, Illinois

InterVarsity Press
P.O. Box 1400, Downers Grove, IL 60515-1426
ivpress.com
email@ivpress.com

©2022 by Sharon Garlough Brown

All rights reserved. No part of this book may be reproduced in any form without written permission from InterVarsity Press.

InterVarsity Press® is the book-publishing division of InterVarsity Christian Fellowship/USA®, a movement of students and faculty active on campus at hundreds of universities, colleges, and schools of nursing in the United States of America, and a member movement of the International Fellowship of Evangelical Students. For information about local and regional activities, visit intervarsity.org.

Scripture quotations, unless otherwise noted, are from the New Revised Standard Version Bible, copyright © 1989 National Council of the Churches of Christ in the United States of America. Used by permission. All rights reserved worldwide.

This is a work of fiction. People, places, events, and situations are either the product of the author's imagination or are used fictitiously. Any resemblance to events, locales, or actual persons, living or dead, is entirely coincidental.

The publisher cannot verify the accuracy or functionality of website URLs used in this book beyond the date of publication.

Cover design and image composite: David Fassett
Interior design: Daniel van Loon
Images: abstract floral background: © andipantz / iStock / Getty Images Plus
        textured gradient cloudscape: © DavidMSchrader / iStock / Getty Images Plus
        sunflower: © Francesco Carta fotografo / Moment / Getty Images
        black ink rolled out: © IntergalacticDesignStudio / E+ / Getty Images
        red cardinal bird: © Jeff R Clow / Moment / Getty Images
        abstract watercolor painting: © philsajonesen / E+ / Getty Images
        designed acrylic background: © Wylius / iStock / Getty Images Plus
        light blue painted texture: ©andipantz / iStock / Getty Images Plus

ISBN 978-1-5140-0062-5 (print)
ISBN 978-1-5140-0063-2 (digital)

Printed in the United States of America ∞

InterVarsity Press is committed to ecological stewardship and to the conservation of natural resources in all our operations. This book was printed using sustainably sourced paper.

Library of Congress Cataloging-in-Publication Data
Names: Brown, Sharon Garlough, author.
Title: Feathers of hope : a novel / Sharon Garlough Brown.
Description: Downers Grove, IL : InterVarsity Press, [2022] | Series:
    Shades of light series
Identifiers: LCCN 2021058499 (print) | LCCN 2021058500 (ebook) | ISBN
    9781514000625 (paperback) | ISBN 9781514000632 (ebook)
Subjects: LCGFT: Christian fiction.
Classification: LCC PS3602.R722867 F43 2022 (print) | LCC PS3602.R722867
    (ebook) | DDC 813/.6—dc23/eng/20211221
LC record available at https://lccn.loc.gov/2021058499
LC ebook record available at https://lccn.loc.gov/2021058500

P 25 24 23 22 21 20 19 18 17 16 15 14 13 12 11 10 9 8 7 6 5 4 3 2
Y 42 41 40 39 38 37 36 35 34 33 32 31 30 29 28 27 26 25 24 23 22

For—and with—my beloved son,
who generously poured out his wisdom, insights,
and creativity on every page of this book.
David, you inspire me with your courage,
kindness, and gentleness. I am so honored
and proud to be your mom.

The LORD bless you and keep you;
the LORD make his face to shine upon you, and be gracious to you;
the LORD lift up his countenance upon you, and give you peace.
NUMBERS 6:24-26

CONTENTS

Part One

THINGS UNSEEN

*Therefore we do not lose heart. Though outwardly we are
wasting away, yet inwardly we are being renewed day by day.
For our light and momentary troubles are achieving for us an
eternal glory that far outweighs them all. So we fix our eyes not
on what is seen, but on what is unseen, since what is seen is
temporary, but what is unseen is eternal.*

2 CORINTHIANS 4:16-18, NIV

1

When the cardinal landed at their bird feeder early that morning, its eyes bulging, its head stripped of red crest feathers, leaving it black and bald, Wren Crawford was sure the poor creature was either sick or wounded. She set her second cup of coffee on the kitchen table and watched him through the glass slider. If he didn't drop dead on the patio now, she would likely find him in the yard later. She hoped she would find him before the neighbor's cat did.

She checked the cupboard beneath the sink for spare gloves. She would get a garden trowel, too, in case she needed to carry him to the woods for a burial.

Just as she was picturing the scene, her great-aunt, Katherine Rhodes, sidled up beside her, wrapped in her terrycloth robe and holding a striped journal. She followed Wren's gaze to the yard. "Molting season," Kit said. "That guy lost all his feathers at once."

Wren felt her shoulders relax. "So, he's not sick?"

"No, he's fine. Just not too handsome right now." Kit's gentle smile indicated she not only perceived where Wren's racing thoughts had landed but understood how they'd arrived there. "Most birds molt gradually," she said, "but every once in a while, you see one that's experienced a more sudden, dramatic shedding of the old."

After living under Kit's roof for nine months, Wren had grown accustomed to her speaking in metaphor. But instead of offering any further insights, Kit patted her arm and said, "He'd make an interesting painting, don't you think?"

Yes. Someday. When she had energy for creative work again. She grabbed her phone off the kitchen table and snapped a photo before the bird flew away.

Vincent would have painted him, she thought later that morning as she loaded her housekeeping cart with supplies from the nursing home storage room. The man who had painted peasant workers and starry nights, sunflowers and kingfishers, would have painted that molting bird with such tenderness, it would have made her weep.

Because he knew how molting felt.

She pushed her cart down the first of three resident hallways she was responsible for cleaning, noting the shadow boxes along the way. Fastened on the wall outside each door were miniature museums filled with curated items to remind staff and visitors of the lives the residents had enjoyed before the loss of occupations, hobbies, health, or loved ones.

As she dusted Mr. Kennedy's box, with its slightly stained Titleist golf ball, a packet of heirloom tomato seeds, and a photo of him as a robust young man in a military uniform, she prayed for him. Molting was a good metaphor, not just for herself but also for the people she served. And not just for the residents but also for the people who loved them. The spouses. The children. The grand-children. The friends. They were all shedding in different ways. Some more dramatically than others.

"Good morning, Mr. Kennedy," Wren said as she placed her hands beneath the sanitizer dispenser on the wall.

He was seated in a faded armchair beside the bed, his thin hair not yet combed, a white towel tucked like a bib into his gray-checkered pajama top. At the sound of her voice, he glanced up from his breakfast tray, where he was trying unsuccessfully to spear a sausage with his fork. The tremor was bad this morning.

Leaning her head back, she scanned the hallway. No nurses or aides in sight. "How about if I help you with that?" She walked over to the tray table and guided the fork to his mouth. He took the bite and chewed slowly. "Is it good?"

He swallowed, then opened his mouth like a little bird. Gently, she loosened his grip on the fork, loaded it with another bite, and held it to his lips. He took it, chewed, and swallowed. Then he sputtered with a cough.

"Are you okay?"

He coughed again.

She reached for the plastic two-handled sippy cup on his tray. "This looks like apple juice. Is that all right? Or would you like me to get you some water?"

With a thin, weary rasp, he replied, "Juice is okay."

She guided his fingers to each handle. "Got it?"

"Yep." His tremor caused the juice to splatter onto his face as he maneuvered the spout to his lips. She waited for him to finish drinking, then helped him set the cup on the tray. Just as she was about to dab his chin and cheeks with a napkin, one of the nurses entered, carrying a small container of applesauce, a glass of water, and a plastic cup with pills. Greta eyed Wren but said nothing. "I've got your morning medications, Pete."

Wren slipped out of her way.

"Whoops," Greta said, "looks like you had a shower." She wiped him off with a corner of his towel bib.

As Wren disinfected her hands again, she surveyed the small memento collection in the room: a golfing statue engraved with his name, a picture of Mr. Kennedy beaming beside his wife on a sailboat, and a few framed photos of his son and grandchildren, who lived in California. Mr. Kennedy said they came to visit sometimes, but he also said his wife came to visit sometimes, and she had died seven years ago.

Greta spooned out a bit of applesauce and placed a pill on top. "Okay, first one, Pete. Open the chute. A little wider. Got it? Good." She watched him swallow. "You need water to wash it down?" When he did not reply, she put a hand to her hip. "Is that a 'no, thank you' or a 'yes, please'?"

He swallowed again and said, "No, thank you."

She loaded up another pill. "Okay, next one coming. You know the drill. Good job. One more, okay? Almost done."

When Mr. Kennedy spluttered and coughed, Greta handed him a cup. "You're scheduled for a bath today. We'll get you smelling nice and fresh."

He murmured something Wren couldn't hear.

"You need help getting to the bathroom?" Greta asked.

"I'm okay," he said.

"Don't wait until I leave and then ring your call button. I'm here now. You sure you don't need to go?"

"I'm sure."

"Okay. Chelsea will be here soon to help bathe you and get you dressed." She turned toward Wren. "You might want to wait to clean until they're finished."

"All right," Wren said. After Greta left, she approached his chair. "Do you want me to turn on the Golf Channel for you, Mr. Kennedy? It's Thursday. I bet there's a tournament somewhere."

He nodded. Wren picked up the remote control from his tray and turned on the television, which was already set to the right channel.

"You want to watch with me?" he asked, his voice not much louder than a whisper.

"I'd love to, but I've got more cleaning to do. Would it be okay if I join you after I'm done?"

He cleared his throat and paused, as if uncertain whether he could project loudly enough to be heard again. "Sure thing."

Wren smiled at him. Sometimes speaking even two syllables was heroic. "I'll be back after your bath to clean, okay?"

"Okay."

She set the remote control down again, close enough for him to reach it. "Is there anything else you need right now?"

He stared at her. "My wallet."

Wren tucked a strand of her dark hair behind her ear. She'd had this conversation with him many times. "Your wallet's in a safe place. You don't need it today."

"You need a tip for cleaning my room."

She patted his shoulder. "It's okay, Mr. Kennedy. Everything's already been taken care of."

"I already paid you?"

"Yes." That was the simplest answer. "Would you like to keep working on your breakfast?"

"Sure." In the three months she had known him, she had never once heard him complain about his sausages or eggs getting cold.

"Okay, I'll see you later." From the doorway, she silently cheered him on as he tried to load his fork. He had probably once been as fiercely determined to sink a long putt. She straightened a few bottles on her cart and waited until he had successfully conveyed his food to his mouth before she proceeded to her next room, celebrating one inconspicuous, monumental victory.

"Wren, can you come help me with this?"

She looked up from the carpet, where she was kneeling to pick up staples that had fallen off a bulletin board the activities director was redesigning. Having removed the Uncle Sam, Liberty Bell, and fire-works pictures, Peyton, who was a few years younger than Wren and working her first job out of college, was now decorating for a tropical beach party.

Wren joined her at a table covered with cutouts of pineapples, palm trees, and surfboards.

"Hold these, will you?" Peyton handed her two streamer rolls, then started unrolling and twisting the red and yellow strands together. "I hope we get a good turnout this time," she said. "I scheduled it for a Sunday afternoon, thinking we might get more grandkids that way."

Wren nodded. Only a few kids had shown up for the Fourth of July barbecue. But more families might be in town mid-August. "Have you done this theme before?"

"Yeah, right after I started working here last summer. But most of these guys won't remember. And we've got lots of new people."

Wren flinched. Given how casually she'd said it, Peyton probably wasn't thinking about the reasons for the high turnover. Becoming immune to death or decline seemed to be an occupational hazard at Willow Springs.

Peyton finished winding the streamers, taped off her end, and motioned for Wren to tear off her side. "Thanks," she said as Wren handed it to her. "Want to help with the bulletin board, or are you still cleaning rooms?"

Wren set the rest of the crepe paper on the table. "I'm done with rooms. I've just got to vacuum the hallways." Since it didn't make sense to vacuum before Peyton finished decorating, she reached for the stack of pudgy letters. "What do you want it to say?"

"I sketched the whole thing there." She gestured to a sheet of paper.

While Wren pinned letters for "Aloha Friends" and "So Happy to Sea You," Peyton described her plans for themed decor, food, and crafts. Kayla, one of the certified nursing assistants, had grown up in Hawaii and was willing to demonstrate a hula dance. "People will love that," Peyton said. "She can teach all of us some simple moves." Wren wondered how Mr. Kennedy would feel, battling to control his arms and hands.

The elevator doors swished open, and she looked over her shoulder. Mrs. Whitlock's daughter Teri, who rarely missed a day of visiting, removed a visitor badge from the basket, then rolled her shoulders and took a deep breath before she realized she'd been observed. When Wren waved to her, she put on a smile and glanced at the bulletin board. "You girls always make it look so festive in here."

Peyton swished her long blonde ponytail and made a mock curtsy. "Thanks. I try."

Wren faced the board again.

"So sorry to interrupt," Kayla said as she strode into the lounge, "but there's a bit of a mess to clean up in Miss Daisy's bathroom."

"I'll be right there," Wren said, and retrieved her cart from the hall.

2

Katherine Rhodes was revising notes for Saturday's retreat when her cell phone buzzed on her office desk with a text from Wren: *Hi, Kit! Staying late to watch golf with Mr. Kennedy. Go ahead and have dinner without me.*

In that case, Kit thought, she might as well stay late too. She typed, *Sounds good. Enjoy!* Then she leaned back in her chair and stretched. With only a few weeks left in her tenure as the director of Kingsbury's New Hope Retreat Center, plenty of work remained.

Nearly four months had passed since she submitted her resignation letter, and the board had planned to complete their candidate search by the end of July. But she could see August from her window, and they hadn't found her replacement.

Or perhaps they had, and she didn't know it yet. The search process had been far more confidential than she'd expected—which was, she frequently reminded herself, the board's prerogative. Though she had provided them with names of people she considered gifted for the role, the job description the board subsequently developed indicated a desire to move in a different direction.

From her desk she withdrew the file folder labeled "Transition" and pulled out the single-page document she'd printed from the website. Her resignation had freed them to re-envision what they wanted and needed. And what they wanted was someone with strong leadership gifts and an entrepreneurial spirit, a digitally savvy marketer with fundraising experience. They wanted someone who could increase the donor base, oversee a building renovation project, develop an active social media presence, and expand New Hope's outreach in West Michigan and beyond.

She had often seen it happen in ministry, how the search team would pursue someone with gifts that addressed perceived or actual deficits in the predecessor. She tried not to take it personally. In all her years of serving at New Hope, she had never pretended to be anything other than a spiritual director and retreat facilitator.

She considered the threadbare carpet in her office. The building was tired. So was she. Ever since she first discerned the need to let go and say yes to whatever next chapter might unfold, her weariness had deepened and accelerated. Though the board had granted her permission to lead a final Sacred Journey retreat after she retired, she had decided it was best to step away completely. Let the new leader have room to establish a presence and vision distinct from hers.

"Knock knock!" a familiar voice called from the doorway.

"Mara!" she exclaimed. Had she forgotten to write down a spiritual direction appointment? She skimmed her open calendar. Nothing listed for four o'clock. "Come on in. Welcome!" She tucked the job description back into her file folder and pushed herself up from her desk. She would need to quickly shift gears to be prayerfully present.

Mara embraced her with a bear hug, then set her beaded bag on the floor. She wore her usual bright colors—a turquoise tunic with orange bracelets and a matching necklace—and her ivory skin beneath her auburn hair showed a hint of sun along her nose and brow.

Kit was about to collect the Christ candle and a box of matches when Mara said, "Sorry to interrupt, but I was talking with Gayle about the catering details for your party, and when I saw your door was open, I thought I'd come say hi. Hope that's okay."

"Of course!" It was more than okay. A casual conversation would require far less mental and emotional energy than a spiritual direction session. "I was just thinking I'd make myself a cup of tea. Would you like one?"

"Sure! Ginger peach if you've got it."

"I keep some here just for you." From her shelf she retrieved two Vincent van Gogh mugs Wren had given her and dropped a teabag in each. "I'll go boil water and be right back."

"I'll come with you," Mara said. "Let me carry those."

Together, they made their way down the hall to the kitchenette, Mara's bangles clinking against the porcelain. "Guess it's been a few months since I was here." She gestured toward the walls. "I like what you've done with all the art. Is it all Van Gogh stuff?"

"Yes. Wren has done all the curating." The corridor was lined with paintings of sowers and reapers, wheat fields, olive groves, and sunflowers in various stages of bloom and decay. If the new director didn't want to keep the art gallery for prayer, he or she could remove all the prints and have the walls painted.

"What's this one?" Mara pointed with her chin to a sketch of an elderly bald man bent forward in a chair, elbows clamped to his thighs, fingers clenched into fists and fastened to his face.

"*Worn Out*," Kit said. She had meditated frequently on that one. She emptied stale water from the kettle and filled it again.

"Poor guy," Mara said. "Don't you just want to kiss him on the forehead and tell him to hang in there?"

Or pull up a chair next to him, Kit thought, and share the silence.

Mara set the mugs down and leaned against the sink. "Is Wren working here today?"

"No, she's at the nursing home."

"Is she working more hours there now? I haven't talked to her lately."

"No, her hours are the same. But she spends a lot of extra time there, keeping the residents company."

"Good for her," Mara said. "I couldn't do it. Way too sad. Strange that she can, though, with her depression and everything." As soon as she said the words, she grimaced. "Sorry, that came out wrong. What I mean is, I'm surprised it doesn't drag her down, being around sickness and death all the time."

Kit had made the same observation herself, how, rather than being weighed down by the sadness in a place like that, Wren seemed comforted by it. Enlarged by it, even. *Companions in sorrow*, she often said. A whole community of them.

"I'm glad she's doing okay," Mara went on. "But I keep telling her that her gifts are wasted scrubbing toilets and mopping floors. She needs to do art therapy somewhere. Not with battered women and kids like she did before. I get how that was too much for her. But someplace where she can paint and draw with people. If I had money in the budget at Crossroads, I'd hire her in a heartbeat to work with our people. They could use some art to brighten their world."

She sounded like Jamie, who often expressed similar concerns and longings for her daughter. Wren might have an easier time hearing it from Mara, though, than from her mom.

When the water finished boiling, Kit held up the mugs. "*Starry Night* or *Irises?*"

"*Starry Night.*"

She poured Mara's cup first, then handed her a spoon. "I'll let you decide how strong you want it."

"Ah, just leave it in today. The stronger, the better."

"That kind of day, huh?"

"That kind of season," Mara said. "I'll spare you the details until we meet for spiritual direction. For now, I want to talk about your party."

Kit stirred her tea. "I'm afraid that party's getting a bit unwieldy." She squeezed out the bag and tossed it into a trashcan that needed to be emptied. She would have to remind Wren to keep an eye on that sort of thing. The new director might not be as lenient.

"Wren told me you'd be happier retiring without any fuss. Not gonna happen, Katherine. You're being celebrated, like it or not. You spend all these years, helping other people know how much God loves and treasures them, you're not leaving here without us reminding you. Orders from Jesus. You can talk to your own spiritual director about your resistance."

Kit laughed. "I've trained you too well, Mara."

"Ha! At sixty, I'm glad I've learned a few things along the way." She linked her arm with Kit's. "Let's go talk about this shindig, shall we?"

She didn't have any special requests for the menu, Kit said as they chatted in her office, but she hadn't expected the affair to include a full dinner. She had assumed they would have light appetizers and cake.

"We're not just gonna do chips and dip from Costco, Katherine. If you've got a problem with that, talk to your daughter. I'm under direct orders from her too."

"Ah," Kit said, throwing up a hand in mock surrender, "it's done, then. Who am I to argue with Jesus or Sarah?"

Mara grinned. "Now we're trackin'."

Kit took a slow sip of tea. New Hope didn't have money in the budget for a party like this. If Sarah had insisted on a sit-down meal, then she and Zach were likely footing the bill. *Just receive it, Mom,* Sarah would say. And celebrate the love and appreciation the gift conveyed.

Mara scanned the office, her expression wistful. "I can't believe you're retiring. We're gonna miss you around here."

"I'm not going far," Kit said.

"You better not. I'll hunt you down, show up on your doorstep."

"And I'll welcome you in."

Mara pressed her hand to her heart. "You always have. And I'll always be grateful you hunted me down when I was ready to ditch my first retreat." She patted the couch cushion. "I've logged an awful lot of miles here with you since then. And I'm sorry I won't be able to come to your last retreat. I wanted to, but I've been leading Saturday morning training sessions for volunteers, and I can't turn that over to anyone else right now."

"No worries at all," Kit said. "You're doing important kingdom work." She couldn't remember how long Mara had served as one of the directors at the homeless shelter, but the job made perfect use of her passions, gifts, and personal experience of having once been a resident there with her oldest son. Hers was one of many beautiful stories of redemption Kit had been privileged to watch unfold.

She wrapped both hands around her mug.

That part of her work wasn't over, she told herself. She could continue meeting with any directees who still desired her companionship as they traveled deeper into God's love and grace—if the Lord continued to empower her for that work. During the past few months, she had been acutely aware of his strength being perfected in her weakness. Which was its own gift of grace.

"Keep reminding me about the kingdom work part," Mara said, "because I'll tell you what. Maybe I'm getting cranky in my old age, but I just don't have a whole lot of patience these days for people who refuse to grow."

"Sounds like there's a story here," Kit said.

"Have you got a few more minutes?"

"Sure."

Mara set her mug on the coffee table. "God knows I'm not pointing a finger at people who say stupid things. I'm the queen of inserting my foot into my mouth. But when you say something stupid that hurts somebody else and then you get angry and defensive when they tell you it hurt . . . when you double-down and blame them for being overly sensitive instead of being open to the possibility that you're blind or ignorant . . ." She pushed her lips to the side and puffed out a long breath, blowing her bangs back. "I know all about that MO, put up with it for way too long in my marriage. So I guess my radar is ultra tuned in when I hear somebody do that to someone else. And it's been happening a lot at Crossroads lately. I'm tired of it. So I've been calling it out and ticking off some of the volunteers. At this rate, we may not have many people left to help."

"I'm so sorry," Kit said, setting her mug down as well. "Is there a certain theme or issue that's surfacing, or is it short fuses in general?"

Mara rested her sandaled feet against the rim of the table. "Seems like no matter where you turn these days, people are ready to explode—the whole 'I'm right and you're evil' mentality—but I'm talking about attitudes and comments some of the White volunteers have made about some of the Black residents and volunteers. Not just about, but to."

Kit felt her shoulders tighten. She hadn't expected this kind of conversation and didn't feel at all prepared to navigate it well. *Help.*

"All the blatant racism stuff is easy to call out and name," Mara continued. "It's the more subtle forms we've been trying to educate our staff and volunteers about. But when you point out why something they said or did is a problem, you get the whole 'Why are you making everything about race?' reaction. And then that shuts down conversation."

Kit sincerely hoped this wasn't the prelude to something political. She was so tired of the divisiveness and didn't feel like asking her usual reframing questions of "What are God's invitations to you in the midst of this?" and "What does the agitation you're feeling reveal about what you need from God?" Those could wait for a spiritual direction session. For now, she needed the grace to listen well and not react, whatever Mara offered. She opened her hands on her lap. Release. Receive.

Mara leaned forward and scraped at some chipped orange toenail polish before planting her feet on the floor again. "So, here's an example, okay? Last week one of our longtime volunteers—a Christian guy—comes in to help serve lunch. The kids love it whenever he comes. He's like a grandpa to them, plays with them, jokes with them. But I've had to talk to Larry in the past about some of the comments he's made—things like telling some of the Black boys they need to study and work hard so they don't end up in gangs or grow up to be crackheads."

Kit raised her eyebrows.

"Yeah," Mara said. "So last week he comes into the kitchen while a couple of us are in there making sandwiches and getting everything ready, and there's a new volunteer helping out—an older Black woman named Ruth. He's friendly to her, wants to make her feel welcome, part of the family. All good. But after talking to her awhile, he looks at her like she's from a different planet and says, 'Wow! You're really articulate.' Ruth cocks her head, sizes him up and down, and gives him this look as if to say, 'Not worth my time answering that.' Then she goes on chatting to Debra, who's next to her, slicing up carrots, and Larry grabs a cookie and strolls out into the dining room to wait for the kids to arrive. And I'm thinking to myself, I don't want to let this go. This is too important. Because this is exactly what we've been trying to train the volunteers to notice, you know? These comments and attitudes we're not even aware of, things that cause hurt and harm. It's all part of trying to be more like Jesus to one another. That's what we want to do. That's who we're called to be."

Kit nodded her agreement with that declaration and desire.

"So I was standing there near the oven, listening to Ruth and Debra chatting, and I didn't want to interrupt and make Ruth uncomfortable by asking how she was feeling—I figured I'd wait until we could have a private conversation—so I followed Larry out into the dining hall. Nobody else was in there, so I sat down with him at one of the tables and pointed out—as firmly and calmly as I could— that even if he meant for his comment to Ruth to be a compliment, what he'd said to her was an example of a racial stereotype. A micro- aggression, just like we'd talked about before. He exploded. Threw up his hands and told me he was done being accused of being a racist when all he'd ever wanted to do was—and I quote—'help those people make something of their lives.'"

Kit stared at her, unsure how to respond. Not only had she never visited Crossroads, but she had never considered how racial prej- udice might affect the community Mara served. She could own that as ignorance. But the truth was, she had always worked hard not to see or call attention to race, and hearing Mara speak so bluntly about color made her uncomfortable. Thankfully, she was so prac- ticed in concealing her thoughts and reactions that Mara probably wouldn't have noticed—even if she had been watching carefully.

"I tried having a conversation with him. I told him we loved having him at Crossroads and said how important he's been to the kids but that I needed him to be open to seeing his blind spots, and that I wanted all of us to keep learning together. But when I told him he would need to do some more training with us about race and justice, he quit right there. Said he was sick and tired of all the political correctness crap and stormed out of the building just before the kids arrived. No reply to any of my emails either. So, I've got to let him walk away, along with a couple of other volunteers he obviously contacted and ranted to. They were so mad about what I said to him and how I'd" —she signed air quotes—"'judged him,' they quit too."

"I'm so sorry," Kit said after a moment. "That all sounds very hard."

"Yeah," Mara said, "but it's not about me. I keep reminding myself of that." She folded her hands in her lap. "I talked with Ruth about it afterward—she and Debra both saw him storm out—and she said she was more concerned about the kids' reaction once they find out Larry probably isn't coming back, even to say goodbye. With all the disruption they've already gone through, now they've lost one more person who meant something to them. And she's right—that's heartbreaking. If he'd just been open to the possibility of seeing something new, we could have moved forward together, as messy and hard and frustrating as it might have been. We could have worked to find a way."

"I know you would have," Kit said. "I admire your commitment to all the people you serve, even the ones who make it challenging for you. That's a powerful expression of love. Especially in times like these."

Mara leaned her head back and closed her eyes. "It's just so loud right now, you know? Everything's so loud. We're not listening to each other. It's constant fighting, constant labeling and condemning. And when did 'justice' become a bad word? When did some Christians decide that working for justice and standing up for people who live life on the margins is a political issue instead of a kingdom one? I don't get it."

"No, neither do I. But I'm so glad you're there, doing what you're doing. That's faithful stewardship of your own experiences."

Mara looked at her again. "Sometimes I wonder, though, if I'd be so passionate about the issues if they weren't personal to me. Like, would I care so much about racism if one of my kids hadn't been the victim of it? I'm not saying that everything Jeremy has struggled with is because of the color of his skin, but being biracial with a racist bully for a stepfather didn't help things. And I guess part of me still regrets all the times I didn't stand up to Tom and tell him to stop. Even though I understand why I didn't, why I didn't feel like I could. But if I can stand up now and advocate for kids who aren't mine or find ways to help empower people who feel beaten down or left out or made to feel 'less than' because of race or poverty or lack of education opportunities or whatever, then I'll give it every breath I've got. Even if it makes some people mad."

Kit wished she could have shown Mara a tape of herself sitting on that same cushion years ago, bound up in shame and guilt and fear and condemnation, convinced she would never make any progress in knowing Jesus' love for her or responding to his love. What a testimony to the grace and power of God. And what an honor, she thought after Mara left her office to go to another meeting, what a joy to have had a front row seat in watching God's work of setting captives free and sending them out into the world, redeemed.

The creaking of the front door to her house later that night startled Kit awake on the couch. Her Bible, which was still open on her lap, slid to the floor. "Hi there," she said as Wren entered, a backpack slung over her shoulder.

"Hey. Sorry, did I wake you?"

"No, it's okay. Must have just nodded off." She straightened her glasses. "What time is it?"

"Almost nine." Wren slipped off her sneakers.

"Good day?"

"Yeah, okay. Pretty quiet, except for Miss Daisy."

Kit picked up her Bible from the floor and set it on the coffee table. Over the past few months, she had heard many stories about the poor woman who clutched her baby doll and hollered for her father and mother to come and take her home.

"She slept most of the morning but then couldn't get settled down this afternoon. Mr. Kennedy kept asking if someone was hurting her. I don't know if he remembers that she has bad episodes almost every day." Wren unzipped her bag and pulled out her housekeeping uniform. "One of the CNAs sang this 'Daisy, Daisy' song to her, and then they must have given her a sedative or something because she was fast asleep when I left."

"That's an old song," Kit said. "My grandmother used to sing that one to me. 'Daisy, Daisy, give me your answer, do.' Something something about a carriage and a bicycle built for two." She pictured Mom-Mom leaning in close, her face beaming as she crooned, her body swaying to the music, her breath smelling of licorice. "I used to make her change the words to 'Kitty, Kitty.' Didn't work quite as well. But I always wanted a bicycle built for two because of that song."

Still clutching her uniform, Wren sat down on the armrest of the couch. "Did you get one?"

"No. Never did. Robert wasn't one for riding, and it's not much use having a tandem if you don't have anyone to pedal with you."

"We should get one."

Kit chuckled. "I'm a little old for something like that now."

"You're not old-old, Kit."

She chuckled again. "Thank you, I think." Wren's soft brown eyes had a hint of sparkle—a more regular occurrence lately. Still not something to take for granted, though. Not when she had to work so hard to be well. Kit wished she didn't have to work so hard.

"What I mean is, you're a youthful, healthy seventy-five. Not like some of the people at Willow Springs."

Kit didn't take that for granted either.

"What color bike did you want?" Wren asked.

"Oh, I don't know. I don't think it would have mattered."

"But if you could choose."

"Don't get any ideas, Wren."

"I won't. I'm just asking."

Kit ran her fingers along one of the throw pillows. "Blue, I guess."

"Light or dark?"

"Light. Like your uniform."

Wren looked down at her scrubs. "Speaking of, I need to do laundry tonight. All three of my uniforms are now officially dirty." She pointed to a large stain on the front of the shirt. "Tomato sauce. I ordered pasta from the cafeteria so I could eat with Mr. Kennedy while we were watching golf. I hope I can get one of them dried in time for tomorrow."

"Are you there again tomorrow?"

"They need me in the morning because one of the other house-keepers is sick. Then I'll come to New Hope and clean after lunch." She paused. "If that's okay. Sorry, I should have checked with you first."

"No, it's fine. You know the hours are flexible. As long as you clean before the group comes in on Saturday, it's all right."

"Okay, thanks." Wren walked to the patio door and gazed into the twilight. "No cardinals lying about?"

"No, I don't think so."

"That's good. I've been thinking about that metaphor all day."

"What's that?"

Wren turned to face her. "What you said about the bald cardinal and molting. I've been pondering that image."

"Have you? I'd love to hear more."

"Okay, cool. I'll get a load started in the washer first. Have you already had your prayer time?"

Most nights she and Wren tried to pray together, whether that was meditating on a Scripture passage, or reading liturgical prayers, or praying with art or collage, or reviewing their day with the examen. "I'll wait for you," Kit said, and stifled a yawn.

When she returned, Wren was scrolling on her phone. "While I was thinking today about the image of molting, I remembered that Vincent used it to describe the losses in his life." She sat beside Kit on the couch and handed her the phone. "Here. You can read it. It's from one of his letters to Theo."

Kit adjusted her glasses to view what Vincent had written to his brother: "What molting is to birds, the time when they change their feathers, that's adversity or misfortune, hard times, for us human beings. One may remain in this period of molting, one may also come out of it renewed, but it's not to be done in public, however. It's scarcely entertaining; it's not cheerful. So it's a matter of making oneself scarce."

"I hear his vulnerability in this," Kit said. "Maybe even shame."

Wren nodded. "I get it. I've felt the same impulse to hide so I don't have to give explanations to anyone. It's easier that way." When Kit handed the phone back to her, she set it on the coffee table. "Dawn told me at our last appointment that she'd love to see me try to make new friends and spend time with people my own age. But I told her it takes way too much energy. I was thinking about it today, how exhausting molting can be. I feel like I need to concentrate just on doing my work until my feathers grow back."

Kit wasn't going to contradict her, but she was glad her counselor had started nudging her out of her comfort zone. "'Until' is a good word," she said. "I hear expectant hope in that word, like you've turned a corner toward something new." When Wren looked confused, Kit said, "I heard you say, 'until my feathers grow back.'"

"Oh!" Wren smiled slightly. "Thanks for catching that. I guess that's progress."

"Great progress. And if Dawn thinks you're ready for a new challenge, take that as a word of hope too."

"Yeah, I guess," Wren replied, but she didn't sound convinced.

Kit decided not to push. "Thinking of birds and molting," she said, "my grandmother—the same one who sang the 'Daisy, Daisy' song—had a parakeet named Socrates. Smart little thing. She used to take him out of his cage when I visited, and he'd do somersaults right in my hand. He could say my name too. 'Kitty-kitty-kitty,' he'd say, and we'd laugh."

Wren drew her knees to her chest and rested her chin on them, her gaze fixed on Kit.

"Whenever he molted, he'd get these sharp little stubs poking up through his skin—pinfeathers, they're called—and they were itchy and uncomfortable for him, like little spikes. Pinfeathers are really delicate. They have sheaths on them—kind of like a toenail—to protect all the new growth. But eventually, that protective cover has to chip off so the feather can expand and unfurl. So little Socrates would preen and preen and try to chip it away, but he couldn't preen the top of his head. So as those pinfeathers grew strong, my grand-mother would gently stroke them so the new growth could emerge."

Kit hadn't thought about that in years, how Mom-Mom would sing to him while she stroked him, and that little bird would nuzzle against her hand as if he knew she was doing something important to help care for him.

"What you said about molting, Wren—how exhausting it is— that's what Mom-Mom used to say too. She always said Socrates needed extra-loving care while he molted and rested. So I would sometimes sit beside his cage and read to him while he sat on his perch, and I'd watch for those little spikes to turn into feathers." She paused. "They always did."

In the silence, Kit listened to the hum and slosh of the washing machine, her thoughts wandering to New Hope and the board and her retirement. After a while, Wren leaned forward and kissed her on the cheek. "Thanks for giving me a safe space where my pin-feathers can emerge. And for being patient with me in the process."

Kit slowly rubbed her short white hair. "I'm going through my own molting process these days, so thanks for being patient with me too."

As a breeze strummed melodic broken chords on a wind chime suspended from the eaves, Kit gazed out the patio door into the darkness, thinking of the bald cardinal and Wren and the Willow Springs residents and Mara and the Crossroads staff and residents and volunteers and all the vulnerable, prickly places of discomfort, loss, and change. And she stroked the top of her head again.

3

As soon as she finished her shift at Willow Springs on Friday afternoon, Wren biked to New Hope. "People are sending in donations for a retirement gift, right?" she asked Gayle, the part-time receptionist, after greeting her in the office.

Nodding, Gayle removed a manila folder from her desk drawer. "I'm keeping track of everything in here. Almost everyone has RSVPed yes, so the chapel will be completely full."

"That's great," Wren said. She hoped Kit would think it was great too. "So, is the board planning to give her a check, or are they also buying gifts?"

"Not sure. Why?"

"I had an idea." Wren peered into the lobby to make sure Kit wasn't nearby. "I found out last night that she's always wanted a bicycle built for two."

"Seriously? Do they still make those?"

"I already went online and found a couple different options." She had even managed to find the right color.

"Does Sarah know?"

"That she wants one?"

"That you want to get her one."

"No."

"Oh." Gayle slid her palm across the file folder. "I don't know, Wren. I mean, if she were my mom . . ."

"Lots of older people ride bikes. I see them all the time. And it's not like we're talking about a mountain or racing bike. I've ridden tandems before. I could take the lead. They're not hard once you get the hang of it."

"But if she fell and broke a hip or—"

"Okay." Wren held up her hand. She didn't need someone planting that kind of anxiety in her. "Never mind. Forget I mentioned it."

"I just worry that—"

"It's fine."

Gayle tucked the folder back into the drawer. "I'm sorry to squash your enthusiasm, Wren."

"No big deal." She picked up her backpack. "I've got to start cleaning. Don't mention the bike idea to Kit, okay?"

Gayle mimed zipping her lips.

If the bicycle couldn't be a gift from the group, Wren thought as she rounded the corner to the hallway, it could be a gift from her. And only she and Kit would need to know about it.

That's the spirit, Wrinkle, Casey replied.

She stopped so fast, she nearly tripped.

Seven months after his death, he could still startle her with a voice that sounded so clear, she could have sworn he was right beside her.

Or behind her.

That was where Casey would often sit when they rented a tandem bike in Muskegon on a Saturday afternoon and cycled along the lakeshore. Though he would joke about taking the backseat so she could chauffeur him for a change, he also knew how to encourage her to take the lead. When he was well, Casey was her champion.

Smiling to herself, she imagined how the two of them might have appeared to anyone watching them ride together, him towering over her with his six-foot-three lanky frame, his wavy red hair flowing behind him, while she directed all her five-foot-two strength into pedaling. It had taken them a few tries to find their rhythm on their first ride—and a fair share of their typical sibling-style bickering—but once they learned how to synchronize their feet, they were off and away.

Dawn was right, Wren thought as she gathered her cleaning supplies from the closet. There came a day in the grief process when

memories of a loved one brought a smile before a tear. Maybe she
was making progress after all.

She inserted her earbuds, found Don McLean's "Vincent" on her
phone, and hit repeat. Then she began dusting his paintings,
watching to see which one would catch her attention for prayer.

But the one that edged into her thoughts didn't hang on these
walls: *La Berceuse*, Vincent's portrait of his friend Augustine Roulin
rocking a cradle. That was the one that had provoked Casey the last
day she saw him alive.

She glanced at the closed door of her painting studio, a classroom
Kit had given her permission to use. Last December, she and Casey
had stood at her worktable, studying the various portraits of Augustine in her art book and arguing about Vincent's style until he
muttered something about mothers being impossible to please and
fatherhood being "overrated." She hadn't understood then what he
meant. She hardly understood now, not with all the mysteries still
swirling around his life and death. Casey had died with secrets. And
as Kit had reminded her multiple times, both in letters and conversations, sometimes you had to bury and relinquish your unknowing so
you could move forward with grief.

"Why does that lady make you sad?" Phoebe had asked her last
spring when they saw one of Vincent's portraits of Augustine in
Chicago. While the rest of their family toured a potential college for
Olivia, she and Phoebe spent a few hours at the Art Institute.

Wren was so taken aback by her little sister's gifts of perception
that she wasn't sure how to answer. So she deflected the question.
"Does she make you feel sad?"

"Yep." Phoebe gripped Wren's hand. "Because she looks mad."

"Does she?"

"Yep." She stood on her tiptoes for a closer look. "Maybe the
baby's crying too much."

"Maybe," Wren had replied. "Babies do cry a lot sometimes."

She wiped a smudge from the frame around *Two Cut Sunflowers*.
Casey wouldn't have had much patience for a crying baby. But even

a colicky newborn couldn't have been the reason why he had abandoned Brooke and their daughter, Estelle. Casey had often been selfish, but he wasn't cruel. Something had pushed him over the edge. Something had triggered a bipolar episode. Maybe Brooke was abusive, just as he'd claimed. Far easier to believe the worst about someone she had never met—and would likely never meet—than to believe the worst about the very first friend she had made after moving from Australia to America when she was eleven. The best friend who had been like a brother.

Except, a best friend wouldn't have concealed the fact that he had become a dad.

A wave of anger swept over her.

Betrayed. That was still the best word to describe how she felt, even all these months later. In May, when she knelt beside Kit in the New Hope courtyard garden to bury her "I forgive you" letter to Casey and to plant the seeds she had plucked from his memorial sunflowers, she thought she was also burying her anger and bewilderment. How naive she had been.

"Forgiveness is a process," Dawn often reminded her. Like grief. And her capacity to feel anger and sorrow without being consumed by them was evidence of her movement forward.

But if she knew precisely what she was forgiving him for—if she could only know the truth about what he did and why—she might truly release him.

Cloth and spray bottle in hand, she opened her studio door and walked to the window overlooking the courtyard. She had hoped the sunflowers would be in full bloom for Kit's retirement party, and the timing seemed about right.

She removed her earbuds and listened to a full-crested cardinal singing on the rose arbor. Maybe she could paint two versions: the bald and the full. Shedding and renewal. Loss and hope. In fact . . .

She thought about Vincent and his plans to flank Augustine with his sunflower paintings: a triptych showing an ordinary saint poised between flaming flowers that brightly blazed, all three paintings gleaming with the radiance of God.

She could paint a triptych of cardinals. Life before molting. Life during molting. Life after molting. The cardinal before the loss would not be identical to the one after. How could it be? Struggle left its mark. Even if new feathers emerged.

Even *when*, she reminded herself. She needed to keep practicing hope. The evidence of things unseen.

"There you are!" Kit called from the doorway.

Startled, Wren spun around. "Yep, I'm here."

Kit gestured at the spray bottle. "Maybe you can clean your studio later. There's quite a lot to be done before the retreat tomorrow."

Wren's face flushed. "I know, I wasn't going to clean in here. I just came in to look outside for a second."

"Ah, okay. I noticed the trashcans are full, so—"

"I know. I'll empty them." *Like I always do,* she added silently.

"Thank you, Wren."

Wren waited until she heard her footsteps recede before stepping into the hallway to resume her slow dusting of Vincent's art.

That'll do for now, Kit told herself later that afternoon. She saved the retreat document on her office computer and looked at the open Bible on her desk.

When she had prayed about good last words to offer the community, the theme of stewardship had come to mind: stewarding love, stewarding affliction, stewarding grace. As you have been loved, love. As you have been comforted, comfort. As you have been forgiven, forgive. That was what she would present on the next three Saturday mornings. Unless the Lord redirected her, which he was always free to do.

Love is patient, she read from 1 Corinthians 13 again. Kind. Not envious or boastful, arrogant or rude, self-seeking or irritable or resentful. Each description from Paul merited a lifetime of pondering.

During one of the personal reflection breaks, she would invite the group to meditate on each word and consider how God had loved them in those ways, to practice receiving that kind of generous love from him before considering what it meant to extend that kind of love to others. Especially to those who were impatient and unkind, envious and boastful, arrogant and rude, self-seeking, irritable, and resentful.

She rubbed her temples slowly. *Long-tempered.* That was the meaning of the Greek word Paul used for "patient," the opposite of short-tempered flares of anger and passion. Long-suffering fortitude extended a long way and a long time over a long haul. She would emphasize to the group that this kind of steadfast perseverance in loving others was a gift of the Spirit and a fruit of abiding in God's extravagant love. She would remind them what Jesus had said: "As the Father has loved me, so I have loved you. Abide in my love." Savoring that kind of divine love took practice. And time.

"I'm heading home, Katherine," Gayle called from the doorway. "Unless there's anything else you need from me."

Looking up from her Bible, she mentally ticked off the to-do list. "Prayer handouts are printed? Registration list is complete?"

"It's all on my desk, ready to go."

"That's great, Gayle. Thank you." She would call it a day too.

After Gayle left, she went to find Wren, whose cart was parked outside the women's bathroom. Not wanting to startle her, Kit called her name from the hall.

Wren appeared, her forearms concealed in yellow rubber gloves. "Heading home?"

"Yes. I'll pick up something quick and easy for dinner on my way. Do you have much left to do?"

"A bit. What time is it?"

"Just after four."

"Okay," Wren said. "I'll see you there."

On her way back to her office to collect her purse, Kit paused in front of one of Vincent's sowers. She might as well take an unhurried moment for the kind of prayer that had become so life-giving to her over the past few months.

Folding her hands, she let her gaze rove over the painting until it landed on the man's large open hand scattering the seeds from his satchel. An abundance of them.

She leaned in for a closer look.

How differently she had approached planting the sunflower seeds with Wren, depositing each one in soil she had amended so they would have the best chance for growth. That kind of deliberate care had felt like faithful, responsible stewardship of what had been entrusted to her.

But this sower seemed blissfully unconcerned about where the seeds might land.

She pictured herself in the painting, trailing behind him with her own satchel, stooping to cover up with earth the seeds he had carelessly flung. She imagined herself kneeling in the dirt, then reaching into her pouch to remove a solitary grain. After carefully burying it, she patted the ground in satisfaction and offered a prayer for its growth.

But the sower tossed seed by the handful and laughed when the wind caught and swirled it, depositing it in places where she was certain it would never take root. The birds were bound to find those seeds and swallow them. And what about the rocky soil or the thorns that would rise up and choke vulnerable seedlings?

"Don't you care about the harvest?" she asked him.

In reply, he gently pried open her fist and poured a mound of seed into her palm, some of it falling to the dirt. Then he blew on her hand, and the seeds floated on his breath to scatter to places unseen, to land on soil that may or may not be prepared. "Listen," he said with mirth in his voice, "a sower went out to sow."

4

When Sarah Kersten entered the New Hope office at eight fifteen on Saturday morning, her mother was muttering at the printer, hands on her hips.

"Misbehaving?" Sarah asked.

Her mom grimaced. "Me? Or the printer?"

Sarah laughed and set her purse on Gayle's tidy desk. "Either. Both." She kissed her mom on the cheek, then shooed her out of the way. "What's the problem with it?"

"It won't do what I want it to do."

What a succinct summary of the human dilemma, Sarah thought. "What do you want it to do?"

"Print, just print. It's a simple Word document, no different from what I've printed hundreds of times."

Sarah examined the printer, then pushed the power button. The machine hummed.

"Good grief," her mother said. "I'm sorry."

"No problem." Sarah checked the paper tray to make sure it was loaded. "Gayle must have switched it off."

"I don't know why she would have done that, no reason to do that."

Sarah stared at the large blue light on the machine. "No harm done, Mom."

"You're right. No harm done." As the printer spat out pages, Kit gathered them one by one, her wrinkled, age-spotted hands trembling ever so slightly.

"I'll get those," Sarah said. "Sit down a minute and take a deep breath."

Obeying, she sank into a chair with a sigh.

Sarah monitored the printer's progress. "Gayle's not helping today?"

"No. She's got a bridal shower. Her son's getting married in a couple of weeks."

"What about Wren?"

"She's going to the nursing home today."

"She works on Saturdays?"

"No, she visits with the residents. Watches golf, plays checkers, that sort of thing."

After all Mom had done for her, Wren might have offered to help with an event like this. But she didn't say that. This was not the time for another round in that conversation. "Put me to work, then. What else needs to be done?"

"Nothing. Wren cleaned yesterday, and Gayle already printed out the handouts and registration list."

Sarah collected the remaining pages and tapped them against the table to straighten the stack. "I'll do the welcome desk. You go sit in your office awhile and re-center yourself." She glanced into the lobby. "Where's the registration table?"

Her mom craned her neck to peer through the office door. "It should be right near the entrance. It's not there?"

"Nope."

She pushed herself up from the chair. "I didn't even notice when I came in. I guess Wren forgot that part. I'll go get it."

"No, you won't. I'll take care of it. You go to your office."

She paused, then gave Sarah a mock salute. "When you use your bossy teacher voice, I know better than to argue with you."

Sarah blew on her fist and brushed off her blouse to simulate an easy victory. "It's my superpower. Works for middle schoolers, mothers, and husbands."

Mom grinned. "Not for teenage daughters?"

"No, less and less, I'm afraid. I'm working on developing different strategies."

She patted Sarah on the arm. "Good luck to you, my dear girl. Seems to me that strong wills run in our family."

Sarah was going to quip, "From your side or Dad's?" but thought better of it. No matter how many years had passed since her parents' divorce or her father's death, he remained a potentially tender topic.

Especially the past few months. While her mother insisted that Wren's presence in her home had led to deeper and fruitful processing of her own grief and losses, Sarah wasn't convinced that ruminating on the past had benefited her.

"Have you got the registration list, Mom?"

"Yes, here. Thank you for helping with this."

"No problem." As Sarah scanned the list of names, she recognized many of them. Over the years her mom had certainly developed a loyal fan base, though she would firmly object to any mention of such a thing. "Go rest and get ready." Sarah kissed her again. "Love you, Mom."

"Love you too, honey. Thanks for being here."

No hint of reproach colored her expression of gratitude, no "Nice of you to come to one of my retreats again, now that I'm retiring." Just sincere appreciation.

In the lounge Sarah found a small round table, which she carried to the lobby. Just as she was setting out pens and name tags, Hannah and Nathan Allen arrived, sporting matching Wayfarer Church T-shirts.

"Hey, stranger!" Nathan called.

"Hey, yourself! They let you come to these?"

"Check your list. Should be right at the top."

Sarah eyed the sheet. "Nope. Hannah is."

"Ah, well, as it should be," he said with a grin. "Bet I'm the only guy, though."

"Nope. There are two of you. Russell's coming."

"Oh, good! Someone to sit with."

Hannah elbowed him. "Don't mind this one. He's had way too much sugar this morning." She swept her hand across the front of her shirt. "Pancake breakfast fundraiser for the food pantry."

"I remember those," Sarah said. Before moving from Kingsbury to Grand Rapids years ago, she had been a longtime member at Wayfarer. "Zach used to be in charge of the bacon."

Nathan chuckled. "The ER doc cooking it up. We all thought that was hilarious."

"I think that's why he did it. He loves his irony."

"Tell him hi from us," Hannah said as she printed her name on a sticker. "Everybody doing okay in the Kersten household?"

"Yeah, just getting ready for the school year. Both the girls will be at the high school."

"Is Morgan already a freshman?" Nathan asked.

"Yeah. And Jessica's a senior."

"Hard to believe," he said. "And you're still teaching?"

"Thirty-three years this fall." That was hard to believe too. Except when she viewed herself in a mirror and wondered who the wrinkled, silver-haired woman was.

"You're a special category of saint," he said. "My college freshmen can be challenging enough. Not sure how you manage middle schoolers, let alone middle school math."

She couldn't imagine doing anything else. She loved being in the classroom, helping kids learn.

"And how about your mom?" Hannah asked, lowering her voice. "How's she doing with everything? I haven't been able to get a good read on her lately."

Sarah shrugged. "She knows it's the right decision at the right time. But it won't be easy to step away, not after so many years here. I'm not sure what she'll do to fill her time. More spiritual direction, maybe."

Nathan peeled the backing off his name tag. "The board still hasn't found anyone?"

"Not yet, as far as we know. They haven't exactly been forthcoming about the process. And you know Mom—she won't be pushy and ask." Even so, Sarah had frequently reminded her that she had a longstanding relationship of trust with a couple of the board members, and it wouldn't be inappropriate for her to request an update. *Let them tell you you're being too nosy,* Sarah had said. *That's what I'd do.*

Nathan held out his hand for Hannah's trash and tossed both pieces into the nearby bin. "Sounds like they're looking for a young CEO-type to come in here and shake things up. I don't know why they don't just find someone with marketing and fundraising experience to join the board. Keep the director as a ministry director."

"Yeah, but Mom would be the first to tell you this place feels tired and needs some re-envisioning. And money to support the vision."

Hannah said, "They're looking for a catalyst rather than a stabilizer."

"That's a good way to put it."

The front door opened again, and more participants entered. Nathan and Hannah stepped back from the table to make room.

"Wren forgot to set up the coffee," her mother called as she rounded the corner from the hallway. When she saw Sarah wasn't alone, she quickly rearranged her frown into a broad smile. "Good morning, everyone. Welcome! So glad you're here."

Several of them embraced her warmly.

"Nate and I can set up the coffee, Katherine," Hannah said. "We know where everything is."

"That's lovely. Thank you. And I'm sorry it isn't ready for all of you. I should have checked as soon as I got here."

No, Sarah silently replied. *You shouldn't have had to. Not your job.*

But if she were a betting woman, she would put odds on her mother not mentioning it to the one whose job it was. "Who's next?" she called. "Step right up, and I'll get you checked in."

During her mother's long tenure as the director at New Hope, Sarah had heard her teach many times. They had even co-led a few retreats and workshops before the girls were born. But it had been a while since Sarah had attended one of her events. Given the discombobulation of the morning, she wasn't sure how quickly her mom would be able to recover or how well she would be able to mask any lack of composure.

She needn't have worried. Listening to her mother teach and respond to questions and comments was like attending a master class in how to shepherd people more deeply into the heart of God. From her seat at the back-corner table near the exit door, Sarah had the perfect vantage point for observing how the group responded, not only to her mother's teaching but to her invitations to reflection and prayer.

Across the table from her, Hannah took copious notes. Even though she had claimed not to have "a good read" on her mom, Sarah wondered what the perceptive pastor might have observed. Hannah may even have attended the Lenten retreat session when her mother had reportedly divulged to the group that she'd been so concerned about her depression after Micah died decades ago, she had admitted herself to a psychiatric hospital.

Would Hannah commend that disclosure as courageous vulnerability or regard it as a puzzling departure from longstanding, unspoken family rules about what was appropriate to broadcast? As small-world and insular as West Michigan could be—and as hard as her mother had worked to recreate a life for herself after their family tragedy—Sarah still found it difficult to understand what had prompted her decision.

Though they'd had several heartfelt conversations and had agreed to disagree, the incident had only deepened her concern over whether her mother could manage having someone who suffered with chronic depression and anxiety live in her home. Harsh as it sounded every time she said it, supporting Wren shouldn't be her mom's responsibility.

And yet . . .

Here stood her mother, speaking to the group about how faithful stewardship was a loving response to an extravagantly kind and generous God and how love—self-sacrificing, costly, inconvenient love— was the way believers demonstrated their family resemblance to their heavenly Father.

So, who was she to sit in judgment on the ways her mother believed she had been called to steward love?

Who was she? A daughter worried about her mom. And if the expression of that concern sometimes manifested as anger and impatience rather than tenderness, it didn't mean she wasn't also trying to love well.

"It's so easy for us to romanticize and sentimentalize love," her mother was saying. "But there's nothing sentimental or cozy or easy about the kind of love Jesus demonstrates and commands. Agape is covenantal love, the kind of love that is committed to the well-being of others, no matter what the cost. 'As I have loved you, so you must love one another,' Jesus says. We have been loved with agape, and now we are called to offer that same kind of humble, generous, merciful, compassionate love to others. Not just to those who have easy access to our affections, but to those who are a trial for us."

No shortage of those in the world, Sarah thought. Or in the body of Christ. She had recently blocked a bunch of them on social media. Life was too short to be continually provoked.

"I'm worried," her mother said, "that a passage like the 'love chapter' in 1 Corinthians can become so familiar to us that we stop attending to it. We relegate it to the realm of greeting cards, inspirational posters, and wedding homilies, then nod and smile and say, 'Isn't that lovely poetry?' But remember that Paul wrote these words about love to a church that was fractured. He wrote these words to a church battling with envy and competition, rivalry and pride, divisiveness and self-centeredness. Set the teaching about love in the midst of a congregation struggling to love, and we begin to grasp its power."

Sarah flipped a page in her notebook and wrote, "What does agape look like?" Then she closed her eyes to listen to her mother read Paul's litany of love.

Patient and long-suffering, Sarah thought later that morning as she watched her mom interact with people waiting in line to talk with her. That was what agape looked like. And kind—determined to serve others benevolently. Even when exhausted. Her mother was a marvel.

From the refreshment table where she was tidying up, Sarah overheard snippets of conversations. Some wanted to ask questions about her retirement plans, others wanted to talk about their insights from the morning, and a few sought words of wisdom about challenging circumstances or people who frustrated their efforts to love well.

Make an appointment, Sarah silently commanded as she loaded a cart with dirty coffee mugs. But instead, she knew her mother would be seeking the grace to remain fully present to each person who asked for her attention. Depleted as she no doubt was, she would practice what she had preached: as you have been loved, love.

When it came to loving others, Mom was far better with the whole "not irritable, resentful, or rude" thing.

"What can we help you with?" Hannah asked as she and Nathan approached.

If Sarah had been confident her mother wouldn't stay late to clean up and would instead leave tasks for Wren to do, she would have thanked Hannah for the offer but dismissed it as unnecessary. "I need to clear this table and take everything to the kitchen to wash or put away."

Nathan lifted the coffee urn and placed it on the top shelf of the cart. "Knowing your mom, I should have expected she wouldn't go with the typical 'Time, talents, treasure' angle on stewardship." He pressed his hand to his chest. "Open heart surgery, as usual."

Sarah smiled. "Mom has a knack for that, doesn't she?" As soon as she spoke the words, she knew her mother would correct her by saying the Spirit had a knack for it and she was only trying to be receptive and responsive to however God led.

Two white-haired women advanced to the lectern, which her mother was now leaning against. "We were hoping you would change your mind, Katherine, and lead one last Sacred Journey retreat this fall. Is that possible?"

Her mother shook her head. This retreat would be her last, she said. "But you'll still lead other retreats and workshops, right?" the other woman asked. "We could host an event at our church. We'd love to have you come."

Hannah said, "I've done imaginative prayer before with Jesus washing the disciples' feet. But today when your mom read that text, I saw whole new things about my resistance—not just my resistance in letting Jesus love and serve me by washing my feet, but my resistance about kneeling to wash the feet of people who, as your mom diplomatically put it, don't have immediate access to my affection."

Sarah brushed cookie crumbs from the tablecloth onto a napkin. "I was thinking the exact same thing. Guarantee you, though, I'm someone else's 'difficult person.'"

Hannah laughed. "Awareness is the first step toward transformation, right? I always tell people that seeing where we're stuck is half the battle. More than half. It's most of it."

As the two women chattered away to her mother, Sarah fought the impulse to extricate her from further conversation. *Love always protects.* That was the manifestation from Paul's description of agape she most resonated with because that was the quality she found easiest to practice. You could protect—fiercely—and still be impatient and irritable. Even rude.

"We had no idea you had suffered like that," one of the women said.

Sarah stiffened. She knew she shouldn't eavesdrop, but covert monitoring of conversations was a middle school teacher's superpower. Since this one potentially involved her as well—at least indirectly—she busied herself at the end of the table nearest the lectern.

"Knowing you've been through it," the woman said, "that you know what that kind of despair feels like, and yet here you are, serving the Lord like you have all these years—"

"Gives hope," the other one interrupted. "And helps break the stigma. That's what we need to do. Break the stigma of mental illness."

When the woman leaned in closer, Sarah couldn't hear what she said next. But given the expression of deep empathy on her mother's face, she was probably listening to details about someone else's struggle with depression.

"What we ourselves have generously and abundantly received," her mother had said in her teaching session, "we freely offer to others." And since sorrow and suffering had carved within her a deep capacity for compassion, that was what her mom generously gave. She was a trustworthy steward of both love and comfort.

Sarah made a pretense of brushing off more crumbs. Though they might disagree about sharing in a public context the details of sorrow and suffering, she couldn't argue against the fruit of her doing it—not when it was on display right in front of her.

"We'll wheel this to the kitchen for you," Nathan said. "Okay to load the dishwasher, or do you want us to handwash?"

"Dishwasher's fine," Sarah said. "I'll be right there."

"You've already been heroic, Barb," her mother said, "just to keep persevering. And as for sharing your story, that's a stewardship issue too—how we tell the stories that have been entrusted to us, in ways that reveal God's love and faithfulness. And who we tell those stories to."

Before Sarah could turn aside, her mother happened to look her direction. As their eyes met, another description of agape came to mind. *Love does not insist on its own way.*

Right, she thought as she pivoted toward the door. Yet another quality of love she doubted she would ever excel at, no matter how many opportunities she received for practice.

🐦🐦🐦

By the time all the participants left, it was nearly one o'clock. Kit pictured herself with a cup of tea on the back patio, gazing into the woods and listening to birdsong. She might even put on her blue cotton pajamas as a declaration of rest. Mental, physical, emotional, and spiritual rest. She had lived through the same pattern for years: a deep sense of being supernaturally empowered for every moment of teaching and group interaction, followed by an internal switch being flipped. She stared at the keys in her hand.

Had she already locked her office door? She walked back down the corridor and jiggled the knob. Yes. Locked.

Sarah emerged from the lounge. "Mugs are in the dishwasher, and the urns are cleaned and put away."

"Thank you so much. That's a huge help. Did Nathan and Hannah already leave?"

"Yes. They said to tell you they both have a lot to chew on for the week. We all do." Sarah stooped to kiss her cheek. "You did a great job, Mom. I'm proud of you."

Kit thanked her. "The group seemed engaged, didn't they? Very receptive." The questions and comments had revealed the Spirit's penetrating work. She breathed her gratitude. Two more sessions, and then she would be done. How grateful she was for that mercy too. She couldn't imagine having to lead another Sacred Journey retreat in the fall.

She tucked her arm through Sarah's as they walked to the main office. "I don't think you've been here since we put up all the art. What do you think?"

Sarah glanced to either side and said, "Yeah, good."

Kit chuckled. "Not exactly a ringing endorsement."

Sarah shrugged. "I've never been a Van Gogh fan. Too chaotic."

"I wasn't one either before Wren's influence." In the past nine months she had come to view his life and work as an invitation to compassion and solidarity and wonder. Vincent knew how to see.

As they rounded the corner, Sarah let go of her arm. "You're going to have to talk to her, Mom."

"I know."

"It's not okay that she didn't do her job setting up."

"I know. I'll talk with her." She locked the main office, then jiggled the knob to make sure it had caught.

Sarah leaned against the wall, arms crossed. "'Cause if the board hires the type of CEO director they're looking for, it probably won't be the sort of person who'll have much patience for that kind of stuff."

"I know, Sarah. I'll take care of it." She had already decided an honest conversation was required for stewarding love well. She would tell Wren the truth with grace and compassion. And hope she wouldn't be triggered by constructive criticism. The two of them had been through enough life together for Wren to be confident of her love and to trust that she was her cheerleader and advocate. She would remind Wren of this so she could receive the truth without feeling rejected or condemned.

"Okay, I won't mention it again." Sarah uncrossed her arms. "How about lunch at the Corner Nook? My treat. And I promise, no more lectures about anything."

Kit smiled at her. It had been months since the two of them had been to lunch together, and Corner Nook was a favorite place. "Thank you. But are you sure you don't want to get home to Zach and the girls?"

Sarah stared at her. "Zach's at the hospital and won't be home until dinner. And the girls are in Florida, remember? They flew down last week to be with Carol and Gary."

Kit felt her chest tighten. Of course they were. Every summer, right before school started, the girls flew to Orlando to spend a week with Sarah's stepmother and her third or fourth husband. She never could remember how many times Carol had been married before and after Robert. "I guess I've lost track of the days. Sorry. I've been preoccupied with things here." She patted her daughter's arm. Her long nap could wait. "I'd love to have lunch with you."

✦✦✦

When Kit arrived home later that afternoon, Wren wasn't there. *Good.* She was too tired to address anything well.

She set her keys on the kitchen counter, took off her glasses, and put the remaining half of her cherry chicken salad sandwich in the fridge. To Sarah's credit, not only had she avoided expressing any further concern over Wren, but she also hadn't mentioned overhearing the conversation with two of the attendees about depression and stewarding stories. If Sarah wanted to discuss that topic in the future, she wouldn't be shy. Kit was confident of that.

Instead of covering old ground, they had talked about Sarah's preparations for teaching middle school algebra and pre-algebra, Jessica's college applications, and Morgan's intensifying desire for a horse. "We've told her no," Sarah said, "not until she proves she's willing to do all the work of taking care of one. If she wants to start mucking out stalls after her riding lessons, that's great. I'm sure the owners would be happy for the help. But until then, no way."

Kit leaned against the counter to steady herself as she removed her sandals. Morgan would find a way to get what she wanted, whatever it took. Tough as Sarah talked, Kit knew her daughter had always appreciated that dauntless streak in both her girls. She had nurtured it. Just as her father had for her. "You fall down, you get up, you move on," Robert had often instructed both Sarah and Micah when they were young. But only Sarah had been able to do it.

Thank God Sarah had been able to do it. Her youthful stubbornness had been sanctified into a tenacity Kit admired, even when that tenacity could sometimes be overbearing.

As she trudged to her room, she pictured the girls in Florida with their "fun grandma," a woman who had always possessed the financial means to spoil them, whether with toys and treats when they were young or with trips and clothes now that they were older.

Strange, how when she'd led the group in the prayer exercise with 1 Corinthians 13, Carol hadn't been on her mind at all, not even when she'd asked the group to listen to the text while picturing the person—or type of person—they found most difficult to love. "When you recognize a lack of love in your own heart," she'd told them, "name it to God and receive God's grace and forgiveness and power. Remember, this isn't an exercise in self-condemnation but an opportunity to diligently seek God for a gift he longs to give you in greater and greater measure."

She removed her pajamas from beneath her pillow. Now that someone specific had come to mind, she might sit and pray with that text again. Later. When she wasn't so exhausted. She changed out of her clothes and sat down on her bed.

Love does not envy. It is not resentful. It keeps no record of wrongs.

Far easier to tick those boxes when you made a habit of ignoring someone's existence. Far easier to love in generalities than in specifics, in theory rather than practice. Because when latent grudges were ignited by the tiniest flame of remembrance . . .

She crawled under her covers.

That could set a heart on fire.

5

In the residents' lounge on the second floor at Willow Springs, Wren sat with her back toward the large glass aviary, where a male and female zebra finch chirped. Though she would have preferred to play Yahtzee in the smaller, birdless lounge near the dining room, Mrs. Clement liked to sit as close as possible to the little creatures, talking and humming to the pair. "Come on, Coco, sing me a song. That's it, Coco-bird. Give me a sweet, sweet song. Aren't you a clever bird?"

Wren rattled the dice in her cup and rolled the three and four she needed for a full house. It had been difficult enough listening to Kit describe little Socrates living life in a cage or turning somersaults in a hand. She had never done well with zoos either.

"Look at Tweety go!" Mrs. Clement clasped her hands together. "Look behind you, missy. Watch her swing on her little perch. Wheeeee!" She laughed like a gleeful child.

With a quick look over her shoulder, Wren made the appropriate sounds of affirmation before recording her points. Poor little things. Whenever she cleaned that lounge, she dusted and vacuumed as quickly as possible. "Your turn, Mrs. Clement."

Mrs. Clement was still watching them. "They need more millet sprays. They like millet."

"I'm sure Audrey will get them what they need," Wren said. Since it had been the housekeeping supervisor's idea to bring caged birds to Willow Springs, she took responsibility for caring for them. According to Peyton, Audrey also took care of replacing Cocos and

Tweetys whenever necessary, with each bird now in its second or third iteration.

She leaned forward to study Mrs. Clement's scorecard. "What do you still need? Sixes?"

Mrs. Clement turned her attention away from the birds to study her list. "Sixes and a large straight." She blew on her cup, then shook it. "Blast," she said after pouring out four twos and a three. Before Wren could advise her about what to keep, she plopped all the dice back into the cup and rolled again.

"Is it game time?" Mrs. Whitlock, wearing a short-sleeved housecoat, shuffled into the room, stooped over her walker. "No one invited me."

Wren patted the chair next to her and rose, making room for her to maneuver past the aviary. "We're just finishing our first round."

"Do you play, Dorothy?" Mrs. Clement asked. "I didn't know you played."

"Of course I play! Are we playing for money?"

Wren stifled a grin. "Not today." Her phone buzzed in her jeans pocket.

"Did somebody press their call button?" Mrs. Whitlock asked, straightening as best she could to peer down the hallway.

Wren reached out to gently tuck long, white, uncombed hair behind her ears. There. Now she could see better. "It's okay, Mrs. Whitlock. It's just my phone buzzing." She pulled her phone partway from her pocket, then stuffed it back in. She would call her mom later.

Mrs. Whitlock was still staring down the hall, brows furrowed.

"Nobody pushed their call button, Dorothy. It was Wren's phone. Come sit down if you're going to play."

Wren helped guide her to the table, moved her walker out of the way, and held the chair for her while she gingerly lowered herself. "I'll slide you in a little closer. Watch your hands."

Mrs. Whitlock lifted her hands from the arms of the chair and pressed them against her breast. "Where's the other girl?"

"Peyton?" Wren asked as she pushed the chair forward.

"The one who plays the music too loud. Always wants me to shimmy in my chair."

Yep. Peyton. "She's got the day off today."

Mrs. Whitlock scrutinized her. "Do you work here?"

"Yes, but I've got the day off too."

Mrs. Clement said, "She's one of the cleaning girls, Dorothy. Haven't you seen her in your room before?"

Mrs. Whitlock didn't reply.

The second Wren sat down beside her, she smelled the soiled diaper. She glanced toward the nurses' station. Nobody there. As soon as one of the CNAs appeared, she would indicate that Mrs. Whitlock needed help. In the meantime, she wasn't going to embarrass her by calling attention to it. Not in front of her friend.

"Is it my turn?" Mrs. Whitlock asked.

"Not yet," Wren said. "We only have two more spaces to fill, and then we'll start a new game. I think you were looking for sixes and a large straight, Mrs. Clement."

"Right you are, missy." She blew on her cup and rolled four sixes. "Ooh, look at that! I'll get my bonus points now."

Wren had just taken the cup from her when the elevator doors opened. Mrs. Whitlock's daughter exited wearing her usual business casual.

"We're over here, Teri," Mrs. Clement called.

Teri clipped her visitor badge to her collar and strode to the table. "Isn't this nice! A game of Yahtzee? You love Yahtzee, don't you, Mother?"

"We're not playing for money."

Teri gave what sounded to Wren like a nervous laugh and ran her fingers through her mother's hair, as if attempting to tame it. "No, Mother. No money involved." She looked at Mrs. Clement. "I didn't know you had a granddaughter, Marjorie. How lovely!"

Wren smiled at her. "I'm one of the housekeepers. Just visiting today."

Teri flung her hand to her forehead. "I'm so sorry! I didn't recognize you without your uniform." Then, with the sort of quick whiff a mother might take of her infant's backside, she crinkled her nose. "We'd better get you to your room, Mother. I don't think anyone has helped you with your hair yet today." She eyed Wren with a quizzical expression.

Wren felt heat rise to her face. Just as she was about to explain, Mrs. Whitlock said, "Don't need my hair done to play Yahtzee."

"I think you'll feel better if you do." She pulled her mother's chair back and reached for her walker. Then she signaled to the CNA who had just returned to the station. "I need some help here, please."

Wren rose from her chair.

Teri faced her. "Next time," she whispered, "you might show more concern for someone's dignity. Even on your day off."

When Wren finished watching golf with Mr. Kennedy several hours later, it was raining too hard to ride home. While she waited for the squall to clear, she sequestered herself in a quiet corner of the lobby and called her mom.

"Did you explain to Teri what happened?" she asked after Wren recounted the story.

"I was going to, but by the time they got Mrs. Whitlock cleaned up, I was with Mr. Kennedy and didn't see her leave." A thunderclap rattled the windows.

"It's too bad she doesn't understand how much you do for people like her mom, way above and beyond what you're paid for."

Wren recognized this as the likely prelude to the "I'm concerned about how much time you're spending there" speech, which was usually followed by questions about her social life. "I wouldn't do it if I didn't enjoy it," she said. Then she changed the subject by asking about Phoebe.

"She's right here. Do you want to talk to her?"

"Sure. Put her on."

"Okay. I love you, Wren. Call or text to let me know how you're going, okay?"

"I will. Thanks, Mom. Love you too!"

She heard her mother say, "Your big sister wants to talk to you," followed by the sound of a chair squeaking against linoleum.

"I'm painting sunflowers like Vincent!" a little voice chirped into the phone.

"You are? Wow! You'll have to send me a picture, okay?"

Phoebe said, "When I'm done."

She grinned at the authoritative tone of a six-year-old. "Okay. Deal."

As Wren watched the rain pound the pavement, Phoebe described her painting in great detail: the number of sunflowers, how many green leaves and yellow or orange petals each flower had, how many black strokes she had already made for the seeds, what color the vase would be, and where she would print her name. Wren wasn't sure if Phoebe was copying a picture of Vincent's sunflowers or if she had simply remembered with remarkable specificity the paintings they had viewed in Wren's art books after their trip to Chicago.

"It sounds beautiful," Wren said when Phoebe finished talking. "I can't wait to see it."

"Maybe you can come here and see it."

"I will someday, Feebs."

"When?"

She knew better than to make any concrete promises. "I'm not sure. But tell you what—how about if we have a Facetime painting date sometime next week?"

"Okay," Phoebe said. "Are you painting sunflowers too?"

"No, I've been too busy to paint anything lately. But I saw this funny bird in our backyard the other day, so I might paint that."

"What was it doing?"

"Eating seeds at the birdfeeder. But it looked funny because it had a bald head."

Phoebe laughed. "Birds don't have hair!"

"No, you're right. But this one had lost all its red feathers on its head, so it looked bald. Like a cartoon bird wearing a red coat that was way too big."

"Oh." Wren pictured Phoebe wrinkling her nose, trying to imagine it. "Did you take a picture?"

"Yes, I'll send it to Mom so you can see, okay? And we'll set up a time to paint together."

"'Kay."

She looked outside. The rain had stopped. All she needed was a ten-minute window to bike straight home. "Tell Dad and Olivia and Joel hi for me."

"They're not here right now."

"That's okay. Just whenever you see them. And tell Mom to give you a hug from me."

"A kiss too," Phoebe said.

"Yes. A big kiss too." Wren made an exaggerated kiss sound, which Phoebe imitated.

Painting with her sister might be just the impetus she needed to return to a life-giving, creative habit, she thought as she cycled home through puddles. Months had passed since she'd completed the Journey to the Cross art, and though she had been personally enriched by meditating on the Scriptures about Jesus' suffering and by painting her response, the project had exhausted her. She hadn't painted recreationally since then, not even abstract compositions as prayer. That could explain why she had felt dry lately. Waiting for her creative well to be refilled before painting again might have been the wrong approach.

Kit probably knew that. But apart from the occasional "That might make a good painting" comment, she hadn't pushed.

When Wren arrived at the condo, she expected Kit to be reading or resting on the couch. But she wasn't there. Her keys and purse lay on the kitchen counter, and from the end of the hallway, through her partially open bedroom door, came the sound of faint snoring.

She set down her backpack and slid off her shoes. Maybe she would call it an early night too. That way she might shake the image of Teri chastising her for being lazy and selfish.

She wasn't lazy. She wasn't selfish. Not when it came to loving and serving the residents at Willow Springs. The accusation wasn't fair. It wasn't true. And yet it stung.

Because it wasn't just Teri. It was Brooke and Casey's mom and all the awful things that had been said about her—how she had deliberately undermined Brooke and Casey's marriage by her close friendship with him and how she had caused "irreparable harm" to his family by "selfishly" holding a memorial service to honor her friend.

When she was tired, the accusations resurfaced. Even though she kept trying to let them go, that grief was an open loop she couldn't find a way to close. No matter how hard she tried.

She poured herself a glass of lemonade and sat down at the table. Kit might remind her to pray with open hands, to release to God the sorrow and churn of accusations and receive his comfort. Grace. Peace. Love. Hope. She unclenched her fingers. It was impossible to release or receive anything with tight fists.

"I thought I heard somebody," Kit said when she shuffled into the kitchen in her pajamas a few minutes later, her short white hair mussed, her glasses askew.

"Hey, Kit." Wren shifted her open hands to her lap.

"Did you just get home?"

"A little while ago."

"Boy, was I out. Sound asleep." She yawned and stretched. "Did you already get something to eat? I've still got half a sandwich left over from lunch."

"I'll get something later, thanks. I'm not very hungry."

Kit straightened her glasses. "Are you all right?"

"Yeah. Just really tired."

She wasn't going to burden her with the details of her day, not when Kit was already exhausted. Maybe she would reread some of her letters instead. Kit knew the pain of being accused. A few of her letters had become so familiar to Wren, she could recite her wisdom by heart.

"How about you?" Wren asked. "How did the retreat go?"

Kit brushed a wisp of hair from her brow. "Great. No problems at all."

Something in Kit's smile didn't seem to match the rest of her face. But it didn't feel right to pry.

6

"Mom forgot the girls are in Florida," Sarah said when Zach arrived home from the hospital.

He hung up his keys on the peg by the kitchen sink and kissed her on the cheek. "Cut her some slack, hon. It happens."

She continued scrubbing the mixing bowl in sudsy water. "I'm not saying that because I'm mad about it. I'm saying she forgot, Zach."

"Okay, she forgot. It happens with age. And with stress. She's been under a whole lot of pressure lately."

True. And retirement would mitigate some of it. But as long as Wren was living under her roof, Sarah couldn't imagine her mom's stress level dropping low enough.

He lifted the Crockpot lid. "Chicken enchilada soup?"

"Yes. And cornbread muffins in the oven."

"I love you."

"I know."

He opened the fridge and brought out a bottle of wine.

"Go change your clothes first," she said as she drained the sink. "You don't need to spread your hospital germs everywhere." He set the bottle on the counter before retreating to their bedroom. Twenty-four years of marriage, and still she had to nag him as if he were a teenager. His nurses said the same thing about having to pester him to complete his charts. He liked to practice medicine, he insisted, not dictation.

As she was removing wine glasses from the cupboard, her phone buzzed with a text from Morgan: a photo of her standing with Jessica and Carol in front of Cinderella's castle, each of them beaming in Mickey Mouse ears. Sarah smiled and typed, *Love it! Having fun?*

Three dots immediately appeared. *Awesome time! Gigi says hi.*

Sarah replied with the like button and enlarged the photo. With her cute, professionally highlighted blonde bob cut and stylish linen ensemble, Carol, who had always been Gigi to the girls, didn't look anywhere close to seventy years old. Travel and hobbies and a posture of playful curiosity had kept her youthful. Her boundless energy had kept Dad youthful too. He had often told Sarah that Carol made him happy. He didn't need to say the rest. Even in elementary school, Sarah had known that her parents didn't make one another happy. Messy as their divorce had been, at least they had both been able to move forward in ways that brought satisfaction, divergent as their paths would be.

Zach emerged from the bedroom in his favorite ratty shorts and his "Who's Your Doctor?" Tardis T-shirt.

"Look at this cute picture," she said, handing him the phone.

As he straightened his eyeglasses, Sarah noticed a price sticker on the corner of the lens. "Seriously, Zach?" She snatched them off his face.

"What?"

"Have you worn these all day like this?" She peeled the sticker off the cheap pair of reading glasses and held it up. He had obviously misplaced his prescription lenses again.

He squinted at her finger. "Need my glasses to see what you've got there."

After she handed them over, he exaggerated adjusting them back and forth on the bridge of his nose. "Ah, so I haven't developed eye floaters. Excellent."

"I swear, Zach. What do your patients say?"

"Nothing. They're so awestruck by my brilliance, words fail."

"Yes," she said, "they do."

Grinning, he studied the phone screen. "Great picture! They sure look happy."

Their suntans, manicured nails, and new haircuts told not only the story of spa days and trips to the beach, but also of Carol's knack for enabling two teenage sisters to enjoy a vacation together. "Morgan looks more and more like Dad, don't you think?"

"Yeah. Like you too, Sarah. Same smile."

"Think so?" People had always said she looked more like her mom than her dad. "I guess I see it around the nose and mouth." She lingered with the photo before setting her phone aside.

"Are we eating in or outside tonight?" Zach asked.

"What's the temperature like?"

"Not bad. Nice breeze." He removed a corkscrew from the drawer. "Let's eat on the deck. I'll dry off the chairs and set the table."

As they ate beneath the patio umbrella, Sarah told him about the morning at New Hope, her frustration over Wren, and lunch with her mom. "Maybe it was a subconscious thing, forgetting about Florida," she said.

"Because of Carol, you mean?"

"And the girls' relationship with her." She took a sip of Merlot. "And mine."

Sarah had worked through those psychological dynamics with a therapist decades ago—how she couldn't take responsibility for whatever journey of forgiveness or reconciliation her parents would or wouldn't make after her father remarried; how she was free to make her own choices about her relationship with her dad and her stepmother, without feeling guilt about being disloyal to her mom; and how she needed to talk honestly with her mom about how she felt and what she needed. To her credit, her mother had encouraged her to find a way forward with her dad. And with Carol. Back then, Sarah hadn't understood what that consistent practice of generosity cost her mom. But over the years she had come to be deeply grateful for her sacrifice. *Love bears all things,* she thought. And her mother had borne much.

"Ask her about it," Zach said as he buttered another corn muffin.

"But if I'm wrong, and it's not even on her radar, I don't want to bring Carol up. Mom's got enough she's trying to deal with right now. I'm not going to pile more on."

You're not responsible for your mother's mental and emotional health, the therapist had told her after her mom was released from the psychiatric hospital. She was only eighteen years old, he said, and she couldn't live the rest of her life walking on eggshells, worried about setting off an episode of her mother's depression by something she said or did.

With her mom's encouragement, she had worked hard to practice that type of freedom too. But she also knew that stewarding love well sometimes meant guarding her tongue and not speaking her mind so directly. That was harder to remember.

"By the way," Zach said, "I traded a couple of shifts, cleared my schedule from Wednesday to Sunday. How about a trip to the cottage before the girls get home?"

She set her wine glass down. It wasn't a bad idea. With only two more weeks before she would return to the school for professional development days and department planning meetings, this would be their best opportunity to get away together. She mentally scanned her commitments for the next week. Nothing that couldn't be rescheduled except . . .

"Mom's leading a Saturday retreat group, and I promised I'd be there."

He looked disappointed. "I think she would understand."

"I know she would. She'd tell us to go and have a great time. But I don't want her to be there on her own, trying to manage everything."

"So, talk to Wren about it. Or tell your mom to talk to Wren about it."

"I already did. She said she would."

"Great." He reached across the table for her hand. "We've hardly been there at all this summer. It would be good for the two of us to have some time away."

She pictured them kayaking on the lake, building bonfires on the beach, enjoying breakfast in bed. "Okay," she said. "I'll sort it out."

He smiled at her. "You always do."

Later that evening, while Zach lay on the couch reading, Sarah sat at her father's baby grand piano, which Carol had paid to transport to her after he died.

Music had always been their common language. Before she could even read a book, her dad taught her to read notes. In her catalog of happy early memories were images of her father practicing his trumpet while she colored in her coloring books on the floor near his feet and the two of them sitting side by side on this very piano bench as his hands flew across the keys. He taught her how to play. When she was skilled enough, she accompanied him when he played his trumpet at church. Sometimes they played duets for anthems. And at her request he played "Trumpet Voluntary" for the recessional at her wedding. She could still see him raise the trumpet to his lips, his eyes glistening with tears as he looked at her with love and pride before she took her husband's arm to walk down the aisle. Dad hadn't missed a note.

She placed the sheet music for "Gabriel's Oboe," one of her mother's favorites, on the scrolled rack and sightread it. Jessica would play the piece on her cello as a retirement party gift, and Sarah would accompany her. She wished her father could hear Jess play. She had inherited his artistic sensibilities and might follow in his footsteps as a high school music teacher. Or elementary school.

Her daughter had far more patience for children than her father ever had. He had never been able to accept Micah's refusal to play any instruments. Or sports. Micah was stubborn that way. And Dad had a temper. He had mellowed in his later years, though. He would have been the first to admit that he became a better version of himself after he married Carol.

"Sounds good, hon!" Zach called from the couch after she finished playing.

"Thanks. It'll work." On her page she marked some fingering in pencil and played a chord progression again. "Not much to it without the solo line. But wait until you hear Jess."

She pictured her mother listening to Dad play his trumpet or watching him conduct a student orchestra. You would have thought she was listening to the New York Philharmonic. But her deep appreciation for music—even for his music—had never been quite enough for him. When he met Carol, a music education and performance instructor at a nearby community college, he met someone who offered not only appreciation and admiration, but who shared a life passion. Though Sarah had never condoned their affair, she also couldn't deny them the happy life they created together. Even if she had tried, it wouldn't have made a difference. She'd had one option back then: forgive and move forward. She hadn't regretted taking that path.

"You'll have to make sure you get video of Mom listening to Jess play, okay? I won't be able to watch her from the keyboard."

Zach held up his phone. "I'll be poised and ready."

She sat down beside him on the couch. "Thinking of video, I managed to get a few more testimonies scheduled. Nathan and Hannah were at the retreat this morning and said they would be happy to record something. So we'll meet at New Hope Monday morning."

"Your mom won't see you doing that? I thought the video was supposed to be a surprise."

"She's taking the day off."

"Ah, perfect."

Though her mom resisted being the center of attention, it seemed a shame to Sarah that people often waited for funerals to offer eulogies. Why not speak encouragement and affirmation and thanks to the living? Why not celebrate a life well lived while that person still lived? "At least I'll be able to see her face when she watches the tribute. I think she'll be overwhelmed—hopefully in a good way—by what people say about her."

Afterward, Mom would no doubt insist it was all too much. But on days when she needed to be reminded about the difference she had made in the lives of others, she might hit the play button and watch it again.

"This will mean so much to her," Sarah said to Hannah and Nathan after they finished recording their video Monday morning. "Thank you for taking time to do this."

"Anything for your mom," Hannah replied.

Nathan took his wife's hand. "Like Hannah said in the video, we wouldn't be who we are today—individually or as a couple—without her wisdom and generosity."

As they entered the lobby, Wren was coasting toward the portico on her bicycle. Nathan held the door open for her as she wheeled it inside.

Sarah glanced at her watch: ten forty. Is that what time she started work on a Monday morning?

Wren took off her helmet and smoothed her dark hair. In her shorts and tank top, she looked more appropriately dressed for a day at the beach than a day at work.

"Missed you yesterday in worship," Hannah said after giving her a hug. "Are you doing okay?"

"Yeah. I helped out with a service at Willow Springs."

"Oh, good for you. That's great."

"I mean, I helped get residents to the service. I didn't help with worship."

Hannah smiled at her. "Don't discount the importance of that. I'm sure they were grateful."

Excusing herself, Sarah headed to the office, where she could monitor Wren while discussing party details with Gayle.

Two minutes. Four minutes. The lobby conversation carried on.

Seven minutes. Ten. At the sound of laughter, Sarah peered through the open door and returned Nathan's wave. "Thanks again!" she called as the Allens left.

Wren removed her phone from her backpack and started scrolling. One minute. Three minutes. Six. Sarah waited to see if Gayle would say anything to her. But Gayle had transitioned from talking about retirement party details to wedding reception plans for her son.

"Excuse me a minute, Gayle. I need to talk to Wren about something."

Like a guilty middle schooler, Wren shoved her phone into her pack and started fiddling with the straps on her bag as soon as Sarah approached.

"I decided not to get one," she said.

"One what?"

Her pale skin flushed. "Oh. Sorry. Nothing. I thought maybe you and Gayle were talking about gifts for your mom."

"No. We weren't." She would ask Gayle about that later. "Listen, Wren, I'm not going to be able to be here to help with the retreat this week. And after what happened on Saturday, I'm worried about Mom being stuck again."

Wren stared at her. "What happened?"

"The coffee not being set up? The registration table? Mom didn't talk to you about it?"

"No."

Sarah sighed. "When I got here for the retreat Saturday morning, nothing was set up."

Wren's eyes widened. "I did the tables before I left on Friday."

"Okay, so the tables in the room were set up. But nothing else. And if I hadn't been here, Mom would have tried to do it all by herself. Not okay. She's stressed out enough as it is. She doesn't need more."

Wren stared at her sneakers. "I'm sorry. I completely forgot. It won't happen again."

"Good. Thank you. But since I can't come on Saturday to supervise, I'd like you to be here so you can help with anything Mom might need. She won't ask you. So I am."

The office phone rang. Gayle answered with a cheery, "Good morning! New Hope Retreat Center."

"Okay," Wren said. "I'll be here."

"Oh, hey, Bill," Gayle said, "how's it going?"

Sarah looked at her watch. "Don't you work afternoons at the nursing home?"

"Yes."

"Not much time for you to get things done here, then, is there?"

"Katherine's taking the day off," Gayle said. "You could call her cell, though."

Wren said, "I have enough time."

"Okay. I won't keep you. Thanks for being willing to help."

Wren mumbled a reply before heading down the hallway.

Good. Message delivered; message received. She waited in the lobby until Gayle finished her phone call, then went into the office to get her purse.

"That was one of the board members," Gayle said. "I bet there's news. I bet they've found somebody."

About time. That news might relieve some of her mother's stress. "Did he say he'd call Mom?"

"No. He just said to let her know he called. Do you want to call her, or do you want me to?"

"You go ahead. I don't want her to know I was here today."

"Oh, okay. I won't tell her."

Sarah pulled her keys out of her bag. "What gift was Wren talking about?"

"When?"

"Out in the lobby just now. She said she had decided not to get a gift for Mom."

Gayle clasped her hands together. "Oh, good, I'm glad she changed her mind. She came in here last week, talking about how your mom had always wanted a tandem bike—"

"What?"

"One of those two-seater bicycles—"

"No, I know what they are." She had just never heard her mother mention wanting one.

"Wren asked me about the board's plans for buying your mom a gift with the donations being sent in, and I said I didn't know what their plans were, but I didn't think it was a good idea to get her a bike. Not when she could fall and break a hip or something."

Sarah shook her head in disbelief. Either Wren had misunderstood what her mother had said, or her mother had confided information she had never told Sarah.

"I told Wren you wouldn't like the idea."

"You're right about that. Thank you." And just in case that message hadn't been received loud and clear, she would hand-deliver it.

She found Wren near the janitor's closet, wearing earbuds and scrolling on her phone again. When she saw Sarah, she yanked the headphones from her ears, shoved her phone into her pocket, and picked up a duster from her cart.

"One more thing before I leave," Sarah said. "Whatever you do, do not get my mother a bicycle."

With her back turned toward Sarah, Wren ran her duster along the frame of a painting of distorted, writhing trees. "Your mom and I were talking about an old song her grandmother used to sing to her when she was little, a song about a bicycle built for two. And she said she had always wanted one and never got one because your dad wasn't interested in riding with her."

Sarah stared at her. Wren kept dusting. After a moment of what felt like hostile silence, Sarah thanked her for her cooperation and walked away. But as she drove home, the question pursued her: What else had her mother confided to that girl?

7

When her phone rang, Kit was lounging on her patio, still wearing her pajamas. She glanced at the number. Gayle knew better than to call her on a day off with anything less than an emergency.

Setting her journal aside, she pitched her voice to soothe as she greeted her.

"Sorry to bother you, Katherine, but Bill just called. When I told him you were taking the day off, he said he would call you another time."

She sat up straighter. "Did he say anything else?"

"No. But I wonder if they've found someone."

Kit had immediately drawn the same conclusion. The chair of the board wouldn't call to chat. "Thanks for letting me know, Gayle."

"Are you gonna call him?"

Kit heard the anxiety in her voice. Ever since seeing the job description, Gayle had been worried about her next boss. She needed the part-time income, and with her adult daughter's chronic mental health struggles, the flexible work schedule was a gift. "I'll let you know if there's any news to share," Kit assured her.

No point waiting in suspense, she decided after they ended their call. She dialed Bill's number.

"Katherine! I thought you were taking the day off."

"I am. I'm enjoying a lovely breeze on my patio." No point beating around the bush either. "Have you got news about the search?"

Yes, he did. After interviewing several candidates, the board had found one who excited them—a young executive pastor from a large church in Tulsa. "I'll be honest with you," Bill said. "We had just about given up on finding anyone who ticked all the boxes. But Logan matches everything we're looking for in terms of executive experience and a passion for spiritual formation. So we've decided to fly him up here for an in-person interview at the end of the week."

Her hand trembled as she reached for her coffee mug. "That sounds very promising. Thanks so much for letting me know."

It was still confidential information, Bill said, and he asked her not to share details with anyone else. "We'll hold it in prayer for now, Katherine, and see how the Lord leads."

"Of course. I'll ask him to guide you in wisdom."

"Thanks," he said. "We'd like for Logan to meet you when he's here so he can ask you any questions we might not be able to answer for him. Is that all right?"

"Sure. I'd be glad to meet him."

"That's great. Could we set a time for Friday?"

"Sorry," Kit said, "my calendar is at my office. Okay if I email you tomorrow?"

He said it was.

Only after ending the call did it occur to her how old-fashioned she must have sounded, not to keep a calendar on her phone. Never mind. The board would soon have their upgrade.

"This is good news," Sarah said when Kit called her later that afternoon. Family, she had decided, didn't count in the "Don't tell anyone else" category. "If they've gotten this far in the process and want to fly him in, Mom, they must be pretty excited about him."

Kit rearranged a cushion behind her on the sofa. "Yes, it sounds as if they are."

"You don't sound so sure, though."

There was nothing to be sure or unsure about. She knew no details about Logan or his gifts, and she certainly didn't presume to know God's plans. "I'm holding it all loosely." She opened her hand in her lap as a declaration of that intent. Release. Receive.

"I would feel relieved if I were you, Mom. You've been worried they wouldn't find anyone before you left. Now you can retire without being stressed over that."

"It's not a done deal."

"I know. But the board has things under control, and if it doesn't work out, they'll figure out the next steps. It's not your responsibility. Not your concern."

No, it wasn't her responsibility or concern. But that didn't mean she didn't care about New Hope's ongoing ministry. At the sound of clicking keys, she asked, "Are you typing something?"

"Just doing a quick search," Sarah said. "How many executive pastors in Tulsa are named Logan?"

Kit hadn't thought of that. She probably shouldn't have mentioned his name. Oh, well. No stopping the freight train now.

"Ha! Got it! One. Logan Harris. Wow, he looks young. Thirty, tops. Let me see if I can get any graduation dates for him."

Kit put her bare feet up on the coffee table. If she said she wasn't interested, she would be lying.

"Okay," Sarah said after more typing, "here we go. He's been the executive pastor at Woodlands Memorial Church for the past five years. Graduated from seminary seven years ago. So he's probably older than he looks. I'm sending you the link. Put me on speaker when you get it."

"I'll check it later, Sarah. I haven't even showered yet today."

Silence. Either Sarah was concerned she was moving that slowly or impressed she was thoroughly resting. "Call me after you've looked, then. I'll see what else I can find out about him."

Kit was going to say, "Don't bother, it's none of my business." But those words got lost somewhere in her throat, and instead, she replied, "Thanks."

Within an hour Sarah had emailed everything she had discovered from the church's Facebook page, archived newsletters, and Logan's website bio. *I haven't looked at YouTube or Twitter yet, but there's probably lots of info there too. He looks like a solid guy! Excited!*

Still in her pajamas, Kit perused the information while picking at
a late lunch. With the day well more than half gone, there didn't
seem much point in showering or getting dressed.

She took a bite of her turkey sandwich. Sarah was right. Given the
board's priorities, Logan seemed like a sound candidate. Born and
raised near Pittsburgh, he came to Christ in college through campus
ministry, completed his MBA at Wharton, and then went on to Beacon
Hill Seminary, where he specialized in organizational leadership.

Kit scrolled through the material, searching. No mention of spiritual direction, and the only mention of retreat ministry referred to
men's events he had led the past few years: "Defeating Goliath,"
"Becoming Men after God's Own Heart," and "Going the Distance."
His bio emphasized his passion for outreach and his desire to help
people become "the best version of themselves, both as individuals
and as communities." His blog, where he posted irregularly, con-
tained personal reflections and book reviews focused primarily on
leadership and Jesus' call to be a servant.

But there was nothing about prayer. Nothing about the role of the
Holy Spirit in empowering ministry or enabling Christlikeness or
transforming lives.

Surely, though, if the board had gotten this far in the interview
process, they would have noticed that sort of deficiency. The board
members knew how to pray and were practiced in discernment.
Even if the job description didn't explicitly state "commitment to
prayer" as a top desire for a candidate, they wouldn't hire someone
with no such passion or commitment, would they?

She took another bite of her sandwich.

Bill claimed Logan not only had executive experience but a "passion
for spiritual formation." Had he only used those words because he
knew she would be listening for them? Or had he used them because
they had heard something in Logan's interviews that indicated more
than what was communicated on the church website or his blog?

Not that her input or impressions mattered. The board wanted
her to meet with Logan not so she could interview him, but so he

could interview her. And no doubt, he would discover many deficiencies, not only in her as a leader but in the organization.

So be it. She had no control over that either.

Her gaze landed on a photo of him standing on a stage, his forward lean and splayed fingers communicating passion and energy as he spoke to a crowded auditorium on a wireless headset. What a stark contrast to New Hope, with its chapel an intimate, reflective space and its classrooms hardly large enough to require amplification, even for her aging voice.

So, what had attracted his attention to this ministry? The thrill of a challenge? The hope of building something entirely new? An appeal to his ego?

She rubbed her brow. *Rein in the rush to judgment,* she commanded herself. *Love believes all things, hopes all things.*

She would practice giving him the benefit of the doubt.

Maybe he felt a deep sense of call toward this type of ministry. Maybe he was tired of the corporate approach to church and wanted to use his gifts and passions in a different way. Who was she to argue with that?

Setting aside her lunch, she did as Bill had asked. She said a prayer for God's will to be done. For all of them.

8

If Sarah hadn't already chastised her for not doing her job properly, Wren might have left the deep cleaning of the New Hope bathrooms for another day. By the time she finished mopping floors, she barely had enough time to get to the nursing home for her shift. If Gayle had still been in the office, she would have asked for a ride. Instead, she pedaled as hard and fast as she could and arrived at Willow Springs sweating, out of breath, and nine minutes late.

"Audrey's looking for you," the receptionist said, then resumed her conversation with one of the security guards.

Great. Wren pulled out her phone. She should have texted to say she was on her way. *Sorry I'm late.*

Audrey replied, *Come see me.*

Without bothering to change into her uniform first, Wren scurried to the head housekeeper's office, rehearsing her excuses. She hoped her boss would remember that in the three months she had worked there, she hadn't been late before. She rapped lightly on Audrey's open door.

"Come on in."

When she entered, Audrey's penciled brows arched. Wren lowered her backpack, attempting to conceal her bare legs. "Sorry. My uniform's in my bag. I can go get changed."

"It's okay. Have a seat first."

Wren sat on the edge of the chair, back erect, knees pressed together, bag on her lap. "I'm so sorry I'm late. I got caught at my other job, and Raymond Road was shut down with construction, so I had to do a detour on my bike."

"It happens. But don't make a habit of it."

"Thank you. I won't."

Just as Wren was going to rise from her chair, Audrey placed her hands on her desk, her expression becoming graver. "I understand you were here on Saturday, playing games in the lounge."

Her gut clenched. She hoped Tweety and Coco were okay. She had told Mrs. Clement that Audrey would give the birds what they needed, but she should have checked the cage to make sure they had enough food and water. Why hadn't she checked? If something had happened to those poor little birds . . .

"I came to watch golf with Mr. Kennedy," she said in a small voice. "And then Mrs. Clement asked if I would play Yahtzee with her. So I did."

Audrey wove her fingers together. "Mrs. Whitlock's daughter lodged a complaint with management this morning."

Wren gasped. "Against me?"

"Against the staff. She said the staff was negligent about her mother's hygiene and that when she arrived on Saturday, Dorothy was sitting with you at a game table. In a dirty diaper." She leaned forward. "It's fine that you come here during your free time. The residents love it. But when one of them needs something—"

"I know. But no one was at the station."

"So, push a call button. Or go find somebody. They're never far away." She paused. "The nurses and CNAs work their tails off and don't get nearly the appreciation they deserve. We're all part of the same team, Wren, and we've got to watch each other's backs. That's the deal. Even when we're not on duty. Clear?"

Not trusting herself to speak, Wren nodded.

"Okay," Audrey said. "We're good. Go get changed."

Wren thanked her. Since she wasn't sure she could stop crying if she started, she bit her lip, strode to the nearest restroom to change her clothes, and asked Jesus for the strength to hold it all together.

Though none of the weekend nurses or CNAs were on duty, word had obviously spread to the weekday shift about Teri's official complaint. When Wren rolled her housekeeping cart past the nurse's station, neither Chelsea nor Greta looked up from their screens to greet her—unlike Teri, who had greeted her by name when they passed one another in the hallway before yesterday's chapel service, Wren pushing Miss Daisy in a wheelchair and Teri walking slowly beside her mother.

"Driving Miss Daisy?" Teri had said with a chuckle. Wren assumed she wasn't holding any grudges behind her wide-open smile. But since Teri had named her in the complaint—along with whichever CNAs she claimed were derelict in their duties—it wasn't surprising the whole nursing staff would band together and scapegoat her. Though Audrey claimed they all served on the same team, Wren had worked there long enough to know that those who wore maroon or evergreen uniforms were in a different category than those who wore light blue.

"You're late today," Mrs. Whitlock said when Wren arrived at her room.

"Yes, a little." Teri's mother was seated in an armchair by the window, wearing a large-print floral blouse and turquoise trousers, her hair combed and pinned back. "All right if I clean for you, Mrs. Whitlock?"

"You left before I got my turn at Yahtzee."

"I know, I'm sorry. We'll play another time, okay?" She donned a pair of plastic gloves and sprayed disinfectant onto a clean cloth. Doorknob. Light switches. Tray table. She wiped in a swift motion, lifting a plastic glass, a crossword puzzle book, a remote control.

"We could play now." Mrs. Whitlock reached for her walker.

"Who's ready to play?" Peyton called from the doorway in her Bermuda shorts and a hot pink polo shirt with the Willow Springs logo. "We're waiting for you, Dorothy."

"What for?"

"Beach volleyball."

Mrs. Whitlock scoffed.

"Ah, c'mon. It'll be fun. We've got a beach ball, a net, and some paddles. You can be on my team."

From the corner of her eye, Wren saw Mrs. Whitlock point at her. "I'll be on that girl's team."

"She can't play with us right now. But lots of other people are in the rec room, ready for you. And we're having ice cream afterward."

"Sundaes?"

"You'll have to come see." As Peyton strode toward the window, Wren stepped out of the way. "Can you get up by yourself, Dorothy?"

"I don't want to play silly games. I just want ice cream."

"We'll get you ice cream, don't worry." She held onto the walker as Mrs. Whitlock pulled herself forward. Then she reached around to support her back as she rose to her feet. "Awesome job."

While Mrs. Whitlock maneuvered around the bed with her walker, Wren pressed herself against the wall to make room. Peyton kept her eyes forward as she passed by.

Best to remain even more inconspicuous than usual today, she decided as she ran her cloth along the television cabinet. Let things blow over. As soon as her shift finished, she changed out of her uniform and left through a side door.

"Heading home?" a white-haired security guard called from his golf cart as she unlocked her bike.

"Yeah."

"Have a good one!" Evidently, Joe hadn't received the "Ignore Wren" memo.

"Thanks. You too." She shoved her lock into her backpack.

See, Wrinkle? Not everyone hates you.

She smiled faintly. That was exactly the sort of thing Casey would say.

She stared up at a canvas of cerulean blue with wisps of clouds. Swish. Swirl. The type of sky Vincent had loved to paint.

She imagined her grip on a palette knife, the smooth wood and contours of the handle, the gleam of the flexible steel blade. Scrape. Press. Layer. Shape. If she were at New Hope, she might retreat to her studio to paint her day. *What color is criticism?* Gran would ask. *What color is sorrow? What color is frustration? Defensiveness? Isolation? Rejection?*

Yes. All of that. She could paint all of that.

She fastened her helmet.

Gunmetal gray. Charcoal. Nickel. Stone. Slate. Ash.

Ashes.

She pictured her painting of Jesus with his penetrating, unwavering gaze and silent mouth, the ashes of accusation encircling him like a halo of smoke. *What color is strength? What color is solidarity? What color is love? What color is presence? What color is faithfulness?*

She had survived the day. She hadn't deteriorated under the gray weight of shame or sorrow. She had asked Jesus to hold her together, and he had. She breathed her thanks.

She could make more ashes to incorporate into paintings. Plenty of content to write down and burn from her ongoing, accumulating collection.

Instead of riding home, she could go to her studio. The empty building would be a quiet, sacred space for processing and prayer. And it would be good to paint by herself before painting with Phoebe. She took her phone out of her backpack and texted Kit her plans.

First, though, a slight detour.

She mounted her bike. Cycling through Casey's childhood neighborhood had lately become a semi-regular ritual. By varying the times of riding past his old house, she figured she was less likely to be noticed. So, on days when she chose to ride rather than walk to work at Willow Springs, she would pedal down his street in the morning or afternoon or evening, slowing ever so slightly in front of the two-story red-brick home with the sugar maple tree and colorful flower beds, and say a prayer for his family.

Mrs. Wilson had always been an avid gardener. Casey used to say his mother could spit out a seed and it would grow. Once, when Wren rode by after a shift, Mrs. Wilson was kneeling in her flower bed, wisps of red hair visible beneath her wide-brimmed straw hat. At first, Wren considered turning her bike around. But then she thought that would look suspicious to anyone who might be watching. So she lowered her head, trusting her helmet to keep Mrs. Wilson from recognizing her if she happened to look up.

She hadn't looked up.

And once, when Wren rode past in the early morning, Mr. Wilson was walking from the front door to his car. He was wearing jeans and a polo shirt, and when he gave the sort of slight wave one might offer a stranger on a bicycle, he looked so much like Casey, Wren nearly burst into tears. Ever since then, she rode past their house almost hoping she would see him again from a distance.

At the corner of Casey's street, she stopped to adjust her helmet, watching to make sure his parents didn't happen to approach in a car. With the coast clear, she turned right on Maplewood and pedaled the first block, then the second. As she crossed the intersection of Maplewood and Oakdale, she noticed a realtor's sign halfway down the block on the left side of the road. But was it the Wilsons' house or their next-door neighbor's? She pedaled faster.

In the shade of the sugar maple tree that she and Casey used to climb stood a metal post and a For Sale sign.

The vise in her gut tightened.

Far too risky to stop. Too risky to slow down. Too risky even to turn aside to look. So she kept pedaling until she reached the end of the next block, then made a U-turn and cycled as slowly as possible toward the house. When she came within two houses, she dismounted her bike, kicked down the stand, and crouched as if to tie an errant shoelace, eyeing the Wilsons' house between the wheel spokes.

What color? she heard Gran say.

Her eyes stung as she stared at Casey's old window. Had his parents kept anything as a memorial? A photography trophy on a shelf? A U2 poster? LEGO sets he assembled for his stop-motion movies? Wren hadn't seen his childhood room since they graduated from high school and didn't know what he had left behind.

She wiped the tears from her cheeks. He had left everything behind.

She mounted her bike and rode away, winding up and down the neighborhood streets with the neighborhood children and neighborhood parents living their neighborhood lives, and pedaled without knowing where she was heading until she ended up there: her old middle school where she'd met Casey after moving from Australia to America. At the edge of the soccer field, she parked her bicycle and lowered herself to the ground.

What color for shock? What color for loss? What color for the kind of change you do not choose and do not want?

She sat in the grass, knees clamped to her chest, until the blue sky turned orange with streaks of red, like grapes pressed and crushed, their juice splattered. She rocked herself in the grass until the cardinals stopped calling to one another and the fireflies hovered and blinked and the bats darted and dove and the sky darkened to a bruise. She lay in the grass until clouds shrouded the stars and the sliver of moon. Then she heaved herself onto her bicycle and pedaled home.

9

I never heard you come in last night," Kit said as Wren entered the kitchen Tuesday morning in a rumpled tank top and shorts. "Good time painting?"

Wren opened the cupboard and removed a mug. "I didn't end up going."

"Oh." Kit shifted in her chair and took another bite of toast. Wherever Wren had gone instead wasn't any of her business. But it was late to be out riding. "Everything okay?"

"Yeah. I'm painting with Phoebe later today, so I decided to wait."

"Ah, good. I'm glad you can do that together."

Wren rubbed her arm, her fair skin blotched with red bumps.

"Looks like the mosquitoes got you. There's cream in the medicine cabinet."

"Thanks, I'm okay." She selected a pod from the carousel on the counter and inserted it into the coffeemaker. "I'm really sorry about forgetting to set up stuff for the retreat. I told Sarah I can come help on Saturday, no problem."

Kit froze, with her slice of toast halfway between the plate and her mouth. "You talked with Sarah?"

"Yeah."

"When?"

"Yesterday at New Hope."

She set her toast down. "Sarah was there?"

"Yeah."

Interesting. Sarah hadn't mentioned being there when they spoke about Logan.

Wren wrapped her fingers around her tank top strap. "She was working on retirement party stuff, I think."

"Ah, I see." She had three more weeks of indulging secrecy about those plans. "I'm sorry Sarah was the one to talk with you about that, Wren. I meant to, but we've both been so tired, and I didn't want to pile more on."

Wren shrugged. "Pile away. What's one more thing?"

Oh, dear. Kit picked up her napkin and wiped crumbs off her hands. Knowing when to press and when to give space was a complicated dance of discernment. "Sounds like you've got a lot going on. I'm sorry."

"Thanks." The coffeemaker whirred, gurgled, hummed.

"Is there anything I can help with?"

"Just pray I'll be able to concentrate at work, that I won't mess anything else up."

Poor girl. "I know Sarah can be a little harsh, but it really wasn't a problem on Saturday. Everything got taken care of. No harm done."

Wren stared out the window. "That's just it, though. If I mess something up at New Hope, no one gets hurt. If I mess something up at the nursing home—if I forget to clean something or I use the wrong product or I don't do things in the right order or don't thoroughly disinfect, then one of the residents could get sick. Even die."

Kit furrowed her brow. In the three months Wren had worked at Willow Springs, she hadn't voiced feeling the weight of that type of pressure or responsibility. At least not to her. Maybe to her counselor. Hopefully to her counselor. When was she scheduled to meet with Dawn? Kit had lost track of the weeks. "Did something happen, Wren?"

The coffee trickled into the sunflower mug. The machine hummed, sighed, and fell silent. "Someone filed a complaint with management yesterday."

Kit's pulse quickened. "Against you?"

"Not just me," Wren said, then told her about the daughter who was upset over people not taking care of her mom.

Seemed that was a theme lately.

Wren took a sip from her mug. "I don't blame Teri for being upset about her mom not having her hair combed or being dressed. It was already noon when she got there. And if she thought her mom had been sitting in a dirty diaper for a while, I can understand why she was angry at me. It wasn't like I hadn't noticed—the smell was pretty bad, and I should have gone for help right away. It wouldn't have been hard to do."

"You'll know next time," Kit said. She carried her breakfast dishes to the sink. "I'm glad you told me, glad to know how I can be praying for you."

"Thanks." Wren removed a box of cereal and two prescription bottles from a cabinet.

"Do you need a ride today? I'm happy to drop you off on my way to work this morning."

"No, it's okay. I'll just ride my bike."

"Are you sure? It's supposed to get hot this afternoon."

"I'll be fine. Dawn keeps reminding me that regular exercise helps, so I want to keep up a routine with that."

"Good for you." Kit rinsed her mug and plate, then put them in the dishwasher.

Exercise. Work. Counseling appointments. Medication. Prayer. Art. Worship. Wren was doing everything she could to battle against depression and persevere with hope. "Let me know if there's anything I can do for you," she said, and retreated to her room to pray.

As soon as Kit opened the front door at New Hope later that morning, Gayle scuttled into the lobby. "You didn't call me back yesterday. Is everything okay? Is there news?"

She tucked her keys into her purse. Bill had told her not to share details about Logan. He hadn't forbidden her to mention they'd found a candidate. "It's what you suspected. The board has finally found someone they think is a good match."

"And?"

"They're flying him in for a face-to-face interview."

"When?"

"Sometime this week."

Gayle trailed her into the office. "Whatever day it is, I'll be here. You don't know what day he's coming? Bill didn't say?"

Kit set her bag on the worktable. Gayle would be in the office on Friday to help with retreat details. She might as well be prepared to meet the man who could be her new boss. "He asked me to check my calendar for Friday."

"To meet him here?"

"As far as I know."

Gayle took a deep breath. "Okay, that's good. What else? Where's he from? What's his background? Is he working at a retreat center somewhere?"

No name, no place, Kit reminded herself. "Bill didn't tell me much, just that the candidate has strong leadership gifts, and they're very excited about him."

Thankfully, Gayle didn't probe. "If you get any other information you can share, please let me know."

Kit promised she would, then headed to her office to check her calendar for Friday: one directee at eleven, one at twelve thirty, and a four-thirty conference call with presenters who would be leading fall workshops and retreats.

Was it better to schedule the appointment with Logan first thing in the morning or after her second direction session? If she met Logan early, would she be preoccupied with the details of their conversation for the rest of the day? If she met Logan late, would she be consumed with anticipating their meeting?

She tapped her pencil against her desk. Either way, she would be battling distraction to remain fully present. But she might have an easier time setting aside an actual conversation than an imagined one.

She emailed Bill to let him know she had an open window between eight and ten thirty and hoped that would work with their schedule. Immediately, he replied, *We'll be there at nine.*

Good. Done.

She glanced at her watch. With almost an hour before her first appointment, she could work on notes for Saturday's retreat. She opened a new Word document and typed the title: "Stewarding Affliction and Consolation."

Glad as she was that Sarah had attended last week's session, she felt relieved she would be out of town for this one. Better to have uninhibited freedom to speak in whatever way the Spirit might lead her, particularly in the question-and-answer segment at the end. If sharing from her own experience of suffering could be a comfort to someone else, then she needed to be a faithful steward of her testimony, just as she had encouraged others to be.

She opened her Bible to 2 Corinthians, which had long been one of her favorite books. Here was Paul, sharing freely from his own experience of pain and suffering, wrestling with insecurity, and expressing his longings with the kind of disarming, humble candor and vulnerability that endeared the normally strident, abrasive apostle to her. Here was Paul, naming his weakness, his need for others, his frustration over being disregarded and unappreciated and misunderstood. Here was Paul, rehearsing his credentials, battling his pride, boasting in his sufferings and his endurance. Here was Paul in his unvarnished humanity, praising the God whose strength was perfected in weakness and whose grace was sufficient for him. *Blessed be the God and Father of our Lord Jesus Christ, the Father of mercies and the God of all consolation, who consoles us in all our affliction, so that we may be able to console those who are in any affliction with the consolation with which we ourselves are consoled by God.*

She reached across her desk for her small holding cross, a gift from her first spiritual director years ago. A comfort cross, Lucy called it, something tangible to clutch as a reminder of God's presence, love, and consolation. *As you have been comforted,* Kit thought, *comfort.* And she curled her fingers around the smooth wood.

Shortly before ten o'clock her phone buzzed with a text from Jamie: *Could you please call me when you get a chance?*

She typed back, *Heading into meeting soon. Everything okay?*

Three words appeared on her screen: *Worried about Wren.*

Her chest constricted. Wren had seemed okay that morning, able to express the challenges she faced while also demonstrating resilience. But what else had happened in the last two hours?

She stared at her phone. Though Jamie was prone to worry about her daughter's mental health and safety, she had also been working hard, with the help of her own counselor, not to monitor or control.

She eyed her watch, then dialed Jamie's number. She could spare two minutes.

"I promise I won't keep you," Jamie said after Kit greeted her, "and I won't ask you to betray any confidences. But Wren just canceled her painting session with Phoebe. One of the residents just died, and I know she's upset. I don't know if she can manage her shift or not."

Kit was going to say, "She's done it before. Several times." But instead, she replied, "I'll be praying. I know it's hard."

"Thank you. And if you could please watch for anything that might concern you when you see her? Just to be safe?"

She promised she would. "I'll let her communicate directly with you about any details she wants to share. And I'll be praying for you too, Jamie."

"Thank you. Whenever she's upset like this, it's a trigger for me. I'm sorry."

"No need to be sorry. It's good you're aware of what your triggers are." She reached again for her holding cross. "If I notice anything that alarms me, I'll let you know." Only at that moment did she remember the anxiety Wren had expressed just that morning about making a mistake that could harm a resident. *Please, God. Let it not be that.* She wouldn't plant that seed of fear in Jamie by mentioning it.

A knock on her open door startled her, and she quickly finished the call.

"Sorry!" her directee said. "Am I early?"

Kit shoved her phone and cross into a desk drawer, then extended her hands. "Right on time, Maureen. Welcome." Inhale. Exhale. Release. Receive. "May I get you some tea?"

10

Miss Daisy's body had already been removed when Wren arrived. A nightshift nurse had found her when she went to give her medication.

Wren stared at the shadow box on the wall outside her room: a blue ceramic cat, a plastic Winnie the Pooh, a few seashells, a Statue of Liberty postcard.

Audrey studied her clipboard. "Her niece lives in New York, and the soonest she can get here is Thursday. But management says we need to get the room ready for a new resident by early afternoon. That means we'll need to box up her things for her family to sort through later." She looked up. "Have you done one of these yet?"

Wren rubbed her arm. "No." Though several residents had died since she began working at Willow Springs, this was the first time she had been on duty when a room needed to be cleared out.

"I'll go get a few cardboard boxes," Audrey said. "You'll want to pack things up first, and then you'll need to scrub everything down, top to bottom."

"Okay."

As Audrey disappeared around the corner, Wren peered into the room. The bed had already been stripped. Miss Daisy's baby doll, Emmy Lou, sat in the chair by the window, her brown hair jagged beneath a tattered crocheted bonnet, her lashless eyes open, her face chipped and mottled.

Miss Daisy had loved that doll like a child. Never went anywhere without her. Until now. Wren pictured her curled up in the bed, clutching her baby to her chest, taking her last breath.

If only she had thought to sketch a portrait of Emmy Lou for Miss Daisy. Or a portrait of Miss Daisy cradling her. She would have liked that. She might even have shown that picture to the other residents as if showing off a family photo.

If only she had thought of offering a gift like that sooner.

Before crossing the threshold to begin her task, she paused to pray, to honor the space as sacred. Miss Daisy, who often hadn't known where she was or who people were, had sung every word of "The Old Rugged Cross" during worship on Sunday, her face lit up as she warbled, "Then he'll call me some day to my home far away." Jesus had. In this very room.

She put on a pair of gloves and stepped toward the bare mattress.

"Here are some boxes for you." Audrey entered carrying a stack. As she passed by the television cabinet, she bumped against it, knocking a larger version of the shadow box's blue ceramic cat onto the floor. It shattered. Audrey cursed.

Wren stared at the broken pieces. "Careful with Ollie," Miss Daisy had always commanded her whenever she dusted her room. "He's very old, you know."

Audrey grabbed a dustpan from the cart, swept up the pieces, and brushed them into the trash bag.

Wren wondered if Miss Daisy's niece knew about Ollie. Or if she would care.

"You got everything under control in here?" Audrey asked.

"Yes." As under control as she could manage.

From the lounge came the snap of a drumbeat and the growl of a saxophone. *C'mon, baby! Let's do the twist . . .*

"C'mon, Dorothy!" Peyton called. "Get those shoulders going! C'mon, Douglas—that's it! Twist and twist and—yeah! You got it! Keep going! Good job, Betty! Way to go! Twist it!" Other voices joined in, cheering on the residents and clapping along with the beat.

"I'll leave you to it, then," Audrey said, and left the room.

Wren took a steadying breath. Then she walked over to Miss Daisy's chair and scooped Emmy Lou into her arms.

Cradling her as tenderly as Miss Daisy always had, she stroked each eye closed.

Three boxes, Wren thought as she ate her sandwich in the courtyard later that day. Three boxes, including her clothes.

She chewed slowly.

Eighty-eight years were now enclosed in three boxes in a basement storage area. Stripped of any evidence of her life, the room was disinfected, gleaming, and ready for the next resident, with an empty shadow box on the wall.

She shut her eyes and listened to the gurgling of the fountain, the hum of bees in the lavender, the cawing of a crow.

Miss Daisy had completed her molting and flown away. Life continued. There and here.

Inside, the residents would be gathering in the dining room for lunch or waiting for meals to be delivered to their rooms. Some would inch by Miss Daisy's room with their walkers and peer through the door. If they hadn't already heard the news of her passing, the empty room would tell the familiar story. Some would ask, "Was she alone? Did she suffer? Does she have family nearby?" The questions would reveal not only their anxieties about the endings of their stories, but their longings for the type of ending they preferred.

Life continued here, pressing forward with ordinary activities. Music. Chair exercise. Bingo. Mall and restaurant outings. Themed parties. Gardening. Visits from therapy dogs. Whatever made life, in all its constraints and limitations, more palatable. Even enjoyable.

Life continued, but in the shadow of death. And was that a terror or a gift of grace, to be reminded that life here was not permanent, that those small rooms were not a final home?

She took another bite of her sandwich.

Three small boxes. Would her niece keep anything from those boxes? Or was Emmy Lou just a shabby toy to be discarded?

A dragonfly darted in front of her. It sped above the fountain, pivoted, and landed on the edge of a nearby concrete bench, its body painted in segments of periwinkle and purple, with splashes of sapphire and ultramarine. Such beauty in the world. Such generous beauty in a broken, weary world.

Life continued.

She waited until the dragonfly resumed its flight before brushing the crumbs from her lap. Then, rising, she returned to her work.

"Got any time for Yahtzee today?" Mrs. Clement called from her chair when Wren went in to tidy up her bathroom.

"Not today, I'm afraid. I'll take a rain check, though."

"You got it, missy." She reached for her remote control and turned off the television. "Sorry to hear about Daisy, poor dear. Guess her niece will fly here to take care of things, huh?"

Wren sprayed her cloth. "I think so."

"I haven't seen her for I don't know how long. Not that I keep track of things like that. I'm sure she's busy with her own life. Or maybe she figured it wouldn't matter, since Daisy probably wouldn't have known her if she'd come."

Wren offered a noncommittal *hmm.*

"I was saying to the others at lunch, they sure do turn 'em over quick, you know? Mattress hardly cools off before the next one arrives."

Wren turned on the faucet and adjusted it to a light stream so she could still hear.

"Saw the name on the door," Mrs. Clement said. "Mercer Page. You think that's a man or a woman?"

Wren switched off the faucet. "Did you say Mercer Page?"

"Yep."

She stared at her reflection in the mirror. "Man, I think." A Mercer Page had taught art and drama at their middle school. How many Mercer Pages could there be? Though her teacher had seemed ancient when she was eleven, he probably hadn't been much older than sixty. She calculated how many years had passed. He might be mid-seventies, tops.

"It would be nice to have a few more men around here," Mrs. Clement said. "Too many of us widows."

As she wiped off the sink, Wren conjured a mental image of her teacher: bright eyes, chalk-white hair, and a habit of saying, "Dig it?" whenever he introduced something new. Wren had thought that phrase was an American thing, and when she said it in her Aussie accent to some classmates one day, they howled with laughter and taunted her with calls of "Crikey!" and "G'day, mate!" until Casey told them to knock it off and privately explained to Wren that "dig it" was a hippie phrase no one used anymore. She had added that to her list of things not to say—along with, "How're you going?" and "my mum."

Mrs. Clement maneuvered out of her chair and steadied herself with her cane. "Maybe he can join us for Yahtzee," she said as she hobbled out the door.

The rest of the afternoon Wren monitored Miss Daisy's old room, watching to see if the new resident would in fact be her old teacher. Shortly before four o'clock, just as she was getting ready to finish her shift, the elevator door opened, and Mercer Page emerged, pushed in a wheelchair by a CNA, his white hair longer than she remembered. Instead of his high-top sneakers and trademark denim jacket—which he always slung over his desk chair when he donned his smock—he wore slippers and an untucked T-shirt. Alongside him stood a gray-haired woman carrying a small suitcase, her face pinched with emotion.

Wren ducked behind an artificial ficus tree in the lounge. Not that he would recognize or remember her. She hadn't been a remarkable student, but he had been kind and had encouraged her to continue with art classes in high school. Thankfully, she had taken his advice.

When the nursing staff greeted him with a chorus of welcomes, he replied with a lopsided smile. His arms—which had always been animated with dramatic expression in the classroom—remained at his side. Just as she was wondering if he had experienced complete paralysis from a stroke, he lifted his left hand from his lap and, with a slight wave and a faltering voice, thanked them.

She pictured him on the cafeteria stage, introducing the school play to a room full of students and parents, his voice booming without a microphone. She pictured him bounding across the stage after the performance finished, his hands raised to lead applause for the cast and crew. She pictured him in his smock in the classroom, paintbrush lifted like a conductor's baton, creating a symphony of color on a canvas, just as Gran had done. Before she had her stroke.

Her throat prickled.

Molting. So much molting.

She waited for him to be guided to his room before she pushed her cart onto the elevator. She would greet him during her next shift, after he'd had a couple of days to settle into his new life. As she pressed the button for the ground floor, she wondered what mementos from his former life he might curate for his shadow box on the wall.

It seemed a strange coincidence, she thought later as she rode through the Wilsons' neighborhood, that Mr. Page would show up at Willow Springs the day after she returned to the middle school to sit in the soccer field.

Was it some kind of sign? Some kind of connection with Casey?

She and Casey had taken an art class with Mr. Page in seventh grade, but Casey's passion was film, not sketching or painting. After a while, his stick figures became part of his class clown routine. Even back then, Wren understood it was Casey's way of defending himself against being teased. Middle schoolers could be awfully cruel toward gangly, freckled, redheaded boys who couldn't catch a baseball or do push-ups or draw a cat.

She turned onto Maplewood.

Mr. Page might remember him.

After trying for weeks, their teacher had managed to persuade Casey to join the crew for the school play. He thought if Casey liked making movies, he might like to help with lighting, sound, or set design. Casey agreed to give it a try. But on the evening of their performance of *The Outsiders*, he missed a cue and left Ponyboy's mic on after Johnny died, and when Ponyboy stubbed his toe on the hospital bed on his way off the stage, he cussed. Multiple times. Mr. Page made him come out after the performance and apologize to the audience.

Casey was afraid Ponyboy and the rest of the cast would beat him up.

She paused at the Oakdale intersection and scanned the block. No sold sign. No one in the yard. No cars in the driveway. She rode toward the house as slowly as possible, looking up at Casey's old window and imagining him stretched out on his bed, fighting tears as he blasted his music through his headphones. He had stayed home from school several days after the play. That was the first of many times Wren had been really worried about him.

She ducked her head, just in case anyone was watching from inside, and said a prayer for Mr. and Mrs. Wilson, Brooke, and Estelle. Then she rode home.

Kit met her on the front porch. "Hey! I was just going to text you. Everything okay?"

"Yeah, fine." Wren punched in the code for the garage door and wheeled her bicycle inside. It was sweltering in there. She took a swig from her water bottle, then squirted some on her face before returning to the porch.

"Go ahead and leave the door open," Kit said. "I thought I'd head out and get us something nice for dinner. What sounds good to you?"

Wren removed her helmet. Her hair was drenched. "I'm not really that hungry. I had a late lunch."

"We can wait, no problem." Kit followed her inside.

Wren kicked off her sneakers. Some days she missed living by herself, with the freedom to come and go without anyone observing her.

"Just let me know what you'd like to eat and when," Kit said.

Her mother had probably called her. Why else would Kit meet her on the porch? "I think I'll just take a shower and go to bed early."

Yep. Her mother had definitely called her. Wren could tell from the combination of concern and compassion etched on Kit's brow.

"I'm okay," she said. "Just worn out."

As if to echo those words, Kit sank onto the couch. "That's allowed. You've had a lot going on lately."

"Yeah." And Kit didn't know the half of it. She didn't need to.

"How about a quiet evening with our friend Vincent?" Kit asked. "I've been praying with his *Worn Out* sketch lately. Lots there to see."

Wren rested her hand on the banister. "Maybe." But at the moment, even a quiet evening praying with Vincent's work sounded like too much to manage.

"No pressure about anything. Just let me know if there's anything you need, anything I can do for you." Kit reached toward a book on the coffee table.

"Mom called you, didn't she?"

Kit halted mid-reach. "Technically, she texted, and I called her back."

Wren smiled. "It's okay. You're not in trouble. Neither is Mom." She knew her mother worried about her because she loved her. But as Dawn often said, her mother's anxiety wasn't her burden to carry.

"You know I don't—and will not—carry information to anyone else about you, Wren. That's my commitment to you. But I did promise her I would check on you to make sure you're okay." She paused. "Are you?"

"Yeah, I'm all right. Just sad. It was Miss Daisy. She was gone before I got there, but I'm the one who cleared out her room." She pictured Ollie lying in pieces on the floor and Emmy Lou lying face up in a box. Why had she hesitated to put a lid on that box?

Kit exhaled slowly. "I'm sorry, Wren. All of that is hard."

"Yes, but I knew when I took the job that I would be facing death all the time." She ran her hand along the banister, a new thought forming. "I don't know. Maybe something deep inside of me knew that I needed to keep confronting it. Keep facing it. So that I can keep moving forward with my own grief."

Raising her eyebrows, Kit said, "That's an intriguing possibility. Something else for you to ponder when you have the capacity for it."

Right, Wren thought. She would add it to her list.

After she finished her shower and changed into a sleeveless night-shirt, she sat cross-legged on her bed, clutching Casey's "inspiration beanie" to her chest.

One item. That was all she possessed of his worldly belongings. If there was any chance his parents had kept anything from his childhood, anything they now intended to discard or give away . . .

But there was no way she could contact them to ask.

She drummed her fingers on the bedside table. *C'mon, think.*

She supposed she could continue to ride by and see if they did a moving sale. But even if she saw a yard filled with items, she couldn't hop off her bike, walk up, and say hi. She was persona non grata.

She chewed on her lower lip. Social media was a dead end. If Mr. or Mrs. Wilson were online, their pages were locked down. Like Brooke's.

She stared at Casey's beanie, then put it on. *C'mon. Think.*

Unrolling the rim, she lowered the fabric over her eyes as he used to do whenever he was problem-solving. With the hem of his cap on the bridge of his nose and a pencil tucked between his teeth, he would sit in silence until inspiration struck.

She leaned her head back against the wall and gripped her knees.

Suddenly, it hit her: listing photos.

Why hadn't she thought of that before? Real estate websites posted photos of rooms. She might even be able to take a virtual tour of the house.

She rolled his cap away from her eyes, grabbed her phone, and punched in the address. *Bingo.* There it was. Exterior, front and back. Side yards. Backyard. And lots of interior shots.

She scrolled through the photos of a remodeled kitchen that didn't look anything like she remembered from ten years ago. Same with the living spaces. All new furniture. The house looked as if it had been professionally staged. No personal items. No photos. Nothing that revealed any details about the family that lived there.

First bedroom, multiple angles. Too big to have been Casey's.

Second bedroom, generic guest room in sage and taupe.

Third bedroom . . .

She tapped to enlarge the image. The size and orientation were so similar to the second bedroom's, she couldn't tell which had been his. She scrolled back and forth between them. Not that it would matter if she could tell them apart, since neither of them showed any evidence of ever having belonged to him.

And when had he been expunged? After he moved out for college? After he got married and moved to Reno? Or after he died?

The ache began deep in her chest, then crept upward along her throat and into her jaw.

She pictured Miss Daisy's three boxes in the corner of a basement storage area at Willow Springs and pulled Casey's beanie down over her eyes.

11

Kit had just finished heating up a bowl of chicken noodle soup in the microwave when her cell phone rang. *Sarah.* Before answering, she carried her dinner to the table. "Hey, hon, doing okay?"

"Yeah, just checking to see what you worked out for meeting Logan."

"Nine o'clock Friday morning."

"Oh, good! That's great. Did you get the links I sent you?"

"Yes. Haven't had much time to look, but thank you."

"No problem," Sarah said. "I haven't looked at everything, but what I see so far is promising."

Kit stirred the broth before taking a sip.

"You don't agree?" Sarah asked.

"I can see why the board is excited."

"Nice dodge, Mom."

"No dodge, just waiting to see." She placed her spoon on the placemat. Still too hot.

"What's the problem with him?"

"No problem," she replied. "The board obviously wants to move New Hope in a different direction, and he seems to match their vision for what they want. So that's a good thing."

Sarah scoffed.

Or perhaps it was a stifled sob from upstairs. She tilted her chin back and stared at the ceiling. Was Wren crying?

" . . . can give him a chance," Sarah was saying.

Kit treaded softly toward the stairs. Yes. Muffled sobs. Poor girl.

" . . . able to trust the process," Sarah said.

Kit stood at the foot of the stairs, wondering if she should give her space or offer a listening ear.

"... play out," Sarah said.

What did love look like, right in this moment? She said a silent prayer. Only when she finished did she realize Sarah had stopped talking.

Kit cleared her throat. "Right," she said as she returned to the kitchen. "You're right."

"Did you even hear what I said?"

"You said to give the call process a chance to work."

The sobs had quieted. The bedframe creaked.

"Mom, are you okay?"

"Yes. Fine. Everything's fine." She sat down at the table. "Tell me about the girls. Are they having a good time? When do they get back?"

Monday, Sarah told her, and yes, they were having a good time. "Since Zach and I will still be up north on Saturday, I asked Wren to help out at the retreat."

Kit sighed. Too loudly, apparently.

"Don't sigh at me. You need help, and she needs to do her job."

Ah, Kit thought, here it comes.

"I thought you were going to talk to her about not setting things up."

"It slipped my mind."

"Mom . . ."

"Well, it did. There are plenty of other things going on that are more important than that." As soon as the words were out of her mouth, she regretted them.

"With her, you mean, or with you?"

Footsteps padded upstairs. A door opened and closed. Bathroom or bedroom? She waited to hear whether the footsteps would continue along the hall, but it was quiet.

"Mom?"

Kit rubbed her forehead. "With things in general. Getting ready to retire, for instance. Trying to finish well. Wondering what Logan will be like. All those things." That might pacify her daughter and divert her from prying any further.

"Don't worry, Mom," Sarah said, her voice softening. "It'll all be okay."

Kit shut her eyes. *All of it, Lord.* The bedframe creaked again. *Please.*

That evening, as she prepared to light her Christ candle, she took from her shelf a collection of liturgical prayers that Ezra, the chaplain at the psychiatric hospital, had given her during her stay. Some of the prayers he had copied from the Book of Common Prayer, others he had written himself. Tucked inside the folder was his handwritten note: "Dear Katherine, These are prayers for when you don't have the words, or when your own words sound hollow, or when the sighs and groans and tears are so deep and so overwhelming that you need a container larger than your own heart to hold them. These are prayers to remind you that you are not alone in your ache and your longings. You are never abandoned in your pain. And when you do not have the strength to reach for God, you are not beyond God's reach. May these words—some of which have long been prayed continually around the globe—bring you comfort and peace."

They had. More times than she could count. She thumbed through the well-worn pages. Not only did the prayers provide words, but they reminded her of her place in the beloved community. Whenever she became consumed by her own preoccupations, the prayers broadened her vision to include God's wider world in her cries for mercy and reminded her she was not alone in her sorrow or suffering. And whenever she became overwhelmed by the needs of the world, the prayers reminded her that others shared the burden of crying out for the kingdom of God to be revealed.

She struck the match and murmured lines Ezra had written. "May our prayers rise as fragrant incense before you, O Lord. Gather into your heavenly bowls our joys and sorrows, our praise and petitions, our gratitude and our longings for your kingdom to come."

At the sound of footsteps on the stairs, she looked up. Wren, in her nightshirt with her arms wrapped tightly around her thin body and her face splotched with red, descended slowly. When Kit slid over on the couch, Wren sank down beside her.

Since they had frequently used this notebook for their evening devotions, Kit pointed to the next words, which Ezra had copied from the Book of Common Prayer. Together, they read them aloud. "Lord Jesus, stay with us, for evening is at hand and the day is past. Be our companion in the way, kindle our hearts, and awaken hope, that we may know you as you are revealed in Scripture and the breaking of bread. Grant this for the sake of your love."

She opened her Bible to Psalm 143. "A prayer for deliverance," she read aloud, "a psalm of David." Wren closed her eyes as Kit read the psalm four times, with silence between each reading, so they could listen for a word or phrase that captured their attention and invited prayerful reflection and response.

Hear. Give ear. Answer me.

At first, all Kit heard in the text was the urgency of the plea, the jeopardy of the one who prayed, the weariness, the crush, the darkness, the pleading for God to rescue and deliver. *Therefore my spirit faints. I stretch out my hands. My soul thirsts for you*

Only after the third reading did a single phrase rise above the clamor: *Let me hear of your steadfast love.*

There. That was the settling word, the light to the path, the reorienting toward the trustworthy foundation of God's mercy, especially in times of distress. *Let me hear of your steadfast love, Lord.* Not only in the morning when the day was new, but at the end of a tiring day when enemies of despair or worry could more easily ambush her and drag her down toward the pit.

Let me hear of your steadfast love. Not only in the morning, but whenever she sat in darkness, whenever her spirit fainted, whenever remembering days of old was not a pathway toward gratitude or an opportunity to rehearse God's faithfulness, but a detour into regret.

Let me hear of your steadfast love.

The more she savored the phrase, the more it widened. *Let us hear. Let them hear. Let all hear of your steadfast love.*

In the quiet after the final reading, Kit tucked her chin to her shoulder and pictured herself nestled against Jesus' breast—and not just her, but the whole weary world gathered near and safely held in a tender embrace of steadfast and compassionate love.

When Kit eventually opened her eyes, Wren was sitting erectly on the couch, staring at the flickering flame. "Closing prayer?" Kit asked.

Wren nodded. Together, they read another excerpt from the Book of Common Prayer: "Keep watch, dear Lord, with those who work, or watch, or weep this night, and give your angels charge over those who sleep. Tend the sick, Lord Christ; give rest to the weary, bless the dying, soothe the suffering, pity the afflicted, shield the joyous; and all for your love's sake. Amen."

Kit let the silence hover before closing the notebook and her Bible. "I'm glad you joined me."

"Me too. Thanks."

The wick crackled. The wax dribbled through a gap and down the side, creating a new pool on the glass base.

Her eyes still on the flame, Wren said, "I think I really messed something up."

Kit did not reply. No need to rush or force a disclosure by asking questions.

Wren drew her knees to her chest. "I found out yesterday that Casey's parents are selling their house, and it upset me. It shouldn't have, but it did. Like I was losing one more connection with his life here."

As soon as she heard that, Kit time-traveled to Micah's room, emptied after the house had been cleared out to sell. She saw herself kneeling there, running her hand back and forth along the carpet where his bed had been, where he had taken his last earthly breath.

She understood.

"And then today," Wren said, "when I had to pack up all of Miss Daisy's belongings—which wasn't much, just a couple of boxes—I started wondering what Casey's parents might have kept that belonged to him."

A few boxes. That was all that had been packed from Micah's room too. Robert hadn't moved any of those boxes with him to Arizona. She had kept them, with Micah's name scrawled in Robert's handwriting on the lids. When she moved into the condo, she asked the movers to put them in the basement beside boxes of Christmas decorations and a few childhood mementos Sarah had left behind.

"I sent a text a little while ago," Wren said, "and I'm wishing I hadn't."

Kit waited a moment to make sure she had control of her tone. "You sent a message to his mother?"

"No. No way I would text her. I texted Casey's friend Chris, one of the guys who was at Casey's memorial service. The one whose mom was so excited about him deciding to follow Jesus, she told Mrs. Wilson all about it."

Kit remembered. Casey's mother had then sent Wren a spiteful text, which Wren printed out and burned so she could incorporate the ashes into her painting of Jesus before Pilate.

"I've seen Chris a few times at church since then, so I figured it wouldn't be weird for him to get a message from me. And since his mom is good friends with Mrs. Wilson, I figured she might know details about their move. So I asked Chris if he knew anything. Or if he could find out anything for me."

Kit hoped her eyes wouldn't communicate her dismay.

Wren ran her hands over her face. "I wish I could take it back. Because what if he goes to his mom, and she tells Mrs. Wilson I'm trying to get information? Then what?"

Yes, Kit thought. Exactly. Then what?

Wren pressed her forehead to her knees. "'Do not enter into judgment with your servant,'" she murmured. "That's the phrase I kept hearing from the psalm. But I deserve it for this. It was a really, really stupid thing to do. But it felt so urgent, like I absolutely had to know." Kit heard her whisper, *I'm sorry.* "Why can't I let Casey go? Why do I keep trying to hold on?"

Kit was going to say, "Be patient with yourself. These things take time." But it didn't seem as if Wren was looking for an answer—just a place to voice the question.

"I think I'll send Chris another text and say, 'Never mind,' and hope it isn't too late, that he won't think it's a big deal." She rose. "Yeah. I'll do that."

After Wren bounded up the stairs, Kit sat a few minutes in the silence. Then, leaning forward, she cupped her hand around the flame and blew the candle out.

12

At her computer in their home office, Sarah watched a video that her mother's first spiritual director had sent from her nursing home in Tampa. "Is it on?" Lucy called from a wheelchair near a panel of windows. The light was so bright behind her, Sarah could hardly see her facial features.

A louder voice said, "I pressed the button." The shot jerked from Lucy to the linoleum floor, then to a scuffed-up sneaker. "Yep, it's going. Go ahead. You can talk now."

Lucy's overexposed face reappeared in the shot. "Katherine?" she said, her voice quavering. "I miss you. It's been so long since we were together. And now I hear you're retiring from"—she slowly turned her head toward the window—"from the place where we met a long time ago. You know the one I mean." She looked back at the camera, then lifted a yellow piece of paper from her lap. "Wait a minute now, I wrote something for you. Get me my glasses, will you, Bea?"

A veined, wrinkled hand came into view, removed the glasses from the top of Lucy's head, and looped them over her ears. The shot pulled back as Lucy adjusted them. "Thank you, that's better." She lifted the paper closer, the lower half of her face now obscured. The picture zoomed in, then out again.

"My dear Katherine," Lucy read, her voice becoming steadier. "I wish I could be with you to celebrate this grand occasion. I know you are surrounded by people who love you as much as I do. I'm glad your daughter, Susan, is making a videotape for you. She said I could read you something or share a memory or pray for you. So I'm going to give you the blessing we used to say together at the end of our meetings." She lowered the paper and, closing her eyes, said with a strong voice, "The Lord bless you and keep you. The Lord make his face to shine upon you and be gracious to you. The Lord lift up his countenance upon you and give you peace." She opened her eyes and looked directly into the camera. "I love you, dear one. I'll see you again when we're both safely home."

Lucy folded her paper and took off her glasses. "Is that good?" she asked, looking at the camera again. Then her image froze on the screen.

Sarah wiped her eyes with the back of her hand.

How could she edit the clip to best honor Lucy's contribution? Not only was the lighting harsh, but whoever Bea was—another resident, she supposed—had trembling hands the entire time she was filming. And how would Mom feel, seeing Lucy struggle to remember names? But if she cut out those lines, the artless beauty of her gift might unravel.

She stared at the face of her mother's beloved mentor, the woman who had first introduced her to the ministry of spiritual direction and had companioned her in prayer and discernment for many years, helping her navigate heartaches and celebrate growth.

Though Sarah had never spent much time with Lucy, her mother described her as a no-nonsense woman with a quick wit, strong opinions, and the ability to speak the truth with a fierce and protective love. Sarah knew there had been times when Lucy's aggressively surgical approach had felt a bit overwhelming to her mom, even wounding. "But I always knew she was for me," her mother often said, "that she wanted me to be free and whole." Lucy had perceived leadership potential in her and had done everything she could to challenge and exhort her as she said yes to God's call. *The next yes,* as Mom liked to say.

How long had it been since Lucy retired and moved south? Seven? Eight years? Losing someone who had been so deeply invested in her life had been painful for her mom, especially after all her other losses.

Eventually, after many months of searching for a new spiritual director and a few false starts, she'd found Russell, who was also gifted, she said, but in an entirely different way.

"Ah, come on!" Zach yelled from the living room, where he was listening to his beloved Mets play. "You're killin' me, Smalls!"

Sarah tapped her fingers on her desk. She would need to find a way to make the video work. Though Jess had promised to help after she returned from Orlando, Sarah had hoped to make significant progress on editing clips before leaving for the cottage in the morning.

Leaning back in her chair, she called out to Zach. "Can you come here a sec?"

"Unbelievable," she heard him say. "How could you walk that guy with two outs?"

She strode to the doorway. "Zach?"

"Yeah?" He was lying on the couch, phone in his hand.

"Do you know if you can adjust lighting on a video?"

"On a phone video, you mean?"

"Yeah, on the video Lucy sent for Mom." She motioned for him to sit up so she could sit beside him.

"Probably," he said, "but I have no idea how. Text Jess." He reached for his Coke can on the coffee table and took a sip.

She motioned for him to share his drink. "What's the score?"

"Don't even ask."

"That bad, huh?"

"Currently thirteen-nothing."

She nearly spat out her mouthful of soda. "Seriously? Why are you still listening?"

"'Cause it's only the fourth inning. Plenty of time for a comeback." Leave it to Zach never to be daunted by impossible odds.

Knowing she would have a better chance of a quick reply from Morgan, she retrieved her phone from the charger and texted her instead. *Hey, hon! Could you pls ask Jess if there's a way to adjust lighting on a video and make the picture less shaky?*

"Nooooo!" Zach yelled as the broadcaster called a double to right field, enabling the runner to score from first. "You had two outs, buddy! Two outs, for cryin' out loud!"

She sat down beside him again and patted his knee. "Deep breath, babe." Three dots appeared on her screen. *Jess says yes.*

Zach leaned his head back, listening. Ball one. "C'mon. If you can't control that fastball, then . . ."

Sarah typed, *How?*

The broadcaster called ball two. Zach muttered something.

Morgan wrote, *She says she can do it when she gets home.*

Sarah typed, *I know. But I want to get a head start on it.*

The broadcaster called the next pitch. A swing and—

Zach leaped up from the couch and stamped his foot as the broadcaster described the ball sailing over the center field fence. "Sixteen!" he yelled. "Sixteen nothing!" He punched a button on his phone. The broadcast ended.

"What about that comeback?" she asked.

He sank onto the couch. "I'm all for miracles, but the writing's on the wall for this one."

"Flatliner?" she asked.

"Yeah. With an ironclad DNR."

Her phone buzzed with another text, this time from Jess. *Hey, Mom. Just leave it till I get back. Plenty of time before the party.*

Sarah sighed. She and Jess had a different definition of "plenty of time."

Okay, hon. Thanks. She set her phone next to Zach's on the coffee table. "I'm beginning to regret my video idea."

"So, scrap it."

"Not when so many people have already taken time to send messages. I need to honor their contributions."

"Yeah, but it's about your mom, though. And maybe the videos don't need to be shown to the whole group. You could give them to her as a separate gift."

She stared at the fireplace. Never one to seek the limelight, her mother had only very reluctantly agreed to the plan for a formal retirement party. So would a tribute video played in front an audience be a gift to her? Or torture? What was the best way to celebrate and honor her? The best expression of love?

She shifted on the couch. "Are you packed and ready to go?"

"I will be." He picked up his phone.

"You'd better be. I told Linda and Ed we'd be there in time to meet them for lunch."

"Great," he said sarcastically.

"Why? What's the problem?" The Coopers had been like family to her ever since she was a little girl, and Ed and Zach had been golfing buddies for years.

He pointed to his screen. "A score like that? He'll never let me live it down."

She patted his arm before returning to her to-do list. "Put on your big boy pants, my friend, and deal with it."

It never failed, Sarah thought as Zach turned onto the lane that wound toward their cottage. As soon as they passed Freda's Ice Cream hut on the corner, with its colorful pinwheels spinning in planters of geraniums and petunias, Sarah was eight years old again, bouncing on her seat in the back of the family Ford, her Nancy Drew mystery temporarily forgotten.

Zach slowed behind a golf cart they immediately recognized. "Don't you dare honk at them," she said. "You'll scare them half to death."

He lowered her window. "Hey, strangers!" he called as they pulled up beside them.

Ed and Linda both waved. "Race you!" Ed leaned forward as if he was going to floor it.

"Don't even tempt him," Sarah said.

Linda grinned. "Always a competition between these two boys."

"All right, Doc," Ed said as he waved them on, "I'll give you this one. Meet you there."

As Zach drove ahead, Sarah watched them in her side mirror. The Coopers lived the life her parents had never enjoyed—laughter, hobbies, friendship. And though Carol and her dad had shared a happy life, they hadn't been able to enjoy a long retirement together. Not like Ed and Linda, who could still travel and garden and sip wine with one another at the edge of their pier, watching Hodge Lake shimmer in gold beneath a setting sun.

They turned left into the driveway, the gravel crunching beneath the wheels. Something about that sound confirmed the leap across a threshold into another world—an older, slower world where, her mother would say, the demands of *chronos* time more readily yielded to the invitations of *kairos*.

Opening her car door, Sarah inhaled the freshness of pine, just as her mother had always done whenever they first arrived. Mom would lean her head back and breathe deeply, a blue checkered scarf covering her hair and tied in a knot beneath her chin. Since she only ever wore kerchiefs on vacation, those colorful bandanas had signified leisure and hope. Her mother whistled or hummed more often when she wore them, and she always donned one before they left home for a weekend at the cottage, a silent declaration of the quest for family fun and harmony.

But the arguments that darkened their house in Kingsbury disregarded geographical boundaries. Sarah had often fled the stress of her parents' bickering by retreating to the woods or the shore to read. Micah usually chose the edge of the dock, where he dangled his feet in the water while sorting his latest rock collection.

When she glanced at the pier, she could almost see him there in his straw hat, ignoring their mother's plea to wear a shirt beneath his denim overalls so he wouldn't get sunburned. She pictured him sitting on the dock, coaxing onto his lap a feral cat nobody could catch or tame and then sniffling quietly on the bottom bunk later that night because their mother was allergic, and Oreo had to stay outside. And behind.

"But who will take care of him when I'm not here?" Micah had sobbed. He had kept his nose pressed against the car window most of the way home, and the next time they went to the cottage, Oreo was gone.

Odd, the images conjured without her consent.

She looked up at two wooden signs fastened beside the front door: one reading, "Simpson," the other, "Kersten." Maybe the Simpson memories returned with such strong force because the girls weren't with them.

"Welcome!" Linda called after Ed parked the golf cart in their adjacent driveway.

"Condolences, Doc," he said with a grin.

Zach pretended to rebuff his handshake. "Don't even start with me, old man."

"Was it a record for runs scored? I haven't looked yet."

"Yes, he has," Linda said. "First thing this morning he checked, just to wind you up, Zach."

Ed laughed. "Twenty-five to four! Whoo-eee!"

"Behave yourself." Linda poked his chest. "I tell you what, Zach, if he ever needed someone working on him in an emergency room, he'd want somebody who doesn't give up, no matter how bad it looks."

"Right you are!" Ed said. "This world needs relentless optimists. Keep it up."

Zach saluted.

"Need any help carrying things in?" Linda asked.

Sarah unloaded a few bags of food from the backseat. "No, we've got it, thanks."

"All right, then, we'll get out of your way and let you settle. Still good for lunch? Or would you prefer dinner? Doesn't matter to us. Ed's grilling burgers either way."

Zach slung his duffel bag over his shoulder and removed Sarah's small suitcase. "I didn't have much breakfast, so lunch sounds good."

"Just come on over whenever you're ready, then," Ed said, "and I'll fire it up." With that, the two of them walked hand in hand across the lawn to a house much larger than the modest two-bedroom cottage Sarah's grandparents had built in the 1950s.

"I think I may go for a quick swim first," Zach said as they carried their bags up the porch steps. "Want to join me?"

"I'll wait, thanks." The second she unlocked the front door and swung it open, she froze, causing Zach to bump into her from behind.

"You okay?"

She stared at the paneled walls. They were white, not natural honey-colored wood. And the dining table had been moved from the small kitchen area to a corner of the living room, where it was drenched in sunlight.

"Sarah?"

Which was all ridiculous, of course, because now that she thought about it, the dining table had been positioned beside those windows since before the girls were born. She had eaten many meals there with Zach, Dad, and Carol as they watched swans bob on the lake or kayakers paddle by.

She stepped inside and deposited the bags of food on the kitchen counter. "I could have sworn when I opened the door that the walls were the wrong color."

"What color are they supposed to be?"

She recognized that look. Give the man his stethoscope, and he'd be busy assessing symptoms. "No, I mean, I know they're white." Carol and Dad had painted them after they got married because Carol said it felt like a cave in there and needed brightening up. Which was what her mom always used to say too, but Dad argued that his father had built the cottage, and it was staying the way he intended it to be. Until Carol requested the change. He had always yielded readily to Carol.

She cast her gaze around the cheery room. She hadn't minded when her stepmother upgraded the space with braided rugs, gingham cushions, nautical wall art, and breezy fabrics in shades of blue to mimic lake and sky. When Sarah inherited the cottage after her father died, she'd seen no reason to change anything, especially since Carol visited occasionally before she remarried.

Her mother, on the other hand, hadn't set foot in the place after the divorce. Whenever Sarah invited her to come and spend a weekend with them, she always made excuses. After a while, Sarah stopped inviting.

She opened the fridge and put away the milk, eggs, and cheese. If she could find a photo of her mother in a kerchief or Micah in his overalls, she might frame and display them alongside the ones of her dad, Carol, Zach, herself, and the girls. To honor all the life lived within those walls.

13

Thirty-six hours after she texted Chris again, the messages still showed as delivered but unread.

Wren shoved her phone into her backpack before putting everything in her Willow Springs' locker. She could check again on her break.

The good thing, she thought as she maneuvered her cart onto the elevator, was that whenever Chris picked up her texts, he would get both at once. There wouldn't even be time for him to contact his mom for information. Not that he would have immediately done so after reading her first message. But it was reassuring that she hadn't missed the window for shutting things down.

As soon as she exited the elevator, Greta greeted her from the nursing station. Evidently, whatever chill Wren had experienced yesterday because of Teri's complaint—real or imagined—had thawed. "I've got revised instructions for the day," Greta said, summoning her over.

Wren parked her cart out of the way.

"Pete has a ten o'clock haircut. That'll be a good time to do a thorough cleaning of his room, including the floors. Betty is resting this morning. If her door is open during the lunch hour, you can clean then. And Dorothy's windows need extra attention. The rest of the schedule Audrey left for you is fine." She handed Wren a pencil to mark the changes on her sheet.

"Audrey isn't here today?" she asked as she scribbled her notes. Audrey was always the one who updated any special requests or schedule changes.

"Problem with childcare," Greta said. "She'll be in later."

Wren thanked her, then pushed her cart along the first hallway. Mr. Kennedy was sitting in his chair, concentrating on his breakfast, the low and soothing voices of golf commentators floating through the doorway. She decided not to interrupt. Across the corridor, where the door was partially closed, a decorated shadow box hung on the wall. Parking her cart beneath it, she peered at the items: a paintbrush, a playbill from a Broadway production of *Les Misérables*, and a black-and-white photo of a young man on a stage, dressed in Shakespearean costume. She leaned in for a closer look. The animation of his arms, the intensity of his gaze, a single raised eyebrow—all these character-istics Mr. Page had carried forward out of his youth into his middle school classroom. That single raised eyebrow had communicated everything from curiosity to skepticism to deep thought to a "Don't even think about trying that" warning to preteen boys, Casey included.

Rather than risk disturbing him by knocking on the door, she peeked through the opening. He was propped up in his bed, the tray table positioned in front of him, his scrambled eggs and bacon un-disturbed. Softly, she called, "Mr. Page?"

He slowly turned his head and looked at her with such cavernous melancholy that she gripped the edge of the door to steady herself. She could only imagine the legion of losses that had dimmed those once lively eyes. If she could have sketched him—if she could have captured the ache as he searched her face, as if longing for reprieve, only to be disappointed again— if she could paint him, those with eyes to see might be moved to tears. Or prayer.

Vincent would have painted him. He *had* painted him. Over and over in his own self-portraits, he had painted that same ache, that same plea for compassion or understanding or help. *Companions in misfortune.* In sorrow. Vincent would have immediately recognized in Mercer Page a brother. And yes, if Vincent had seen his work, a fellow artist too.

She entered the room. No photos. No paintings. No silk plants. No magnets on the small fridge or decor on the walls or mementos on the shelf. Just an ash gray chair and dark hardwood floors and beige walls and brown blinds battened down against the window and a mustard-colored blanket tucked around the lower half of his body like a burial shroud.

She approached the bed, where a white wand with its red call button was wrapped around a small silver bedrail. They must have determined he was at risk for falling. "Hey, Mr. Page," she said. Though his eyes were locked on hers, he showed no sign of recognizing her. Why would he after all these years? "I don't expect you to remember me, but you were my art teacher at Kingsbury Middle School."

She wasn't sure if the flicker of emotion that swept across one side of his face was pleasure or pain.

"I'm Wren Crawford."

She waited. No verbal response. If her unusual name didn't ring a bell, one more detail might spark a connection. "You were really kind to me when I moved here from Australia."

One side of his mouth curled slightly upward. "You've lost your lovely accent, Wren." Whatever damage a stroke might initially have caused to his speech, the old stage veteran could still project and enunciate well enough to be heard—if not to the back of a room— at least within one.

"My mum still has hers," she said, slipping on the old accent like a favorite wool jumper.

"Some things never leave us," he said. As his gaze drifted toward the window, she wondered what things he had in mind.

"Would you like me to open those blinds for you?"

"No, thank you."

"Are you sure? It's a nice day out."

"All the more reason to keep them closed."

She cleared her throat. "Is it all right if I clean your room for you, Mr. Page?"

He appeared to be considering this. "Is that what you do here? Clean rooms?"

Her face flushed. "Yes, sir." Immediately, she felt compelled to explain. "I was a social worker. But it became too much for me, so I'm taking a break."

He shut his eyes. "The best laid schemes o' mice an' men," he said in a Scottish brogue, "'Gang aft a-gley an' lea'e us nought but grief an' pain for promised joy.'" He opened his eyes. "Do you know that one?"

"Only the first line."

He lifted his hand ever so slowly to scratch the side of his nose. "Learn the rest while you're still young. It'll save you a lot of disappointment."

Not sure how to reply, she shifted her weight from one foot to the other.

"Morning, Mr. Page!" a cheerful voice called from the doorway. Kayla entered with a broad smile, waved to Wren, and said, "You need help with that breakfast?"

He stared at her.

"Looks like you haven't touched it. Can I get you something else? A muffin or toast or something?"

"No, thank you."

"Okay. If you get hungry, though, remember we've got yogurt and bananas and granola bars in the lounge. And a good lunch to look forward to." She moved the tray aside. "We're gonna get you dressed and into your wheelchair so you can get a good start on the day. Peyton has lots of fun things planned."

Wren watched his jaw set.

"I'll come back later to clean, Mr. Page," she said as Kayla untucked the towel from his shirt.

"'To a Mouse,' by Robert Burns," he replied, his sad eyes locked on hers. "Be sure to read it."

Following his advice, she spent her lunch break near the courtyard fountain, reading on her phone a modern translation of the Burns poem about a man who, while plowing his field, inadvertently destroyed the home of a little mouse, who scampered away, terrified.

Not only had the tiny mouse's labor been obliterated, but it was winter, and there would be no rebuilding. *Poor wee beastie.* All that effort, all the resources invested into creating the comfort of that humble dwelling place, all the hope and expectation to shelter there from snarling wind, and with one horrific crash, it was gone. Forever.

The buzzing of her phone startled her. A text. Not from Chris, though. From her mom. *Still good to paint with Phoebe after work today?*

Wren typed, *Yes.*

Her mom replied with a thumbs up.

She took a bite of her sandwich. Maybe Chris wouldn't reply. And would that matter? As long as he didn't do what she had first asked him to do—and why would he?—all would be well. No harm done.

Unlike the man in the poem, who had inadvertently caused irreparable harm.

At least he had compassion on his fellow creature and regretted what he had done. But there was no remedying the destruction, no caring for the vulnerable little one now exposed to menacing cold. She read the last stanzas again.

> But little Mouse, you are not alone
> In proving foresight may be vain;
> The best laid schemes of mice and men
> Go often askew,
> And leave us nothing but grief and pain,
> For promised joy!
>
> Still you are blessed, compared with me!
> The present only touches you.
> But oh! I backward cast my eye
> On prospects dreary!
> And forward, though I cannot see,
> I guess and fear!

Poor creature, poor man, enduring the cruel uncertainties of this life, no matter how carefully they planned. What circumstances, she wondered, had prompted the man to ponder their solidarity in disappointment? What burdens of the past made his suffering more acute than that of the little mouse? Regret? Guilt? Cumulative losses that made it painful to hope? And those losses, combined with the anxieties of an unknown future, could lead to despair.

Perhaps he was only naming the reality of the human condition rather than reflecting on the circumstances of his life, how the past and the future could encroach on the present and taint it with gloom and fear.

She pictured Mr. Page in his barren room, waiting for someone to help dress him, and imagined the storms of destruction that had hurled him there. She would tell him she had read the poem. And if he asked if she understood it, she would say yes. And if she felt brave enough, she might ask this companion in sorrow about the ways he had lived those verses and see if he might become a companion in hope as well.

When she returned to the second floor to clean the public spaces, a dozen residents, including Mr. Page, were seated around a long table frequently used for games or arts and crafts. Peyton stood at the head, holding toilet paper tubes in each hand. "Anyone want to guess what we're making today?"

"I've got a guess," Mrs. Clement called out, casting a sidelong look in Mr. Page's direction, "but I'd rather not say in polite company."

From the corner where she was dusting, Wren suppressed a chuckle.

Peyton was undeterred. "Tropical fish! We're going to make cute little fish to decorate for our beach party. You're all excited for our party, right? Only ten more days!" She set down the tubes and fetched a sample from a nearby shelf. "Here, I've made one to show you. All we have to do is flatten out the rolls, make a couple of cuts with scissors, and voila! Ready to decorate." After raising it above her head and rotating it for people to see, she gave it to Mrs. Whitlock, who was sitting closest to her. "Take a look and then pass it to your neighbor."

When Mrs. Whitlock finished looking, she passed it to Mr. Kennedy, who, without taking it from her, nodded slightly and said, "Isn't that something."

"Pass it along, Pete," Peyton said, "so everyone can see."

But his hand was shaking so badly, he dropped it. Kayla stooped to pick it up and then gave it to Mrs. Clement.

"Now, I'm very excited today," Peyton went on, "because we've got an actual artist with us. You've all met Mercer, right? Mercer was an art teacher for many years, weren't you, Mercer?"

Wren clutched her cloth, wondering what Mr. Page was thinking as he stared forward.

Peyton plowed ahead. "So we'll have an expert who can give us pointers for our art projects, won't we?" She scanned the table. "Who's got my little fish?"

Chelsea, one of the CNAs, retrieved it from Mrs. Vanderwaal's lap and handed it to Peyton. "Okay, so you've seen my example, but you can do anything you want to decorate yours. We've got lots of different colored pens and stickers, plenty for everyone. And construction paper—lots of bright and cheerful colors to choose from. And if you want to use some little googly eyes, we've got those too." She held up a sample eye and wiggled it. "So cute, right?"

Mr. Page had set his left hand on the table and appeared to be trying to push himself backward in his wheelchair, but the brake was locked.

Kayla stepped forward. "Hey, hey, where you goin', my friend?"

"Away."

"How about staying here with the group awhile? We've got a great snack planned for after our art project."

"No, thank you."

"You sure? We could use your help with our art."

Wren watched him lift his hand. If he had made that single gesture from the front of a stage, the entire auditorium would have immediately fallen silent. "What you're doing here," he said, "needs no help from me. And since you cannot take me where I want to go,

I'll go instead to my room." He turned his face toward Peyton, the motion made all the more dramatic because of how slowly he pivoted. "And you, young lady, may call me Mr. Page."

As she gathered her painting supplies in her studio later that day, Wren pictured Peyton's mortified expression while she stammered out an apology. If she hadn't felt so fiercely loyal to her former teacher, she might have felt sorry for Peyton—especially after she happened to overhear a tearful bathroom conversation in which Peyton confided to Chelsea how tired she was of trying so hard to make life fun for them and how unappreciated she felt. "Let it go," Chelsea replied. "You're doing a great job. We all have moments like that." And then she invited her to happy hour at The Tavern. Wren had waited in her stall until she heard them leave.

On her worktable she spread out her brushes and palette knives. Though she had told Phoebe she might try painting the bald cardinal, the sunflower heads near her courtyard window had started to open, and rather than painting from imagination or a photograph, she would prefer to paint directly from nature. Like Vincent. She removed from her box the tubes of cadmium yellow and orange, yellow and red ochre, phthalo and chrome oxide green, and burnt umber. She studied the sky. Cerulean with hints of lilac.

After setting up her easel near the window, she perched her iPad against a stack of art books on the table so Phoebe would be able to see both her face and her canvas while they painted. At first, she had considered moving all her material outside, but that felt like too much effort. Now that she had decided to return to her art, though, she could set aside time for plein air painting too.

Mr. Page had taken his students outside to draw and even paint a few times. She remembered sitting on the front lawn with a small canvas panel and a paper plate with her palette colors, staring up at orange leaves of a maple tree set against a bright blue sky. But she couldn't capture the beauty of the sunlight converting the leaves into flames. Her orange paint on the canvas was only orange. No life. No luminosity. Until Mr. Page suggested she look more closely at the leaf to see if she perceived any other colors she might layer on top of the flat orange. So she layered a splash of red and streaks of yellow, and though it wasn't nearly as radiant as what she saw, the leaf became textured, with a slight glow. He had nodded his approval and said, "Now, what can you do with the sky?"

As she squeezed colors onto her palette, she pictured him in his cheerless cell. If only his room faced the garden courtyard with the fountain. Someone social like Mrs. Clement preferred the parking lot view, which enabled her to monitor the comings and goings of visitors and cars and activity in and out of the building. Miss Daisy had sat in the chair that now belonged to Mr. Page, clutching Emmy Lou while watching and waiting for people who would never come.

No wonder he insisted the blinds remain closed.

She had hoped to talk with him again before the end of her shift, but his door had also remained shut. While he was at lunch, she cleaned his room, hoping to find cardboard storage boxes stashed away in the closet, indicating a work in progress. But the only personal items in the room were a few shirts and trousers hung along the rod. She pictured the gray-haired woman—wife? sister?—who had accompanied him with a suitcase and wondered if she was the one who had gathered items for the shadow box. At least she had taken the suitcase away. A suitcase communicated a temporary situation and might only magnify the losses. Hopefully, she would soon return with photos, mementos, or even some of his paintings to decorate the walls.

Then again, he might not be comforted by a touch of home. The reminders might be too painful. Still, she couldn't imagine an artist like him bearing such a sterile room for long.

An incoming call buzzed on her iPad. "Hey, Phoebe-girl!" Wren called when her little sister appeared on the screen. She wore shorts and an oversized tie-dyed T-shirt Wren recognized as a hand-me-down from Olivia.

"Wait a second," Phoebe said. "Mommy says I have to put on my smock."

"Good idea. I'll put one on too, okay?" She reached for her canvas apron.

"Hey, hon, how're you going?" Her mother stepped into view with a small red waterproof smock and held out the neck hole for Phoebe to duck into. "Feeb's been pretty excited about this."

"Me too," Wren said as she looped her apron strap around her neck.

"Do you have pockets?" Phoebe displayed hers.

"That's so cool! No, I don't have any."

"I can put my brushes in here, see?"

"That's perfect, Feebs. But don't put them in there when you've got paint on them, right?"

"Right." She ran her hand over her smock and set her brushes down. "But we can wash it all off when I'm done."

"That's good." Wren eyed the canvas she had prepped months ago. "I thought I would paint sunflowers like you, okay?"

"Yep. I'm going to paint more." Turning her head, she giggled at something Wren couldn't see. "Daddy, stop!"

"What's Dad doing?"

He appeared onscreen wearing a royal blue felt beret and sporting a mascara handlebar mustache. "I thought I'd paint with the Crawford girls tonight."

"That's my hat, Daddy!"

"Oh, all right, then." He whipped it off his head and placed it on hers. Then he planted a kiss on her cheek. "Doing okay, Wren?"

"Yeah, thanks. You?"

"Hanging in there."

Phoebe adjusted her beret, then leaned closer to the screen to inspect herself. "Okay, I'm ready." She stepped back to her easel.

As they painted, Phoebe reported on the latest Doc McStuffins episodes, her playdate with a new girl at church, and the speckled fawn she had seen in their yard that morning while sitting on her swing. "But then he ran away from his mom, and his mom was so mad because he ran across the street without looking."

Wren braced herself for a bad ending. "Was he okay?"

"Yeah. But his mom was making this snorting noise with her mouth like this"—she opened her mouth and breathed in and out heavily—"and then she ran across the street too." Phoebe dipped her brush into a blob of yellow and carefully painted more petals on her sheet of paper. "But there were no cars."

"That's good."

"Yeah. They were lucky."

Wren studied her own canvas, the spiky green bracts surrounding an unopened sunflower like a rosette on an award ribbon. She mixed her phthalo green with a tiny bit of cadmium yellow. Yes. A nice bit of contrast to the chrome oxide green. The variety of August greens astonished her as much as May greens did.

Olivia walked into the kitchen and waved at the screen.

"Hey, Liv!" Wren said. "Nice to see you!"

"Yeah, you too." She patted Phoebe's beret. "Okay if I start making cookies, Feebs?"

"Yep." Phoebe dunked her brush into a glass of water and swirled it around. "We're having movie night tonight because Daddy doesn't have a meeting, and it's summer."

"Lucky you!" Wren took a narrow palette knife and played with the greens on the canvas, layering the rosette.

"I get to stay up past my bedtime because I took a nap," Phoebe said. Behind her, Olivia pulled out mixing bowls from a cabinet.

"Wish I could be there with you to watch a movie and eat cookies," Wren said.

"And popcorn. Joel's making it."

"What are you going to watch?"

"*Inside Out.*"

"I'm jealous, Feebs! I love that movie! One of my very favorites."

"Me too. Because it's okay to be sad sometimes, right?"

"You're right. It is." She wiped off her knife and squeezed more ochre onto her palette. "Do you feel sad today?"

"Nope."

Wren caught herself before saying, "That's good." If her sister could learn at an early age that sorrow and joy could coexist and that healthy and appropriate sorrow had an essential role to play in emotional and mental health . . .

Phoebe was staring at the screen, her brows furrowed. "You okay, Feebs?"

"Your sunflowers are better than mine."

"Your sunflowers are gorgeous!"

"No, they aren't. They look bad."

Wren wasn't sure if she should hide her canvas or let Phoebe continue to examine it. She left the screen where it was. For now. "When I was your age, I didn't even know how to paint. You're an amazing artist." She pointed at her screen. "Look at how you've done your flowers there, all facing different directions, just like Vincent's. See? Each one is unique."

Phoebe didn't look convinced.

"And the way you've painted the leaves—some of them straight and some of them droopy. See? Hey, Olivia!" But Olivia, who had her back turned while measuring ingredients at the kitchen counter, was wearing earbuds and didn't hear Wren calling. "Phoebe, ask Olivia or Mom and Dad to come see your painting, okay?"

Phoebe was now standing with her hands on her hips. Before Wren could say anything else to her, she snatched the painting from her easel—"Phoebe, careful with that!"—and ripped it in half.

Wren shouldn't have smiled. But Phoebe's defiant stance in her smock and beret struck her as comical.

"It's not funny!" she shouted.

Wren covered the corners of her mouth. "I know, I'm sorry. It's not. Mom or Dad can tape it for you, don't worry."

But instead of setting it aside for repair, Phoebe shredded it into smaller pieces.

"Oooh!" Joel said as he sauntered up behind her. "Look at the artist having a temper tantrum. Cool!"

She butted her head against Joel's waist, then tried to box his chest. He laughed, which made her angrier.

Olivia, now aware of the commotion behind her, yanked out her earbuds, and yelled, "Hey! Stop it! Both of you."

But Joel just laughed harder, and Phoebe just boxed harder until Mom and Dad swept into the room. They didn't need to say anything for Joel to exclaim, "Okay, okay! I'm sorry I laughed." But by now, he couldn't stop.

Phoebe burst into tears. Dad scooped her up into his arms. "Hey, hey, I've got you. You're okay."

Mom leaned toward the screen and said, "I'm sorry, Wren, we'd better go." Just before she ended the call, Wren could see Phoebe nestled against their father's breast, her sobs quieting. The tenderness of that image lingered long after the screen went dark, and as she stared at her canvas, she thought of Casey, remembering with joy and sorrow the comfort and gift of that kind of embrace.

Two hours later Wren was still hard at work in her studio, adding texture, value, and details to her sunflowers. Though dusk had fallen and the courtyard flowers were cloaked in shadows, her painted versions exploded like starbursts beneath the fluorescent lights. Not bad for an amateur.

She leaned back and stretched. Time to call it a night. She put away her paint tubes and gathered her brushes and knives to rinse them off in the hallway kitchenette. But just as she was about to head out of her studio, she heard a man's voice from the direction of the lobby. Panicked, she flicked off the lights and shut her door as quietly as possible, then locked it from inside, her heart hammering her chest.

No one should be in the building. The only man who worked there was the part-time maintenance guy. That wasn't Mike's voice.

Neither was the second one.

She sank to her knees. Had she left the front door unlocked or had they jimmied it open? And what would they think when they saw a bike in the lobby? Would they assume someone was still inside?

She pressed her ear to the door. Silence. That was worse. She was completely blind. No way to check the hall. No view of the front parking lot.

She crawled across the floor, grabbed her phone, and called Kit, who answered on the third ring with a sleepy, "Hello?"

Huddled beneath her worktable, she whispered, "Kit, it's me. I'm still in my studio, and there are men's voices coming from the lobby. I don't know who they are or how they got in."

"Did you say men are inside?"

"Yes. Two. At least two." She heard muffled voices. Maybe they were trying to break into the front office. If she heard glass shatter, she might try to make a run for it down the hall, into the chapel, out a back door.

"Wren? Are you still there?"

"Yes."

"I want you to dial 911."

Her heart pounded in her ears. She had hoped Kit might tell her she had hired workmen to come in late on a Thursday night to fix plumbing or something. "You're not expecting anyone to be here?"

"No. Call 911 right now. Stay in your studio. Lock your door."

Hands shaking, Wren punched the emergency number. "Please," she said after spitting out all the details, "could you stay on the phone with me?"

The operator promised she would. "Help is on the way," she said, her voice calm and authoritative.

Crouched beneath the table, Wren commanded herself to breathe. She needed to stay alert. *Jesus, help.* How long had she already hidden there, phone glued to her ear? Minutes? Hours?

"Still with me, Wren?"

"Yes."

"Do you still hear voices in the building?"

"Yes, I think they're coming closer."

"Okay, stay right where you are."

She rocked back and forth as the voices grew louder. "The chapel's down this way," one of them said, and the other replied, "Okay, great."

Wren stopped rocking.

"Wow, somebody likes artwork, huh?"

"Yeah. Katherine and her niece put them up for prayer."

Wren crawled out from under the table and inched closer to the door.

"Gotta confess, I'm not much of an art guy," the younger-sounding one said, and the other said, "Me neither. But she's led a few retreats using art, and some people seem to like it."

"Ummmm," Wren whispered to the operator, "I think it's actually okay."

"You think they're gone?"

"No, they're still out there, but I can hear them talking, and it sounds like they know my aunt."

"Like they're targeting her?"

"No, I mean, like one of them might be a friend of hers or something." But that still didn't explain why he would be in the building this time of night.

"Bill!" Kit's voice shouted. "What in the world?"

Still gripping her phone, Wren leaped up and yanked the door open. The man nearest the door jumped back, hands up, while the older man staggered a few feet forward, hands to his chest, and exclaimed, "You just about gave me a heart attack!"

"It's okay, Wren," Kit said, bustling toward her in a bathrobe and slippers. "Everything's okay." She threw her arms around Wren and kissed her cheek.

"It's okay," Wren said to the operator, her body starting to shake. "We're okay."

Just then, an officer appeared at the end of the hall. The older man turned to the younger one and grimaced. "Welcome to Kingsbury, Logan. Guess I'll have some explaining to do."

14

After Bill went to talk with the officers, Kit sank to the floor beside Wren and draped her arm around her. Poor girl. She looked as if she was trying as hard as she could to keep her breathing steady. Kit was too. During the short but interminable drive from her house to New Hope, she had barely managed to pull herself back from the brink of a full-blown panic attack. It had been a long time since she'd been catapulted that close to the edge of one too severe to conceal.

She unclenched her left fist and opened her trembling, clammy hand. Release. Receive. And breathe.

Logan raked his fingers through his dark hair. "It's my fault. I just arrived from Tulsa and told Bill I wanted to see the place before our official meetings start tomorrow." He crouched in front of them. "You must be Kathcrine. I'm Logan Harris. And I'm really, truly sorry."

Before she could introduce Wren, Bill called to her. "They want to check out my story, Katherine."

With another deep breath, she accepted Logan's outstretched hand and rose to her feet. "You're lucky I'll vouch for you, Bill."

He responded with a suitably remorseful nod.

Clutching the collar of her robe, she explained to the officers that Wren had been painting in her studio when she heard someone enter the building. "I told her to call the police because I couldn't think of any reason why anyone would be here this time of night."

Wren, still sitting on the floor, wiped her eyes. When one of the officers asked if she was okay, she murmured, "Yes, I'm fine. I'm sorry I caused so much trouble."

"You didn't cause the trouble," Bill said. "I did." He looked at Kit. "And what were you thinking, driving here and racing in when you thought there was a robbery underway?"

She shrugged slightly. "I wasn't sure how long it would take the police to get here."

The other officer said, "Ma'am, in the future . . ."

"I know, I know, but as soon as I pulled into the parking lot, I recognized his car and pieced together what had probably happened. I didn't run into the building expecting to confront armed men. I just wanted to get to my niece." She motioned for Wren to join her. "Is there anything else you need from us? Or are we free to go home?"

"We've got what we need," the officer said.

"Good. Thank you so much for your help." She faced Bill. "Since you have a key, you can lock up whenever you're done."

Only after they reached her car did she realize she hadn't spoken a parting word to Logan. Never mind. If he judged her for being angry and upset, so be it.

"The board found somebody to replace you?" Wren asked as she fastened her seatbelt.

"I didn't tell you?"

"No."

"I'm sorry." She hadn't meant to keep that general information from her. "Bill told me I wasn't allowed to share details, but I should have thought to tell you they were flying in a candidate." She turned her key in the ignition. From her rearview mirror, she watched Logan in the lobby with Bill, talking with animated gestures and laughing. She clenched her jaw. It was far too soon to be laughing about anything that had happened tonight. If he thought any bit of it was funny—

"He's not an art fan," Wren said.

"Who isn't?"

"The new guy."

"How do you know that?"

"I heard him tell Bill he wasn't. And then Bill said he wasn't either, but that some people seemed to like it."

"*Some people?*"

"Yes."

Kit inhaled, then exhaled slowly. If she felt offended, then there was pride to offend. As she turned left out of the parking lot, she silently confessed her sin and prayed God's blessing on them. She knew no better way to resist the gravitational pull toward anger and resentment. "Were they dismissive about people who find value in it?"

"I don't know. Their conversation got interrupted when you shouted and scared them to death." Wren sighed. "Thanks for coming to rescue me. I shouldn't have freaked out like that. I should have recognized Bill's voice, should've known there was a good explanation."

With one hand still on the wheel, she patted Wren's shoulder. "Dear one, 'should've, could've, and would've' will get us nowhere fruitful. We did what we did for good reasons. We can leave it at that." She smiled sheepishly. "But maybe don't tell Sarah what her mother did tonight."

The next morning, promptly at nine o'clock, Logan rapped against her partially open door with a jaunty, rhythmic knock. "Come on in," she called from her desk, and rose to meet him.

"Hey, Katherine," he said, extending his hand, "nice to see you again." His chummy tone bordered on patronizing. Without waiting for an invitation, he sat down in a chair facing her desk, removed a water bottle from his canvas briefcase, and crossed one leg over the other, his ankle resting on his thigh.

She frowned at the back of his head. Make yourself at home, she thought. Then she pushed the door shut.

Open your heart, she heard the Spirit whisper.

She kept her hand against the door.

The whisper came again. *You've already made your decision about him. Open your heart. And listen for his.*

Rubbing her palms against her slacks, she pivoted toward him.
"You doing all right?" he asked.

Too intrusive a question. He had no right to—

Keep your heart open, the Spirit repeated.

She nodded, both to Logan's question and the Spirit's command.
"Yes, thank you. Just saying a short prayer." The words—which
probably sounded sanctimonious—had flown out of her mouth
before she could restrain them. Not exactly an auspicious beginning.
If she didn't have control of her thoughts or her tongue, this meeting
would not go well.

He lowered his foot to the floor. "It would be great to pray together, if you're willing. Honestly, I'm feeling a little nervous after
last night." He set his bottle on the carpet. "When I called my wife
after everything happened, she was horrified. Again, Katherine, I'm
so sorry."

See? Sarah would say. So might the Spirit.

She took a moment to compose herself. Then, rather than sitting
behind her desk, she chose the chair beside his. "My very first spiritual director used to love to say, 'Always we begin again.'"

He clasped his hands together. "Thank you. Maybe we can
start there."

The next hour flew by as she listened for his heart, not only in the
questions he asked, but in the vision he articulated: to enhance New
Hope's presence in the local community and beyond so more people
could benefit from the gift of retreats, workshops, and seminars that
provided space for life-transforming encounters with a living God.

He was concerned, he said, by the number of books he'd read
and events he'd attended that emphasized spiritual formation as a
self-improvement exercise designed to promote self-discovery rather
than discipleship, self-fulfillment rather than dying to self. "We can
get so focused on looking within ourselves, we ignore the well-being
of others," he said.

"A spiritualized narcissism," Kit replied.

"That's it exactly. God knows I don't need to be encouraged to be even more self-absorbed. I can get so curved inward, I hardly see the needs of others. Just ask my wife."

She laughed. "Family members are great at holding up mirrors so we can see ourselves more clearly."

"Oh, yeah. My kids do that constantly." He eyed the clock on her wall. "I know our time's almost up, but there's something else I wanted to ask you about, and it might not be a comfortable question to answer."

"That's all right. That's why we scheduled this time together, so you could ask whatever's on your mind." She waited, wondering where his thoughts were traveling during the silence.

"My in-laws are the ones who told me about this job. Nicole grew up near Muskegon, and we've been talking awhile now about trying to move closer to her family. With Savannah starting kindergarten this year, it seems like a good opportunity for making a big switch, not just in terms of location, but to find something that matches my emerging sense of call."

Ah, she thought. Mystery solved.

"I did as much internet research as I could about the programs here, and the retreats and workshops have looked great. I mean that sincerely. A good range of topics and presenters."

She readied herself for the inevitable "but."

"I was wondering what type of demographic usually attends the events. Is it mostly women?"

"Yes. Even for the events that male presenters lead." No matter how hard they had tried to appeal to men—

"And what about age?" he asked.

"I'd say the majority are middle-aged and older." They had tried to design programs for intergenerational groups but—

"How about in terms of ethnic or racial diversity?"

She felt her face flush. "Mostly White."

He held up his hand. "I'm not criticizing. I'm just asking."

"No, I know." But for the second time in a week, a mirror she wasn't comfortable looking into had swung toward her.

Keep your heart open, the Spirit again commanded.

"I know a bit about West Michigan," he said. "My father-in-law's from the whole 'If you aren't Dutch, you aren't much' background."

Kit had heard that insider jest plenty of times—sometimes with barbed wire concealed behind the smile. When she and Robert moved to Kingsbury from Ohio as newlyweds, she'd had no idea Dutch heritage had played such a significant role in shaping West Michigan culture. "Maybe we need to add 'van' or 'vander' to 'Simpson,'" Robert had quipped.

Logan took a drink from his water bottle. "I've been in touch with a couple of seminary friends in Grand Rapids who have been trying to promote antiracism efforts. They've been reaching out to pastors of predominantly White churches, just trying to get conversations started about racial brokenness and our kingdom responsibility in working toward healing and restoration. Not just pursuing a surface-level appearance of diversity to make ourselves feel better, but doing the really hard work of addressing underlying patterns of sin and resistance and fear. Long and slow spiritual and cultural formation work. Believe me, I'm not naive about the challenges. But I'm wondering how open the board would be to that kind of ministry. Would they support offering programs that specifically address racial justice issues? Is there room for hosting tough conversations here?"

Kit forced herself to look him in the eye. "There hasn't been any focus on that, Logan, but that's not because the board has resisted ideas or recommendations. It's because I haven't pursued it as a priority."

For a moment she was tempted to explain herself, to defend the work she had done at New Hope. Even if her teaching hadn't focused on specific issues in culture and society, she had tried to encourage people to practice receiving and responding to the love and grace of God in ways that impacted all of life—individually and in community—for healing and transformation.

But she didn't say that. "We've had occasional workshops and retreats about justice issues from a spiritual formation angle," she said, "and every once in a while, we've hosted community conversations about local and global needs. But during my long tenure here, we've never had a program that specifically addressed racism." She paused. "And the responsibility for that oversight falls squarely on me."

There was nothing judgmental in his expression. "I get it," he said. "I'm only beginning to confront my own blindness and complicity. Being in Tulsa the past few years has opened my eyes a little, but I've still got a whole lot to learn. And honestly, one of the reasons I've been looking for a new ministry context is that every time I try to nudge our church forward into racial justice conversations, I hit a wall. Major resistance and fear, not just from the congregation but from the staff. And since I'm not the senior pastor, I don't feel like there's a whole lot I can do to respond to how the Lord has been stretching me—not at an organizational level, anyway. I feel like I need to start fresh somewhere so I can keep growing."

A loud knock sounded on the door, causing Kit to jump in her seat. Before she could rise to see who was there, the door inched open, and Bill said, "Sorry to interrupt, but Logan has another appointment, and we've got to get going."

"Give us another couple of minutes, please," she said. "We're almost done."

He glanced at his watch, then closed the door.

Logan lowered his voice. "I want to do whatever I can to advance God's purposes, even if it's just using my fundraising background to support some new initiatives. And I'd love to establish collaborative opportunities with local agencies and partners who are already doing the hard work. I think there's a lot of potential here, as long as the board is open to it. They say they are. But I wasn't sure if they were just telling me what they thought I wanted to hear. That's why I wanted to get your honest input."

She studied his earnest face. "I've never known the board to be anything but supportive of what I've offered in terms of programming.

So if they tell you they're open, I think you can trust that. Even if it becomes uncomfortable."

"Well, that goes with the territory," he said. "But if we can at least begin to see and name the places where we get defensive or protective, then that's a start, right?"

"Yes. A great start." Good thing she had left herself ample time between this meeting and her first spiritual direction appointment of the day. She had plenty to process in terms of her own defensive reactions.

"Please don't get me wrong," he said. "What I'm talking about isn't intended to replace what New Hope is already providing to the community. I just see opportunities for more."

"I'm glad you do." She stared at her hands, aware of the gravitational pull toward shame regarding her own failures and oversight. And really, how self-centered was that, making her response about her own guilt and discomfort? One more thing to confess to God in prayer.

"You know what the Spirit used in order to wake me up and help me see?" he asked. "I was at a meeting about a year ago with a group of pastors and community leaders, and at lunch I caught up with one of them—an African American pastor I hadn't seen in a while— and asked how he was doing. He told me he'd just had to have The Talk with his ten-year-old son, and I smiled and said I remembered when my dad had that talk with me and how uncomfortable we both were and that I didn't look forward to having it with my son, Eli. He listened and then gently corrected me. He wasn't talking about the sex talk. He was talking about the talk that Black parents have been having with their sons for generations—a talk I'd never even heard about—and his eyes filled with pain when he described how his little boy's lip quivered when he told him that the older he got and the taller and stronger he got, some people would see him as a threat. Some people would be scared of him. And he would need to make sure he didn't wear his hoodie over his head or keep his hands in his pockets when he was in the store to buy candy."

This wasn't about her shock or horror, Kit reminded herself as she tried to remain fully present. This wasn't about her discomfort or ignorance. But as Logan shared more details about what the father had told his son, she thought of Mara and wondered if she'd had to have similar conversations with Jeremy when he was young. Though Mara had often spoken about her concerns for him, in all their years of spiritual direction together, she had never mentioned what it had been like to be a White woman raising a brown-skinned son. In Kingsbury. Kit had never asked her. It never would have occurred to her to even wonder what kind of grief or fear Mara might have experienced, watching Jeremy get taller and older.

Logan said, "He told me later he wasn't sure why he opened up like that, why he felt compelled to be honest with me. Because we could have just done the typical superficial check-in and talk about how ministry was going. But he honored me with his story. And I told him the Holy Spirit must have put the words in his mouth because that conversation—brother to brother, dad to dad got through to me, in a way that none of the news stories ever had. I could distance myself from all of those, live in my protected little bubble, kid myself by thinking we had all moved forward and evolved into a post-racial society. But hearing him talk that day and seeing his heartache and fear . . ." He clutched his water bottle. "Truth is, I worry about lots of things for my kids. But the color of their skin isn't one of them. And the very fact that I don't have to think about it shows my privilege. That's what I'm starting to see."

He sat in silence, looking pensive. "I know my voice won't be the important one to hear in these kinds of conversations," he said after a while. "But if we can steward our gifts and resources by making room at the table for diverse voices to speak and be heard—really heard and understood—then that's a start too." He set his bottle on the floor. "Would you be willing to pray for me, Katherine?"

A lump rose in her throat. *Always we begin again,* she thought, and took his hand in hers.

Part Two

OUT OF DARKNESS

*For it is the God who said, "Let light shine out of darkness," who
has shone in our hearts to give the light of the knowledge of the
glory of God in the face of Jesus Christ.
But we have this treasure in clay jars, so that it may be
made clear that this extraordinary power belongs to
God and does not come from us.*

2 CORINTHIANS 4:6-7

15

I told you so!" Sarah exclaimed on the phone when Kit finished giving her all the details about her meeting with Logan. "I told you he was a solid guy."

Kit leaned back in her patio chair and gazed up at spokes of sunlight streaming through the branches of the neighbor's honey locust tree. "Yes, you did. But I was so caught up in looking for my own watchwords, I was blind to the gifts he brings that are vastly different from mine." After Logan had left her office, she'd spent half an hour in the chapel praying. But there was far more to process. Thankfully, she had a spiritual direction appointment scheduled on Monday with Russell.

"Logan asked me if it's okay for him to come to the retreat tomorrow, and I told him, sure. I suppose it's fine that he'll see exactly what we talked about today. Very little diversity with age and gender and none with race."

She shut her eyes. What did she honestly expect to contribute to conversations about race or the work of promoting issues of justice, especially at her age? She didn't have the gifts of a prophet. She had always considered herself an ear in the body of Christ, listening attentively, offering whatever wisdom God supplied, and exhorting others to trust his love and grace and faithfulness. But had she been precise enough in her teaching and her encouragement so that the ones she served had been enlarged by the love of God to love others generously? Or had she, while appealing for prayerful self-examination, only reinforced the kind of self-absorption and spiritual narcissism they had talked about—and lamented?

"I know what you're doing, Mom. You're beating yourself up, aren't you? You're second-guessing everything about your ministry because of what Logan asked."

"Not everything. Only some of it."

"Well, don't let the enemy drag you to condemnation."

"I'm not. I'm just being honest with God about what I'm seeing. I'm naming my need to address my hardheartedness and blindness. Whatever that might involve."

"Okay, fair enough," Sarah said. "But being enlarged by the Spirit for something new doesn't mean discounting the faithful work you've already done. You're the one who always says we see what we need to see when the Spirit reveals it."

Right, Kit thought. Light always came as a gift to expose whatever lurked in the dark. But sometimes the gift hurt her eyes.

"As far as advocacy goes," Sarah went on, "that takes lots of different forms. Your ministry has focused on the poor in spirit. The spiritually captive. You've preached good news to people oppressed by sin and regrets and grief. So don't feel guilty about a call or gifts you don't have. We've all got different parts to play in the kingdom."

Sarah was using her teacher voice. There would be no arguing with her, no explaining how she felt about what she had seen—or her bewilderment about where to go with it. So instead, she replied, "Thank you, honey. I appreciate your encouragement."

"And another thing," Sarah said.

Kit stared again at the tree.

"It isn't like Kingsbury has a ton of racial diversity, Mom."

"Not in some neighborhoods, no. But that doesn't mean there isn't any. Or that I couldn't have tried to encourage diversity in the programs I offered."

"You haven't excluded anyone," Sarah said.

"No, but I haven't been deliberate about including, either. Sometimes our sins are ones of omission." And those, it seemed, were always harder to see.

Logan's words came to mind again. "The way I look at it," he'd said after Kit thanked him for their conversation, "justice is all about pursuing what Paul calls 'the more excellent way' of love. We've got to put flesh on what we say we believe about God's kingdom priorities and really confront the ways we haven't loved our neighbors as we've loved ourselves—especially neighbors who are different from us. It's all about seeing and confessing how we've privileged our own comfort, how we've worked to preserve and defend the status quo that benefits us while ignoring people who aren't flourishing like God desires." Then he'd paused and said, "Change all those 'we' statements to 'I.' I'm guilty of all of it. And now that I see it, how will I respond? That's the question, right? If I say I see, then what will I do with what I see?"

And that, Kit thought as she and Sarah finished their call, was a stewardship issue too.

After Wren completed setting up the New Hope refreshment table early Saturday morning, she found Kit sitting on the memorial bench in the courtyard, clutching her small wooden cross. "Am I interrupting?"

"Not at all," Kit said. But her smile seemed weary as she scooted over on the bench.

Wren sat down beside her. "What else can I help you with?"

"Trash is emptied? Bathrooms are clean? Registration table is in the lobby?"

"Yes to all that." After hearing that Logan planned to attend, she had double-checked everything.

"Then I think we're ready," Kit said. "At least, I hope so." Again, that weary smile. Ever since the incident with the police, she hadn't seemed quite herself. But whenever Wren asked if she was okay, she gave the same answer: just tired. And though she had hoped Kit might share details about her meeting with Logan yesterday, she'd seemed reluctant to say anything other than, "I think he has strong gifts the community needs." Wren hadn't pushed for more.

"Are you sure you're okay, Kit?" It didn't hurt to ask again.

She took a slow breath. "I didn't sleep well at all last night, just couldn't get settled down. And now I'm second-guessing all the content I've prepared for today. I'm not sure, though, if it's the Lord prompting a different direction, or if it's weariness and anxiety, or my own ego and vanity rising up."

Wren responded with a gentle scoff. "Katherine Rhodes, you are the least vain person I know."

"Oh, dear one. You have no idea. If I've given you the impression of being free of it, then that's just further evidence of my vainglory."

"What do you mean? What's vainglory?" She couldn't remember ever having heard that word before.

Kit slowly rubbed the cross with her thumb. "It's all about wanting to maintain an image with a high approval rating. One of the so-called deadly sins."

"If that's what it is," Wren said, "then I'm guilty too. Big time. I care way too much about what people think of me."

Kit eyed her with compassion. "Wanting a good reputation isn't the problem. It's when we become attached to it as a source of our identity, security, or worth, when we'll do whatever it takes to earn the approval or applause of others, even if that means practicing deceit and manipulation to gain that good opinion."

"So, wearing a mask."

"Yes. Whatever mask will work in the situation."

Wren watched her rotate the cross several times in her hand. "I still don't see it in you, Kit. And I don't think that's because you've fooled me with a really good mask."

Kit thanked her. "But I've had lots of years to practice noticing and naming it. And what makes this one so tricky is that even when you try to combat it by confessing your sin and weaknesses to others, you might just be trying to impress them with your own humility." She smiled slightly. "I say that from personal experience, not as a hypothetical possibility."

Wren clasped the edge of the bench. "So, what are you supposed to do with it? How do you get rid of it?"

Kit stopped rotating the cross and stared into space. "Offer it to God whenever I notice its grip. And then practice receiving from him the love and approval I'm attempting to get from others. That's pretty much the remedy for counteracting all our disordered desires—drinking deeply of the love of God."

She would need to keep finding ways to practice that, Wren thought as she watched a few sparrows splash about in a nearby birdbath. It was way too easy to forget, way too easy to drift.

"You're welcome to join us for the session," Kit said after a while. "We're talking about stewarding sorrow and suffering today. Unless I hear differently from the Lord." She set her cross on the bench and looked at her watch. "At this point, there's not much time left for him to redirect. But I'll keep listening."

Wren took that as her cue to leave. "I'll be praying," she said, and Kit thanked her again. As she left the courtyard, she glanced over her shoulder. Kit remained on the bench, head in her hands, like the elderly man in Vincent's *Worn Out.*

Through the open door of her studio, Wren heard Hannah's smooth alto voice and Nathan's hearty laugh as they arrived in the lobby.

Maybe she would worship at Wayfarer tomorrow instead of going to the Willow Springs service. She might even see Chris there. And if she saw him, she might casually mention that she'd sent him a text he might not have received and that it was no big deal, really. Just missing Casey, you know? And he might say, Yeah, I get that.

She blew a speck of dirt off the corner of her sunflower canvas. Once she added more definition to the leaves and shadows behind the green bracts, she could sign her name and be done. Then she could start on a new project. Like the molting cardinal triptych.

From the lobby rose the sound of a male voice she recognized. "Just visiting today," Logan said. She wondered if the board had devised a cover story to offer the inquisitive. Or maybe they had already made their decision and didn't care who figured out his identity.

She looked out the window. Amazing, how much the sunflowers had changed in just a couple of days. If she wanted, she could paint them in other stages of life, just as Vincent had done with his. And when the heads were weighed down with seeds, she could collect them and plant again. If not at New Hope, perhaps at Willow Springs.

At her worktable she opened one of her Van Gogh art books and flipped the pages to the sunflower section, the petals of his cut flowers teeming with life. Or were the flowers technically dead the moment they were cut off at the stem? Vincent had painted them in their final burst of vitality, even as they began to wilt in the vase. They were dying and decomposing before her very eyes. A *memento mori*, one of her art history professors had said about Vincent's collection of sunflowers. *Remember you must die.*

She leaned in for a closer look.

And let that reminder shape the way you live.

She found nothing morbid or despairing about that message. She even found comfort in it. Because the promise of life remained—even in the dead flowers. For those with eyes to see, the hope of life was even more visible in the dead ones. Because they were the ones that showed the seeds.

Yes, she thought. There was a promise of life, both in the molting cardinal and the dying sunflowers. The images were connected. In fact, from what Kit had described about pinfeathers and the sturdy sheaths protecting the vulnerable new growth, those casings sounded a bit like seed coatings, protecting the tender embryo inside.

That could make an interesting visual juxtaposition: pinfeathers and seeds. She could play with that. Maybe she would paint her bald cardinal surrounded by sunflower seeds. Eating sunflower seeds. Did cardinals like sunflower seeds?

"Hello there," a voice called from the doorway, causing her to jump. She spun around. "Oh, boy," Logan said, "my bad again. Sorry to startle you."

She slid her hand from her neck to the sleeve of her T-shirt. "Hey, Logan."

Without waiting for an invitation, he stepped inside her studio. "It's Wren, right?"

"Yeah." She quickly closed her art book.

The overhead lights reflected off the top of his polished shoes as he surveyed the room. "Cool space. Are you an artist in residence or something?"

"No, I'm the housekeeper. But Katherine lets me use this room as a studio."

"Oh, right. Bill mentioned that." His expression seemed to indicate he knew more than he was letting on. He pointed to her easel. "Is that your work?"

Seized by the impulse to throw her body in front of her latest creation to protect it from scrutiny, she opted instead for a simple, more reasonable, "Yes."

Without asking her permission, he sauntered toward her painting and, with his hands tucked into his trouser pockets, glanced back and forth between the canvas and the window. "Pretty cool," he said, then looked over his shoulder at her. "So you're part time here?"

"Yes."

"Is that because you've got another job somewhere or . . ."

She rubbed her throat. "There aren't enough hours available here, so yes, I work two jobs."

"Ah, okay." He seemed to be considering this as he turned again toward the window.

She wished she could rescue her canvas from any further inspection and clasp it to her breast, the back side facing him, but the paint was still wet.

"Hey, Wren!" Hannah's voice called from the doorway. For some inexplicable reason, Wren felt the urge to burst into tears and run to her. *Get a grip*, she commanded herself, and strode toward her pastor for a hug.

Maneuvering around them, Logan excused himself with a wave and a "See you later!"

After he disappeared, Hannah asked, "Is that a candidate for Katherine's job?"

She nodded.

"Are you okay, Wren?"

She wasn't sure. But she didn't know why she wasn't sure. "I think so." She reached for her bag. "Is it all right if I sit with you?"

"We'd love to have you join us," Hannah replied, and escorted her down the hall.

The back-corner table near an exit door provided an ideal position for being inconspicuous while also affording a good view of other people in the room. Wren wondered if that was why Hannah liked to sit there. Though her pastor took extensive notes, her gaze periodically drifted to the back table opposite them, where Logan sat across from Russell, frequently checking his phone. From the expression on Hannah's face, she didn't approve of his lack of etiquette.

"Stewarding affliction faithfully," Kit was saying, "means naming it for what it is. When we deny or minimize our distress, we join the father of lies in his campaign of deceit. When we refuse to acknowledge the truth about our suffering—when we try to shrink our suffering and our sorrow to a size where we can manage or control it, we're only fortifying our flesh. Self-sufficiency and self-reliance— those great American values of pulling yourself up by your bootstraps—are symptoms of pride."

She picked up her Bible from the podium and thumbed through it. "Let me read to you what Paul says about his distress, how he honestly and vulnerably names the truth of his affliction. Listen to 2 Corinthians 1:8-9: 'We do not want you to be unaware, brothers and sisters, of the affliction we experienced in Asia; for we were so utterly, unbearably crushed that we despaired of life itself. Indeed, we felt that we had received the sentence of death so that we would rely not on ourselves but on God who raises the dead.'"

She looked up from her Bible. "Think of that. The great apostle felt so overwhelmed and weighed down by distress that he despaired—the Greek word there means to be totally at a loss with no way out—Paul and his ministry partners felt so completely defeated, they despaired of life. Does that sound anything like the saying 'God never gives you more than you can handle'?"

There were murmurs around the room.

"If we can handle our circumstances," Kit said, "why would we need God? No, the gift in being overwhelmed—and the invitation to steward our affliction faithfully—is to be able to say with Paul, 'I'm pressed beyond what I can bear. I have no human power or resources I can rely on. And so, I will not trust in myself or my own strength to persevere, but I will trust the God who raises the dead.'"

From the corner of her eye, Wren watched Logan fold his hands on the table. Kit, meanwhile, was scanning the room with an expression Wren recognized. She had seen the same look on her face when Kit led a retreat session about lament this past spring.

Kit was listening. Wren could tell. She was listening for whether the Spirit was directing her to speak about her own personal experience. With Logan in the room. Maybe he was the reason she had second-guessed her topic for the morning.

Kit motioned to her Bible. "If you've ever felt so burdened you could hardly breathe and struggled to imagine ever finding your breath again . . . If you've ever despaired of life, no matter what circumstances led you there, then you're in good company." She paused. "I'm in good company. And I'm so deeply comforted by this detail from Paul's journey. I'm so grateful he was honest about how he felt."

Companions in distress and despair, Wren thought. And in comfort. From the expressions on a few other faces, she and Kit weren't the only ones who sympathized with how Paul had felt.

Kit shuffled a few pages on the lectern. "Before we look at the rest of this passage together, I'll press a pause button here and give you space for personal reflection and prayer. Let me offer you a few prompts as you think about honestly naming distress as a first step in stewarding affliction."

Wren stared at her. That was it, then. Whether she had discerned a leading away from sharing her own story or had simply decided not to, the moment for vulnerability and disclosure had apparently passed.

"The word Paul uses for 'affliction,'" Kit said, "is a word that means 'pressed.' Think of times when you've felt crushed under the weight of suffering, when you've felt like there was no way of escape, when you've felt hemmed in or claustrophobic with the pressure. That's the word Paul uses here. Like the compression of grapes in a winepress. Or olives being crushed for oil. This is the kind of suffering when you feel confined and squeezed, and you aren't sure how much more you can take. That's *thlipsis*. It's not just intense tribulations we might experience but also disappointments that crush the life out of us."

When their eyes met, Kit's expression was so tender, Wren thought for certain she was going to divulge something about their common journey with depression or grief or loss.

But Kit wouldn't do that. She wouldn't expose her like that. Not without first asking permission to share her story.

Wren steadied herself with a slow breath. Silly, the irrational grip of panic that had overtaken her.

"Some of you were here for our Journey to the Cross during Holy Week," Kit said. "For those of you who may not be familiar with this part of our ministry"—Wren watched her make eye contact with Logan—"for more than twenty years now, we've hosted an opportunity for the wider community to come and pray with art and Scripture texts that help us keep company with Jesus on his journey to Golgotha. This year, we were deeply enriched by Wren Crawford's contributions"—Wren froze in her seat as multiple eyes, including Logan's, were now fixed on her—"and as I was praying about what we might use in our first exercise today, one of her exquisite paintings came to mind."

Kit retrieved her painting of Gethsemane from behind the podium. Wren clutched the edge of the table. Kit hadn't mentioned she intended to show one of her paintings. If she had known Kit planned to display one, she wouldn't have come to the session. She would have locked herself away in her studio until everyone was gone and it was time for her to clean up. It was one thing for her paintings to be on public display when she wasn't in the room. But to have to sit there and watch people react to her work? That just created anxiety. If that was evidence of vainglory or pride, fine. Whatever. Guilty.

Kit rotated the painting so everyone could see. "This one is called *Pressed*. It's a beautiful invitation to consider how we have been pressed—to name to God the times when we have felt crushed and overwhelmed, even possibly despairing of life. And to find in our own places of pressing the companionship and comfort of Jesus, who was bruised and crushed for us."

Though Kit kept talking, Wren stopped listening. In the corner across the room, Logan picked up his phone again and started typing in his lap. She felt a surge of anger—not just at Logan for being disinterested or even dismissive, but at Kit, for exposing her to scrutiny and judgment. Even rejection.

"Are you okay?" Hannah quietly asked after Kit finished speaking. A few people moved closer to the painting. Others began journaling at their tables.

"Just feeling agitated," she whispered. "I think I'll go sit awhile in my studio."

"Do you want company, or would you rather be alone?"

Who better to process her feelings with than Hannah? "Company would be good," she said, and together, they left the room.

16

R*elease,* Kit commanded herself as she watched Hannah trail Wren into the hall.

If she had considered the possibility that Wren would object to her art being included in a retreat session, she never would have shown it. Or she would have asked permission first.

Straightening her notes on the lectern, she pictured Wren's horrified expression when she held up her painting. Whatever needed to be resolved between them would need to be addressed later. For now, as exhausted as Kit felt, she had to remain fully present to the work and the people in front of her. If Wren had overreacted enough to be in significant distress, Hannah was more than capable of helping her.

"Is the courtyard open for prayer?" a woman asked.

"Of course! Feel free to go there. Or the chapel."

While others around the room engaged in silent reflection, Logan was typing on his phone. Again.

She felt her body clench. Again.

Throughout the session he probably hadn't been using his phone to read along with the Scripture passages or to verify her interpretation of Greek words. More than likely he was texting—even after she had given her usual opening reminder about turning off cellphones to diminish distractions.

How hard would it have been to put the phone away? Or, if something urgent needed his attention, he could have left the room.

As if in reply, he stood, phone pressed to his ear, and exited.

Release, she commanded herself again. *And receive.*

But hard as she tried to settle down for her own prayer and re-flection, she couldn't quiet her soul. After fifteen minutes of glancing up every time the back door opened—only to find it wasn't Hannah or Wren—she made her decision. If Wren was that wounded by what she had done, then she needed to leave her gift at the altar and go seek forgiveness now. Before she tried to lead the next portion of the retreat.

The corridors were empty, and Wren's studio door was closed. Before knocking, she listened for voices inside. Nothing. "Wren?" she called softly.

At the far end of the hall, Hannah emerged from the bathroom and disappeared around the corner just as Wren flung open her door, her eyes wide. "Did Hannah tell you?"

"Tell me what?"

Urging her to come in, Wren scanned the corridor, then shut the door behind them. "About overhearing Logan on the phone. He obviously didn't know we were in here, and I don't know who he was talking to, but after listening to him, there's no way I'm—"

Kit threw up her hand. "Hold on. I don't need to hear about a private conver—"

"But he was criticizing you and New Hope! He said he wasn't surprised the finances were such a mess because if this was the kind of"—Wren signed air quotes—"'dire and depressing' content being offered, then it wasn't the sort of thing that would motivate donors to contribute."

Her pulse quickening, Kit leaned against the edge of the worktable. "I'm sorry," Wren said. "I shouldn't have told you."

"You shouldn't have been eavesdropping."

"He was right outside! We couldn't help overhearing."

"I'm surprised Hannah was complicit in that."

"Complicit?" Wren echoed. "We didn't do anything wrong!"

Kit motioned for her to lower her voice. "We can talk about it later."

"Please don't treat me like I'm twelve."

"I'm not. I'm just saying, I don't have the margin to talk about this right now. I'm still trying to lead a retreat."

"Then why did you come here?"

"To apologize for showing your painting without asking you first."

Wren yanked open the door. "We can talk about that later too."

As soon as the door slammed behind her, Kit sank into a chair, her hands quivering. There was no way she could process all this before she needed to return to the group.

She stared at the ceiling. For now, she would need to set aside the conflict with Wren. She wasn't going to chase after her. *Release.* She pictured Jesus placing his hands on Wren's head and prayed a blessing on her. *Receive.*

She rubbed her temples slowly.

As for the rest . . .

She took a ragged breath.

That would have to wait too.

If she'd had her bicycle, Wren would have ridden away as fast as she could pedal. Instead, she stormed toward a nearby neighborhood, each angry step providing percussive accompaniment to the soundtrack of their argument, which she played on repeat.

Kit had no right to scold her like that. She hadn't done anything wrong. It wasn't her fault Logan was stupid enough to have a private conversation where he could be overheard.

His fault.

She knew something was off with that guy the second he crouched in front of them Thursday night. Sure, his lips spoke words of apology—to Kit, mind you, not to her—but his cavalier smile showed he had no clue—or couldn't care less—about the terror she had experienced because of him.

Jerk.

And to come into her space—without her permission!—to stride right in and start grilling her about why she was there and how many hours she worked, and what business was it of his, whether she worked somewhere else?

None.

If the board chose that guy, she wouldn't work for him. Not after what she heard him say. Kit didn't know the half of it. Because she had cut her off and scolded her. Like she was a little kid.

Kit blamed her for eavesdropping? Well, the only reason she was in her studio in the first place was because of what Kit did. *Her* fault.

She slowed her pace behind an elderly jogger who was making such painful progress, she couldn't bear to pass him as a pedestrian. So she crossed to the other side of the road.

Come to think of it, the painting thing wasn't really Kit's fault. That was Logan's too.

If he hadn't been in the room, would she have cared that Kit used her art as a prayer prompt for the group? As Hannah had reminded her, most of the people at the retreat had probably already seen it during the Journey to the Cross. "Would you really begrudge them the opportunity to pray with a beautiful piece like yours?" she'd asked. Hannah agreed it would have been better for Kit to ask permission, but maybe it was good, she said, that Wren hadn't been given an opportunity to deny it.

That was when they'd heard Logan talking right outside her studio. "Maybe they're all depressed," he said. "I am too after listening to that for an hour." And then he chuckled and made some crack about the tomb being empty and how maybe Kit hadn't heard that news.

Wren cursed him under her breath. What if Kit had shared intimate details from her own story? Would he have laughed about that too?

She picked up her pace.

Audrey might be willing to give her a few more housekeeping hours. It wouldn't hurt to ask. If working more hours at Willow

Springs wasn't an option, she could find hours somewhere else. Anywhere else. Because she wasn't going to work for Logan. Ever.

Much as she hoped to leave aside her agitation, the instant Kit returned to the room, the sight of Logan at his table with his phone beside his notebook caused her heart to race again. She removed her drinking glass from the lectern shelf and raised it to her lips with both hands, the water sloshing onto her chin.

Inhale: *I can't.* Exhale: *You can, Lord.*

She set the glass down and wiped her chin with the back of a trembling hand. Inhale: *I can't.* Exhale: *You can, Lord.* She rubbed her chest slowly with her fist. Back and forth. Back and forth. Somehow, she needed to find a way to complete the task entrusted to her without being consumed by resentment toward Logan for being— what? Critical? Dismissive?

Honest?

She unclenched her hand, her heartbeat pounding beneath her palm. Inhale. *I can't.* Exhale. *You can, Lord.* Logan was entitled to his opinions. His wrong opinions.

Then again . . .

She took a sharp breath. What if the Spirit *had* prompted her to change direction for the session? Her heartbeat throbbed in her ears.

She stared out at the group, their faces blurred at the edges.

Inhale.

Exhale.

What if she had disregarded God's leading? Inhale.

What if she had failed to listen to—Inhale.

No time to change direct—Inhale. *I can't. Catch.*

Her skin prickled. No. Not—

She couldn't swallow. *Jesus.*

She grabbed hold of the podium. No exit. No escape.

"Katherine?" someone called from inside a tunnel.

She bowed her head, the sweat beading on her brow. *Don't fight.*

"Can you lift your arms?"

She gripped her blouse.

"Can you raise your arms above your head?"

Too close. She tried to brush a hand off her shoulder. Too heavy.

"Get her to smile!"

She sagged in slow motion to the floor.

"Give her space!"

She clawed at the carpet.

"Everybody, back away!"

She pressed her forehead to the floor. Tingling. Gasping. *Back away.*

"See if you can focus on my voice, Katherine. I'm going to start counting, okay? One . . . two . . . three . . ."

She rubbed the carpet. Back and forth. Back and forth. Rough. Smooth. *Jesus.*

"Six . . . seven . . ."

A shallow inhale.

A trembling exhale.

"Ten," she gasped as she stretched out an open hand. "Ten."

🐦🐦🐦

So much for her plan of returning to her studio unseen. As Wren crossed the New Hope parking lot, she checked her phone. It was way too soon for people to be leaving the building. Had Kit finished forty-five minutes early?

A sudden wave of nausea swept over her. What if Kit had been too upset to continue after their conversation?

"I thought for sure it was a stroke," she overheard one woman say to another as they walked to their cars.

"Me too. Or a heart attack. I'm glad she didn't hit her head on the way down."

Wren bolted to the entrance and flung open the lobby door.

"There you are!" Nathan strode toward her. "I've been looking for you."

"Where's Kit?"

"She's okay. Just exhausted. Hannah's already taken her home."

She felt her knees buckle with relief. *She's okay*, she repeated to herself several times as she sank into the nearest chair. "What happened?"

"She had a panic attack. A pretty bad one."

Wren drew back, eyes wide. "While she was teaching?"

"Right before she started the second half."

She covered her mouth. It was all her fault. She never should have upset Kit like that. Not when she was already so worn out. "You're sure it was panic, not a heart attack or something else?"

"She told us she's had panic attacks before," he said. "She recognized the symptoms. And they eased up after a little while. But Hannah will keep an eye on her for a bit, make sure she's okay, that she doesn't need any medical care."

"Did she call Zach and Sarah?"

"She doesn't want to bother them while they're away."

"Oh. Okay." Wren hoped that was the right decision.

He lowered his voice. "Hannah told me what happened with Logan. I'm sorry to hear it."

As she sat there trying to digest everything, a possibility occurred to her. "Is he still here?"

"I think so. He was on his phone, last I saw him."

Okay, then. She made her decision. If she didn't take care of this now, she might not have another opportunity.

"I told Katherine I'd be happy to give you a ride back to her place, Wren."

Squaring her shoulders, she rose to her feet. "Thanks. But I've got other plans."

He studied her a moment. "Is there anything I can do for you?"

"No. I'm okay, thanks."

He glanced toward the parking lot, where a couple of cars remained. "I promised I'd lock up after everyone left."

"You can lock me in," she said. "I want to get things cleaned up and put away."

"Already done. A few of us got it all taken care of."

"Oh." Then she needed another excuse. "I'll go work in my studio, then. Thanks so much for helping. I appreciate it."

"No problem. I'll just wait here until everyone else is out."

She thanked him and rounded the corner. With any luck . . .

Yes. There he stood in the hall, typing on his phone. At the sound of footsteps, Logan looked up. "I was hoping to catch you," he said as he ambled toward her.

Funny, she silently replied. *I was hoping to catch you too.*

She stepped aside as two women emerged from the restroom. "Tell your aunt I'll be praying for her," one of them said, and the other nodded.

Logan stowed his phone in his trouser pocket. "Yeah, Wren," he said as the women continued to the lobby. "I was hoping to talk with her before I left, but with everything going on . . ." He took a pen and a small notepad out of his briefcase, then scribbled a number. "Would you ask her to call me?"

She bristled. So he could do what? Kick her while she was already down? No. Not on her watch.

Instead of accepting the paper from him, she planted her feet on the carpet and folded her hands in front of her. Now or never. "I heard you talking about Katherine on the phone earlier and how depressing you thought the retreat was. You were standing right outside my studio door."

His hand froze in the space between them, a shadow darkening his face.

"I told her some of what I heard you say. So, whatever you hope to talk to her about, you might want to throw in an explanation or apology."

He slowly crumpled the piece of paper in his hand.

She took a fortifying breath. "You have no idea what my aunt has been through. None. You have no idea how brave and wise she is, how everything she does is because of her love and compassion for other people, especially people who suffer. You want to know what faithful stewardship of affliction or comfort looks like? Look at her."

She rocked back and forth on her heels. "You want to criticize what she offers, fine. I doubt she cares. But don't criticize people who need what she offers."

He lowered his gaze.

"And just so you know," she said, "both of us got the memo about the tomb being empty."

She pictured Casey bolstering her with a *Way to go, Wrinkle. You tell him.*

"Everything okay here?" At the sound of Nathan's voice, she spun around.

"We're okay," Logan said before she could reply. "Just sorting out a misunderstanding."

Misunderstanding? She pivoted toward him. "I didn't misunderstand anything. I know exactly what I heard. And my pastor"—she pointed over her shoulder—"his wife heard it too."

Nathan tucked his hands into his pockets. "Yes. She did."

Logan blew out a slow sigh. "Okay, can we sit down a minute and talk?"

Wren stayed anchored to her spot. If he was going to minimize what he said or make excuses for why he said it, she wasn't interested in listening. And besides—she wasn't the one who needed an apology.

"Are we the last ones here?" he asked.

Nathan nodded.

"Okay, listen." Logan shifted his briefcase to his other shoulder. "I was blowing off steam to my wife after getting some tough news. I don't say that to excuse myself—just to explain the context of my rant. Because honestly, after getting the board's final numbers this morning, she and I are wondering whether we can make this work for us. So yeah, I'm feeling frustrated that this place isn't in a different financial position. I'm not interested in fundraising my salary or benefits. I want to fundraise initiatives that bless the community."

If he thought that passed for an apology, he was sorely mistaken.

Nathan said, "I don't think it's appropriate for us to be privy to your contract negotiations with—"

"Fair enough," Logan said. "I'm just saying, the comments Wren and your wife overheard had a larger context. And no, I'm not proud of what I said or the way I said it, and I'll apologize to Katherine for it. I was harsh and unkind. And I'm sorry for that."

Maybe, Wren thought. But if he hadn't been overheard, would he have apologized? Was he sorry he said it or only sorry he got caught?

He looked at her. "I don't want to upset Katherine any more than I already have. But I can't leave town without trying to apologize." He uncrumpled the piece of paper. "Would you please give her my number and ask her to call me as soon as she feels up to it?"

Wren hesitated, then took it from him.

"You sure I can't give you a ride home?" Nathan asked her.

She had her own apology to make to Kit. But knowing how draining a panic attack could be, it seemed best to give her space to rest and recover. Especially since she herself had been a primary source of Kit's stress. Not just today, either. She had been the cause of long-term, ongoing, cumulative stress. *Her fault.* "Thanks, Nathan, but I've got work to do here." She waited until he and Logan left the building. Then she sank to her knees beneath Vincent's *Two Cut Sunflowers* and wept.

17

Just because she wasn't answering her phone or responding to texts didn't mean there was anything wrong, Sarah told herself as she dangled her legs over the edge of the dock. She waved to Zach as he swooped by on one of Ed and Linda's jet skis, then reread a few sentences of her novel. Mom was probably taking a long nap, which she often did after leading an event. She might even have switched off her phone.

From behind her a bicycle bell dinged in syncopated rhythm. She turned to see Ed and Linda riding toward her on a tandem bike.

"Why aren't you out there racing him?" he called to her as they dismounted.

"I'm getting too old for that."

"Nonsense. Age is a state of mind."

Linda scoffed. "Speak for yourself." She rubbed her knee. "I thought when we got the tandem that it would slow him down. Instead, he just yells over his shoulder for me to pick up the pace."

"Once a drill sergeant, always a drill sergeant, huh?" Sarah stood and shook off her towel.

Zach sped by again, revving the engine before he did a figure eight.

"Ah, see?" Ed said. "He's taunting me."

Zach waved, then stood up and popped a wheelie.

"Not bad, Doc!" He looked at Linda. "How long we got before dinner?"

"Ah, go on. It'll wait."

He jogged to the house like a much younger man.

"He may not be skipping so happily when he finds out we're having cold cuts," she said. "Not much to invite you to, but you're welcome to join us."

"That sounds great, Linda. Thank you."

"I've got peach pie for dessert, and I'm making potato salad."

"Can I help you with that?"

"Wouldn't mind." She started wheeling their bike across the lawn. "It's your mother's old recipe."

"Is it?" She hadn't tasted Mom's potato salad in years.

"She made it once for a picnic, and Ed fell in love with it. I've made it ever since."

As they passed a row of sunflowers in Linda's garden, Sarah gazed up at the Fibonacci sequence, with hundreds of tiny florets radiating from the center in precise spirals. Dad had taught her and Micah about how that mathematical pattern was revealed in everything from starfish and pinecones to ocean waves and galaxies. She and Micah had turned spotting the sequence into a competitive sport.

Reaching up, she touched the center of the flower. People sometimes asked why she loved math so much. Here. Right here. The elegant beauty of structure and order underpinning a chaotic and broken world. That was one of the realities she tried to show her students. Having something predictable and reliable seemed an important gift to offer middle schoolers.

"Life jacket!" Linda called as Ed exited the house in swim trunks.

Zach slowed the jet ski near the shore. "You comin', old man?"

"Somebody's gotta teach you how to do proper wheelies!"

"Ed!" Linda yelled. "Watch it!"

He waved her off. "I know, woman, I know."

"Those boys," she said as she opened the garage door.

"When did you get your bike?" Sarah asked.

"Beginning of the summer. You and Zach are welcome to ride it anytime." She wheeled it into an immaculate space. Ed had always taken great pride in organizing every tool and gadget he owned.

Someday she ought to ask him to teach Zach how to do that. Far more useful than wheelies.

"I found out recently that Mom always wanted a tandem bike."

"Really? That surprises me."

"I know. Me too."

"She never seemed like the riding type," Linda said. "Not from what I remember, anyway. Now, Carol? Sure. She was always up for adventure. She and your dad used to ride bikes around the lake all the time. Jet skis too. Competitive as all get out, the two of them. In a playful sort of way." She sighed. "I miss having them around. What do you hear from Florida? She and the girls are having a good time?"

"Yeah, great."

"Bet she's spoiling them rotten. Grandmother's prerogative, you know."

Yes. That was what Carol always said.

"Tell her hi for me when you talk to her. She and I are way overdue for a phone call."

Sarah hadn't realized they were still chummy enough to chat by phone. Linda and her mother, on the other hand, had never been close. Friendly, but no relationship. Her mother had always been more private and self-contained than Carol.

She scratched a mosquito bite on her wrist. "So, tandems are pretty safe, then?"

Linda grinned. "If you trust the person at the front, sure. Why? Are you thinking of getting one?"

"Maybe."

"Try it out before you leave. See how you like it."

"Okay. Thanks." On their way into the house, she draped her towel over the back of an Adirondack chair and set her book down. "I keep forgetting to ask you, Linda. Do you have any old photos of us here at the lake?"

"How old?"

"Anything from when I was little? Maybe something with all four of us together?"

She slid their patio door open. "I've got lots of old albums you're welcome to look through. And possibly more pictures in boxes. You want to look now?"

"After dinner's fine."

Linda washed her hands at the kitchen sink, then turned on the stove, where potatoes were already soaking in a pot. "Since you mentioned your brother, I'll tell you that for some reason, I've been thinking about him a lot the past few days."

"Yeah," Sarah said. "Me too." No mystery why, though. Not only had her mother mentioned him more frequently the past few months, but being at the cottage had churned up many memories of him, all of them tinged with melancholy. If she saw him smiling in a photo, it might help.

As she rinsed off her hands, she regarded a pie cooling on the counter, its ruffled edges browned to perfection, its center decorated with cutout leaves. The golden syrup of peaches seeped through its perforated shell. "That looks and smells amazing."

"Thanks. Micah used to love helping me bake pies."

Hearing Linda speak his name caused unexpected emotion to well up. Sarah couldn't remember the last time someone other than her mother had named him. "I remember he used to help you pick strawberries and raspberries."

"Yeah, that boy would eat as many berries as he picked. We used to make a right mess in here." She opened the fridge and removed a celery stalk and an onion. "I don't think your mother had much patience for his messes."

Sarah fixed her gaze on the pie. Hadn't she? She didn't remember that.

"I used to tell him, 'Don't you worry about making a mess in my kitchen. Anything you spill can be cleaned up.' After we finished, I'd hand him a rag, and he'd take care of it. Don't remember him complaining. I think he was just glad for the company."

Sarah slowly dried her hands. With one brief recollection, Linda had indicted both mother and daughter.

Ask anyone who knew him, and they'd say her brother was a loner. But what if he hadn't wanted to be one? She quickly scanned for any specific memories of her shunning his desire for company or attention. Nothing came to mind. But that didn't mean there wasn't anything there.

She collected a knife and cutting board from the counter and started dicing the onion. "What else do you remember about him?"

Linda sighed. "That my boys teased him something awful. I tried best I could to get them to stop, but I know they did it when I wasn't around. Micah never tattled on them, though. Not to me, anyway."

Sarah had also overheard their verbal abuse, and she hadn't tattled on them either. "Sticks and stones," Dad always said, and he expected both his kids to abide by that.

Linda sliced off the leaves and base of the celery, then rinsed it. "I remember Micah went after them one night with a stick because they were catching fireflies in glass jars. He was so angry—worried the bugs wouldn't be able to breathe. Ed snatched the stick away from him before he could hurt anybody, but my boys wouldn't let it go. Called him Bug Boy and other names I won't repeat. Ed washed their mouths out with soap for saying those." She began peeling off celery strings with a paring knife. "In hindsight, I probably didn't help things, letting Micah cook with me. But it gave him something to do. And he always seemed to enjoy it."

"I'm glad you were kind to him, Linda. Thank you for that."

She shrugged slightly. "I remember after getting the awful news, wishing I'd done more." She inspected a celery rib. "But that's water under the bridge."

Sarah kept dicing. Easy for an outsider to say something like that.

"I always got the impression from your dad that your mother never recovered. Not that he and I talked much about it or that I'm judging her for that—I've got no idea how I would have survived if one of my boys had overdosed—but Ed and I often said we were glad your dad was able to move on and find happiness with Carol. I'm sure you saw it too, how he was a different man after he married her."

Sarah clenched her jaw. Yes, but—

"Your mom always was more serious than your dad, though. Maybe that's why she was able to be a chaplain like that. Suited her personality, I guess."

Sarah was going to say something about her mother's gifts, how she had stewarded pain in ways that helped others and gave them hope, but she didn't want to seem defensive. And she suspected Linda wouldn't understand. Once opinions were entrenched—

"I was trying to remember the other day, when I would've last seen your mom. Must have been Morgan's baptism."

"Yes, probably." When her dad had informed her that he and Carol wouldn't be able to fly in for the service, she'd felt relieved. One less occasion for stressful interaction between her parents. With strategic planning over the years, she and Zach had been able to avoid most of those landmines.

"You think she might come with you to the cottage after she retires? Or are there too many bad memories here?"

Sarah pitched her voice to sound convincing. "Oh, no, I don't think that's why she hasn't come. She's just been so busy with work, so devoted to ministry that she hasn't had time."

"It would be nice to see her again."

"Thanks. I'll tell her that." But she suspected that in her mother's mind, the cottage had become too closely associated with Carol.

"Anyway," Linda said as she chopped the celery, "we'll look for those pictures and see what we can find."

"Look at this one, Zach," Sarah said later that evening as she picked up a Polaroid photo from the pile on their kitchen table: Mom in a swimsuit, kneeling in the sand beside Micah, both digging with red plastic shovels. Sarah, meanwhile, crouched beside their sandcastle-in-progress, helping her father add another turret. "I remember that castle. It got to be about as tall as Micah before it toppled over. Best one we ever did."

"Impressive," he said.

"Dad loved designing them. Mom was never a fan of sand, but she did it because it was something we could all do together."

He leafed through a few more. "Linda found some good ones."

"Yeah, I'm glad I asked. I don't think I've ever seen any of these. Or if I did, I don't remember. Wonder if Mom does." She grasped one of the few where Micah grinned broadly, his face and hands covered in flour as he proudly displayed a pie in Linda's kitchen. "I don't know if seeing these would make Mom happy or sad."

"Give her the opportunity to decide, hon."

"Good idea." Only a few photos showed the four of them together, and none showed her parents in any affectionate interaction. Pictures didn't lie. The only one of her with Micah showed them standing beside Ed and Linda's old pontoon boat, a foot apart from each other, arms straight at their sides. Her eyes stung. How she wished she could wrap her arms around that lonely boy.

Her thoughts wandered to her students, especially to the solitary ones with sad eyes. Nowadays, Micah might be the sort of troubled kid faculty would monitor. But Micah hadn't been a danger to others. Only to himself. She snapped a picture of that photo so she would have it on her phone as a reminder to show a little more kindness, a little more patience and attentiveness to the students who didn't have easy access to her affection. Because that was what love looked like.

Her phone buzzed with a text. Finally! A reply from Mom. *Fell asleep as soon as I got home. Sorry! All's well. Doing evening prayers, then heading back to bed.*

Okay, Sarah typed. *Talk to you later.*

Mom replied with a thumbs up.

"She's okay," Sarah said. "Just tired."

"Told you." Zach kissed her cheek. "Stop worrying so much about her. She'll be fine. Retirement's gonna be great for her. Just watch." He peered out the window. "Looks like it'll be a clear night. I think I'll pull your dad's telescope down from the loft and set it up."

"Sounds good."

"Okay if I invite Ed and Linda to join us for a bonfire and planet gazing?" he asked.

"Okay if it's just the two of us instead?"

He massaged her shoulders. "You know I'll never say no to that."

When I consider your heavens, the work of your fingers, Sarah thought as she gazed through the telescope at the rings of Saturn. Seeing that white saucer fixed on the black sky like a cutout on dark paper summoned memories of cloudless nights when she would share the deck with Dad, wrapped in a blanket and holding a steaming cup of cocoa Mom had made on the stove. Micah would be there too, waiting his turn to look through the eyepiece, asking in his high voice, "Did you find it yet?" and their father saying, "Hold your horses. Almost." Then Dad would tell them again about how light traveled from the stars and how some of the light they were seeing had left those stars thousands of years ago, and Sarah would try to comprehend how it was possible that she could be staring at light that had burst forth when Jesus was born or when Moses was leading the Israelites through the Red Sea.

"Timey wimey stuff," Zach would say.

Considering the heavens in that way had been part of her own path toward wonder and worship. *Who are we that you should be mindful of us?*

When Saturn disappeared from the field of view, she stepped back from the eyepiece.

"Amazing, isn't it?" Zach asked. "I never get tired of looking at this." He gazed at the sky. "I'll focus in on Jupiter next."

Jupiter had been Micah's favorite planet. He could bore anyone with details about its stripes and moons and magnetic field and mass, and for some reason she now regretted, she had always insisted on arguing with him about which was better, Saturn or Jupiter, until Dad would throw up his hands and say, "Enough! I'm putting the telescope away." And Micah would storm off into the darkness and head for the pier, where he'd hurl stones from his collection into the water.

Sarah closed her eyes. She could hear the angry plunk of the rocks, hear her mother calling for him to come back and work things out with his sister. Then, when the splashing was replaced by an uneasy quiet, her mother would wrap her robe more tightly around her body and plunge into the darkness to find him and cajole him into returning while Dad said, "Ah, leave him be." But Mom never did.

On those nights, Sarah would lie as still as she could on the top bunk, listening to her parents argue in their bedroom about how to deal with him. Then Sarah would hang over the edge of her mattress and hiss at Micah, "See? It's your fault." And he would hiss back, "No, it's not. It's yours."

If only she had climbed down the ladder to sit beside him when she heard him sniffling in the dark.

"Forgive me," she whispered. Perhaps in the realm of mystery and things unseen, Micah might even hear as well.

18

I'm going to head upstairs to bed," Wren said. "Are you sure there isn't anything I can get you? Anything I can do for you?"

Kit rearranged the blanket on her lap. Having slept most of the afternoon and evening, she might be awake awhile, weary with the kind of tired sleep wouldn't fix. "I'm fine, thanks. Just spent. You know how that goes."

Wren crouched in front of the armchair and took her hand. "I know I already apologized but—"

"We both already apologized, dear one. And we both already forgave. No guilt. No regret. No condemnation."

As for Logan . . .

Kit eyed the coffee table, where the scrap of paper with his number remained. Not only had she been too exhausted to pursue any conversation with him, but she still had her own resentment to address, especially since Hannah had confirmed that Wren hadn't exaggerated what he'd said. Processing that would have to wait, though. During their evening prayer time, she had been too spent to do anything other than listen to Wren read a psalm.

"Let me know if you need anything, okay, Kit? I mean, if anything else happens, I'm here. Wake me up if you need to."

"I will. Thank you."

Wren rose and kissed her on the cheek. "I wish we didn't have to be companions in this kind of affliction too. And I'm really sorry I wasn't there to help. Especially after all the times you've helped me."

"I had everything I needed, Wren. No guilt about that either."

"Okay."

In the disorientation of everything, she still wasn't sure who had knelt beside her after she crumpled to the floor. Someone who knew what to do—likely, someone personally acquainted with panic attacks—had protected the space until she had recovered enough to leave with Hannah and Nathan's help.

Long after Wren went to bed, Kit remained in her living room, staring into the dark.

She couldn't remember the last time she'd had a panic attack that severe. Years. Decades, even. And she had never succumbed to one in front of a group. Not like that. The smaller ones she had usually managed to pray her way through and conceal. But this one—this one had ambushed her right in the middle of her breath prayer about her weakness and God's strength. What cruel irony.

Words she had spoken at the retreat session returned to her. *Pressed. Crushed. Overwhelmed. Breathless. Hemmed in. Squeezed. Confined and claustrophobic.*

She could have been describing a panic attack. That was what it felt like, being stripped and vulnerable, without human strength or resources to depend on.

The place of pressing was a place of terror. To deny that was to deny the truth.

She pictured Wren's Gethsemane trees, the roots and branches resembling thorns. Like a thorn in the flesh designed to torment and afflict. Or like thorns plaited into a crown for the King of Kings.

Yes, the place of pressing was a place of terror. But it was also a place of solidarity with Jesus, the place of divine strengthening, the place of yielding that would end not in death but in resurrection. The place of pressing was the place to discover and rediscover God's power made perfect in weakness, the place where despair and help-lessness could be transformed into defiant and joyful boasting. *I can't. You can, Lord.*

She closed her eyes, remembering. Ezra had introduced her to that breath prayer while she was at the hospital. That dear chaplain had visited her after she experienced a panic attack so severe, so debilitating, she had plunged into even darker anguish. If this was to be her life going forward . . .

Then it was a life where the glory of God could be revealed, he said. Because if the Lord in his wisdom chose not to remove the thorn, he would transform it into a holy instrument, able to achieve his purposes.

She hadn't been convinced. Not at first. Especially as it seemed her mind and body were determined to betray her. But after a while she stopped trying to fight off the attacks—what could she achieve by that?—and instead tried to regard them, at least in retrospect, as reminders of her desperate need for God.

She shook her head slowly. Oh, the delicious irony. The second half of the retreat was supposed to be about stewarding thorns. Boasting about weaknesses. Relying on God's strength. If the Lord did not remove the thorn designed by the enemy to discourage and torment, then he would use it to deepen humility and sculpt Christlikeness.

Maybe she had enough energy to ponder her own collection of thorns from that morning.

She lit the Christ candle again. As the flame sputtered and caught, she reviewed them one by one, beginning with her public collapse and the potential for shame to attach itself to the event.

She stroked the fringe of her blanket.

Strangely enough, that was the most straightforward thorn to address. Hadn't she just spoken with Wren about her perennial battle with vainglory?

So, let the Lord use the display of her weakness for his own good purposes. It wasn't uncommon for him to require her to live out what she taught. She just hadn't expected such a dramatic, real-time example. So be it.

She pulled the blanket up to her chest.

What about her anxiety over the content she had prepared and presented? A triggering, thorny series of "What if" questions had so tormented her, she hadn't been able to catch her breath.

She watched the candle flicker in the dark.

She knew better than to listen to those questions. The Lord didn't drive by fear or guide by condemnation. She knew that. Even if she had missed his leading, couldn't she trust his ability to take the gift she offered and bless it and break it and use it to feed someone who needed a word of affirmation and hope and comfort in the midst of suffering or despair? And honestly, what did she think she could have offered instead? There hadn't been time to change course, especially since no alternative content had come to mind. Not content she felt equipped to present, anyway.

No, the movement of her soul toward unrest had been a movement away from God, not toward him, and had borne only the fruit of agitation. She needed to let go of any second thoughts. Even with Logan's censure. The Lord didn't require a perfect offering—only a willing and humble one. She had given that as wholeheartedly as possible. She needed to let that go too.

Her gaze shifted from the candle to the scrap of paper with Logan's number, the shadows darting across it. His words had been words of death, not life. A thorn that continued to provoke. If, as Wren said, he seemed more upset over being caught than over being uncharitable, if he sought only to explain his tirade rather than recant it, then . . .

She wove her fingers together.

For one thing, she had seen the New Hope financials too. Month after month, year after year, decade after decade. There was nothing wrong with them. Those records stood as a testimony to God's faithfulness. God had always generously supplied all their needs, even in lean years. Even if they didn't have surplus amounts stored away and earning interest, their provision had come like manna. She and the board had often expressed delight and surprise over how their needs had been met, not only through programs that generated adequate revenue but through faithful donors who believed in the ministry— "dire and depressing" as it was. Trusting the Lord to provide their daily bread had been part of their faith journey together. If the board wanted to trust God in a new way through aggressive marketing campaigns and fundraising—or stop trusting him to supply the needs of the ministry and start trusting their own ingenuity or Logan's gifts—that was up to them. She could wash her hands of it.

And for another thing—she set her blanket aside and stood up—what right did Logan have, sitting in judgment on those who needed a word of hope? If life had been easy for him, if he hadn't yet been seasoned by suffering or loss, if his concern for those who suffered was theoretical rather than integrated, if he had no room in his theology for a theology of the cross, then she hoped the people who had been best served by her ministry would find other places to receive what they needed. But don't smile and nod and say how great the programs have been—"I mean that sincerely"—and claim you aren't looking to replace but to expand. Don't patronize. Be man enough to say what you want to say directly.

She paced back and forth. And really, what kind of man— what kind of *kid*—waltzed in and condemned her for not caring enough, for not trying hard enough, for not being inclusive or "woke" enough, for being hardhearted or bigoted or worst, *racist*, when she had only ever tried to extend the grace of the gospel to whoever she met, no matter what color or ethnicity they were? What kind of man would—

Daughter.

The startling word entered as a whisper but filled her entire chest, like a deep breath of bracing mountain air. Cleansing. Pure. Settling. A holy interruption opening a sacred space.

She stopped pacing and stared again at the flame.

My beloved daughter.

She bowed her head, listening, waiting.

He is your brother.

Gripping the armrest of the chair, she sank slowly to her knees.

That kind of man.

19

Did you end up calling Logan last night or were you too tired?" Wren asked as she scrambled eggs for their breakfast early Sunday morning.

Kit poured two glasses of orange juice and set them on the table. "I texted him before I went to bed." It hadn't seemed fair to make him wait any longer to hear from her, and she didn't want to postpone the opportunity to resolve things. Avoidance required too much emotional energy. "We're planning to chat before I head to church."

"Hope that goes well," Wren said.

"Me too. I saw some things about my own hardness of heart last night, so I'll confess that to him."

Wren raised her eyebrows. "You don't have anything to apologize for, Kit."

"Not visible things, maybe. But the invisible ones are just as real. Just as deadly."

Wren didn't look convinced.

"I got off on the wrong start with him long before he showed up on Thursday, Wren. I had already devised a scoresheet against him, rooted in my own insecurity and pride and envy. I need to own that. I judged him harshly and assumed the worst about him." She paused. "Truth is, I was just as uncharitable about him as he was about me. But mine didn't get exposed."

Wren blew out a long sigh. "Fine. When you put it that way . . ."

Kit smiled at her. "Grace upon grace," she said. "For ourselves and for others."

As they ate breakfast together, she told Wren everything that had happened in her conversation with Logan on Friday and how the Lord had used his questions to help her see her own blind spots. "Whatever his faults are—and I think he would admit he has a lot to learn—he seems to have a sincere passion for racial justice and reconciliation ministry, and he's asking good questions about how New Hope might participate in that work. If the board can find a way to provide what he and his family need financially, then I think it will be good for everyone."

Wren was silent, then said, "If he actually follows through with trying to implement a vision like that, I'd be interested in participating."

Yes, Kit thought. If the right opportunity at the right time presented itself, so would she.

Shortly after Wren left on her bike for worship at Wayfarer, Logan called from the airport. "I can only imagine how exhausted you must be, Katherine. Thank you so much for being willing to talk with me."

"Of course." She sat down in her armchair.

"I'll cut straight to it," he said. "Bottom line, I sinned against you—not just in the critical words I spoke about you but in my attitude toward what you offered. I was spiteful and mean and arrogant. No minimizing or denying it. And no excuses either. I'm so sorry for wounding you, Katherine. Would you please forgive me?"

Specific. Honest. Humble. If only all apologies were so forthright. "Yes, I forgive you. Thank you, Logan. But my own ego and sin were wrapped up in what happened yesterday. I was distracted by wanting to prove to you that my ministry has had merit, even with all my blind spots and failures."

"I'm so sorry," he said after a moment of silence. "I didn't mean to communicate condemnation to you when we talked in your office."

"No, I know. But when those mirrors of truth go up and we see ourselves more clearly . . ."

"Right," he said. "I know. Wren held one up for me yesterday. And I was too stunned and ashamed to respond well. Would you please thank her for me?"

"I will." That candid acknowledgment and expression of gratitude might soften Wren's heart toward him. "Before I let you go, Logan, let me say how sorry I am about my own judgmental attitude toward you. If my ungracious thoughts and opinions had been revealed, I would have been ashamed too." What she had named to Wren she briefly confessed to him. "Would you please forgive me for not loving you well as a brother?"

In the background a voice made an announcement over a loudspeaker. "Of course," he said. "Thank you. If we can't practice reconciliation well between individuals, we don't have much credibility for trying to practice it in communities, do we?" Another loudspeaker announcement sounded.

"I know you've got a flight to board," she said, "and you can tell me it's none of my business, but I hope things are moving forward for you to come here."

He didn't immediately reply. "Lots to pray about," he finally said. "We've got some tough decisions to make. I'd appreciate your prayers as the board tries to figure things out."

No one had sought her advice. No one was seeking it now. But if she were standing in front of the board, she might say to them, Do whatever you can to make it happen.

Wren hadn't even had a chance to wheel her bicycle all the way into the New Hope lobby Monday morning before Gayle bombarded her. "Is Katherine okay? I've already gotten several emails this morning, asking."

Wren parked her bike in the corner and unfastened her helmet. "She's fine. Just very tired."

"But she quit early or something?"

Seriously? That was how someone had framed it? "She didn't quit anything. She had a panic attack. A bad one."

Gayle's eyes grew wide. "Oh. Poor Katherine. I'm so sorry. Is there anything I can do?"

"No, she just needs to rest. She's taking the day off."

"I know. That's why I asked you. I didn't want to bother her."

Wren hung her helmet on her bike. "Actually, there *is* something you can do."

"Sure, anything!"

"Sarah's been out of town, and Kit wants to talk with her in person later today about what happened. So if she calls here this morning about the party or anything—"

"I won't say a word. Promise."

"Okay. Thanks."

Gayle pursued her around the corner to the housekeeping closet. "So, what did you think of Logan? I mean, he seemed like a nice guy, but I didn't really get a chance to talk to him."

"Yeah, he's okay." What else was she free to say about him?

"Just okay?"

"Kit likes him," Wren said. "And it sounds like he has some good ministry ideas."

"You think they'll offer him the job?"

It sounded like they already had. But she wasn't going to tell Gayle that. After all, he might decide the financial package wasn't good enough. "I don't know."

Gayle twirled her silver pinkie ring around and around. "I just wonder if he'd be as flexible as Katherine. I never know what a day might bring with my daughter and grandkids, and she's been so good about letting me work from home when I need to. I just hope . . ." She stopped twirling her ring. "For both our sakes, I guess."

Wren bristled. She had never discussed her mental health struggles with Gayle. Not that her affliction wouldn't have been apparent earlier in the year when she was so unwell, but she wondered what conclusions Gayle had drawn. Or maybe she simply meant that both of them had benefited from a flexible schedule.

When the phone rang in the office, Gayle scurried back to her post, any further probing mercifully cut short. Wren dragged the vacuum out of the closet and inserted her earbuds. There. Double protection against ongoing conversation.

As she listened to Beethoven's Pastoral Symphony, she pondered how best to use the time with Dawn during her counseling appointment later that day. So much had happened in the two weeks since she'd last seen her, she wasn't sure where to begin.

For one thing, Dawn would likely be concerned by her frequent rides past the Wilsons' house. But if she didn't mention riding past their house, she couldn't mention seeing the For Sale sign. And if she couldn't mention seeing the sign, she couldn't mention her grief over losing one more connection with Casey. And if she didn't mention her grief over losing one more connection with Casey, she couldn't mention texting Chris for information and then changing her mind and trying to cancel that request by texting him again to say never mind, and then going to Wayfarer yesterday, hoping to see him, but not seeing him and wondering if he would ever reply. Or if he'd even read it. Maybe he was ignoring her. Maybe he had turned off his "Read Receipts," and she would never know if he'd seen it.

She could mention to Dawn that she'd happened to find out the Wilsons were moving, and she could discuss her grief without mentioning her investigative efforts. They could talk about her triggers and how to process them, and she wouldn't have to disclose what she knew to be unhealthy, ongoing attempts to stalk people with connections to Casey.

The truth was, no matter how hard she tried, she couldn't find closure for his death. And what more could Dawn offer regarding that? They had already mined that topic. They needed new talking points.

She slid the vacuum back and forth.

They could talk about Logan. That would be new. She could start by telling Dawn about the police incident and how Logan's response had predisposed her not to like him or trust him. Then she could talk about how Kit showing her art had felt like a betrayal, and they could explore the reasons why, and that might be fruitful. She could also tell Dawn what she overheard Logan tell his wife and why she was triggered by that, not just for Kit's sake but her own. That discussion would probably yield lots of insight. And Dawn would be interested to hear how she had confronted him, and she would ask why Wren did it and how she felt about doing it and how she felt about it a few days later.

She might also mention to Dawn what Kit had told her about his desire to partner with local agencies or churches for racial justice ministry, how New Hope might host workshops or seminars or panel discussions to raise awareness and highlight needs for compassion and advocacy in the community, and how she would be interested in attending those. Some of her social work colleagues at Bethel House had taken continuing education courses in how to address trauma—including racial trauma—and though Wren had focused more on cycles of domestic violence and victimization, she was open to learning more. She felt ready to learn more.

But would that topic be awkward for Dawn?

In the nine months they had met together, Wren had been so focused on her own struggles, she hadn't thought about the particular challenges Dawn might have faced as a Black woman, either personally or professionally, or how any experiences of racism or even racial trauma might have shaped her work as a therapist.

It wasn't as if she could ask Dawn probing personal questions. Dawn might have strong opinions about Logan's plans and intentions, but she wouldn't be free to share them in a therapy session.

Maybe she could name to Dawn her apprehension over causing offense or being insensitive while talking about race. That could be a place to begin. Dawn would know how to handle the rest.

From her peripheral vision, Wren spied Gayle, the stricken look on Gayle's face causing her to yank out her earbuds and switch off the vacuum. "What's wrong?"

Gayle's lips were trembling. "That was Bill," she said. "I'm done."

"Wait—what?" Wren snatched her phone from her pocket and stopped the music.

"They've hired Logan, and they don't need me anymore. He was calling to give me two weeks' notice." Before Wren could reply, Gayle said, "I had a bad feeling about all this. I knew something was up. I could sense it. I just didn't know it would happen so soon. Didn't I just say a little while ago? Didn't I just say to you I hoped . . ." Her eyes welled with tears. "I told Bill, 'But my son's getting married on Saturday!' What a crazy thing to come out of my mouth. As if that would make a difference. For what? For them to change their minds? Or maybe because I don't know how I'm going to celebrate a wedding when I've got two weeks to figure out a new place to work."

When her shoulders started to heave in sobs, Wren draped her arm around her. "I'm so sorry, Gayle. I wish there was something I could do."

Gayle wiped her nose on her sleeve. "I know she's taking today off, and I don't want to upset her. But could you please call Katherine and see if she knows anything?"

"Sure. I'll do that right now." But just as she was getting ready to dial Kit's number, her phone began to buzz. Her heart raced when the name appeared.

"I think I'd better take this in my studio," she said. "It's Bill."

Kit had just stepped out of the shower when her phone rang on her nightstand. Wrapping her terrycloth robe more tightly around herself, she stooped to check the number. *Wren.* Whatever she needed could wait a few minutes.

As she selected a pair of slacks and a blouse from her closet, she mentally scanned her day: spiritual direction with Russell, then lunch with Sarah in Grand Rapids before she went to the airport to meet the girls. "You could come with me," Sarah had said when she called from the cottage yesterday. "It would be a fun surprise for them to see you." But Kit wasn't convinced that two teenagers exhausted by an enjoyable but busy vacation would be thrilled about having to interact with a second grandmother as soon as they landed.

On top of that, she wasn't sure how exhausted she would be after talking with Sarah about what happened on Saturday. In fact, with so much to process in spiritual direction, she might already be worn out before they even met for lunch.

She sank onto the edge of her bed, clothes draped across her lap. Who was she kidding? She was already worn out, and the day had barely begun. She pictured Vincent's old man, slumped forward, head in his hands. *Come to me, all you who are weary and heavy-laden, and I will give you rest.*

She rubbed her brow. Lately, it seemed all she did was come to Jesus weary and heavy-laden. Not that he judged her for that. Lucy would have reminded her to stop judging herself. "If you're exhausted, that's your offering," Lucy would say. "Don't pretend to bring anything else."

Her phone buzzed with a text. *Strength and patience, Lord,* she prayed before leaning over to check.

Please call me asap, the words read.

Kit sighed. She had just enough time to get dressed, collect her thoughts, and drive to her appointment. As she was about to type, *Can it wait?* one more word appeared on the screen: *Emergency.*

Bracing herself, she dialed Wren's number.

"They fired us," Wren said as soon as she picked up. "Well, technically, laid us off. Bill called Gayle, then me. They're axing both of us."

"What? No! That can't be."

"It's true. I just got off the phone with him."

Kit crumpled the hem of her blouse in a tight fist. "That doesn't make any sense."

"So, you didn't know?"

"Of course not!"

"I told Gayle you wouldn't."

That it might occur to either of them that she could have been silently complicit . . . "I'm as stunned as you are, Wren. I promise." *Tough decisions to make,* Logan had said. But did he know about this plan when he said that? She hoped not. "What did Bill tell you?"

"That the board has decided to restructure staff. That's it. No other explanation."

"But it still doesn't make sense. Even if they're restructuring, they need support staff."

"Unless Logan plans to clean the bathrooms himself," Wren retorted, "and I don't imagine he does."

Kit didn't think that was likely either. "They've hired him for sure? Bill said that?"

"Yes. And he told me I'll be done after the twentieth. They want me to come in and clean up after your retirement party, and then that's it. Finished. Same for Gayle."

Kit exhaled slowly. "I don't even know what to say. I'm so sorry."

"I bet Logan told the board he didn't want to work with me."

"Why would he do that?"

"After my angry outburst on Saturday. It's not like I gave him a great impression."

"That's not what he said about it, Wren. I told you, he was grateful you held up a mirror."

"Yeah, but maybe he was lying. Or being manipulative. Who knows? That whole vainglory thing, right? Playing to an audience, saying things designed to impress."

Even if that were the case—and she sincerely hoped it wasn't— that wouldn't explain them laying off Gayle. Something else was going on.

"Could you please call Bill for us?"

Kit stared at the clothes on her lap. "Yes. Right away."

She texted Russell first. Spiritual direction would have to wait for another time. And by then, she might have plenty more to share and process with him.

"I was just getting ready to ring you," Bill said when he answered her call. "I imagine you've already heard, though."

"Wren just phoned." She tramped to the kitchen in her robe. "I don't understand what's going on."

"It's all part of the contract negotiations with Logan," he said.

Blood rushed to her face. "He wants them cut?"

"No, no. It's nothing personal against either of them. Not at all. It's just that we're trying to make a salary package work for a family of four."

She had assumed that. "But the building still needs to be cleaned, Bill. And unless he wants to handle all the admin duties on top of everything else he'll be doing—"

"Nikki is willing to help."

"Nikki who?"

"His wife, Nicole. She's willing to take over cleaning the building and answering phones and emails as part of a package deal for them."

Kit slumped into a chair at the table.

"This was an eleventh-hour idea from one of the board members, Katherine. Happened late last night. It was the only way we could figure out how to get him here. And we need him to come. We're convinced he's the one God has called. And if that means we have to let two good people go, then that's part of the cost. I'm sorry for it, believe me. But we don't see any other way."

She pictured Gayle, distraught over how she would find a job that allowed the flexibility she needed whenever her daughter was unwell and couldn't care for her children. Arnie was nearing retirement, and they wouldn't be able to make it on his social security alone. "It's a pastoral issue, Bill, providing work for people who need it."

"I realize that, but Wren is young and able-bodied, and I'm sure she can find something else."

Able-bodied? He had no clue.

"And as for Gayle," he went on, "it's not like she's made a lot of money working for us. She'll probably do better financially by going elsewhere."

She doesn't want to go elsewhere, Kit silently fumed. Bill was right to say she didn't make a lot of money at New Hope. Couldn't they find a way to keep her on staff?

"Don't Logan and Nicole have young children?" she asked. Surely, the cost of babysitting or childcare while they—

"Nikki's parents live nearby. They can help with the kids."

She stared out the patio door to the birdfeeder, where house sparrows flitted to and from the perches. It was finished, then. No appeal to make. "When will Logan start?"

"Well, that's the other thing. We thought we'd let you retire a bit early. Logan gave notice to his church this morning, and they can stay with Nikki's parents until they find a house. So he's going to officially start the day after your retirement party."

She wondered if reports of her panic attack had prompted that decision. Give the old woman a break. Let her rest.

"We'll pay you through the end of the month, of course, but we thought it might be a gift to you, not to have to work after he arrives. There's no need, really. He's got such a good sense of what next steps need to happen, we've got no worries about him hitting the ground running."

What an interesting, illuminating phrase for describing the work of a director at a contemplative retreat center. "Okay," she said. "We move forward."

There was silence. Then Bill said, "With no hard feelings, I hope."

"I won't speak for anyone else," she said. "As for mine, I'll find a way to sort them out."

"Katherine—"

"I need to connect with Gayle and Wren. Thank you for telling me the truth."

"I'd be happy to meet with you face to face if that would be helpful."

"No need, Bill. But perhaps you might extend the same courtesy to each of them."

As soon as they ended the call, she threw on her clothes and texted Sarah to say she was sorry, but they would need to reschedule lunch. *Urgent pastoral care need,* she typed. Sarah would know better than to ask for any details.

20

While she sat in an empty waiting room outside Dawn's office, Wren drummed her fingers on her lap. She wouldn't have wanted to work for him anyway. Sure, she would lose her studio space by leaving New Hope, but since Logan didn't value art or artists, he probably wouldn't have let her keep it even if she had continued working there. She pictured him at the retreat, looking at his phone while Kit displayed her painting. Rude and dismissive.

She would remove all her art from the chapel before he could, and she would recommend to Kit that she return original work to the other artists before he dismissed theirs as well. And since Kit had personally paid for all the Van Gogh prints, they could rescue those from Logan's rejection pile too.

Poor Gayle. She was the one Wren felt sorry for. When Kit arrived at New Hope shortly after Wren called her, Gayle collapsed into her arms. "Who would hire a sixty-three-year-old administrator with only basic computer skills?" she'd cried. And now that their long-term bachelor son was getting married, they couldn't ask him for financial help if they needed it.

Kit told Gayle to take the rest of the day off. The rest of the week, if she wanted. "The timing of this is terrible," Kit had said, "and I'm so sorry. I hope you and Arnie are able to focus just on the wedding, hard as that is."

Through the receptionist's window, Wren saw Dawn's office door open onto the hallway. Wanting to afford privacy to whoever was exiting, she averted her gaze. But when a woman called, "Thanks for the tune-up!" Wren immediately recognized the voice.

Mara Payne. She had no idea they shared a counselor. As soon as their eyes met through the glass, Mara beamed, and when she entered the waiting area, she greeted Wren with a bear hug. "Small world!" Mara exclaimed. "You're here for Dawn?"

"Yes."

"Oh, I'm so glad. She's great, isn't she?"

"Yeah."

"She's been a lifeline for me for years," Mara said. "Hadn't seen her in a while, but sometimes you just need to be reminded of what you already know."

Right, she thought. And try not to feel guilty for forgetting or not implementing the wisdom.

"I've been meaning to call you, Wren. How about coffee sometime?"

"I'd love that, thanks."

Mara adjusted her oversized beaded bag on her shoulder. "You doing okay?"

Wren gave a wry smile. "Just got laid off, but other than that . . ."

"No! From the nursing home?"

"From New Hope."

"Are you kidding me?"

"Nope. New guy coming in, and he's cleaning house."

Mara cocked her head. "Sounds like there's a bigger story going on here. How soon can you get together?"

She could keep her entire social calendar on a Post-it note. "I'm working the next couple of days. How about later this week?"

"Good. I'll text you some open times."

Dawn appeared in the doorway. "Hi, Wren."

"Hey."

Mara hugged her again. "Hang in there, okay? You're in good hands."

"I'm hearing more frustration than sorrow," Dawn said after Wren filled her in on everything that had happened with Logan since his arrival. "Would that be accurate?"

"Yes. Way more." She picked up a pillow from Dawn's sofa and clasped it to her abdomen. "I think anger feels less frightening to me than sorrow right now, like it has more energy to it. I don't know if that makes sense or not."

"Say more about that." Dawn leaned slightly forward in her chair.

"Sorrow can take me to a dark place, a numb place. I guess with anger, at least I'm feeling something that might help me take action and move somewhere helpful." As long as she didn't become consumed by it. She supposed there was always that danger.

"Where would you say your anger is directed?"

Wren shrugged. "I could try to give you a holy answer and say I'm most angry about what happened to Gayle. But it's mostly about me. I'm mad that Logan doesn't seem to appreciate the things that are important to me. Like art."

Her gaze drifted to Vincent's painting of *The Good Samaritan* on the wall behind Dawn's chair, the weak and wounded young man with his arm looped around the older man's neck as he was hoisted onto the donkey. The swirl of Vincent's brushstrokes portrayed the energy and strain of the kind Samaritan.

Her throat burned. Logan dismissing art—*her* art—only scratched the surface of her anger. "It's about Kit too," she said.

"You're angry at her?"

"No. I mean, I was. But mostly I'm angry over what Logan said about her." She pointed at the scene. "That's Kit and me."

Dawn turned briefly to look.

"That's what Kit did for me. She poured out compassion and care and comfort when I couldn't care for myself. When I didn't care about caring for myself."

Though many of those days were blurred, she remembered presence. Strength. Kindness. Understanding.

With her gaze still fixed on the painting, she said, "Kit and I have been companions in sorrow because she knows what despair feels like and hasn't judged me for my weaknesses. So when she talked at the retreat about stewarding suffering and then Logan said how depressing it all was—when he said that Kit obviously hadn't gotten the news about the resurrection—I lost it. It's not just that he dismissed Kit and all the comfort and compassion she offers other people, but I felt like he dismissed what she's done for me. She's the one who helped me focus on Jesus' suffering and compassion, to see his solidarity with us. With me. So when he said that, it felt like he dismissed everything we did together for the Journey to the Cross. Everything we've become together." She took a deep breath. "So, even though he supposedly apologized to her, I still feel angry."

Her focus shifted toward the two figures who had passed by the wounded man, disregarding his suffering. One of them appeared to be reading as he walked. God's Word, probably—which made it even worse. The way the scene was composed, two self-absorbed, self-righteous men remained in view. If they had just turned their heads to look, they might have seen the Samaritan bowing under the weight of his generosity and compassion, determined to help, no matter what it cost him. But if they had seen, would they have turned around to help him? Probably not.

"I feel like that's Logan," she said, pointing at the figure with his head bowed toward his scroll or book. "It seems like he was so caught up in himself—his own ministry or financial package or whatever— that he didn't bother to pay attention to what Kit was saying about people who have felt crushed by despair." If Logan *had* heard what Kit said and didn't care, that made it even worse.

"Kit says he claims to be committed to racial justice and advocacy and everything, but if he thinks talking about suffering is depressing, then it makes me wonder how sincere he is. Maybe he only talks about those issues to try to impress people." Like all the virtue signaling posts she'd seen from people online, claiming to care. Was that just vainglory on display? Or did their words result in compassionate action?

Now that she thought about it, did hers?

She stared at the painting again. "I'm so tired of being the one on the donkey. I'm tired of being the one who needs help. I see how worn out Kit is, and I keep adding to her stress and exhaustion. She tries so hard to be patient and compassionate toward me but . . ."

Dawn waited a moment, then said, "Keep going, Wren. What else are you seeing?"

She rubbed one of the gold pillow tassels between her fingers, the strands silky and soothing. "I'm the one who's been doing all the taking," she said. "There are so many big things happening in the world. So many needs. And for a few years I was on the frontline, helping lift people up and care for their wounds. I was helping them move forward with hope. And now all of that feels like a lifetime ago."

Even though Kit often told her that her presence at Willow Springs made a difference to the residents, it wasn't hard to sit with someone and watch golf or play Yahtzee. That cost her nothing. She wished she could be more like Kit, more like the generous, self-sacrificing Samaritan. Or even like the steady, patient donkey in the painting. The donkey served simply by holding still and doing his part to carry the load, without complaining. Vincent often painted animals with human qualities. He saw something sacred in them.

She gestured toward it again. "Van Gogh painted that when he was at the asylum."

Dawn's eyes widened. "Did he?"

"Yeah. He was tired of needing other people's help. Like me. He felt guilty for being dependent on Theo for financial support. He was really frustrated that he hadn't been able to make a living selling his work, and he was upset that Theo's investment in him had never paid off. But he also still longed to make a difference. He wanted to comfort people through his art. He hoped he could be well enough to do that."

She studied the face of the good Samaritan, his orange beard suddenly catching her attention. How could she have missed that detail before? Yes, it could have been an artistic choice of color, but what if it were a self-portrait detail expressing Vincent's longing to help others? To see himself not only as the wounded one needing help but also the wounded healer offering help?

She shared that theory with Dawn. "That's a powerful insight, Wren. What might that mean for you?"

She thought a moment. "I know I'll never be able to repay Kit for what she's done. I just don't want to be a burden. And I want to make a difference in the world. I know that can be a selfish, self-centered pursuit, a way of making ourselves feel good. Even look good. But when I heard Kit talking about Logan's vision for promoting justice issues, I got excited. Like I could participate in something like that and help make a difference."

"Could you still do that?"

"No. Not there. Not with him. At least, not now. Or not yet." She would have to wait and see what kind of person he proved to be before making that decision.

Wren eyed the clock on the wall. They were almost out of time. "Maybe I just need to focus on the opportunities at Willow Springs. Not just with the residents, but with the staff. I've been too preoccupied with my own life to pay much attention to them or their stories. But I know some of the housekeepers and CNAs work multiple jobs just to make ends meet. Some of them are single moms. I bet none of them have been given the same luxury I've been given, with a free place to stay while I sort out my next steps." She paused. "I guess that's stewardship too, isn't it? Instead of feeling guilty about what I've been given, I can look for ways to give what I have. And not just to alleviate my own guilt. But to really try to love well."

Dawn was silent. "There are always opportunities to do justice, love mercy, and walk humbly," she said after a while. "Wherever we find ourselves."

Kit was staring into her pantry cupboard, trying to figure out what they could eat for dinner, when Wren entered with a shopping bag. "I stopped at the store on my way home. Thought we could have fajitas." She set the bag on the counter. "Or if you had something else in mind, we could save this for tomorrow."

"No, that sounds good. Thank you." Kit closed the cupboard and removed a skillet from the drawer beneath the oven.

Wren shooed her away. "You go rest. I'll take care of everything."

She wasn't going to argue with that. By the time she filled the birdfeeder and replied to several emails, the chicken was sizzling on the stove. Wren set her phone aside. "Mom says hi."

"Hi back. Is she doing okay?"

"Yeah. Just her usual worry about me. I told her I'm doing fine with everything. I really am. But I wouldn't mind if you reassure her too."

"If she asks me, I can do that."

"Thanks."

Kit slid a chair out from the table and sat down. "Good appointment with Dawn today?"

"Yeah. Really good timing." Wren flipped over the chicken breasts. "I told her everything that happened with Logan, how he completely dismissed what we did for the Journey to the Cross and—"

"Wait, Wren. I'm not sure that's an accurate picture of what he said."

"Yes, it is. You didn't hear him on the phone. I did."

"But I'm not sure he was dismissing everything," Kit said, "just that he didn't hear enough emphasis on hope and resurrection in what I presented."

Wren held up the tongs. "Why are you so quick to defend him, especially after what he did to Gayle?"

"That was a board decision. Not Logan."

"I'm not so sure about that. Because Logan told me on Saturday that the reason he was spouting off to his wife was because the financial package wasn't good enough for them. That's probably why he was asking me questions about how many hours I worked and whether I had another job. He was doing his mental calculations. He had it all planned out." She poked at the chicken again. "And he blamed you for New Hope not having enough money to hire him, because the programs you offered were too depressing."

Kit rubbed her temple slowly. She didn't need Wren to bring any kindling to the embers of resentment she had been trying all day to douse with prayer.

"Sorry," Wren said, "but it's true. Not what he said about you. But the fact that he said it. I know what I heard."

"I know, Wren. But I also know how corrosive anger is. It does no good to keep rehearsing the grievances. It just keeps things stirred up."

"But you also can't cover it up and pretend he didn't say it or think it."

"It's not about pretending. He already asked for my forgiveness. So we move forward."

Wren set her free hand on her hip. "Do you really think he's sincere in what he says?"

She wasn't sure. But loving him as a brother meant giving him the benefit of the doubt. That much she knew. "It's not our place to judge motives or sincerity," she said. "The heart is for God to see, not me. All I know is that the measure I use to judge someone else is the measure that will be used to judge me. And I want mercy. I have enough to deal with in my own heart without focusing on someone else's. I don't need that distraction."

Wren sighed.

"Give him a chance," Kit said. "The fruit always reveals the heart. But it takes time for the fruit to be evident. Love is patient, remember? Patient with us so we can be patient with others. Hard as that can be."

Wren slid the chicken breasts onto a plate. "I won't have to give him a chance. Because they fired me. So I won't be there to see what he does."

"I'm sorry for that, Wren."

"No, it's okay. I'd planned to quit anyway. It won't be the same without you, so I might as well move on."

Since Kit didn't want to cause her stress by asking questions about work options, she watched silently as Wren scraped slices of yellow, red, and green peppers into the skillet and stirred them around.

"Don't you ever get angry?" Wren asked after a while.

"Of course I do."

"You just don't explode with it?"

She shrugged. "Maybe that's part of my vainglory. I keep the full force of it concealed."

"You didn't ever explode at Robert? Even after he abandoned you?"

Kit thought of Jesus and his stark warnings about anger. "I murdered him a thousand times with my raging thoughts, wished terrible things upon him. Since I couldn't punish him or Carol, I wanted God to." She paused. "Even if we aren't the sort of person who erupts in shouting and rage, the quiet version can be just as deadly. So I wrote lots of angry letters that I destroyed, and I prayed lots of imprecatory psalms. Plenty of those to choose from."

"Text me the numbers," Wren said. "They might come in handy."

Kit smiled slightly. Those raw and heartfelt cries for God's judgment had expressed the honest desires she'd harbored in her heart—that God would bring calamity or punishment or destruction upon them. "Spit it out," Lucy used to say. "Don't swallow that. It'll make you sick." Having a way to voice her anger in prayer had helped her release the toxic resentment by vomiting it to God, who, Lucy always reminded her, was big enough—and gracious enough—to receive it without her trying to tidy it up first.

Kit rubbed the finger where she'd once worn a wedding ring. "After a while I saw that my anger was only consuming me, not them. My spiritual director helped me see how I had dehumanized them with my contempt. I reduced them to the size of their offense, where it was easier to hate and disregard them as human beings created in the image of God." Seeing how shriveled her own heart had become had been a wake-up call from the Spirit and had launched her on a journey of forgiveness that kept unfolding.

Wren lowered the heat on the stove and started slicing up the chicken. "I get what you're saying about anger being destructive, but Dawn and I were also talking about anger being a catalyst for change—not just for individuals, but for communities. I think it can be channeled for good. For fighting against unjust systems."

Kit wasn't going to argue that point. The Scriptures were filled with prophetic anger and calls to repent over injustice and oppression. "Just remember, though, that righteous anger never depletes love. If our anger isn't rooted in love, then it isn't holy. And I've got a lifetime of personal experience with the unholy kind. It can be a consuming fire. And not in a good way."

"Right," Wren said. "But one of my social work profs used to say that anger and hate aren't the opposite of love. Indifference is. I don't want to become so numbed out or overwhelmed by the suffering in the world that I become apathetic or hardhearted or completely self-absorbed. Not that I'm saying I'm filled with the holy kind of righteous indignation Jesus had. But if I start feeling passionate about mercy and justice issues again—like I was when I worked at Bethel House—that seems like an important step forward. And given how dead I felt for so long, I'll take it as a positive sign."

May it be so, Kit thought, and she rose to set the table for their meal.

21

Rather than wait in the cellphone lot for the girls to text and say they had their luggage, Sarah met them as they emerged from the concourse, Jess in designer skinny jeans and fringed hoop earrings that brushed the top of her sheer peasant blouse, Morgan carrying a large plush Tigger and wearing denim shorts, a princess shirt, and mouse ears.

"How about a hug for your mom, Jess?" she asked after Morgan embraced her.

Jess glanced up from her screen long enough for a one-armed version before returning to her phone.

"'Hey, Mom,'" Sarah teased, "'nice to see you. How've you been?' 'Good, thanks for asking, Jess. So glad you're home! I've missed you!'"

Jess smiled and tucked her phone into a Coach bag Sarah didn't recognize. "Hey, Mom. Missed you too."

As they walked to the baggage claim area, Sarah wrapped an arm around each of her daughters. "Gigi took you shopping, huh?"

"A few times," Morgan said.

"Did you come home with extra luggage?"

"Gigi bought Jess a set. So I used her old one for my souvenirs."

"What's wrong with your old suitcase?" she asked Jess.

"Nothing."

Morgan straightened her mouse ears. "Gigi is taking her to Europe for a graduation present."

"Morgan!" Jess snapped.

"Well, she is."

"And getting you a horse," Jess replied.

"Wait! What's all this?" Sarah stopped in her tracks, causing someone from behind to bump into her legs with a wheeled carry-on. Muttering an apology, she stepped out of the way and motioned for the girls to do the same. "Okay. Back up. Gigi is doing what?"

Jess elbowed Morgan. "You weren't supposed to say anything before she called Mom."

Morgan stuck out her tongue.

"Stop," Sarah said. "Both of you."

"She's not getting me a horse. She just said she'd talk to you about it."

"Fine, we'll talk. But the answer is still no."

"Mom!"

"No, Morgan. Dad and I have already gone around and around with you about this. You need to show your commitment first. Not just to the fun stuff. To the hard stuff."

"I have!"

Sarah signaled her to lower her voice. "We'll talk about this later."

"What about Jess?"

"We'll talk about that later too."

"You can't say no to that one," Jess said. "You and Dad already said I could do a graduation trip."

"We never talked about Europe, Jess. We talked about going to see shows in New York or touring DC."

"Well, Gigi offered to pay for everything."

"I'll talk to her," Sarah said.

"Mom!" Jess exclaimed in the same exasperated tone as Morgan's.

"I said I'll talk to her."

"Yeah, but what are you going to say?"

She wasn't sure yet. But she would wait until she calmed down so she wouldn't say something she would regret.

As soon as they got home, the girls—who had provided polite but clipped answers to all her questions about their trip—disappeared to their rooms. Zach, who was working a long shift at the hospital, didn't reply to her *Have you got a minute?* text. She stared at her phone, wondering if her mother was still navigating whatever urgent pastoral crisis had disrupted their lunch plans.

If the issue with the girls involved anyone other than Carol, she would call her mom for a reality check. But her mom's feelings toward Carol could potentially cloud her judgment. And Sarah didn't need to rope her in as an ally. That wasn't fair.

She didn't think she was overreacting, though. Not regarding Morgan and the horse. If Carol wanted to take Jess to Europe, she couldn't think of a good reason to say no. Except that they would need to take the trip right after graduation so Jess could still work full time during the summer to help pay for college. No negotiating on that one. If that meant the trip needed to be shorter than Carol or Jess hoped for, so be it.

There. They could move forward on that one. As for the horse. . .

She scanned her memory. Had she ever talked with Carol about that? With Mom, yes. But maybe she hadn't mentioned to Carol that she and Zach had said no. Morgan certainly wouldn't have supplied that information to her grandmother. She would have told Gigi how much she loved her riding lessons, how beneficial it would be for her to have responsibility for owning a horse, and how all the other girls at the barn owned theirs. She would have laid it on thick. Sarah pictured Carol listening sympathetically, trying to find a way to "keep the girls equal," despite their age difference.

Okay. She could give Carol the benefit of the doubt. To do otherwise—to jump to conclusions about someone's actions or motives, her mother would remind her—was a way of bearing false witness against a neighbor.

She took a deep breath. Get the facts. Then interpret the facts with mercy.

She texted Carol. *Good time to talk?*

"I'm so sorry," Carol said. "I had no idea. I would never undermine what you and Zach told her."

Sarah sat back in her patio chair. "No, I didn't think you would. Morgan already has finely honed manipulation skills. We've got to watch that with her."

"I'll admit I did see evidence of that a few times. Nothing major. She just knows how to get what she wants," Carol said, chuckling. "Like her Gigi."

True, Sarah thought. She pictured her dad throwing up his hands in mock surrender and saying to Carol with a grin, "I heard you the first time, woman!" Whatever Carol wanted from him, she received.

"I'm happy to talk to her, Sarah. I'll tell her that once you say it's okay—once she does what she needs to do to prove she's responsible enough to handle it—then I'm happy to help her purchase one. Within reason. No world champions."

Sarah laughed. "I figure that someplace there's an old horse that needs a retirement home. And Morgan will have to contribute toward all the expenses."

"She told me she's been saving her babysitting money."

Sarah hadn't seen much evidence of saving—only spending. But a goal like this might prod her toward better financial stewardship.

"As for Jess," Carol said, "I should have checked with you first on that one too. We didn't finalize any plans, mind you. We just talked about what she might like to see."

"Is Gary joining you?"

Carol scoffed. "That man still refuses to get a passport. So I told him, Fine. I'll travel with my granddaughter instead. I've been wanting to get back to Europe ever since your dad died, to see some of the places he and I visited, and this gives me a good excuse to do it. Think of her as my Jane Austen–style companion."

"*Little Women* comes to mind," Sarah said. "But you're way more hip and fun than Aunt March. Wish I could go with you."

"Could you?"

"No, I wouldn't take that unique opportunity away from Jess. Zach and I will get there someday."

"You should plan a special wedding anniversary trip. That's what your dad and I did for our twenty-fifth. Remember?"

Yes, she did. Seeing their photos from places her mother had always hoped to visit—London, Edinburgh, Paris, Munich, Vienna, Rome—had caused a twinge of sadness. The life he and Carol shared had been so vastly different from the life of her parents.

"I've never regretted doing that. Not for a second. We had no idea it would be our last big trip together. *Carpe diem,* I always say. Or as your dad always said, 'Time to carp the day.'" Carol sighed. "How I miss that man."

Though it was none of her business, Sarah wondered how Gary felt about that. Or if he knew. "I miss him too," she said.

"I know. That's something you and I will always share. The girls too. I'm so glad they were old enough to have memories of him." Sarah heard her sniffle. "Anyway. I'll work it out with Morgan. And you and I can stay on the same page going forward."

There, see? Sarah thought after she thanked her and ended the call. Far easier than she had even hoped for. She stood and stretched as her phone buzzed with a text from Zach. *Everything okay?*

All good, she typed, and went back inside.

When Zach called on his way home from the hospital, Sarah withdrew to the basement laundry room so the girls wouldn't overhear her relaying details from the conversation.

"She knew," Zach said after Sarah finished updating him.

"What do you mean, she knew? Knew what?"

"That we told Morgan no way on the horse."

Sarah stared at a pile of cottage laundry. "Are you sure? I know I told Mom about it but—"

"No, you told Carol. I heard you on the phone with her."

"When?"

"I don't know, hon. A few weeks ago? I remember thinking it was good you said something to her because we know how she likes to spoil them."

Sarah stroked her brow. "You're sure it was Carol and not Mom?"

He hesitated. "Now you've got me second-guessing it. So call it 95 percent sure instead of a hundred."

With her free hand she tossed light-colored shorts and shirts into the washer. "I need to be sure before I accuse her of lying."

"Don't accuse," Zach said. "Just ask her. You can find a way to be diplomatic about it."

Diplomacy wasn't exactly her superpower, and confronting her students was a far different ball game than confronting her stepmother about deceit. She would give herself twenty-four hours, then call.

Email?

No. Call.

"In the meantime," she went on, "we need to make sure we're a united front with Morgan. And with Jess and the summer job stuff."

"Yep."

"You're sure we're on the same page, Zach? That you aren't going to back down?"

"When have you known me to back down?"

"Um, Jess's car?"

He chuckled. "Okay, busted. But you gotta admit, she ended up with a much better vehicle than the one you'd found for her."

"Hmmm. 'This cute one's way safer, Dad.' Three thousand dollars safer. With a sunroof."

"A cool sunroof."

Sarah set the phone down and put him on speaker while she added detergent to the load. "United front, Zach. Summer job. Shorter trip if necessary."

She pictured him saluting as he said, "Got it."

"And we tell Morgan she has to wait, no matter what Carol said."

"Right, but let's give her a timeframe, hon. Something to work toward with definable goals."

That seemed reasonable. She started the wash cycle, then picked up her phone. "As long as she doesn't meet those goals only to slack off after getting what she wants. That wouldn't be fair to a horse."

"Agreed."

Morgan would need to make a task chart, Sarah decided as she headed upstairs after finishing their call. She would need to ask the owners of the stable what she could do to serve them, and then she would need to agree to a schedule and keep it as if she were getting paid for a job. No excuses. No begging off during bad weather or complaining she wasn't getting enough time with friends. Schoolwork first, then barn and babysitting. With those parameters, she might decide that owning a horse would cramp her style.

Morgan, still wearing her mouse ears, was sitting at the kitchen table, hunched forward as she typed on her phone. "Did you talk to Dad?" she asked without looking up.

"Yes." Sarah sat down across from her.

"And?"

"And when you're done typing and want to have a conversation, we'll talk."

Morgan typed a bit more, then slid her phone a few inches away.

"Off the table," Sarah said.

Morgan sighed, snatched up the phone, and deposited it in the living room before returning to the kitchen with her arms crossed.

"Given this is about a negotiation, Morgan, I would think you'd drop the attitude."

"I was in the middle of texting with Gigi."

"And what did Gigi say?"

Morgan didn't reply.

"You can tell me, or you can show me. You know that's the rule." Whenever the report of what texts said didn't match the actual content, there were consequences. Morgan knew that. It saved everyone a step by exacting an honest response on the first try. Usually.

"She said she was sorry and that she shouldn't have gotten my hopes up."

"It isn't about getting hopes up, Morgan. Dad and I haven't told you that you can't ever get a horse. We've told you that you have to work for it."

"I know that."

"Then walk me through your conversations with Gigi. Not just in the texts, but in Florida."

Morgan said, "She cares about the things I care about. That's why she wants to help."

"I know that. Dad and I care about what you care about too. We're just trying to help you grow in being responsible. That's our job. And Gigi doesn't disagree with that. In fact, she told me she felt manipulated by you, that you weren't honest with her about what we told you."

Morgan's eyebrows shot up. "I did tell her!"

"You told her what?"

"That you and Dad said I couldn't get a horse until I proved I was serious about taking care of it, and she said she would talk to you. She said she agreed that owning a horse would be good for me and that she would be happy to buy one. Not a fancy one, she said. But I don't need a fancy one."

Sarah stared at her daughter. Someone was lying. And for the first time ever, she hoped it was Morgan.

"I didn't manipulate her, Mom, I swear. I didn't even bring it up. She's the one who asked me about it. She wanted to see pictures of me riding, so I showed her. And yeah, I probably would have mentioned that I wanted one, but I didn't have to. She did."

Morgan had no idea that by exonerating herself, she had indicted her beloved Gigi.

"I can show you the texts. You can see for yourself."

The offering of verification was evidence enough. "It's okay, Morgan. I believe you. Thank you for telling me."

Morgan looked distressed. "Is she in trouble now?"

"Nobody's in trouble."

"Don't tell her I told you."

Sarah leaned toward her. "I'll need to tell her the truth so we can work things out."

"Please don't!"

"Listen, Morgan, your relationship with Gigi is special, and I'll always protect that. I promise. But what she did undermined Dad and me, and for trust to be restored, I have to talk with her." Enough said. No reason to tell Morgan she had lied.

Morgan covered her eyes. "I shouldn't have told you."

"That's not the lesson here. And you didn't do anything wrong."

"Neither did Gigi! She just wanted to help."

"Okay. I know that. And she and I will work it out. I promise."

But as soon as Morgan retreated to her room, Sarah texted her mom. *Need some advice. Free for breakfast or lunch tomorrow?*

Her reply was quick. *How about 8am at Corner Nook?*

22

Sarah was already seated at a table for two near the window when Kit arrived a few minutes late. "So sorry I had to bail on you and the girls yesterday," she said as Sarah rose to embrace her.

"No problem. Everything work out okay?"

"Yes, fine." Whatever advice Sarah needed took precedence over giving an update about New Hope and Logan. She would wait for the right opportunity to tell Sarah about her panic attack too. And while she was at it, she probably needed to mention the incident with the police. No way to know how many people Bill and Logan had told. Best to preempt the grapevine and control the narrative Sarah heard. "Did you already ask for coffee?"

"It was burnt, so I asked them to make a fresh pot for us."

"Oh, okay." She was glad to have missed Sarah complaining about bad coffee. Robert would have done the same—not make a fuss but be firm with the server, whereas Kit might have taken a sip and set it aside.

Sarah gestured toward the menu. "Are you getting your usual?"

"Yes."

Sarah waved to catch the server's attention. "We're ready," she said when the young woman approached. "Go ahead, Mom."

She placed her cloth napkin in her lap. "One scrambled egg and one wholegrain pancake, please."

"With real maple syrup," Sarah added.

"If you have it," Kit said to her, smiling.

"Sure thing."

"And I'll have the avocado toast," Sarah said, "with eggs over easy. Make sure they're over easy, okay? Not medium."

"Okay." She underlined the words on her pad.

As soon as the server left their table, Sarah said, "So. Remember the horse thing with Morgan?"

"Don't tell me she came home from Florida with one."

"What makes you say that?"

"I'm only kidding. Sorry."

"No, you're not far off, Mom."

As Kit listened to her describe what Carol had done, she tried to conceal her strong emotions. It was one thing to set aside triggers during a spiritual direction session and remain prayerfully present even when the directee's story tapped her own experiences of loss or suffering. But when the tale of deceit involved a woman who had directly betrayed and wounded her, practicing detachment from her own thoughts and feelings was far more challenging. Especially when it seemed that Sarah was more uncertain about how to confront Carol than angry about what she had done.

Odd. Sarah didn't usually shy away from confrontation. And though she had tempered her approach over the years, there was a time in her life when she hadn't much cared how people received what she needed to say.

At least, Sarah had been that way with her. Maybe she had been different with Carol. Kit had seldom had the opportunity to observe them together. Or, more accurately, she had avoided opportunities to do so. It had been easier that way.

The server returned with a pot of coffee. "Let me know if it's okay," she said after pouring two cups.

Sarah took a sip and responded with a satisfied sigh. "Perfect. Thanks so much."

With a nod, she proceeded to another table.

"Obviously, I don't want to do anything to jeopardize Morgan's relationship with her," Sarah went on.

No, of course not, Kit thought. The time to sever a relationship with a woman practiced in deceit had passed by decades ago. Ancient words she had once spat in angry prayers about Carol and Robert rose again from the depths. *You destroy those who speak lies. The Lord abhors the bloodthirsty and deceitful.* But he didn't destroy them. They continued to flourish, never once expressing remorse over the destruction they had caused.

"I also don't want to start off by accusing her," Sarah said. "I'd like to give her the opportunity to come clean."

Good luck with that, Kit thought. A woman who had smiled and offered condolences to a grieving mother at her son's funeral, only to move into her bedroom shortly after she was admitted to a psychiatric hospital, was unlikely to confess to lying about something as small as a horse.

"I'm just trying to figure out a way to be gracious with her. And I figured you might have some words of wisdom about how to do that."

Kit added two creamers to her coffee and stirred slowly. No. She had nothing to offer that might benefit Carol in the kind of conversation that could lead to reconciliation and restoration of trust. In fact, it might be beneficial for Sarah to feel the sting of betrayal so she could name it and forgive it, not just gloss over it. "Sorry," she said after prolonged silence. "Nothing is coming to mind."

Sarah scrutinized her, then said with a half-shrug, "I thought it was at least worth asking."

At neighboring tables, silverware clinked, conversations hummed, a cell phone rang, a toddler squealed in a highchair.

"Here you go," the server said. "Avocado toast with eggs over easy." Sarah immediately pierced an egg with a fork and nodded when the yolk streamed onto the plate. "And one wholegrain pancake and scrambled egg." She set Kit's food in front of her. "That's real maple syrup in the pitcher," she said, and Kit thanked her. "Anything else I can get you?"

"No, I think we're all set, thanks," Sarah said. She unfolded her napkin and placed it in her lap as the server stepped away. "You want to pray the blessing, Mom?"

Kit stared at her breakfast. "I think I'll let you do it today."

Bad idea, Sarah thought as she sliced into her toast. Evidently, Mom wasn't in a good enough frame of mind even to discuss how to have a healthy, fruitful conversation with Carol. Or maybe she was just too weary to pretend she could. "Sorry I brought it up," she said.

Her mother poured syrup onto her pancake, then wiped the dribble from the spout with her finger. "I'm sorry you're going through it with her." As she rubbed her hand on her napkin, she mumbled something under her breath.

"What did you say?"

"Nothing."

"Don't play passive-aggressive with me, Mom. You're obviously upset. What did you say?"

"I said, Not that I'm surprised."

Ah, okay. "Do you want to have that conversation here?" Sarah asked.

"I'm just saying, when you have a relationship with someone who has a long history of treachery—"

"*Treachery?* That's a little harsh, don't you think?"

"Is it?"

Their eyes met across a table that had become a canyon. Her mother didn't blink.

Sarah swirled a piece of toast in the egg yolk. "Don't think I didn't catch the barb about me having a relationship with someone treacherous. Or letting my daughters have one."

Without responding, her mother picked up her knife and cut her pancake into vertical, then horizontal strips. Slowly and methodically.

"Everything good here?" the server asked.

"Yes, thank you," Sarah said. Though her mother hadn't yet tasted her food, she nodded.

Sarah waited until the server was out of earshot before saying, "Why don't you just be honest and admit you've always resented my relationship with Carol? And with Dad."

Her mother's eyes flashed with uncharacteristic anger. "I never, ever did anything to interfere with your relationship with your father. Or with Carol. Ever."

"I didn't say you did. I said, be honest and confess you've always resented it."

Her mom took one bite of pancake and chewed slowly. Then she set down her fork. "I always encouraged you to maintain a relationship with your dad. I did everything I could to stay out of the way so you could do that. I never badmouthed either one of them to you, never leaned on you for support—"

"I was eighteen, Mom. It would have been inappropriate if you'd tried."

"You think I don't know that?"

"I'm just saying, we both found a way forward. And I've told you many times how grateful I am that you never did anything to jeopardize my relationship with Dad. Just like I won't do anything to jeopardize Morgan's relationship with Carol."

Her mother shook her head slowly.

"What?" Sarah demanded.

"That's your business, not mine."

"Right, Mom. You're right. But I thought you might care about it. I thought you might want to help me navigate all of this well. For my sake. And your granddaughter's."

The jab landed. She squared her shoulders. "Don't accuse me of not caring about you or my granddaughters. Just because I'm not able to fly them around the world or buy them hor—"

"Ah, see? There it is, Mom. There it is. The jealousy and resentment. It's good, right? Let it all come to the surface. Let it all be flushed out into the light. That's what you always say. So don't stop there. Keep going. What else are you angry about?"

Her mother picked up her fork and resumed eating.

"My relationship with Carol, right? That's what this is about. It's not about what Carol has or hasn't done. It's about me. Why don't you just say that? Why can't you just say that?"

"Don't bully me, Sarah. I didn't come here for a fight."

"Neither did I! I just want an honest conversation. This is what love looks like, right? Caring enough to tell the truth?" She waited. No reply. "I'm not eighteen anymore. You don't have to shield me from anything. I promise. Please. Say the hard things, Mom. I'm listening."

As Sarah watched her slowly push her plate to the side, she wondered what uncensored thoughts had presented themselves as candidates. Several times her mother's lips parted, but rather than words, only punctuated breaths escaped.

From the corner of her eye, Sarah saw the server approach. Before the girl could say anything, Sarah waved her off. "We're good here, thanks. You can bring the check after we're done eating."

"I'm finished," her mother said in a faint voice. She had hardly touched her pancake.

"Are you sure?" the girl asked.

"Yes."

"Do you want me to box it up for you?"

"No, thank you."

Sarah watched her remove the plate. "So that's it, then?" she asked once the server had left. "We're done here?"

Her mother's gaze shifted from her lap to the window, then back to her lap.

Sarah speared a piece of toast with her fork. "By all means, feel free to go. No need to stay on my account."

Her mother closed her eyes and bowed her head.

Fabulous. Passive-aggressive with a side of piety. Perfect combo. Come to think of it, that was how Mom often ended arguments with Dad. Squeeze him out, shut him down, take control by taking it all to God in prayer. No wonder he left. He couldn't compete against the Almighty for her attention or her words.

She snatched the piece of toast from her fork and chewed. She could outlast her mother in this showdown. Refuse to change the subject. Keep on eating and drinking until Mom picked up her purse and left or deigned to speak.

She thrust her fork into her second egg, the yolk spurting onto the plate. And they said she had her father's stubborn streak? No. She'd received a double portion. *Tenacious,* Dad used to call her whenever Mom complained. Her tenacity had helped her survive. She wouldn't apologize for it.

"Katherine!" a voice exclaimed from behind. "How nice to see you!"

Her mother rearranged her lips into a smile and said hello.

"Barb and I were just talking about you this morning," the woman said. When she stepped into view, Sarah recognized her from the retreat. "We've been wondering how you're doing. We were all so worried about you."

Sarah stared at her mother, eyebrows arched.

"Are you feeling any better?" the woman asked.

"Yes. Fine. Thanks." She looked down at her lap.

"Oh, that's good. And having breakfast with your daughter? How nice." She turned toward Sarah. "I'm Joan. Big fan of your mom's."

Still eyeing her mother, she replied, "I am too."

Joan laughed. "That's good to hear!"

Sarah took a slow sip of coffee. Clearly, something had happened at the retreat. And if it had anything to do with Wren—anything at all—

"We're looking forward to Saturday, Katherine. Just awfully sad it's your last one. But I guess you're ready to be finished, eh? You'll need a good long rest when it's all over."

Glancing up, she gave a wan smile. "Yes, I will."

"I'm sure everybody's praying for you," Joan said, "and we'll keep praying."

She thanked her.

"I'll let you get on with your breakfast. See you Saturday!"

As soon as she left, Sarah leaned forward. "Anything you want to tell me, Mom?"

Her mother twisted her napkin and took a slow breath. "Yes."

23

Wren's supervisor said she was sorry, but she didn't have any more housekeeping hours to give. "I haven't gotten any complaints about your cleaning, so if anything changes, I'll let you know." Audrey folded her hands on her desk. "But I'll tell you this, it wouldn't be full time. The higher ups don't want to pay benefits, so they'd keep you under thirty hours."

"I know," Wren said. "I figured that." If she could at least recoup her lost income from New Hope, though, she would have enough to pay her bills—as long as she stayed with Kit. *If* she could stay with Kit and not feel like she was becoming even more of a burden. "Thank you. I really appreciate it." She started to rise from her chair.

"Let me ask you something, Wren."

She sat back down.

"I said when I hired you that you seemed way overqualified for the job, and you told me you needed something that didn't wear you out emotionally. I thought that was kinda funny at the time, 'cause lots of people can't stand coming into a place like this."

"I know. But it's not depressing for me. I like being here."

"I can tell. I've watched you with the residents. You're great with them. Not just when you're here on your own time but when you're cleaning their rooms. I can tell you care about them."

"Thanks. I do." Hearing Audrey say that—especially after the mishap with Teri and her mother—was a gift.

"You're the kind of employee I'd love to keep on staff as long as possible. But I figured you'd be long gone by now, that you'd go back to social work. And yet here you are, asking me for more hours." She opened her hands in a question. "Is it really because you want to mop floors for a living? Is this what you want to do?"

Wren rubbed her palms slowly against her cotton scrub pants. How much truth did she owe her supervisor? "I want to make a difference in people's lives. But I can't manage the stress of what I used to do."

Audrey looked as if she was trying to decide what to say next. "Okay, Wren. Listen. If a different job opened up here—something that wasn't housekeeping but would still give you a chance to help the residents—would you be interested?"

"What kind of job?"

"Again, only part time. Maybe fifteen hours a week."

"That would be perfect!"

"And I'm giving you this as a confidential heads up, okay? I'm trusting you not to say anything."

"Sure. Promise."

Audrey steepled her fingers. "The volunteer coordinator just gave her notice. She got a full-time job somewhere else, so her job will be posted soon."

"Seriously? Oh, my word, Audrey, I would love that job!"

"That's what I figured."

Her mind sped forward. "Would I be allowed to do both? I mean, if I got that job, could I keep cleaning?"

"It wouldn't be a problem as far as I'm concerned, but I don't know what admin would say."

"Right. Okay. I know I'm running ahead, but . . ."

"You would need to work closely with Peyton. She would still be the one planning activities. You'd be finding volunteers to help support what she plans."

"Okay. I'd be happy to do that." Maybe Peyton would be open to new ideas about activities the residents would enjoy—without feeling threatened by suggestions.

"I'll put in a good word for you," Audrey said. "The management already knows you spend a lot of time here."

Her thoughts leaped to Mrs. Whitlock and the soiled diaper. "You don't think they'll hold it against me, what happened with Teri and her mom?"

"That's over and done with, Wren. We all make mistakes. If you put in an application, I'll vouch for you. They may say what I said—that you're way overqualified. But I think you've demonstrated your commitment to this place, and that will probably go a long way." Audrey stood. "Remember, not a word to anyone about this."

Wren crossed her heart. "You'll tell me as soon as they post the job?"

"The second I hear."

If she could have been sure she wasn't being observed, Wren might have skipped her way to the housekeeping storage room.

How much longer would it take? she wondered as she pushed her cleaning cart down the hall. How long until she stopped wishing she could call Casey and tell him news? "Give yourself time," Kit would remind her. It hadn't even been a year yet.

She parked her cart outside Mr. Page's room. If someone had told her when she graduated with her social work degree that in a few years she would be this excited about the possibility of working fifteen hours a week as a volunteer coordinator—or seeking to increase her hours as a housekeeper—she would have been too proud to have believed it.

Good thing God didn't reveal many details about the future ahead of time. She might live in constant dread or despair. Enough to receive grace for the moment, a daily gathering of manna that couldn't be hoarded. Hannah had preached about that on Sunday, how *manna* literally meant, "What is it?," and how believers were called not only to trust God for daily bread but also to daily ingest the mystery of what God provided. Sometimes, Hannah said, grace didn't look or taste like grace.

She leaned closer to inspect the photo in Mr. Page's shadow box. If someone had told that lively, fresh-faced actor he would one day be mostly confined to a wheelchair, living in a single sterile room at a nursing home, what would he have done? What would any of them have done? It was grace, not knowing the endgame too far in advance.

She peeked through the partially open door to make sure he was awake, then gently knocked. "Mr. Page?" she called softly as she entered.

At the sound of her voice, he looked up from the tray table wedged in front of his chair, his meal untouched. "Decided to come back, did you? I thought perhaps you'd had enough."

"Oh, no—sorry! I've been off the past few days. Working at my other job, I mean." The walls were still bare, the shelves empty. Had no one returned to decorate? Or had he refused the help?

"The other girl is not a conversationalist," he said. With a slow and deliberate hand motion, he ran one finger along the edge of the tray table. "Neither is she one for cleaning. I'm not sure what she does when she comes in here. Except make a fuss about opening those confounded blinds."

Wren eyed the window, where the blinds remained shut against the sunlight.

"I told her, why do I want to stare at a parking lot? What purpose does that serve, except remind me of all the places I cannot go?"

"The other side of the hall faces the garden," Wren said. "You could ask about moving into a different room."

"And what would that require? Someone dying so I get their view? A bit of *Arsenic and Old Lace*? You could be my accomplice."

She decided her safest bet was to change the subject. "Would you like me to help you with your lunch?"

"Finish it off, you mean?" He shifted his good hand a few inches and pushed the plate farther away. "Have at it. I think they call that a chicken sandwich."

Kayla came into the room with her characteristic cheer. "Mr. Page! What's this, my friend? Still haven't finished your lunch? I told you, if I let you stay here instead of going to the dining room, you need to cooperate with me. I'll have to call your sister again and tattle on you. And I don't think Miss Mary will be happy about that."

He muttered something.

"What's that?" Kayla asked.

"I said go right ahead."

In his younger days his tone could silence a classroom of teenage boys. Now he only sounded resigned. Wren stepped away from his chair to give Kayla more room.

"C'mon now." Kayla picked up his knife and fork. "How about if I cut it up for you? Would that help?"

In reply, he seized his plate and, with far more force than Wren could have predicted, flung it like a frisbee, narrowly missing Kayla's shoulder. After bouncing off the empty bookcase, it landed with a durable clatter on the floor, French fries launching across the room like errant Nerf darts.

"Mr. Page!" Kayla exclaimed. "You could have hurt someone!"

Too shocked to speak, Wren stooped to pick up a piece of lettuce, then remembered she ought to wear gloves.

"What's all the racket in here?" Greta demanded as she stormed into the room. She took one look at Kayla, another at the floor, and immediately assessed the situation. "Are you hurt?"

"No," Kayla said, visibly shaken.

"Then you are a very, very lucky man, Mercer. We take assault extremely seriously around here. You're well enough to know better."

Wren wondered what his expression might have been if he'd had full use of both sides of his face. But the former thespian didn't even attempt to convey horror or regret over what he'd done.

"I'll take over in here, Kayla. Wren, give us a few minutes, and then you can come back in and clean." Greta met Mr. Page's stare with one of her own. "Leave the door open," she directed them.

As soon as Kayla stepped into the hallway, she leaned against the wall, then slowly sank to the floor, head in her hands. "Lord Jesus," she murmured.

Wren knelt beside her, waiting to speak until Kayla looked up. "Can I do anything for you?"

She shook her head. "I'll be all right."

Inside the room, Greta was speaking in too low a voice to be overheard.

"I try to treat everybody the same," Kayla said, "but some of them are easier than others."

"Has he done that before?"

"Not a plate, no. Flung a towel at me once when I was trying to get him into the shower. I thought maybe it was just me that upset him, but the others have had trouble too." She gripped the nape of her neck and sighed. "Lord, have mercy. He's gonna be a tough one."

Wren sat cross-legged on the carpet. "He was my middle school art teacher."

"He taught children?" Kayla gave a low whistle. "Ever throw anything at you?"

"No. He raised his voice at kids sometimes. But middle schoolers can be a handful." A memory surfaced. He *had* hurled something across the room once—a paintbrush. But his intended target snared it like a line drive. The class cheered, and Mr. Page grinned and congratulated him. She wouldn't mention that to Kayla. "What he did just now was awful. But that man in there isn't the man I knew years ago. Mr. Page was kind. Passionate and kind. Maybe he'll settle in after a while."

"Yeah, some of them do. But strokes are hard. Especially when they get aggressive like that." She rose and offered a hand to pull Wren up. "I'm glad you told me about him, though. It helps to remember where they've come from and what they've lost."

Eyeing his shadow box, Wren breathed a prayer for him.

"Mercer is ready to apologize to both of you," Greta announced from the doorway, her expression like that of a daycare teacher who had successfully chastened a toddler.

Wren motioned for Kayla to go ahead of her, then picked her way across the floor to avoid stepping in splattered mayonnaise or trampling stray fries. Side by side they stood in front of his chair. "I'm sorry for throwing a plate. I didn't intend to hit you with it. But my aim isn't what it used to be."

Greta raised her eyebrows. "I think the issue is, you won't throw objects, period."

"Correct," he said. "And I'm sorry I've made a mess for you, Wren. If I could get out of my chair, I would help you clean it up."

"It's okay, Mr. Page. I'll take care of it for you."

Kayla bent down so she was eye level with him. "I want to do everything I can to help you, Mr. Page. I know it's really hard, moving in here."

"Do you?" he asked, his tone sad rather than hostile.

She cupped her hand over his. "My grandpa was in a care facility for a long time. So, yes. I know a little bit about how it feels—not just for you but for the people who care about you."

"Not many of those left," he said.

"Then let us be some of them for you."

When he didn't reply to Kayla, Wren stooped beside her and looked into his eyes, searching for a connection. "We want to help you, Mr. Page. Dig it?"

He stared at her a moment, then said, "Dug."

She and Kayla both straightened up. "Okay," Kayla said, "I'm going to hold you to that."

"I'll be back with your pills," Greta said before leaving the room.

Kayla surveyed the scattered remnants of his lunch. "You want to try something else from the kitchen? I'll get you whatever you want."

"I just want to sleep."

"I'll get you back in your bed a little later," Kayla said. "You've got occupational therapy soon."

"Not today."

"That's part of the deal, Mr. Page. You've got to do whatever you can to cooperate with us and get stronger."

He stared at the closed blinds. "And what good will that do? I won't be able to go home."

"No, that's true, but Wren told me you were her art teacher. You managed to fling that plate pretty good. Maybe you could paint again."

"I'd paint with you," Wren said as she donned gloves.

Kayla smiled. "There. See? Bet you could still teach her a thing or two."

He gestured to his right side, where his arm hung limply. "See? No good."

Kayla was undeterred. "You could learn to paint with your left hand. Or, you ever seen those videos of people painting with a brush between their toes or their teeth?"

"Like Joni Eareckson Tada," Wren said.

"Yes! Like Joni. You could experiment."

Wren could tell he was shutting down. "If you'd be willing, you could be my teacher again. You wouldn't have to paint if you don't want to. But maybe you could help me."

He closed his eyes. "I don't need to be made to feel useful. Those days are done."

Wren and Kayla exchanged glances.

"If you change your mind about lunch," Kayla said, "push your button, okay? I'll be back to check on you soon."

When Kayla left the room, Wren carried the dirty plate to her cart, then began sweeping fries onto her dustpan, trying to decide if she should clean in silence or attempt to engage him in conversation. After a while, she said, "I read the poem you suggested."

He remained motionless, his eyes still closed.

She kept sweeping. "Do you think Burns was speaking about his own experience, or did he create the narrator?"

He did not reply.

"I guess it doesn't matter, does it, whether he destroyed a nest with his plow or someone else did? Or whether he just made up the story to illustrate a theme." She looked up. He was watching her. She decided to keep going. "But if it actually happened to him—if he's the one who caused a mouse distress and then he wrote about it, then

I like him. I like that he noticed and cared about the little creature
and what she lost because of him. I like that he saw the consequences of what he did and that it mattered to him and prompted
him to think about his own losses and disappointment."

He turned his face toward the blinds.

Wren peered under the bed and swept up a few more fries. "I
won't be able to do the brogue like you but"—she cleared her
throat—"'Och! I backward cast my eye on prospects drear! An'
forward, tho I canna see, I guess an' fear!' That's the burden, isn't it?
When our present moments get clouded by the pain of the past or
the fear of the future. That's why he says the mouse has the ad-
vantage over us."

"Us?" he echoed, turning toward her again. "Is there an 'us,'
Wren, young as you are?"

She sat back on her heels. "Does age have a monopoly on suffering or losses or fear?"

He lowered his gaze. "I'm sorry to hear it, then."

"Thank you," she said. "And I'm sorry for yours."

Just as she was wondering whether to try to engage him about his
own story, he said, "As far as prospects go, however, I'd say you're in
a far better place than I am. Not much guesswork as I gaze into the
future. What do I have to look forward to? Weeks of this? Months
of this? Years of this? Seems to me it would have been merciful if
the plow had destroyed not only the nest but the mouse."

In the heavy silence, she searched for something to say. "I'm sorry,
Mr. Page. I wish I could do something to help."

"Then you can leave me alone. And tell the others I want my door
to stay closed."

She took a slow breath, then pushed herself up from the floor.
"Okay." Though Greta would insist otherwise, Wren didn't tell him
that. Let the two of them fight a battle of wills. "I'll come back to
finish cleaning later."

"Tell the other girl to do it," he said. "Not much for conversation,
that one." He paused. "Dig it?"

Grace and compassion, Wren reminded herself as she strode to her locker after cleaning the other residents' rooms. Whenever people lost patience with Casey—and it had happened frequently—she would become even more determined to stick with him. Not necessarily defend him. Sometimes there was no defense for his volatility. But she had always found a way to remain when others walked away. Like Theo with Vincent. Vincent had lost plenty of friends because he was outspoken and passionate, irritable and moody. But he was also tenderhearted and generous and devoted. Theo witnessed the best and the worst of his brother and remained fiercely loyal to the very end.

She dialed her locker combination.

If someone as buoyant and kind as Kayla lost patience with Mr. Page, who else would put up with him? Sure, the staff would do their duty, but they might grow tired of trying to go above and beyond. She would need to find a way to remain alongside, even if he continued to rebuff her. He had once been kind to her. And to Casey. That was enough reason to be kind to him now. She had no idea what he had lost. People who cared about him, he'd said, *Not many of those left.* But was that because they had died? Or abandoned him?

She swung open her locker door and took out her lunch bag and phone. For the sake of the memory of who he had once been—and for the sake of Casey's memory too—she would not abandon him. "Dig it?" she said aloud as she checked her messages. One from Mom: *Let me know what your supervisor says about adding more shifts,* and one from Sarah, two hours ago: *No emergency. But please call me asap.*

She stared at the screen. Great. What had she done now?

She scanned the last several days.

Oh. The retreat. Sarah had probably heard about what happened on Saturday and planned to chastise her for causing more stress.

That phone call could wait. She shut her locker and carried her lunch down the back stairs. She would call her mom later too and try to reassure her that she was okay and that she wasn't worried about not getting more housekeeping hours. Something else would open.

She exited the stairwell onto the back patio. Several residents sat in wheelchairs near the fountain while others worked with volunteers at the raised flower beds, pulling weeds. Wren returned their friendly waves. Soon she might be working with those volunteers. She wished she could tell her mom. But then her mom might get her hopes up, and if the job didn't come through, that would be harder. Better to strictly interpret Audrey's admonition. Once the job was posted, she could tell others she had applied for it and ask for their prayers.

She gazed up at a powder blue sky with fleecy clouds. Maybe she would go to her studio after work. She might as well do as much painting there as possible before she had to pack it up. With no natural light, Kit's basement wasn't an ideal substitute, but any space—even a corner stacked with boxes—was better than nothing. If she got the coordinator job, they might let her store supplies in one of the closets, and she could paint with the residents at the arts and crafts table. Or outside on a day like this.

She strolled through the courtyard and sat down on the lawn beneath a towering oak. If she hadn't been wearing her uniform, she might have climbed onto a branch to eat her lunch. It had been years since she'd climbed a tree, and this one, Casey would point out, had the perfect shape.

Just as she removed her peanut butter sandwich from her bag, her phone buzzed with an incoming call. *Sarah*. Adrenaline surged. Something must have happened with Kit. She wouldn't call just to chew her out, would she?

"I'm so sorry," she said when she answered, "but I only just got your text. Is everything okay?"

"Are you at work?"

"On my lunch break. Why? What's going on?"

"I was with Mom all morning. She filled me in on everything that's happened the past few days."

Then again, Wren thought, Sarah might call for just that reason. She pressed her forehead.

"I'm worried about how exhausted she is," Sarah said. "All the stress the past few months has taken a huge toll on her. She can't keep going like this. She needs a rest. A break."

Yes, and a break was coming. In less than two weeks Kit would be retired. Then she could rest as much as she wanted.

Unless Sarah was talking about her needing a break from something —or someone—else. "What can I do to help?" Wren asked, hearing the quiver in her voice.

"Move out for a bit."

Though she wasn't sure she had heard Sarah correctly, she couldn't find the breath to ask her to repeat herself.

"Just for a little while," Sarah said. "Maybe stay with friends?"

Friends? she thought. What friends? Casey was gone. And before he was gone, he took up enough space for a dozen.

"I tried to persuade Mom to move in with us for a little while so we could keep an eye on her. But she insists that what she needs is quiet. Solitude. Not a house with teenagers."

Wren pulled her knees to her chest. Or her own house with a great-niece who caused her stress.

Message received.

Wren made sure she had as much control of her voice as possible before asking, "How soon should I plan to go?"

Sarah paused, then said, "I think the sooner she has some extended time to herself, the better."

Wren stared at her scrubs. Okay. She could go home—no, not home. She could go to Kit's house. Pack a duffel bag. Find a cheap hotel for the night. Then figure out what to do next.

"I'm sorry to ask you to do this," Sarah said.

Was she really? Or had she had this in mind for a while and only just found the excuse to make it happen?

And why was Sarah the one delivering the message? Why hadn't Kit been brave enough to tell her she needed a break? She'd thought the two of them were closer companions than that.

Evidently not. And that wound cut deep.

Long after they finished the phone call, Wren remained beneath the tree, her sandwich still in her lap. She pictured Mr. Page alone in his room. *Not many people left,* she heard him say.

No, she thought. Not many at all. And when a plow destroyed a nest, where was a mouse to go?

24

Kit turned her head on her pillow and eyed her bedside clock. Three thirty. She had slept for almost four hours. She couldn't make a regular habit of that. Not even after she retired.

She lay on her back, watching her abdomen rise and fall. In all the years she had served at New Hope, she had seldom canceled spiritual direction appointments for any reason other than being sick. "If you don't cancel them," Sarah had said when she escorted her to the Corner Nook parking lot, "I'll tell Gayle to do it. You need to rest."

She hadn't had the strength to argue. She'd only wanted to drive away as quickly as possible. Sarah had waited until she was buckled in. Then she kissed her on the cheek, said she was sorry for upsetting her, that she loved her and would call later to check in.

Kit inhaled slowly. After everything she had revealed to Sarah that morning, there would be no convincing her she didn't need to be monitored. *I can't, Lord.* She couldn't bear the thought of living under Sarah's increased scrutiny or well-meaning attempts to dictate the life she would lead, now or in the future. *I can't, Lord.*

But she was too tired to fight.

Favorite lines from a psalm came to mind: "O that I had wings like a dove! I would fly away and be at rest; truly, I would flee far away; I would lodge in the wilderness; I would hurry to find a shelter for myself from the raging wind and tempest."

Sarah's suggestion about getting away for an extended time of retreat after her retirement party wasn't a bad idea. But she didn't want to accept her offer of the cottage. That place was tainted by too many painful memories. Better to flee to a wilderness where no one knew her, where she would be free to walk and rest, sit and pray, and ask the Lord to restore her soul.

In the meantime, she needed to seek his strength for leading one last retreat session. Sarah had urged her to cancel that too. "If you can't do it, Mom, you can't do it. You've got limits. People will understand."

But she didn't want to let it go. Especially since the topic she'd chosen months ago now had deep personal relevance again: stewarding grace.

She propped herself up on her pillow. *As you have been forgiven, forgive.* That was the only way to confront the sprouting resentment. What she had been too tired to practice when she got home from the restaurant, she decided to do now. Before it took deeper root.

She closed her eyes and pictured Carol, not with her arms wrapped around Robert but with her arms wrapped around Sarah and Jess and Morgan. Then she spoke the words aloud. "Forgive Carol for her deception, Lord, and deliver her from her sin." Her flesh always resisted the next step. "Bless her and bring her to life in you." The words felt halfhearted, but she said them anyway. "Bless and do not destroy."

She leaned back against her headboard. Not only were the words halfhearted; they were dishonest. She *did* want God to destroy—not Carol, but her relationship with Sarah and the girls. Again, she pictured Carol with her arms wrapped around Sarah and Jess and Morgan—not as a stepmother or step-grandmother, but as a fully integrated, deeply loved member of their family. Not just the "fun grandma." The preferred one.

Carol wasn't the one with her arms wrapped around them. They had their arms wrapped around her. That was the image that stung.

Could she ever confess to Sarah the satisfaction she'd derived from hearing about Carol's latest breach of trust? Could she ever confess to cherishing the hope that this infraction might generate a rift too severe to be mended?

With a heavy sigh, she rose from her bed and plodded to the kitchen to make herself a cup of tea. No doubt about it: Joan's interruption at the restaurant had been a well-timed gift of grace, diverting Sarah's attention away from who and what her mother resented and why. After hearing everything that had happened with Wren and the police and Logan and the panic attack, Sarah had launched into problem-solving mode, all conversation about Carol mercifully abandoned.

For now.

She stared out her window as the water boiled.

Confessing her envy and resentment toward Carol wouldn't have been any new revelation. Sarah knew she had struggled to be supportive of Carol's close relationship with her family, especially after Robert died.

But Sarah had also accurately discerned a reality Kit had been reluctant to name. She hadn't only resented what Carol had taken, but what Sarah had given. Sarah was right: she resented that her daughter had remained loyal to the woman who had betrayed her. Plain and simple. And she had tried to keep that part concealed. Until she was too weary to conceal it.

She blew out a long breath as she poured boiling water into her mug.

She supposed she would need to name that as a gift of grace too, the light shining into the dark and revealing the truth. And someday—when she wasn't so exhausted—she could confess to Sarah that yes, she had attempted to mask her hurt and pretend she hadn't cared how quickly Sarah embraced Carol after the affair was exposed or how readily Sarah forgave—or overlooked—Robert and Carol's sins.

No mystery why.

She carried her tea to the table and sat down facing the patio door.

She had pretended it wasn't important to her because she knew how much Sarah needed her father. She had just lost her brother, and her mother had suffered a nervous breakdown. Robert was a stabilizing force for their daughter, even after he abandoned their marriage, and he and Carol were a package deal. Kit had known and understood that. By not interfering with Sarah's relationship with the two of them, she had protected their own.

Ah, now. That was interesting.

Had she considered that before? She couldn't remember. But the revelation struck with fresh force.

Why had she pretended?

Out of fear.

And why had she been afraid?

She watched the steam rise from the cup. The Holy Spirit was stealthy. Persistent. She followed the thread of emerging insight.

She had already lost Micah and Robert. She couldn't have borne losing Sarah too. So she had striven to demonstrate to Sarah that she wouldn't be the sort of mother to make things difficult.

She steepled her hands against her lips.

What did that cost you, beloved? the Spirit whispered.

She blew out another long breath. "Freedom, Lord."

The truth always set captives free. Even when it was painful to embrace.

And this was the truth: what had appeared to be generosity of spirit had also been tinged with self-protection and fear. There she was, accusing Carol of deceit while refusing to acknowledge her own. "Forgive me," she whispered. She had refused to be honest with Sarah because she had privileged her own security. She had avoided speaking the truth because it might have cost her personally.

In fact, come to think of it, she had probably confided far more truth to Wren regarding how she'd felt about Carol and Robert than she ever had to Sarah. Expressing her thoughts and feelings to Wren about those losses had felt safer. More objective. But Sarah was right. She didn't need to be protected. She could handle the truth. The truth would come as no surprise.

She took a sip of tea. She could journal about all this when she wasn't so tired. And figure out the best time for a follow-up conversation. Not today, though. No more today. *Oh, that I had wings . . .*

On second thought, she would be too weary even to fly away to rest.

Her stomach growled, and she eyed the wall clock. Wren would be home soon, and she hadn't yet given any thought to dinner.

She was too weary to cook, and a bowl of cereal wouldn't suffice. Maybe they could order pizza for delivery and watch a movie in their pajamas. Something light and fun. Both of them had been living under the weight of stress and change lately. With all the weariness of molting and the discomfort of new pinfeathers emerging, a bit of mindless distraction might be exactly what they needed. It was what *she* needed. If she could quiet her thoughts, she could fly away while reclining on her couch.

The front door creaked open. "Hey there!" she called.

No reply. Maybe Wren was on the phone.

She set her mug down and shuffled into the living room. Wren was sitting on the bottom stair, removing her shoes, "Hey there," Kit repeated. "You doing okay?"

As soon as Wren looked up, it was clear she wasn't. "I found someone to take me in for the night, so at least I don't have to go to a hotel."

Kit furrowed her brow. "What are you talking about?"

Wren stood and slung her backpack over her shoulder. "Sarah passed along your message. I'll be out of your hair shortly." She started up the stairs.

"Wait, Wren—what do you mean? What message?"

"The one about me moving out," she called over her shoulder.

What in the world? "Wren, stop—please. There's obviously been a big misunderstanding."

Halfway up the stairs, Wren pivoted toward her. "I didn't misunderstand anything. Sarah was perfectly clear. She said you told her you need a break and that I need to move out."

Kit pursed her lips. This was exactly the sort of well-meaning interference she had dreaded. *Oh, to have wings like a dove . . . Truly, I would flee far away.*

With a sigh, she said, "I told Sarah I needed some peace and quiet. But I didn't mean you have to move out. I'm sorry she took it that way. I'll work it out with her." Add this to the list of things to resolve with her daughter. But not tonight.

"It's fine," Wren said. "I already figured it out."

Kit picked up her phone from the coffee table, where she had left it hours ago. One unread text from Sarah: *I talked with Wren. She's willing to stay with friends for a few days so you can have some silence and solitude. Hope you can rest well. Love you!*

She clenched the bridge of her nose with her fingers. "I'm sorry, Wren. I never saw her message. And I didn't know she was going to call you." She sank onto the couch. "Whenever she worries about me, she can get bossy. I'm sorry. I'll handle things with her, don't worry. What you and I work out is our business, not hers."

Wren didn't reply right away. "It's okay," she finally said as she descended the stairs. "Don't worry about it. I found a place to go."

"Who will you stay with?"

"Mara."

Kit smiled weakly. "Ah, well, you might have a better time with her."

"Sounds like you aren't unhappy for me to leave."

"No. I didn't mean—"

"It's okay. I get it. I know it's been stressful, having me here. Sarah's right. You need your space for solitude."

"Don't let Sarah tell you what I need. That's not her place."

"No, but like you said, Kit, she's worried about you. She wants what's best for you. I get that." She set her backpack on the floor and sat down beside her. "I want what's best for you too. Even though it seems like I only care about myself and my own health sometimes. Sorry. I can be really selfish."

"So can I."

They shared the silence.

"I'm sorry I got upset with you," Wren said after a while. "I should have known you wouldn't kick me out without talking to me first."

Kit cupped her hand over Wren's. "I have no plans to kick you out. I've told you before, you can stay here as long as you need to. As long as you want to."

"Thank you."

"I enjoy having you here. Truly. I enjoy your company. That's not to put any pressure on you about staying—just that there isn't any pressure for you to leave."

"Okay," Wren said. "Thanks. But having a few days for your own mini-retreat might be a gift for you right now."

With so many things needing her attention, Kit wasn't sure how feasible that was. But as wrong as Sarah had been to determine a course of action without consulting her, the instinct might have been correct. *I would lodge in the wilderness. I would hurry to find a shelter for myself from the raging wind and tempest.* No wings required. A few days of silence and solitude in her own home might serve her well, especially as she tried to prepare for one last teaching session. No stress. No drama. No distractions.

No company. She would miss the company.

Wren kissed her on the cheek. "I'll go pack a bag."

"Is Mara cooking dinner for you?"

"Pizza and a movie, I think."

Kit pitched her voice to sound cheerful as she said, "That sounds like fun." After Wren disappeared upstairs, she shuffled back to the kitchen, opened the cupboard, and removed a cereal bowl.

25

One pack of dry erase markers, six spiral notebooks, two three-ring binders. Sarah inventoried the supplies she had loaded into her shopping cart, checking each item off her list. All she needed were two more packs of highlighters and some Post-it notes, and she would be all set. At least for now.

As she pushed her cart toward the shortest checkout lane, she glanced at her phone. Nothing from Mom. She would wait a while longer before she called to see how she was feeling. By then, Wren ought to be settled with friends. She might even decide she preferred being with people her own age. That wouldn't be a bad outcome in all this. For everyone.

Can you preheat the oven to 375? she texted Zach. *And ask Jess to make a salad.* They would have just enough time to eat before he needed to leave for his shift.

Jess is out with friends, he texted back. *Just dropped Morgan off at the library. She said she'll eat when she gets home.*

Sarah sighed. Why did she bother trying to fix family dinners? *Fine. Throw in a frozen pizza. We'll save the casserole for tomorrow.*

"Hey, Mrs. Kersten," the cashier said as Sarah began unloading items onto the conveyor belt.

She looked more carefully at the girl with the striped headband and tattooed arms. She had acquired quite a few designs since eighth grade. "Taylor! How are you?"

"Okay." Taylor surveyed the items. "Shopping for school?"

"Getting the classroom ready." She mentally calculated when Taylor would have been in her algebra class. "Are you a senior this year?"

"No, I graduated already. Just going to community college and trying to figure out my life."

Sarah nodded. "Good for you, taking time to do that. Community college is a great option. No sense spending lots of money on tuition if you don't know what you want to do."

"Yeah, well, my dad's been sick—he's got MS, and my mom had to take an extra job to pay for medical bills, so college isn't really an option for me right now. Maybe someday."

Sarah felt a lump rise in her throat. And her daughters were thinking about horses and trips to Europe? "I'm sorry to hear that, Taylor."

Taylor shrugged. "It is what it is, right?"

She watched her scan the first of the notebooks, wishing she could hide the pack of motivational posters about determination and diligence and positive attitude. "That doesn't mean it isn't hard, though." She took her wallet out of her purse.

"My little sister's gonna be in your class this year."

"Is she?" Sarah hadn't studied her rosters yet.

"For a little while, anyway. Mom's trying to sell our house so we can move in with my grandparents."

"Where do they live?"

"Kalamazoo." She pressed a button on the register. When the total appeared on the screen, Sarah swiped her card and thought of all the teachers who couldn't be so cavalier about paying for classroom expenses. And moms who worked multiple jobs to make ends meet.

"I don't want to move, but I need to help out my family."

And all the young people who, unlike Jess and Morgan, didn't have the luxury of options and routinely sacrificed their own desires. "I'm proud of you, Taylor," she said as she scribbled an illegible signature with the stylus. "What you're doing shows real maturity."

Taylor thanked her as she printed out a receipt.

"What's your sister's name?"

"Macy."

"Tell Macy I look forward to having her as my student, even if it's only for a little while."

Taylor thanked her again, then greeted the next customer with a warm hello and a, "Did you find everything you need?"

Perspective, Sarah thought as she pushed her loaded cart to the parking lot. That was one of the posters hanging in her classroom. *Sometimes you need yours turned upside down.*

When she arrived home, Zach was shaving for his hospital shift. "I'm rethinking the Europe and horse plans," Sarah said as she sat down on the edge of their bed.

He eyed her from the bathroom mirror. "Because?"

"Because I'm not sure it serves them well."

"Why not?"

"Just because Carol has the means to do it doesn't mean it's the right thing to do for them."

The blade scraped against his whiskers like a rake grating on pavement. "Is this because of what happened with your mom?"

"No."

"You sure?"

"Positive."

"Okay." He tilted his head and leaned closer to the mirror. "So, why wouldn't it be good for them?"

"Because I don't want them thinking everything comes easily in life. Struggle is good for the soul. It forms character."

He rinsed the razor. "We already talked about Morgan working for this. Not exactly glamorous, easy stuff, mucking out stalls."

"I know. But owning a horse smacks of privilege. So does going to Europe."

He observed her over his shoulder, his neck and chin still covered in shaving cream. "Jess isn't going over there to goof off. It's an educational opportunity. A cultural one. She's worked her socks off in school. I think she deserves a celebration trip, especially if her grandmother wants to give her one." He resumed shaving. "And as for privilege, both the girls have done mission trips."

Sarah folded her hands in her lap. "A few days in Mexico with their youth group friends, followed by trips to the beach. And then they get to come home and forget about it. They've been glorified tourists."

"They're teenagers, Sarah."

"I'm just saying, I don't think we've done enough to encourage them to serve locally, to see what's right around them in terms of need."

"Jess has done plenty."

"Because she's had to, Zach. For her NHS volunteer hours. And because she knows it looks good on college applications. But I don't get the sense that she's been shaped by what she's seen or that serving has deeply impacted her."

"So, that's a different conversation."

"No, it's not."

He rinsed off his face, then reached for a towel. "Where is all this coming from?"

"I'm just thinking, that's all."

He seemed to take extra time drying off. "I for one am not going to apologize or feel guilty that they have opportunities like this. And neither should you." He turned toward her, towel still in hand. "We haven't spoiled them, hon. They're good kids. And if their grandmother wants to do something special for them, it won't do them any harm." He studied her. "It seems to me there's something else going on here, like you not wanting to have the real conversation with Carol."

"That's not true."

"Have you called her?"

"Not yet."

He shrugged as if to say, *Case proved.*

"Fine. I'll call her. But I'm not done with this other conversation."

He draped the towel over the rack. "If you want to tell Jess no on Europe, that's on you. If you want to give her a lesson plan or goals to accomplish while she's there, that's on you."

Much as the two of them joked about her being the boss in the family, when Zach felt strongly about something, there would be no changing his mind. Jess would go to Europe, and Morgan would get her horse—eventually.

"As for both of them serving locally," he said, "I'm all for that. We can encourage Jess to look for opportunities beyond her own self-interests. That's great. But she's also old enough to make her own decisions about how she uses her time—within reason. And she's never given us any reason to question her judgment about that." He stepped into the bedroom and placed his hands on her shoulders. "Do you have any idea how lucky we are? Don't fixate on the negative, hon. Just be grateful for what we have."

"I am." But being grateful didn't mean being lazy about discerning how to steward their abundance. Or teaching their daughters to do the same.

The oven timer beeped. "Do you want me to make a salad?" she asked.

He let go of her shoulders. "Nah, don't bother. I'm not that hungry."

She sighed with frustration. "If you had said that earlier, we could have saved the pizza for another time. I swear, between you and the girls . . ."

"You sure this isn't connected to what happened with your mom today?"

She pictured him with his stethoscope, listening and assessing. "Positive."

As soon as Zach left for work, she called Carol. Might as well be done with it before the girls got home and Morgan started pestering her for information.

"Hey," she said when Carol answered after the first ring. "Good time for conversation?"

"Just got home from yoga," Carol said. "I keep threatening to Gary that I'm going to sign up for goat yoga sometime. Have you seen that?"

"No." But it sounded ridiculous. She settled herself in the armchair near the bedroom window.

"Check out videos online. So cute. Those baby goats climb right up onto your back while you do your plank. I don't think I could stop laughing. So maybe that defeats the purpose." She paused. "Then again, does everything need a purpose? Your dad would say no. Gary says yes. Aye, there's the rub."

Again with the husband comparisons. If Carol was trying to telegraph plans for a divorce, that was none of Sarah's business, and she didn't want it to be. Making a mental note not to encourage Carol's fond reminiscing about her dad, she forged ahead. "If it's a bad time, I can call back."

"No, it's okay. I'll put you on speaker while I mix myself a drink. What's up?"

Sarah monitored the driveway in case Jess got home early. "I wanted to follow up with you about Morgan and the horse."

"Don't tell me she's already picked one out."

"No. But as I've been thinking about it, I'm wondering if we've had a miscommunication." She heard what sounded like rhythmic clicking of fingernails against wood and pictured Carol deciding which bottles to take out of her liquor cabinet. "When you offered to get Morgan a horse, did you already know what we had told her?"

"Of course not!"

That wasn't the answer Sarah had hoped for. She pictured her mother shrugging slightly as if to say, "What did you expect?"

She decided to give Carol another chance to come clean. "You're sure I didn't mention it to you a few weeks ago?"

"Positive."

She had hoped she wouldn't have to enlist Zach as a witness. But better Zach than Morgan. "Are you sure? Because Zach says I did."

Silence. Then, "Maybe I forgot."

Again, not the reply she had hoped for.

"Listen, Sarah. I haven't mentioned it to you, but I've been under a tremendous amount of stress with Gary. Terrible. So it's very possible I'm not remembering things correctly. If I forgot a detail from a conversation a few weeks ago, then I'm sorry. I've had other more important things on my mind."

Not the apology she would have hoped for either. "I'm sorry to hear about you and Gary. I'm sure that's hard. But—"

"You have no idea," Carol said. "I knew when I married him that he wasn't anything like your father, and we didn't have many things in common. But he said he loved me. And I knew he wasn't marrying me for my money because he was already loaded. I figured we could have some fun together."

Sarah heard her vigorously stir a spoon in a glass.

"But ask the girls. Ask them if he showed even the slightest interest in me while they were here. They'll tell you. When he's not playing golf, he's glued to his phone or lying on the couch watching news. I can't stand it. I can't stand being around him. I'm about ready to walk out, I tell you."

Sarah pressed her fingers against her temple. She wasn't going to let her stepmother change the subject. "I'm really sorry to hear this, Carol. And I don't want to add more stress, but I also care too much about our relationship to let this go."

"Let what go?"

"The truth about what we'd told Morgan and what I told you."

"Oh, for cryin' out loud! Did you hear anything I said to you? I'm talking about my marriage breaking up, and you're talking about a horse? Gimme a break."

"It's not about the horse, Carol."

"I told you I forgot!"

She figured she had one more chance to extract a confession before she would need to mention Morgan. "Seems to me it wasn't just a matter of forgetting," she said as calmly as possible. "I think you lied to me. And I'm trying to give you an opportunity to tell me the truth."

"Oh, gawd. You sound just like your mother."

"Don't bring Mom into this."

"Then spare me her condescending, sanctimonious tripe. I don't have time for that."

Sarah gripped the armrest. "You can't bear to tell the truth, can you?" Even when caught in a lie, she kept digging and digging, making excuses, blaming other people.

"Don't you ever accuse me of something I didn't do," Carol snarled.

"You're sure about that? Because your texts with Morgan say otherwise."

Silence.

"I actually defended you to my mom this morning. I told her she was being harsh, calling you 'treacherous.' But you know what? It's not a bad word. Not a bad word at all."

"You should be ashamed of yourself," Carol hissed. "I'll tell you this much, if your father were here, he wouldn't put up with it."

Sarah dug her nails into the fabric of the chair. "No," she said, her voice shaking. "You're right. He always protected and defended you." She paused. "If you want to move forward with me, then it needs to be with truth. I'll let you decide."

During the ensuing silence, Sarah entertained the hope that her stepmother would care enough about their relationship to be brave and humble.

Instead, the woman Dad had chosen and loved said, "Your father would be ashamed of you," and ended the call.

Trembling, Sarah stared at her screen. Then she sank to her knees and, with her face pressed to the floor, gave herself permission to cry.

26

You don't have a problem with dogs, do you?" Mara asked as she drove her SUV into her garage. "Sorry, I should've asked you sooner."

"No, it's okay," Wren replied. "We had sheepdogs when I was little."

Mara unbuckled her seatbelt and opened her door. "I never had pets growing up, but my ex got Brian a little mutt for Christmas one year, and when Brian left for the army, Bailey was lonely. So I got him a friend." From inside the house came the sound of deep barks, followed by little yaps. "Oy! Brewster! Bailey! That's enough!"

Wren lifted her duffel bag from the backseat. "What should I do with my bike?"

"Leave it on the rack for now. Gotta clear out some crap to make room first."

Wren maneuvered around recycling bins overflowing with cardboard and Diet Coke cans, then followed Mara indoors, nearly tripping over a scruffy little dog who raced in circles before lunging at her knees. "Bailey! Down!" Mara grabbed his collar, then scooped him up. "You're a monster, I tell you. A little monster." He licked her face.

Wren stroked his head, brushing fur away from his eyes. He licked her hand before Mara set him down. Then he leaped toward the chocolate lab, who was sitting beside the kitchen table, watching Mara expectantly. The lab didn't budge.

Mara hung up her keys and put her bag on the floor. "Shake," she commanded. Brewster held up his paw. "Good boy." She patted his head, then reached into a jar on the counter to remove a treat, which she handed to Wren. "He'll be your friend for life if you give him that."

Wren placed her duffel bag beside Mara's purse, then held the edge of the biscuit, making sure her fingers wouldn't get caught in his teeth.

"I know, I know," Mara said as Bailey stood on his hind legs and took a few steps backward. "There's one for you too. Sit!" Bailey immediately obeyed. Mara pointed at the open canister. "He gets half of one."

Wren broke a treat into two pieces and set one on the floor in front of him. He snatched it up, then trotted off into another room. Brewster raised his paw again. Mara laughed. "He'd like the other half, please."

Wren let go before he could seize it from her hand. Brewster snagged it mid-air, then followed Bailey.

"Do you want me to take off my shoes?" Wren asked.

"Not unless you want to. No rules around here."

"Oh, okay. Thanks."

Mara leaned back against the kitchen counter. "I usually take them for a walk right after I change my clothes. You're welcome to come with us. Then we can eat after."

"Okay, sounds good."

"I'll show you where you're gonna sleep. Nothing fancy. Just Brian's old room."

Wren picked up her bag and followed her through a small living room with two dog kennels, a couch, an armchair, and a television. "My room's here"—Mara pointed to the left as they proceeded down a short hallway—"yours is here"—she pointed to the right—"and that's the bathroom. Like I said, not much to it."

Wren scanned the bedroom walls, which were plastered with military-themed posters of soldiers riding in tanks, wielding guns, and crawling in fatigues. *Brothers don't always have the same mother,* one caption read.

"Sorry I don't have a different space to give you."

Wren set her bag on the twin-size camouflage comforter. "This is great, Mara. Thank you. I'm just grateful you were willing to help out on such short notice."

"Anything for Katherine," she replied, then quickly added, "and for you too." She patted Wren's arm. "I'll go change out of these clothes, and we can get a move on."

Wren sat on the edge of the bed to wait. When Bailey appeared in the doorway a few minutes later, she tapped the bedspread. "C'mon." He leaped onto the bed and plopped down beside her. "Don't get too comfortable, though. We're going for a walk." At this, his ears perked up, and he bounded off the bed to spin in circles near the door.

"Wouldn't know he's almost ten, would you?" Mara said as she emerged from her room wearing loose-fitting long shorts and a jade green top. She bent over and vigorously rubbed both sides of his face. "My ex thought he was screwing me over, getting this dog when he knew I didn't want one." She modified her voice. "But we showed him, didn't we, Bailey? Yes, we did. We sure did!" Bailey bounced alongside her as she strolled to the kitchen. "C'mon, Brewster. Walkies!"

Mara plucked two leashes from a peg on the wall and attached them to their collars. "You take Brewster. He's far better behaved."

As they walked down the street, keeping pace with Bailey's good clip, Mara shared information about her neighbors, seeming to know details about every single resident on the block. Mr. Jones, who lived next door with his cats, Misty and Jujube, was beginning to suffer early signs of dementia. His daughter, who lived in Benton Harbor, was just about ready to move him to a facility near her. "Don't know what will happen to the cats, though. If I didn't have the dogs, I'd take them." Mr. and Mrs. Hassan, who lived across the street with their four children, had immigrated from Syria. "Not even gonna tell you the horror those little kids have seen." Sometimes Mara babysat for them on weekends when both parents were working. "Six people in a tiny two-bedroom house," she said. "It reminds me not to complain about my little place."

As Wren listened to Mara describe details about her neighbors' lives, she pictured Kit's cul-de-sac. After living there almost a year, she didn't know a thing about any of them.

Mara waved to a little girl careening by on a tricycle. "You ever hear about turquoise picnic tables?"

"No. But I saw one in your front yard."

"It's like this national thing," Mara said. "You paint them turquoise, put them on your front lawn, and it's a symbol for people to gather. No agenda. Just a place to hang out for conversation or food or games." She laughed. "Sometimes I look out my window or drive home from work and see people sitting there, just being together. It's been the coolest thing to have space for community like that. Especially since so many people on the street don't have family nearby."

Wren stopped as Brewster raised his leg on a shrub.

Mara tugged on Bailey's leash to get him to wait. "There's no pressure for you to join in while you're staying with me. Nobody will think bad of you if you go in and out of the house without socializing. But if you look outside and see a bunch of random people hanging out, you'll know why."

Wren chuckled. "Glad you gave me the heads up."

Mara said, "My old neighborhood would have freaked out about something like that. My ex would have hated it. Brian wasn't thrilled either when I put one out there, but I told him, hey! You're not here often enough to get a say in things. But sometimes when he's home on leave, he'll put on his uniform and hang out with the kids. They think he's a hero. And he is. I'm proud of him. Worry about him like crazy when he's over there, but proud of him."

"Where is he?"

"Afghanistan. I'm hoping he'll be home next spring, and then he'll be done. Don't know what he'll do next. College, maybe." Bailey strained against the leash, making choking noises. "Oy! Cool it, little man. Patience." But when Brewster continued sniffing leisurely around the shrubbery, she said, "Give him a yank, Wren. Otherwise, we'll be here all day."

When she gave a gentle tug, Brewster responded.

"So, how are you holding up with everything?" Mara asked as they rounded the corner onto a street that looked identical, with small homes set close together, no sidewalks, and mature trees. "You've had an awful lot of change in a short time."

She thought of the bald cardinal with, as Kit had put it, his "sudden, dramatic shedding of the old." Later, she might share with Mara how that image had spoken to her and what Kit had said about pinfeathers. Mara could probably relate, both to the vulnerability and the emerging hope. "I'm actually doing okay," she said. "Better, now that I know it wasn't Kit who wanted me to leave."

Mara gave a low whistle. "Man, that Sarah. Don't know what to make of her. I've been working with her on the retirement party, and let me tell you, she's got strong opinions about everything."

That was Sarah, all right. "She loves her mom," Wren said, trying to be generous.

"Yeah. Doesn't make it okay, though, what she did to you."

Wren wasn't sure how to reply.

"Maybe you're just way more gracious than I am," Mara said. "I would have been really upset."

"I was."

"You hid it well when you called me."

"I think I was still in shock."

"Well, I'm glad you reached out. I was going to text you this week to see about having dinner. Now we can have a good old-fashioned slumber party instead. Always wanted to have one of those when I was little. Never did."

It was Bailey's turn to stop. Mara pulled a plastic bag out of her pocket.

"Do your grandkids come and stay sometimes?"

"No. Kevin's wife doesn't like to travel, and it's way too expensive for Jeremy and his family to fly here from Texas. And besides all that, life for them right now is"—she appeared to be searching for the right word—"stressful. So I'm trying to give them space."

Given the sorrow in her voice, Wren wondered if that was the reason why she'd needed a "tune-up" session with Dawn.

Mara stooped to clean up after Bailey while he kicked up grass. "Crazy hard world, isn't it? Everybody's dealing with something." She knotted the bag, then patted Bailey's back. "Except you, little monster. Right? Life's pretty darn good for you."

As Bailey led the way prancing, they returned to Mara's house, where two little girls with long dark curly hair tied back in bows sat at the picnic table, coloring. "Nana, look!" One of them jumped up and skipped toward her, waving a piece of paper. Wren took Bailey's leash and the trash bag as Mara bent forward to embrace the child. "What have you got here, Yasmin?"

"Flowers!"

"Oh, how pretty!"

As Brewster lay down on the grass, Wren looked over their shoulders at a drawing of a purple vase and purple flowers, with "For you" and several x's and o's scrawled in purple crayon at the top of the page. Yasmin bounced on her toes. "It's for you!" she chirped.

"How did you know purple is my favorite?"

"Because it's my favorite too!" She grasped Mara's hand and swung her arm as they strolled to the table.

"And what are you drawing, Bibi?" Mara asked.

The other little girl held up a picture of a blue dog. "Bailey."

"He's very handsome, isn't he?" Mara motioned for Wren to join them, then removed both leashes. Bailey jumped up beside Bibi and rested his head on her lap. "This is my friend Wren. She's an artist too."

"Do you want to color with us?" Yasmin asked, her large brown eyes wide with welcome.

Mara gave Wren a look that said, *Totally up to you.*

"Sure, I'd like that. Thanks."

Yasmin patted the bench. "You can sit next to me."

Later that evening, Wren stood at the living room window, counting heads.

"How many have we got?" Mara called from the kitchen.

"Fifteen. No, wait." Two more children skipped up the driveway. "Seventeen."

"Kids?" Mara exclaimed.

"No, hold on." She counted the adults congregating around the table. "Five grownups, twelve kids."

Mara stepped into the doorway and wiped her hands on her hot pink "My favorite people call me Nana" apron. "The adults won't eat as many as the kids, so we should be fine."

Wren backed away from the window. "I think the news spread pretty fast."

Mara grinned. "World-famous snickerdoodles. At least in this neighborhood. Come help me with delivery and distribution."

As the two of them carried out trays of warm cookies, Yasmin and Bibi walked ahead of Mara like heralds for a celebrity, while their older brothers commanded the other neighborhood kids to sit down and wait. "There's enough for everyone, right?" one of the boys asked Mara.

"Right you are, Tariq. Plenty for everyone." They set the trays in the middle of the table. "Everyone," Mara called, "this is Wren. Wren, this is everyone."

Wren waved to a chorus of greetings.

Yasmin tugged on Mara's shirt. "Mr. Jones needs some."

"Right you are, young lady. Take two from the tray to deliver to him. I'll make sure there are still some left for you when you come back."

"Save some for my sister!" Tariq called out as she skipped to the next-door house, a cookie in each hand. Bibi chased after her.

As Wren observed the lively gathering, two thoughts emerged: first, that she wished she had a sketchbook to capture this moment, and second, that moments like these defied capturing.

"Join us, Wren!" a woman with long gray braids called from the table, scooting over to make room.

When the woman held out the tray to her, she could imagine Jesus smiling, saying, "Take and eat."

An hour later, while a few neighbors remained at the table chatting, Wren and Mara lounged on her couch, Brewster asleep with his head on Mara's bare feet and Bailey curled up on Wren's lap. "Tell me more about this Logan guy," Mara said. "I'm not sure what to make of him."

"I'm not sure either," Wren said. "He's this odd mix of White middle-class business guy who's focused on budgets and bottom lines while claiming to have a passion for racial justice." As she reached for her glass of water, she tried not to disturb the sleeping dog. "Not that those things can't go together. But I still can't get past what he said about Kit and her content being depressing. How do you say you're passionate about serving people who have been marginalized or oppressed and then say that talking about suffering is too depressing? I don't get it."

Mara shook her head slowly. "Nope. Neither do I. If you've done that kind of work, then you know how important lament is. You gotta know how to see and name the hard and ugly. Really face it and grieve it. If you're not willing to go there, you don't really get it." From Mara's expression, it appeared she spoke from personal experience. Though she hadn't shared many details about her son Jeremy, Wren suspected that being biracial had been a challenge for him, especially in certain pockets of Kingsbury. And if her son had struggled, her heart would have ached too.

"If Logan's truly serious about it," Wren said, "and if he wants to connect with people who are already doing the work, you would be a good resource for him." Through her ministry at Crossroads and her experience of worshiping as a White woman at a multiracial church, Mara could provide invaluable help. If Logan was open to receiving it.

"I'd have to think about that," Mara said. "I'd need to know he was the real deal before I started introducing him to people. You don't just get to waltz into a Black community and ask people to tell you

what it feels like to be Black. Nobody owes you their stories. If he's
committed to the hard, long-haul work, great. But building relationships takes trust and time. And the whole image of a woke White guy
coming to"—she signed air quotes—"'help' has its own problems.
He'll need to demonstrate he's ready to serve. Ready to listen. Not
just come in and try to take the lead. Or assume that good work isn't
already taking place, that somehow it's starting with him." She took
a sip of her peppermint tea. "From what you've described, I'm not
sure he understands what he says he wants to do. But who am I to
judge? Been there, done that, got the T-shirt. Whole closet full."

Wren watched the rise and fall of Bailey's flank, the rhythm
soothing. "Logan and I didn't click, that's for sure. Kit's much better
than I am at giving someone the benefit of the doubt. I just feel angry."

"Join the club," Mara said. "Plenty to be angry about these days."

"Yeah, Dawn and I talked about that."

"Did she tell you to keep an anger journal?"

"No. I try to keep a gratitude journal, but sometimes I forget."
In fact, had she written anything in it the past couple of weeks?
Probably not.

"I try to keep one of those too," Mara said. She pointed at a
couple of notebooks on the floor near the armchair. "That pretty
one with the flowers is for gratitude. The cheapo black and white
one is for anger. I can buy those in bulk."

Wren chuckled. "So, you just write down whenever you get angry?"

"Yeah. You write down all the details and then you rate your anger
from one to five—one for 'mildly irritated,' five for 'raging mad.'
And then once a week you review all your angry reactions and see
how many times you got angry for selfish reasons, like every time you
didn't get what you wanted or somebody offended you or your own
agenda got blocked. And then you look for how many times you got
angry for someone else's sake—when someone else didn't get what
they needed. And you look for how often you got angry because of
injustice." She set her mug down. "I tell you what, I usually get way
more angry over things that affect me personally than I do about

things that affect other people, especially when they're outside my own circle. I don't like it, but it's the truth."

Wren quickly scanned the last several days. Plenty to notice and name. "I might have to try that. I'm sure I'll see the same thing as you, though—that most of my anger is self-centered."

"We could make T-shirts if you want," Mara said. "*Angry but self-aware.*"

Wren laughed, startling Bailey. "Oh, sorry!" She stroked his head and then his belly when he stretched and flopped to his side.

"I know this sounds weird," Mara said, "but I found this verse in Romans one day that really comforted me: 'Leave room for the wrath of God.' It's good for me to remember that God can't be fooled and won't be mocked. He's just way more patient than I am. And way more generous. Dawn's always reminding me that I don't really want fairness. I want grace. It's just hard to want grace for people who don't deserve it." She chuckled. "And that's exactly the point, isn't it? None of us deserve it."

Wren was just about to ask which situations made her most angry when the doorbell rang. Bailey and Brewster sprang to their feet, barking. "Hey, boys! Enough." Mara peered through the front window. "That's the girls, ready for their bedtime story."

Wren followed her gaze to the front porch, where Yasmin and Bibi waited in pajamas, each holding a book and a stuffed toy. "Do they come every night?"

"No, mostly Fridays. Sorry. Should have told you. Okay to do a movie tomorrow night instead?"

"Sure."

Mara rose and stretched. "You're welcome to join us. Or if you'd rather have some quiet, feel free to head to your room."

Wren thought of Phoebe and how much she would enjoy more regular phone calls for stories, especially if painting together wasn't a good idea. Making a mental note to text her mom to set up a time, she scooted over on the couch. "Is there enough room for four?"

"Plenty," Mara said. "They each get one of my knees."

27

She wasn't going to burden her mom with anything else. That much was clear. She would need to find a way forward with Carol without drawing her mother into the drama.

From the library parking lot, Sarah texted *Here* to Morgan and waited. She would also need to find a way to communicate to the girls what had happened with Gigi—without disparaging her.

Morgan emerged from the building wearing shorts and her Winnie the Pooh T-shirt, flanked by a girl in a spaghetti strap shirt and a miniskirt that left far too little to imagination. If a student walked into her classroom dressed like that, she had a cupboard filled with sweatshirts and elastic-waist skirts they could choose from. No arguing. Once they had to wear clothes from Mrs. Kersten's closet, they never came to class inappropriately dressed again.

Morgan adjusted her backpack, gave the girl a hug, and ambled to the car. "Hey, Mom!" she said as she got in.

"Hey, sweetie." Sarah waited for her to buckle up before asking, "Who's that?" The girl remained at the entrance, eyeing her phone.

"Someone from school."

"I figured that much. Is that who you were meeting?"

"No, I ran into her afterwards. Lily and Michelle already left."

"Oh, okay." Sarah rubbed Morgan's shoulder. "Don't take any fashion advice from that one, okay?"

Morgan rolled her eyes. "I know, Mom." She put her phone into her bag. "Did you talk with Gigi yet?"

"A little bit."

"And?"

"We're still working things out."

"What did you tell her?"

Sarah watched her rearview camera as a woman passed behind them, pushing a stroller. "I gave her a chance to tell me the truth. But she has some other stressful things going on in her life right now, so it's not a good time to try to work things out." She slowly reversed out of the parking space. "That doesn't change what Dad and I told you, though. You work hard, show you're committed, and we'll see where it goes."

She still wasn't convinced Morgan wouldn't lose interest once she realized how much work a horse would require. That would solve a whole bunch of issues. Rather than reneging on any promises they had already made, they could let Morgan decide she didn't want one. If she still wanted to ride, she could find opportunities for helping disadvantaged kids work with horses. That would be worth investigating. Match her privilege with her passions. Win-win.

When they arrived home, Jess was at the kitchen table, eating out of a pint of cookie dough ice cream while scrolling on her phone. "Is that the last one?" Morgan asked as she set her backpack on a chair.

"Don't know."

Morgan marched to the freezer and yanked the door open. "Why do you always do that? You could've put it in a bowl."

"Forgot," Jess said. "Sorry. Want me to go to the store and get you some?"

"No."

"Get a spoon," Jess said. "You can have the rest." She slid the pint over on the table.

"Dinner first, Morgan," Sarah said. "There's leftover pizza in the fridge."

"I'm not hungry."

Jess scoffed, then picked up the pint again.

"Did you have dinner with your friends, Jess?" Sarah asked.

"Yeah." She took another bite of ice cream.

Sarah reached around Morgan, who was still staring into the freezer, and removed a bag of frozen strawberries. "Want a smoothie instead?" She interpreted Morgan's shrug as a yes and hauled out the blender from the cupboard.

"What's up with Gigi?" Jess asked, still scrolling on her phone.

"You want bananas in it too, Morgan?"

"Yeah, okay."

"Get the milk you want. There's almond or low fat." She poured strawberries into the blender, then turned toward Jess. "What do you mean, what's up with her?"

Jess held out her phone. "She sent me this weird text saying she doesn't know if we'll be able to go to Europe."

Fabulous. "Did she say why?"

Jess read from her phone. "Your mother might prefer a different traveling companion for you."

Seriously? Sarah stripped the peel from a banana. It didn't matter that she had second-guessed the wisdom of the trip. She didn't like Carol pulling that kind of stunt. She wanted to play passive-aggressive with her? Fine. But not with the girls. No way. "Gigi and I are working through a disagreement. I'm sorry she roped you into it."

"Why wouldn't you trust her to take me to Europe?"

"I never told her that."

"Because Gigi lied about the horse," Morgan said as she poured milk into the blender. "She told Mom she didn't know I wasn't allowed to have one."

"Morgan, for the last time, that's not what Dad and I—"

"Okay! Fine. Whatever."

Sarah dropped the banana into the blender, then stepped away. "You can finish this up. Get another banana, and don't forget to put in ice."

"Are you going to call her?" Jess asked as Sarah tossed the peel into the compost bin.

"Yes."

"Right now?"

"Give me some space, Jess, okay?"

Jess scraped around the pint's circumference with her spoon. "I'm just wondering if I should reply."

"Completely your call," Sarah said. She strode to her room and closed the door firmly behind her.

It would be so much easier to play Carol's game and fight by text. But one of them needed to be a grownup. She pressed her number and waited, the rings eventually yielding to a cheerful, "Hey, it's Carol! You know what to do!"

Sarah hung up before the beep and texted, *Call me.* Then she retrieved her laptop from her desk and sat down in the armchair to check email.

Video for your mom, a subject line read. She opened it. "Hi, Sarah. Hannah Allen mentioned you're collecting tribute videos for your mom. Hope I'm not too late to submit."

Sarah clicked on the video, which showed a young woman—maybe thirty—with short dark hair and an intricate butterfly tattoo on her shoulder. Sarah wasn't usually a fan of tattoos, but if Jess or Morgan someday showed up with something similar, she wouldn't criticize.

"Hi, Katherine, it's Becca Crane. Just wanted to say congratulations on your retirement. I know how much you've meant to so many people, and I wanted to thank you again for everything you did for my mom before she died. You made a big difference in her life in the short time she knew you." Becca tucked a stray strand of hair behind her ear. "I don't know if you remember this or not, but Mom told me you prayed over me when I was only a few hours old. She didn't get to live long enough to see how your prayer and all her prayers for me were answered. But I wanted you to know they were." Becca's large brown eyes brimmed with tears, and her voice quavered. "So, anyway . . . thank you. I hope to make a difference in people's lives like you have."

When Becca's image froze on the screen, Sarah kept the window open. Collecting the videos had been as much a gift to her as she hoped it would be to her mother. With many of the testimonies, she had learned new stories about the way her mom had impacted others. A faithful stewarding of life. Of opportunities. Of affliction. Of comfort. Of hope.

Of love.

Just as she was about to hit play again, there was a knock on her door. "Mom?" Jess called.

"Yeah, come on in." As the door opened, she closed her laptop and set it on the floor.

"Gigi said she's going to bed and please stop harassing her."

"Is that what she said? That I'm harassing her?"

"Yeah. Without the 'please' part."

Sarah sucked in her cheeks. So, first her mom accused her of bullying, and now Carol accused her of harassing. Could no one manage direct conversations?

"Sorry," Jess said.

"Not your fault, sweetie. I'm sorry she put you in the middle."

"No big deal. It's just Gigi being Gigi."

"What do you mean?" Seldom had she heard either of the girls say anything even remotely critical about her.

Jess sat down on the edge of the bed. "She can be a drama queen sometimes. Don't get me wrong, I love her and everything, but she can be over the top. I kept trying to tell her I didn't need all the stuff she wanted to buy me, but I think sometimes she bought it just to make Gary mad. Could be wrong, though."

Given what Carol had said about him, Jess probably wasn't far off.

"She talks about Papa all the time, Mom. Like, all. the. time."

"Has she always done that with you guys?"

"Yeah, but I think it's worse now. She kept talking about how we could go visit all the places she went with him, which is fine. I mean, it's Europe. But I also don't want to be traveling with a ghost, you know?"

What a mature observation. "Do you want to go with her?"

"I want to go to Europe."

"I know. But do you want to go to Europe with Gigi?" From the expression on Jess's face, Sarah's internal dilemma over that kind of graduation gift smacking of privilege might resolve itself too.

Jess sighed. "Too bad Gigi's the rich one."

Sarah sat back in her chair. "How come?"

"Because I would probably have a better time traveling with Gram."

For some reason, Sarah's throat burned at hearing those words. She waited until she was sure she had control of her voice before asking, "Why's that?"

Jess said, "I guess because Gram would be slower, and there would be more time to really see and experience things. Everywhere Gigi goes, it's like she's on a mission. And if she's going there because she wants to relive her trip with Papa, then I'm not sure how much room there is for living it with me."

When did her girl get so wise? You blink, and they're out of diapers and off to college.

"Anyway," Jess said, "maybe she's looking for a way out and blaming you for it instead." She stood up. "Don't stress about it, Mom. It's not the end of the world if it falls through with her."

Hearing Jess relinquish her desire made Sarah all the more determined to pursue different options. Better ones. Plenty of time to explore those. Another win-win. "Okay, hon. Good to know."

After Jess left the room, she opened her laptop and played Becca's message about their praying moms one more time.

When her phone rang with a call from Sarah just before nine o'clock, Kit nearly didn't answer. But if she didn't answer, Sarah would worry. "Hey there," she said as she switched off the kitchen lights and trudged to her bedroom. How very quiet the house was. Not just silence, but palpable absence. "Everything okay?"

"Just checking on you," Sarah said. "Are you heading to bed?"

"Soon." She wasn't sure she could endure many more long, eventful days like this one. Not just one, actually, but a whole string of long, eventful days. No wonder she felt spent.

"Did Wren go to a friend's house?"

As casually as Sarah said it, you might have thought she and Wren had hatched the plan together. Never mind. It wasn't worth fighting over. "Yes."

"Oh, that's good. I hope that gives you the peace and quiet you need."

Again, not worth arguing about. Sarah had done what she thought was best. Leave it at that. "Sometime when I'm not so tired," Kit said, "I want to talk with you about our conversation at the restaurant. I've been pondering what you said about me being resentful over your relationship with Carol, and you were right. I—"

"Don't even mention her to me right now, Mom. You wouldn't believe the latest. Or actually, you would."

Exhausted as Kit was, the whiff of vindication revived her like ammonia waved beneath her nose. "What did she do now?"

That was all the encouragement Sarah needed.

None of the details she shared about Carol's deceit, deflection, and bid for sympathy came as any surprise. Kit was too jaded to share Sarah's indignation and too tired to feign astonishment. She could validate Sarah's thoughts and feelings, though, and that was enough. She sat on her bed, listening and offering the occasional, "Terrible. I'm so sorry."

But she wasn't. The truth was, she wasn't sorry at all. Having Sarah personally and bluntly experience the core of who Carol was—painful as it might be for her—felt like a long-awaited gift, something they could now share as mother and daughter. Grand-daughters too. It wasn't too soon for the girls to figure out what kind of woman their Gigi was. The only thing that surprised Kit was that it had taken so long for Carol's sin to affect them directly. *Welcome to the club.*

"She told me Dad would be ashamed of me," Sarah said, her voice suddenly breaking.

Kit sat up straighter. "She said what?"

"That he would be ashamed of me for attacking her like that."

Kit set her jaw against a surge of unanticipated fury. How dare she speak for the dead? How dare she use that weapon to wound? "Your father adored you," she said, barely able to control her voice. "Your father couldn't have been any prouder of you, Sarah. Don't let that woman serve her own purposes by telling you otherwise."

Sarah was silent. Kit pictured her with lips flattened and head tilted back to fend off tears. That was how she had sat at Micah's funeral. Sarah, who so rarely cried, had sat between her parents, grasping their hands and attempting to hold herself together. To hold all of them together, maybe.

"Thanks, Mom," she said after a while.

"I'm so deeply sorry," Kit said. And she was. She truly was.

"You know what Jess said about all this?"

"Tell me."

"That she wished she could go to Europe with you instead."

Kit was too stunned to reply.

"She said she didn't want to travel with Dad's ghost, and she knew you would be the sort of person who wouldn't rush her, who would give her space to experience everything to the fullest."

Preferred to Carol? Really?

Kit pressed her hand to her heart. She could sort the movement of her soul later. For now, how sweet it was.

Part Three

INTO LIGHT

Thus says God, the LORD,
who created the heavens and stretched them out,
who spread out the earth and what comes from it,
who gives breath to the people upon it
and spirit to those who walk in it:
I am the LORD, *I have called you in righteousness,*
I have taken you by the hand and kept you;
I have given you as a covenant to the people,
a light to the nations,
to open the eyes that are blind,
to bring out the prisoners from the dungeon,
from the prison those who sit in darkness. . . .
I will lead the blind
by a road they do not know,
by paths they have not known
I will guide them.
I will turn the darkness before them into light,
the rough places into level ground.
These are the things I will do,
and I will not forsake them.

ISAIAH 42:5-7, 16

28

On a wall near the nurses' station hung a large whiteboard where staff daily recorded information for the residents. As Wren dusted in the lounge area, she watched Kayla fill in the details with a green marker and large letters.

Today: Thursday, August 9, 2018

Weather: sunny and hot!

Kayla drew a picture of a smiling sun wearing shades.

Peyton called to her from the art table where she was setting out craft supplies. "Write on there, Countdown to party 3 days!"

Kayla obliged and drew a picture of a pineapple, also smiling.

"That's pretty good," Peyton said. "I didn't know you could draw."

"Not well at all! Wren's the artist."

"Is she?"

Wren pretended she wasn't listening as she stood on tiptoe to swipe the top of a bookcase with her duster.

"Mrs. Clement showed me the drawing you made of her with the birds yesterday," Kayla said.

"Oh, it wasn't anything," Wren replied. Just a quick outline she had sketched during her lunch break.

Kayla put the cap back on the marker. "That's not what she said. She told me she wants to frame it and hang it on her wall."

"I'll have to go see it, then," Peyton said. Wren could feel her gaze boring into the back of her head.

"I think you're going to have more customers wanting art from you," said Kayla.

From her peripheral vision, Wren watched Peyton remove bags of popsicle sticks from the supply box. Then she took out a sheet of paper. "Maybe you can demonstrate for us, Wren."

"Oh, I don't know."

"C'mon." Kayla picked up a pencil from the nurse's station. "Draw something for us."

Peyton struck a mock Vogue pose. "Draw me."

Kayla laughed.

Reluctantly, Wren set down her duster. Best to be quick and get it over with.

"Where should I stand?" Peyton asked.

"How about in front of the bulletin board?" She could sketch her with the palm trees and tropical fish in the background.

Peyton unpinned one of the toilet paper roll fish and held it next to her face. Then she widened her eyes, puckered her mouth into fish lips, and poked her cheek.

Good. If she wasn't taking it seriously, that ought to relieve any pressure to perform.

As Kayla stood beside her to observe, Wren drew a quick outline, making sure to capture the shape of her lips and eyes before she got tired of holding that expression. Then she added depth and shadows to her cheeks, chin, and forehead with cross-hatching. "That's really good," Kayla said.

When Peyton shifted forward to look, Wren motioned for her to hold still. "Almost done." She sketched Peyton's fingers clasped around the fish and drew a few palm trees behind her. "There." She slid the page toward Peyton, who looked at it without commenting.

"I think you need to draw at the party," Kayla said. "You could sketch the residents with their families. They'd love that."

Peyton pinned the fish to the board again. "We've already got someone lined up to take pictures. Kids won't sit still for drawings."

"The residents will," Kayla said.

"We'll see." She resumed her rummaging through supply boxes.

"Do you want to keep this sketch?" Wren asked her. She wasn't going to leave it lying around.

"No, it's okay. You can add it to your collection."

Kayla scooped it up as if it were a rejected child and walked over to the nurses' station, waving it. "Look what Wren can do!"

Wren retrieved her duster.

"You should do that as an activity someday," Chelsea called as she wheeled a resident toward the elevator. "People would love it."

"See?" Kayla said. "Told you!"

Greta looked up from a cart where she was dispensing pills into plastic cups. "Dorothy is ready for her bath, Kayla. Don't keep her waiting. And I'm sure Wren has other duties right now, instead of drawing."

With her back turned toward Greta, Kayla rolled her eyes at Wren. "Sketch me later?"

"Sure," she said, and resumed her dusting.

When she arrived at Mr. Page's room to clean, he was seated in his wheelchair beside his bed, dressed and wearing sneakers instead of his usual slippers. "Heading out?" she asked, then immediately regretted it.

"If by 'out' you mean being taken somewhere I do not wish to go, then yes."

Since he had replied, she decided to continue. "Sometimes even a small change of scenery can help."

He scoffed.

She removed the dirty towels from his bathroom and put them in her soiled linen bag. As she passed his closet, she noticed a few framed landscape paintings propped against the wall. His sister must have returned with them. "Maintenance can hang those paintings for you," she said.

"I told Mary not to bring them. But it seems I can't command even that."

Wren replaced the towels. "They look original. Did you paint them?"

"Favorite places from a past life," he said. "They don't belong here."

"They don't belong in a closet either. If you won't hang them in your room, why not put them someplace where others can enjoy them?"

He waved dismissively with his good hand. "Take them. They mean nothing to me."

She lifted one depicting a covered bridge. "When I was little, I used to imagine I could jump into paintings and explore the landscape. Or just sit and dream awhile. I would have done that with this painting. I would have sat right here"—she pointed to a grassy knoll with a view of the river—"and imagined the sun warming my back or the fish jumping in the stream or the sound of water rippling over the rocks."

"A poet, are you?"

"No. But beauty has always made me cry."

He studied her face intently, as an artist might study a model. "The world is harsh and unkind to sensitive souls, Wren Crawford."

She wondered if he included himself in that description. But it felt like too tender a place to probe. "True," she said. "But maybe sensitive souls are more open to seeing beauty in unexpected places. Even if it's not the kind of beauty we long to see." Like a tiny sword of a new feather, she thought, piercing through the bare scalp of a weary bird.

"Ah, Mr. Page, looking good!" Kayla said as she entered. "You're ready for OT?"

He curled the fingers of his left hand over the wheelchair armrest. "If it saves me from having to do another confounded craft project, then yes."

Wren suppressed a smile as Kayla looked at the covered bridge. "Did you change your mind? You're going to hang your beautiful paintings?"

Before he could reply, Wren said, "He's given them to me to hang wherever I choose. And since we all need beauty, we'll hang them in the hallway." Right beside his shadow box, where people could see and appreciate the plumage he had lost.

To her surprise, he didn't immediately voice his objection. Progress. "We could do a whole wall of resident and staff art," Kayla said. "Have you seen Wren's drawings, Mr. Page?"

She immediately voiced her own objection. "They're nothing. Just quick line sketches."

"No, look here." From one of her pouches Kayla pulled out the folded-up drawing of Peyton with the fish lips and held it up for him to see. Wren wished she could run and hide somewhere. For an artist like Mr. Page to see a silly sketch like that . . .

He looked at it. And as he looked, his lips curled into a half-smile reminiscent of his former self. "You've captured that woman precisely," he said. "See what I've been spared this morning?"

Kayla tucked the drawing back into her pocket. "Everybody's doing the best they can, Mr. Page. I'm sure Melissa will appreciate you doing your best in OT too." She released the parking brake and wheeled him toward the door.

"I look forward to seeing more from you, Wren Crawford," he said as he passed by.

She stared at the back of his head.

Progress. A pinprick of hope.

She fetched her cloth and dusted his closed blinds. Someday she might open them without his permission and see if he complained. If he could begin to see beauty in an unexpected place like this, that would be progress too.

She had just finished her shift and was unlocking her bike from the rack when Audrey appeared. "I was hoping to catch you before you left, Wren. Job just got posted. Like, just this second."

"That's great! Thank you so much for letting me know." Now she could ask her mom and Kit and Mara and Hannah to pray.

"You in a hurry to get somewhere?" Audrey asked. "'Cause I'd be happy to let you use my computer if you want to fill out the application before you leave."

Even though half an hour wouldn't make any difference to the process, she would be hot and sweaty and tired when she got to Mara's. Why not do it now? "That's really kind of you. Thank you."

"I saw the picture you drew of Marjorie and the birds," Audrey said as they headed to her office. "I told her I'd find her a frame so she can hang it on her wall. And when you get a chance, I'd love you to draw me with those little guys."

"Of course! I'd be happy to." Since the poor creatures would never know anything other than their cage, they might as well be honored and remembered as beloved pets. And if more residents and staff wanted sketches, she should keep her drawing pencils in her bag.

"You don't paint, do you?"

"Yes, a bit."

"Like, real paintings? Faces and stuff?"

"Yes."

Audrey pushed open her office door. "Put all that down on your application. Could you lead a class for the residents?"

Wren tried not to bounce on her heels. "I'd love to."

Audrey signaled her to sit down at the desk, then opened her laptop. "We used to have a volunteer who did that. People loved it. She was an art therapist. But she moved away."

It was more—so much more than she could have hoped for. "I used art with the kids at the shelter."

"Put that down too," Audrey said. "You wouldn't get paid for it here, but if you're willing to do it as a volunteer . . ."

"I'd love to."

"Good." Audrey leaned forward and opened her browser to the application link. "You'll need to play it cool with Peyton. She tries. She really does. But sometimes she treats the residents like pre-schoolers. And some of them can't manage her craft projects."

Wren pictured Mr. Kennedy with his tremor, trying in vain to glue popsicle sticks together for a beach party picture frame.

Even though Mr. Page refused to do the craft projects, he might be willing to participate as a supervisor if she started leading an actual art group. The residents could paint abstracts on canvas. They could paint their feelings as Gran had encouraged her to do. *What color is waiting? What color is loneliness? What color is molting? What color is hope?*

"I'm gonna go feed Coco and Tweety. If you finish before I get back, close the door behind you."

"Thank you so much, Audrey. I really appreciate it."

"I'm cheering for you. Hope this works out. I think you'd be great at it."

Reading the job description, Wren agreed. *The staff and volunteers at Willow Springs are committed to loving and serving our residents as if they are family. The volunteer coordinator plays the crucial role of recruiting, training, scheduling, and equipping volunteers to serve according to their gifts and passions so they can help meet the social, mental, and emotional needs of our residents. Applicants should be well-organized, creative, flexible, and compassionate.*

The more she read, the more excited she became. She could do this job and do it well.

Except . . .

Her heart sank. *Please include two professional references who can verify both competency and character.*

When she applied for the cleaning job, she had only needed to provide a single character reference, and she had named Hannah. Since Kit was a family member, she couldn't list her for this. Gayle had only ever observed her as a housekeeper—and not a particularly reliable one. At least, not in the early days of trying to manage the job while still battling to recover from her depressive episode. Given the experience Willow Springs required, she would need to highlight her training and skills as a social worker. And to do that, she would need someone from Bethel House to vouch for her.

Except. . .

She hadn't ended well, quitting without giving notice.

And now what? Email her former supervisor and say, "Hey! Wondering if you'd be a reference for me. They need to know I'm responsible and reliable and won't suddenly quit because things get too hard and I can't manage it"? She had never told Audrey she struggled with mental health. Would she have hired her if she had?

She closed the window. If she couldn't even provide a reference for a job like this, how would she ever provide a reference for something full time?

Audrey was chatting with the receptionist when Wren entered the main lounge. "Done already?"

"No."

Excusing herself from conversation, Audrey beckoned her to a quiet corner. "Everything okay?"

Wren slung her backpack onto her shoulders. "I need to figure out references."

"Put me down."

"Thanks, but I need two."

"Put down your boss from your other cleaning job."

"She's my great-aunt."

"Doesn't matter. They probably won't even check since you already work here."

Wren didn't want to argue about the integrity of listing Kit. "It sounds like they want someone who can specifically talk about my ability to do the job."

"You were a social worker, Wren. You can do the job."

Could she? She hoped she could. She wanted to. She needed to.

"You're way overthinking this. Just put someone down from where you used to work." She furrowed her brow. "Unless you got fired from there or something?"

"No. Nothing like that."

"Okay, then. Solved. You want to finish it up here?"

Wren gripped her shoulder straps. "No, it's okay. Thank you. I need to check current contact info for them." She wasn't even sure her old boss still worked there.

But maybe Allie did.

Why hadn't she thought of that sooner? She could send Allie a casual "Hey! Sorry I dropped off the planet" text and ask if she might be willing to be a job reference and see if she might like to get coffee sometime, just to catch up with life. Very casual. A "no big deal if you can't, but thought I'd ask" sort of text. Allie wouldn't say anything negative about her. They had worked well together for a couple of years, and Allie understood the stress of the job. She wouldn't fault Wren for quitting.

Unless her quitting had created far more work for Allie and the others. Which it no doubt had. But she couldn't worry about that now. That was over and done.

Audrey was staring at her. "You okay?"

"Yeah. Sorry. Just thinking." She raked her fingers through her hair. "Thanks for all your help, Audrey. I'll see you tomorrow."

"Don't wait too long to get your application in. Best to get on their radar as soon as you can."

Wren promised she would, then retrieved her bike. En route to Mara's, she could take a slight detour through the Wilsons' neighborhood. A few days had passed since she'd last checked on the house, and a sold sign could go up anytime.

As she rode, she let herself dream about getting the job. Willow Springs already had a devoted group of volunteers who helped with everything from music to gardening to outings to games to parties. But she could develop and expand their pool of students. The residents loved when young people visited. Mara might have connections with teenagers willing to serve. In fact, the same compassionate curiosity Mara had demonstrated in learning her neighbors' stories could be modeled to students. What if teens interviewed residents and then wrote down their stories for family members? Having that sort of record would be a gift. The students would need to be patient if they heard the same stories over and over again. But those repeated stories often had the most significance. Or perhaps they were the ones that were unresolved.

She thought about the stories she had shared with Mara the past couple of days—stories about her childhood in Australia, her years at Bethel House, her battle with depression. But most of her stories revolved around Casey and their friendship and the mysteries that remained. Mara had shared stories about her life too—stories about being bullied and rejected as a little girl, her struggles with failed relationships, her joys and challenges in serving at Crossroads. She spoke frankly about her ex-husband and a trail of ex-wives he'd abandoned—a serial adulterer, she said—and how their two sons had given up on having any kind of meaningful relationship with him. Whenever Brian or Kevin shared updates about him, she said, he ended up in her anger journal.

From what Mara described, Tom sounded a lot like the men whose wives and girlfriends sought refuge at Bethel House. Wren would have filled pages about him in an anger journal too.

At the corner of Maplewood and Oakdale, she stopped to take a drink from her water bottle, then scanned the next block: a few kids riding bikes, a couple of teens shooting hoops, a woman pushing a lawnmower, a For Sale sign still in front of the Wilsons' house. She put her bottle back in its holder. Nobody was in the yard, but a couple of cars she didn't recognize were parked in the driveway. A realtor, maybe, with prospective buyers.

Pedaling leisurely down the block, she said a prayer for Mr. and Mrs. Wilson, asking God to bless them and guide them forward and help them honor Casey and—

A guy in a baseball cap and blue T-shirt exited the house, accompanied by an attractive blonde woman in denim shorts and a pink sleeveless top, carrying a baby.

A baby with bright red hair.

My God.

Wren narrowly avoided colliding with the curb. Shaking, she sped past, head lowered, then dismounted her bike across the street and crouched behind the front wheel spokes, pretending to inspect her chain.

After they reached the car, the man spun his baseball cap backward, then leaned in to kiss the baby on her cheek. When he stepped away, the baby stretched out her hands. Laughing, the woman handed her over, and he raised her high above his head.

He held Estelle high above his head. And Brooke laughed while Chris held his friend's baby high above his head.

Dear God.

Transfixed, Wren knelt on the pavement, trying to make sense of the scene. Too far away to hear their conversation, she watched Brooke smile as Chris played with her daughter. Up and down he lifted her, Estelle squealing with uninhibited delight. Then Brooke held out her arms. As Chris handed the baby to her, the two of them leaned in for a lingering kiss above Estelle's head.

Oh, God.

No wonder he hadn't replied to her texts.

If she could have persuaded her body to move, she would have hopped onto her bike and ridden away as fast as possible. But she didn't trust her legs to support her if she tried to stand. So instead, she remained anchored to the spot and low to the ground as a maelstrom of new questions assaulted her, all of which could be summed up in two words. When? How?

Brooke stepped back from the car as Chris got in and closed the door. Shifting Estelle on her hip, she spoke to her. In reply, the baby thrust her hand into the air and waved. Brooke waved too, then blew kisses, exaggerating the motion until Estelle copied her. Laughing, Brooke blew kisses with her daughter while Chris, his arm stretched out the window toward them, slowly backed the car out of the driveway.

Wren willed him to head the opposite direction. When he obeyed, she released the breath she had been holding. Only after Brooke disappeared into the house with Estelle did she manage to rise and walk her bike to the end of the block, gripping the handlebars for stability.

"You all right?" called a neighbor watering a flowerbed.

With a feeble wave, she mounted her bike and rode away.

29

J ust one more, Kit reminded herself as she stared at her computer screen in her office Friday morning. One last retreat session to write and deliver.

It shouldn't be this difficult to get across the finish line, especially after a few days of rest.

Clutching her holding cross, she read the theme verses from Ephesians again: "And be kind to one another, tenderhearted, forgiving one another, as God in Christ has forgiven you. Therefore be imitators of God, as beloved children, and live in love, as Christ loved us and gave himself up for us, a fragrant offering and sacrifice to God."

As you have been loved, love. As you have been forgiven, forgive.

Such straightforward principles to articulate. Such difficult principles to practice.

Through her open window, a gentle breeze drew her attention to the courtyard, the bright blue sky in glorious contrast to the canary yellow and amber and burnished gold of the sunflowers. Wren would be impressed she could name three different shades of yellow.

She set her cross on her desk, then gathered her *Starry Night* mug and an Earl Grey tea bag from her shelf. Best to take a break and shift gears before leaving for her spiritual direction appointment with Russell.

On her way to the kitchenette, she noticed Wren's studio door was open, and a new painting was propped on her easel. Kit stepped in for a closer look at a bald cardinal with a protruding orange beak and dull rust-colored feathers on his breast and wings. Around the bird's feet lay black seeds. Many of them. In fact—she adjusted her glasses as she examined the canvas—both the cardinal's black head and the black seeds had been rendered not with black paint but with charcoal mixed with ashes. She recognized the technique from Wren's painting of Jesus, the accused.

Evidently, she had burned more paper. The ashes remained in a bowl on her worktable. Whatever had prompted the burning, she had painted that vulnerable creature with such dignity and tenderness that Kit stood utterly transfixed.

"Hey there," came a familiar, beloved voice from the hall.

Spinning around, Kit smiled sheepishly at Wren. "You caught me. I'm sorry. I shouldn't have been spying on your work without your permission, but this bird . . ." She set her mug on the table and embraced her. Three days of not seeing her felt like weeks.

"Do you like it?" Wren asked.

"Like it? It's absolutely compelling. I can't think of a better word."

"Thanks. It's coming along."

Together, they gazed at her work. "I'm no expert," Kit said, "but it seems to me you could sign your name on this one right now. Leaving it unfinished fits the molting theme."

"Yeah, you're probably right."

Kit picked up her mug again. "I didn't expect you this morning. Are you here to clean?"

"I figured I'd get it done early."

"That's great. I was just going to boil some water. Want a cup of tea first?"

"No, that's all right. Thanks."

"Come with me, then, while I make mine." They walked down the corridor. "I'm heading out shortly to meet with Russell, but I'm eager to hear how you're doing. Anything new?"

"Yes," Wren said. "A lot, actually."

Kit raised her eyebrows.

"Brooke is in Kingsbury with Estelle. They're at the Wilsons' house."

Kit gasped. "Are you sure?"

"I saw them yesterday in the driveway as I was riding by. Chris was with them. It's obvious he and Brooke are in a relationship. So that explains why he never replied to my messages. She's probably told him hideous things about me."

Kit didn't disagree with that conclusion. No wonder she was painting with ashes again. "I'm so sorry, Wren."

"Mara thinks I should send him another text. She says this is my chance to get answers and that I'll never forgive myself if I don't try to talk with Brooke and see Estelle. She thinks this is God's open door so I can move forward."

"What do you think?" Kit asked as they reached the kitchenette.

Wren leaned against the wall opposite Vincent's *Worn Out* sketch. "I don't know. But I knew it wasn't right for me to do anything when I was upset. So at least there's that."

"Good choice," Kit said. "They didn't see you?"

"No. But I'm fighting like crazy not to keep riding by." Her eyes brimmed with tears. "She looks just like Casey. Same red hair. And when I saw her reach for Chris, when I saw him play with her and kiss her, my heart broke. Because it should have been Casey watching her grow up. And I don't know if it feels like a betrayal, seeing one of his friends with his daughter, or if I should feel happy the three of them found each other—however they found each other. I just wish I knew more. About everything." She swiped each cheek with the palm of her hand. "Mara's right. If I want to know everything, this is my chance. And maybe I just need to lay aside my own pride and fear and text Chris again and ask to meet up with him. Because I know I shouldn't keep stalking them on my bike. And I can't find any details about their relationship online." She gave a rueful smile. "I've checked."

Kit switched on the kettle.

"I know I'll have to live with the consequences of whatever decision I make. I'm just trying to figure out which consequences will be easier to live with."

Kit leaned back against the counter, hands curled over the edge.

"I think the possibility of knowing more about what happened to Casey outweighs everything else. Whatever they think about me, that's already set. And if I text Chris, he can decide what to tell me. If he shuts me down, at least I tried. But I think I have to try. As long as there's an opportunity to get closure, I have to try."

Kit rubbed the edge of the counter with her thumbs.

"You're not going to tell me what to do, are you?"

No. She wasn't. But offering a crash course in discernment wouldn't hurt. "You already took a good step by not acting quickly, Wren. If you want to take another good step, then take a bit more time to prayerfully consider your choices. See what happens in your spirit when you imagine contacting Chris. See if you experience an increase in hope and peace or agitation and fear. Then do the same thing for your other possible choice. See what happens in your spirit when you imagine not contacting him and letting it go. Then make a decision. Don't act on it, just live with it for a couple of days. See if peace and hope increase or decrease. Then you can move forward from there."

Wren appeared to be considering this. "But I don't know how long Brooke and Estelle will be in town and whether or not they'll ever come back, especially since I don't know when the Wilsons are moving or where they're going. And if there's a chance to meet Estelle, then I need to text Chris as soon as possible. It feels urgent."

Kit wasn't going to attempt to redirect her. Whatever decision Wren made needed to be hers. "I'll pray for you. I'll ask God to guide you forward and confirm his way with peace."

"Thank you. I think I already know what I need to do. But I'll clean first. And see what happens in my spirit when I imagine texting him."

"Sounds like a plan." Kit removed a carton of milk from the small fridge. "I'll be back in a couple of hours to finish up my notes for tomorrow. Have you already got plans for dinner?"

"A neighborhood picnic."

Kit cloaked her disappointment with a cheerful, "That sounds like fun!"

"Yeah, her neighbors are great." Wren paused. "Mara says I can stay with her longer to give you more time on your own. If that would help you, I mean."

"Choose what's best for you, Wren. I'm fine either way." But her thoughts and feelings weren't nearly as detached as her words claimed to be.

Add that to the long list of things to discuss with Russell, she thought as she made herself a cup of tea. When she waved goodbye half an hour later, Wren was dusting Vincent's sower, humming.

"I've been praying for you, Katherine," Russell said as he welcomed her into his office. "How are you feeling?"

"After my very public breakdown, you mean?"

"Is that how you see it?"

She smiled. "No. And people were very kind and gracious about it." She took her usual seat in the armchair across from his. "But if I told you that my panic attack wasn't even on my radar of things to talk about today, does that put my week in perspective?"

His eyes widened. "Well, then. Let's quiet ourselves and begin."

But after he gave extended space for silence, the situations she had intended to lead with—the latest conflict with Carol, her insights about her relationship with Sarah, and her experience of Wren's absence—instead gave way to a discussion about Logan and all that she had been trying to process since their initial conversation in her office.

"He and I probably have some theological disagreements about how much to emphasize the cross and Jesus' suffering," she said. "And I'll be sorely disappointed if I discover he played a direct role in the board's decision to lay off Gayle and Wren. But those things aside, the point he raised about the lack of diversity at New Hope was right and true, and his questions were painfully incisive. With everything else clamoring for my attention right now, I want to make sure I give this the time and weight it deserves." Otherwise, she thought, an opportunity for growth would be lost in the tyranny of the urgent. She didn't want that to happen.

Russell leaned forward in his chair. "What are you already seeing?"

She took a moment to collect her thoughts. "I'm aware of a variety of responses in myself—everything from shame and guilt to defensiveness and wanting to make excuses for everything I've neglected to do at New Hope. Not just with the programs we haven't offered but with the people we haven't been deliberate about including."

It was more personal than that, though. She pictured herself across from Mara, listening with masked discomfort as she spoke bluntly about the color of people's skin and the forms of racism she was attempting to address at Crossroads. She thought of Logan and his story about how the Lord had used his African American colleague to help him see his own blind spots and to awaken him to the things he didn't have to think or grieve or worry about because of the color of his skin. She hadn't thought or grieved or worried about those types of struggles either.

"Let me change that *we* to *I*," she said. "The programs I haven't offered and the people of color I haven't been deliberate about including. I want to own that directly. Because one of the things I'm starting to see is that my determination to be colorblind has made me blind. Pure and simple. I've always thought that making note of race was a form of racism. So I completely disregarded the issue, not just in my personal life but in the ministries I led at New Hope. I focused my attention entirely on individuals, not on unjust systems or the transformation of communities. And yes, I know part of that has to do with my own call and giftedness. But in all my years of ministry, I did nothing to promote diversity or actively advocate for justice. And I regret that."

Logan had described justice as the "more excellent way of love," the way of living rightly with God and others, the call to love not just with words, but with embodied mercy that made God's righteousness and heart of compassion visible to the world. She wanted to say a wholehearted yes to joining the Spirit in that kingdom work.

"The truth is, Russell, I have the luxury—the privilege—of forgetting about the struggle for racial justice and reconciliation because it doesn't directly impact me. I can have a moment of awakening and confess my sin and even offer heartfelt lament, but then I can move on with my life and not think about it again. And I don't want to do that. If my repentance is sincere, then it means going forward from here in a different way. I'm just not sure what that is."

In the burgeoning quiet, Russell appeared to be listening deeply. "The story of Jesus healing the blind man comes to mind," he finally said. "The one that took two touches."

She stared at him. She hadn't prayed with that text in a long time. "That's a perfect one for me to meditate on. Thank you." In some ways, she thought, the discomfort she had experienced in her conversation with Mara had been Jesus' first touch with this blindness. The conversation with Logan had been the second.

Russell said, "I think sometimes we can be too quick to disregard the preliminary stage of awakening. But it's a necessary part of the process."

She exhaled slowly. That was a good reminder. A word of grace and comfort. And also a gentle admonishment to her inner perfectionist, who, after processing the agitation of being confronted and exposed, could be too eager to rush toward some kind of solution.

"Your word, 'preliminary,' catches my attention," she said. "I hear that word and immediately think of preliminary research or testing—something that might need to be corrected because it's incomplete or flawed. Like it's not good enough."

He smiled. "Well, you know me—the etymology wonk. So I can tell you it's literally 'pre-limen.' From the same Latin word as *liminal.*"

Her eyes widened. "Is it really?" She loved the word *liminal.* She loved the possibilities of it, the anticipatory excitement of inhabiting a fertile threshold space filled with the potential for growth and change. Thinking of *preliminary* as *preparatory* could reorient her toward hope.

That night as she sat at her kitchen table with her Christ candle lit, she read the story of the blind man in Bethsaida. "I can see people, but they look like trees, walking," the man confessed after Jesus touched his eyes the first time. At least he was honest about his limits. Far more dangerous to pretend you could see clearly when you couldn't.

She pictured herself in the scene, warm bodies wedged together as they moved en masse along a dusty road. She yielded to the insistent tug of hands and stumbled when someone nudged her from behind. Multiple voices cried out in unison, begging for a man named Jesus to touch her.

Then they came to an abrupt halt. The two hands gripping hers released. She turned her head from side to side, listening for familiar voices, searching for familiar scents, aching for the protective cover of those who had now withdrawn. She was left alone, waiting.

No, not alone. Calloused fingers curled around her own, and she felt herself relax into the care of someone whose grasp was both decisive and infinitely gentle. Silently, Jesus led her along the dusty path until the hum of voices ceased, leaving only the buzz of insects and the distant screech of a hawk.

He let go of her hand. She lifted her head toward his breath. "Lord?"

She heard the click of his tongue, then felt water spray into her open eyes. Had he just spat on her?

Before she could wipe off his saliva with her sleeve, he placed his palms over her eyes. She circled his wrists with her hands, flesh to bone. Not content to command her with a disembodied voice, he had given her tactile gifts of presence.

She leaned in. Suddenly, the inky darkness yielded, the warmth of the sun's rays becoming gold light filtered through his fingers. She blinked. He touched her chin, then stepped back.

"Can you see anything, Katherine?" His soft voice reverberated in her spirit.

She blinked again, the features of his face still unfocused.

Could she tell him the truth, like the blind man had? Or would she pretend that one touch sufficed, that his power had already supplied what she needed and that seeing things dimly was good enough?

Which impulse would cause her to attempt to conceal the truth from the One who saw everything clearly? Fear of criticizing him for an incomplete healing? Or pride that kept her from admitting that even after being touched by the Son of God, she still couldn't see?

"Can you see anything, Katherine?" he asked again.

She swallowed hard. "Only a little, Lord. And I don't know how to interpret what I see. Or how to respond to what I see."

He touched her eyes again. "Stay awake with me, beloved," he said. "Keep watch and pray."

30

When Sarah's phone rang after ten o'clock on Friday night, she was sure something had happened to her mom. She leaped from the couch, where she had been watching a movie with Zach and the girls, and raced to the kitchen to answer her phone. "Mom! Are you okay?"

"I'm sorry. Did I wake you up?" Her mother's voice was perfectly calm.

Her shoulders relaxed. "No, just watching a movie. What's up?"

"I just finished a rather intense prayer time and wanted to talk with you before tomorrow. But if I'm interrupting . . ."

"No, it's okay. I want to hear what's going on." She signaled for Zach to hit play, then retreated to their bedroom, where she could listen without distraction.

"I've been trying for the past three days to write my retreat content for tomorrow, and I wasn't getting anywhere. I kept praying about the resentment you and I talked about, and I thought I had plumbed the depths of it. But tonight, I saw more. And before I attempt to offer any gift on the altar tomorrow, I need to address it."

"Okay." Sarah switched on the lamp beside her armchair and sat down.

"I've done nothing to encourage you to pursue reconciliation with Carol. I've actually savored the breakdown in your relationship."

Though that didn't come as a surprise, Sarah appreciated that she could name it.

"Your anger with her made me feel vindicated, like you and I are on the same team. And I'm sorry for that, Sarah. My grudge doesn't serve you well. Or her, for that matter."

At the moment, Sarah couldn't care less what served Carol well. If Carol wanted to give her the silent treatment, fine. But don't play that game with the girls. "It's just Gigi being Gigi," Jess said whenever Morgan expressed hurt. "She'll get over it." But that brand of pettiness only made Sarah angrier. And texting Carol to tell her to knock it off and be a grownup hadn't worked. She'd tried. Twice.

"Lucy used to remind me that forgiveness isn't about forgetting. Forgiveness is about remembering without bitterness. That's the evidence of the Spirit's deep work. Because amnesia is easier. I'm far more holy when I don't remember offenses. But when new ones expose the old roots, that's when I see again how desperately I need Jesus and his grace."

Before Sarah could comment, her mother said, "I'm asking for your forgiveness. Everything you said the other day is true. I haven't just been resentful about your relationship with Carol. I've been resentful that you were loyal to her, that you didn't share my anger and woundedness. I tried to hide it, and so I was dishonest with you about how I truly felt. I'm sorry for that too. I'm sorry for not trusting you enough to share the truth with you. That fear says far more about me than it does about you."

What a brave and vulnerable confession. "It's okay, Mom. I understand. And I forgive you. Thanks for being honest with me." This kind of good resolution seemed well worth the stress of arriving there.

"You said it so well at the restaurant, Sarah. This is what love looks like. Love rejoices in the truth. It doesn't rejoice in wrongdoing. And I've been rejoicing in Carol's wrongdoing." She paused. "I need to practice extending grace to her. And that means affirming and celebrating the love she's shown you and Zach and the girls over the years. I need to call her love good. Because it's been a gift to you and your family."

From the living room came the sound of laughter, Zach's guffawing mixed with Jess's giggling and Morgan's signature snort.

Carol had often sat right in the middle of that laughter, an arm around each girl, a popcorn bucket on her lap. "Thanks, Mom. I appreciate that. But she's going to need to own what she did. True reconciliation isn't possible otherwise."

"No, I know that. And you'll need to work out your own process with her, at your own pace. But I also know you can be stubborn. You got that fair and square from both your dad and me." She paused. "You asked for my advice the other day. So, here it is. Don't make it difficult for her to move toward you. Affirm your love for her and your desire to have an even stronger bond."

Sarah slowly rubbed her arm. "She won't stomach any conversation about forgiveness. She hates any kind of God-talk." She decided not to repeat what Carol had said about spewing sanctimonious tripe. Why spoil her mother's sincere effort to practice magnanimity?

"You might need to work out your own process of forgiving her without expecting her to ask for it," her mother said. "If you reassure her of your love and your commitment to her, you might be surprised what shifts."

If only relationships were as predictable as math equations, Sarah thought. Or as elegant as the Fibonacci sequence, the pattern emerging as you kept adding the numbers together to find the next one. She sighed. "I've been hoping she would be mature about this. But you're right. It might have to be me." Otherwise, the stalemate could last forever.

A glance at the window revealed her reflection in the lamplight. Both her mom and her dad. She smiled. "By the way, I can't remember you ever admitting I got my stubbornness from your side of the family."

Mom laughed. "Tenacity, right? It can be a holy thing."

"I'll remind you of that in the future."

"I'm sure you will." There was playfulness in her voice. Sarah couldn't remember the last time she had heard that kind of lightness in her. The days of rest had clearly been good for her soul.

"I'm planning to be there tomorrow, Mom. Do you have everything you need?"

"I think so. I'll let you get back to your family."

Sarah thanked her. "I know you wanted some space for yourself this week, but after you finish up everything, we'd love to have you join us for dinner and a movie night. We've got a bed with your name on it."

"Thank you, honey. I look forward to that."

More laughter floated from the living room. "I love you, Mom. I'll see you in the morning."

If there was going to be any possibility of an elegant solution with Carol, she knew the next number in the sequence was hers to play. Before rejoining Zach and the girls, she typed a message to her step-mother: *Just wanted to say I love you. I'm sorry things are hard for you right now. I'd love to talk anytime you're up for it.*

As for whether any beauty would emerge from it, that wasn't hers to control.

"Fill me in," she said as she resumed her place on the couch. "What'd I miss?"

Early Saturday morning when Sarah arrived at New Hope, several cars were already in the parking lot, and Wren was sitting at the welcome table, looking at her phone. As soon as she saw Sarah, she shoved it into her bag. "Hey," she said as she rearranged a few Sharpies and name tags.

"Hey. Is Mom in her office?"

"She's in the chapel."

"Who else is here?"

"The trustees."

Sarah raised her eyebrows. "Is there a problem?"

"I'm not sure. Bill and one of the others got here right after I did, and they went straight to her office. I think they're meeting in one of the classrooms now."

Odd. This didn't sound like a "We came to support you for your last session" visit. "Did you see Mom after they talked to her?"

"Yeah, that's when she told me she would be in the chapel. She seemed okay, though."

Clearly, she wasn't going to get any useful information from Wren. Depositing her keys in her purse, she headed there. Her mom, seated near the cross, looked up when she entered.

"Wren said the trustees are here. Everything okay?"

She beckoned Sarah closer.

"What's going on?" Sarah drew up a chair beside her and sat down.

"Someone they're counting on to be a major donor for their building renovations found a recent blog post from Logan. Evidently, tomorrow is the one-year anniversary of the protests and violence in Charlottesville, and he voiced his support for antiracist protests scheduled in DC." She paused. "The donor is threatening to pull his pledge if they move ahead with hiring him."

Sarah gaped at her. "You have got to be kidding me."

"Wish I were."

"So why did they come to you?"

"They wanted to know if Logan said anything in our conversations that indicated—and I quote—'radicalized views.'"

Sarah shook her head slowly. "What did you tell them?"

"The truth. I told them he has a passion for justice and a heart for promoting diversity. I told them I was personally challenged by the good questions he asked and that I hoped they wouldn't be swayed by one donor's power play. And I reminded them that we have a long history here of not being held hostage by donors who attempt to wield influence like that."

"Good. I'm glad you said that. What now?"

"They called an emergency board meeting this morning to discuss it."

Sarah sat back in her chair. "You think they'll rescind their offer?"

"I don't know. Bill didn't give me any other details. But I got the impression it all happened late last night." She gestured toward the cross. "So before I lead a retreat about stewarding grace, I figured I'd better come in here and try to work through my anger."

"Better you than me, Mom. I'm not sure I could shift gears that fast."

Her mother gave a weary smile. "I'm hoping I can."

Sarah squeezed her hand. "I'll give you space for that." As she left the chapel, she prayed for Mom and Logan and the board. Not for the donor, though. Her mother's prayers would have to suffice for him.

Settling into a secluded corner in the lounge, she did a quick search for Logan's post. Two clicks, and she found it. *Stewarding Privilege.* She opened the link to read.

He had been thinking a lot lately, he said, about what it meant to be a faithful steward of everything that had been entrusted to him— not just time or talent or treasure, but the gifts that were harder to quantify and name. Like influence and privilege.

He hadn't grown up in affluence, he said. His dad worked factory jobs in Pittsburgh while his mom took care of five kids and then did general transcription for a small insurance company, often working long after everyone else went to bed, bent over her typewriter on the kitchen table. So whenever he'd heard people talk about "White privilege," he'd felt angry and defensive. He hadn't grown up with a silver spoon in his mouth. Like most people, he'd had his fair share of trials and losses. That was part of living in a broken, fallen world.

But in the past year, he said, a friend had helped him see what he had inherited, simply by being born White. "I had bought the lie that we were living in a post-racial society. But that's because the color of my skin has never made my life more challenging than it already is. And this is my privilege. The very fact that I lived in Tulsa for three years without ever knowing about the Race Massacre demonstrates my insular disregard for people who have suffered in ways that make me feel uncomfortable."

Part of faithful stewardship meant naming the hard truth, he said, not just to himself but to others—especially to the body of Christ, which was called to reject every form of partiality and superiority and to become humble servants willing to lay down their lives in love and to advocate on behalf of the poor and the marginalized and the oppressed. Just as Jesus had done. Then he quoted 1 John 3:17-18: "How does God's love abide in anyone who has the world's goods and sees a brother or sister in need and yet refuses help? Little children, let us love, not in word or speech, but in truth and action."

What the antiracism protesters were highlighting, he said, was the need for fundamental and widespread change. Not just in awareness, but in response. Not just for individuals, but for communities. It was far too easy to distance himself from overt racism and blatant bigotry—to identify racists like the White nationalists marching last August with their tiki torches and Confederate flags as "those people" and to congratulate himself for not being like them. But Jesus was all about demonstrating active, costly, incarnational love. "Do unto others as you would have them do unto you" was different from "Don't do to others what you don't want them to do to you." Engagement was harder than avoidance, and he had come to see it wasn't enough for him not to be a racist. He needed to find ways to promote antiracism and racial justice, and he wanted to practice listening well to the struggles of people of color without making it about his own feelings.

"As I continue to think and pray about how to steward my privilege more faithfully, Paul's words to the Corinthians about using their abundance to serve those in need have challenged me: 'As it is written, "The one who had much did not have too much, and the one who had little did not have too little"' (2 Corinthians 8:15). May God help us name the abundance we've been given and share generously with others what we have received."

"Sarah?"

She looked up at Wren. "Yeah?" Leaving the blog post open, she set her phone face-down in her lap.

"I just got a message from someone, and it's kind of an emergency, and I don't want to interrupt your mom while she's praying, but I'm just checking to see if it's okay with you if I head out for a little bit. I'll be back in time to clean up afterwards. I promise."

Sarah knew her mom wouldn't deny the request. "Yeah, okay."

"Sorry, it's just—if I don't take care of this now, I might not get a chance later, so . . ."

"I said okay." Sarah picked up her phone to read the post again.

Wren looked as if she was about to say something else.

"Ah, there you are!" her mom exclaimed as she entered the lounge. "Two of my very favorite people."

Wren embraced her. "Are you all right?"

"Yes. Nothing to worry about. I'll fill you in later."

Sarah wondered if her mother planned to give Wren specifics or just the broad strokes. Specifics, probably. They had that sort of relationship.

"I was telling Sarah I just got a text. From Chris." A knowing look passed between them. "He's free for coffee this morning."

"Go! By all means, go. We can cover everything here."

"Are you sure? I didn't want to miss your final session, but. . ."

In a gesture of motherly tenderness, she pressed her thumb to Wren's cheek. "Don't you worry about that. This is more important. And don't rush back. You can clean up anytime."

Wren thanked her, then hurried down the hall.

Sarah watched her round the corner. "Boyfriend?" she asked.

"No."

Clearly, no further details would be forthcoming. And Sarah knew better than to ask for them.

31

With its food truck, hammocks, and firepits, the new Great Out-doors Café was the sort of spot Casey would have loved. As she entered through the wrought iron gates, Wren pictured him ensconced in one of the garden igloos, editing video on his laptop while drinking a skinny vanilla latte, his inspiration cap covering his brow.

She scanned the garden, half-hoping to see Brooke and Chris playing with Estelle. But if Chris had told Brooke he had received another text—and he probably had—Brooke wouldn't have wanted any part in their meeting. She likely would have told Chris not to agree to it either. Wren hadn't thought he would. She hadn't even expected him to reply.

Maneuvering around other patrons vying for prime spots, she headed for a secluded table under a tree, where she would have a good view of the entrance. While she waited for him, she read their text thread again.

Hey, Chris! I was riding home from work yesterday and thought I saw you with Brooke. Was I imagining things? Hope you're doing okay. I'd love to connect sometime for coffee.

She would never confess to him how many hours she had spent last night trying to compose those few sentences or how many lines she had edited or deleted. If he hadn't replied with his, *10am at Great Outdoors?* would she have tried again?

Probably.

She set her phone down. Maybe Brooke hadn't told him not to meet. Maybe she had urged him to meet up as quickly as possible.

Maybe the simple "gotcha" was enough to catch their attention. Maybe Brooke was sending Chris with new cease-and-desist orders. Maybe the reason he suggested meeting outdoors was to give Brooke the opportunity to observe them from the coffee shop across the street. If he suggested moving closer to the road, Wren would look for her.

From this distance she would be able to observe his posture and body language before he saw her. She didn't know Chris well, but she could detect plenty from a few strides or a quick change of expression when their eyes met.

She breathed a prayer to settle herself.

Maybe she would leave the café with answers to questions about Casey's life and death. Maybe she could reassure Chris that Brooke had nothing to fear from contact with her, that she had only ever wanted to support her and Estelle in prayer.

Which she could do with or without contact.

That approach wouldn't work. She breathed another prayer, trying to slow her racing heart, and opened her hands on the table. *Release. Receive.*

She didn't need to see Brooke. She wanted to meet Estelle. Desperately. But she knew better than to ask for that. She had seen her once. She ought to be satisfied with that gift. Riding past the house at just the right time was too big a coincidence to believe that God hadn't orchestrated it.

Then again, Casey would argue that if you did something like that frequently enough, you stacked the odds in your favor.

"Are you getting ready to head out?" a woman asked as she approached carrying two cups.

"Sorry, waiting for a friend."

With an irritated sigh, the woman surveyed the rest of the courtyard.

Normally, Wren would have jumped up and apologized for taking up space before she had purchased a drink. But she needed this table, not only to watch for Chris's entry but to provide a secluded place for what might become a difficult conversation. She lifted her bag from the ground and placed it on the table near the other chair to indicate an imminent arrival. Then she picked up her phone and pretended she was talking to someone. *Come on, Chris. Any time now.*

But as the crowd continued to swell, she could no longer defend her territory against coffee-carrying customers. Rising, she gave her table to a young mom pushing a double stroller, then stepped closer to the tree. Just when she was wondering whether to pester him with a text, Chris strolled through the front gate in sunglasses and cargo shorts, his baseball cap drawn low. So much for being able to monitor facial expressions.

She wiped her palms on her capri pants and commanded herself to smile. Casually. "Hey, stranger," she said as she met him on the gravel path.

"Hey, sorry I'm late."

She wasn't sure whether to extend a hand or offer a hug. He offered neither. She rubbed her bare arm.

"Crowded here, huh?" he said.

"Saturday morning, I guess."

"Yeah."

She didn't tell him she had secured and lost a table.

"You want to go somewhere else?" he asked.

She didn't mind waiting. Being in the fresh air felt less claustrophobic. But if they stayed outside, he might keep his sunglasses on, and she preferred seeing his eyes. "Up to you," she finally said.

"Guess we can stay here. I don't have a whole lot of time."

She felt herself deflate. If she was going to secure the information she most wanted, she would need to move more quickly than she'd planned. "I'm really grateful you agreed to meet me. When I didn't hear anything back from you, I worried that maybe I had offended you somehow. And I haven't seen you lately at Wayfarer, so . . ."

He moved forward in line. "Pastor Hannah helped me get a media job at a different church, so I've been there on Sundays."

"Oh, I didn't know that. That's great." She should have thought to ask Hannah if she'd seen him. "I'm glad she was able to help you."

"Yeah. She's been really supportive."

Wren wondered what "supportive" included. Did Hannah know about his relationship with Brooke? And if she did, had she deliberately withheld that information? Or had it simply not occurred to her to mention to Casey's best friend that his wife was dating again?

That oversight seemed unlikely.

She chewed on her bottom lip.

Then again, if she had benefited from her pastor's commitment to confidentiality, why shouldn't Chris?

"Hannah is amazing," she said. "I don't know what I would have done without her this past year. Especially after everything happened with Casey."

He didn't reply.

"I'm glad she's been alongside to support you. I guess I didn't realize you had connected with her like that after Casey's memorial."

He stepped forward again.

She studied his profile, noting his set jaw as he perused the chalkboard menu. "What do you want?" he asked.

"Oh, no, it's okay. I'll get mine. Thanks."

He didn't ask twice.

She reached into her bag and took out her wallet, gripping it as if it could ground her whole body in the gravel. Too late for regrets now. Whatever message he'd been sent to deliver, she needed to be prepared to receive.

"Go ahead," he said when they got to the counter.

She ordered a chai latte, then moved aside. "I asked you to meet me, Chris. The least I can do is buy your coffee. What would you like?"

He hesitated, then ordered a small caramel macchiato. "Thanks, Wren. I'll leave the tip."

"Okay." She swiped her card.

As he removed a couple of bills from his pocket, a coin fell out and rolled toward Wren's sandals. Stooping to pick it up, she recognized the silver token, with "24 hours" enclosed in a triangle and Unity, Service, and Recovery printed along the sides.

When she handed it to him, he clenched his fingers around it as if clutching a jewel. Or a lifeline.

"We'll call you when they're ready," the barista said.

Wren thanked her and moved out of the way.

He opened his fist to display the token. "You know what this is?"

"Yes." Some of the women at Bethel House had kept sobriety coins to celebrate progress.

"I've got a five-month one too, but I keep this one with me to remind me it's one day at a time."

She nodded. "I'm proud of you. That's wonderful."

"Thanks. Pastor Hannah helped connect me with a rehab program in the spring. I've been clean since then." He pocketed the token. "It was a wake-up call after Casey died. I decided I had to get help. I didn't want the same end."

"What do you mean?"

Chris said, "It coulda been me, crashing into a tree like that. Driving drunk."

She felt her breath escape. "They determined that for sure? The toxicology report said that?"

"I thought you knew."

"No. I don't know anything." Her eyes filled with tears. "Please. If you can tell me anything that would help, anything that would help me move on and get some closure, please. That's all I want."

He glanced over her shoulder. "I'll wait for the drinks. See if you can snag that igloo." He pointed at a young couple on the verge of leaving. "Quick."

She hurried toward them. "Good timing," the guy said as he held the zippered door open for her.

She breathed a prayer of gratitude. If she was going to break down in tears, being isolated in a tent was the perfect place for it. She hoped Chris wouldn't feel uncomfortable, though, being in an enclosed space. Or maybe the enclosed space would make him feel safe enough to share firsthand details. After all, he'd suggested it. She opened her hands again.

"Sorry to get emotional on you," she said when he came in a few minutes later and set the cups on the table. "It's just, I've spent the past eight months trying to make sense of his death, trying to figure out if it was an accident."

He sat down across from her and sipped his drink.

"He left me a goodbye note. But I didn't know if it was a suicide note or not. I still don't." She curled her fingers around her cup. "I'm not asking for confidential information. But Casey was my best friend. If it's possible to get answers, that's all I'm asking for."

If only he would take off his sunglasses. With his eyes covered and cup pressed to his lips, she couldn't read him.

She decided to try a different tack. "I didn't realize you knew Brooke. And I'm not looking to upset her. I promise. I'm just trying to move forward in grieving my friend." She gripped her drink with both hands. "Can you help me? Please?"

He set his coffee down. "Where did you see me with Brooke?"

That was the question she had hoped he wouldn't ask. But she had rehearsed her answer, just in case. "I was riding my bike to a friend's house after work and thought I saw you."

"Where?"

This was a test, wasn't it? And if she weren't honest, their conversation would be over.

She fought to steady her voice. "I often ride by the Wilsons' house on my way home from work. I know it seems weird, but it's a way for me to connect with Casey. That's how I found out it was for sale."

He seemed to be waiting for a further confession.

"As I was riding by yesterday, I saw you walking to your car in the driveway. And I guessed it was Brooke coming out of the house." She bit her lip. "Because Estelle has Casey's hair."

She watched his shoulders lower, and he nodded slowly. "She looks just like him," he said, his voice full of such unexpected tenderness, Wren almost burst into tears. He picked up his coffee again. "Brooke was really freaked out by your text."

"Freaked out, why?"

"Because it seemed too big a coincidence that you would see us together."

"I had no idea she was in town. I promise."

"I told her that. But you gotta admit, it was weird. She was threatening to put a restraining order on you, so I told her I would come talk to you instead."

My God. *Breathe.*

When she felt as if she had control of her voice, she murmured, "Thank you."

Breathe. Please, Lord. Not here. Not now.

She concentrated on the café logo on his cup: a black bear beside a pine tree. *O.U.T.D.O.O.—*

"Sorry to upset you," he said. "I just thought you should know."

R.S. . . .

She pictured Jesus standing beside her, his hand gripping her shoulder, and imagined him saying, "I am with you." She filled her lungs with air. Once. Twice. Again.

"I'm glad you told me," she said weakly. "Thank you."

He took off his glasses and set them on the table. "Brooke doesn't know much more than you do—just that it looks like he was on his way home and somewhere along the way, he either changed his mind, or the stress of everything drove him to drink and drive. I don't know. It's something we'll never know. And I know that's hard. I'm sorry."

She took another deep breath.

So, that was it, then. Done. No more searching for answers. Closure would need to come by accepting the fact that she would never know the full truth. She blinked back tears. "I'm just glad he decided to head home."

Chris raised his eyebrows.

"You look surprised," she said.

"Yeah, for sure. I didn't expect you to say that, not after you guys were looking for a house together."

"Wait—you don't think . . ." *Dear God.* "We were friends, Chris. Just friends. Nothing more. Ever. He needed a roommate because he couldn't afford to live on his own." Casey must have told Brooke they were house hunting. That was the only way Chris would have known. "I know Brooke thought we were too emotionally attached. Codependent. I won't disagree with her about that. Our friendship was always complicated that way because of our mental health challenges. But I promise you, there wasn't anything else. Ever. We were planning to find a few more people to live with. He was making calls."

Chris didn't reply.

"He told me he had to leave Reno because Brooke was abusive"— at this, his eyebrows shot up again—"and I believed him. He never even told me about Estelle."

"Wait—you didn't know he had a baby?"

"No."

He puffed up his cheeks and blew out the air slowly.

"If I had known about Estelle, I would have done everything I could to encourage him to be her daddy. All he said was that it wasn't safe for him and Brooke to live together. He said she was violent and unstable."

Chris scoffed. "Hardly."

"Okay, see? I told you. He wasn't honest with me. But I didn't find that out until later."

He lowered his gaze. "Dude had his demons and secrets, that's for sure."

Wren couldn't argue with that. "Whatever happened at the end, I have to believe he wanted to return to Estelle." She didn't say "and Brooke." She wasn't confident of that part.

"He didn't want to be a dad," Chris said after a while. "He did everything he could to make Brooke kick him out and give up on him. Got fired from his job, started drinking and spending like crazy, had an affair with somebody—Brooke never figured out who. She assumed it was you. That's why she told him to cut off contact."

Wren felt as if she had been punched in the gut.

"And then when you texted him in the delivery room . . ."

Another punch to the gut. "I was worried about him," she said. "I felt like it was a nudge from the Holy Spirit to contact him, so I did. I had no idea where he was. I never would have intruded if I'd known." Her throat burned. "Please tell Brooke I'm so sorry. No wonder she hates me."

He didn't correct her. "Brooke was worried about him being around Estelle because he was so unpredictable and wouldn't take his meds. So she told him to leave, said she didn't care where he went, but that he needed to get straightened out before he came back. She'd been pleading with him to go to rehab, but he refused. Next thing she knew, he texted her from a burner phone to say he was in Kingsbury, and the two of you were moving in together. And then a few days later, his parents called to say you'd called them, panicked, because you didn't know where he was, and you thought he was heading back to Reno."

"They didn't even know he'd left Reno," she said.

"No. Brooke hadn't told them. She was trying to keep his chaos a secret. She was still hoping they would have a different ending, that he would make different choices."

"He never called her from the road to tell her he was heading home?"

"No."

Wren pictured that beautiful little girl with the red hair and the open hands, squealing with laughter. *If only . . .*

No. There were no more "if onlys." Only, "What next?"

Casey had asked for her forgiveness in his goodbye letter. Maybe when he wrote his note about the rooster crowing and the thief on the cross and Jesus saying, "Father, forgive them," he suspected that someday she would find out how he had deceived and betrayed her. *Think of me,* he'd said.

She would need to forgive him again. A whole new layer of forgiving him. She'd had no idea what he had stolen from her in terms of her integrity and reputation.

She straightened up in her chair. "Would you please tell Brooke the truth? Would you please tell her I never meant to hurt her or Estelle? I'd love to talk with her myself, if she'd be open to it."

"I'm not sure about that. I mean, I'll try but . . ."

She attempted to conceal her disappointment. "Okay. Thank you." She couldn't ask for more than that.

He tilted his head back for an emptying sip from his cup, then set it aside on the table. "I should probably get going."

"Okay."

"Are you all right?"

His kindness in asking the question caused her eyes to well up again. "Yes. Thank you."

He gave her a compassionate smile. "If it weren't for Pastor Hannah, I wouldn't have gotten my own life straightened around. And I never would have met her if you hadn't invited me to the service for Casey. So, thank you for that."

Not trusting herself to speak, she nodded.

"I went there high. I guess you knew that."

Again, Wren nodded.

"I don't even know for sure that I understood what I was signing up for when I said I wanted to follow Jesus. But he knew. He took my blurred yes and rescued me." Chris paused. "I know Brooke was upset when she heard about the service and everything, but she's grateful for it now. She knows that was a turning point in my life. And the fact that it was connected with Casey"—he swiped his eyes with the back of his hand—"I don't know how to explain it. Like he and I both got raised from the dead, you know?"

Yes. She understood.

"And then meeting Brooke a few months ago," he said, "and getting to be part of Estelle's life . . . it sounds weird to say it, but it feels like I've got Casey's blessing on everything."

Wren gaped at him. "You're getting married?"

"No. I mean, not yet. We don't want to rush into anything. But I love them both and want to spend my life with them."

She had a thousand questions and didn't feel free to ask any of them. "I'm happy for you, Chris."

"Thanks." He reached for his sunglasses and fiddled with one of the arms. "Before I go, I need to apologize to you for something."

She eyed him quizzically.

"I met Brooke a few months ago at a dinner party at the Wilsons' house—our moms arranged it—and we immediately connected because of Casey. She wanted to know everything I knew about him, wanted all the details about the video projects we did, the documentary we were working on, that kind of thing. She was grieving and looking for answers. I didn't have any. But I had funny stories to share and some good memories about his passion and heart. Casey was a good guy at the core, but tormented, you know? The whole bipolar thing plus addiction. Brooke didn't know any of that when they got together, and by the time she found out, she was pregnant." He stopped fiddling with his glasses. "Anyway. We ended up going out for coffee a few times when she was in town, and she told me everything that had happened. I didn't have any reason to doubt what she said. I didn't know you well, and I knew you and Casey were close so . . ."

She wrapped her hands around her cup and commanded herself not to break eye contact with him.

"I'm sorry I never asked you for your side of things," he said. "Whenever I saw you at Wayfarer, I tried to avoid you because I knew how Brooke felt about you. Then when I got the job at the other church, I figured I wouldn't have to worry about running into you anymore."

"And then I texted you about the Wilsons moving."

"Yeah. And that freaked Brooke out. So I decided it was best to ignore you." He ran his thumb along the rim of his glasses. "I'm sorry about all that. It wasn't fair to judge you. And I'll do what I can to help Brooke see the truth."

"Thank you, Chris. I appreciate that."

He stood. "Casey thought the world of you, you know?"

She swallowed hard.

"He often talked about what you meant to him, how you were always there for him, no matter what. You were the kind of friend who laid down her life in love. He knew that."

She pressed her palms against her eyes.

"Aw, come 'ere." Chris gently drew her to her feet and wrapped her in a comforting embrace, her tears falling onto his chest.

Be well, Wrinkle, she heard Casey say. *Be well.*

32

No minimizing. No denying. No excusing. Forgiveness, her mother reminded the group, looked squarely at sin and called it sin. To do otherwise, she said, was to avoid the cross.

At her back-corner table, Sarah flipped a page in her notebook. Calling a spade a spade had seldom been her difficulty. Seeing the offender with compassion—offering fellow debtors the sort of gut-level mercy Jesus spoke about in his parable of the unforgiving servant—that was the challenge. She could tick the box of forgiveness without ever being moved by sympathetic groaning for the offender. She could be obedient, fulfill her duty, and move on. Holding a grudge had never been her style. But not granting someone access to her affection? Sure. Guilty. Writing someone off? Yeah. That too.

Speaking of . . .

Her gaze wandered to the other side of the room, where Wren, having quietly entered a few minutes ago, now sat beside Hannah, staring off into space.

What was it about that girl that so provoked her?

She clicked her pen.

Simple. Wren was a freeloader who caused her mother way too much stress. Bottom line. That was her problem with Wren: her impact on Mom's well-being. Especially during a vulnerable time of loss and transition. Wren was a taker.

So, okay. Maybe she *had* been holding a grudge. She could admit that to God and forgive Wren for her selfishness, even if Wren didn't recognize her sin or ask for mercy. But as far as moving toward her in a process of reconciliation, that seemed unnecessary—especially when, family connections aside, she had no intention of being in close relationship with her.

She smoothed her blank page.

It had been different with Dad and Carol. By necessity. If she hadn't immediately moved toward them after finding out about their affair—if she hadn't worked through her own process of forgiving both of them—that wouldn't have kept Dad from moving forward in his new life. He still would have chosen Carol. And then he and Carol—together—might have moved away from her. She hadn't been willing to let that happen. Not after so many other losses.

Across the top of her page, she doodled geometric shapes.

So why was it that she resented and rejected Wren for causing her mother stress when she hadn't resented and rejected Dad and Carol for the devastation they had caused her mom? Why harbor grudges against Wren, who hadn't wounded or betrayed or deceived or abandoned her mother, while forgiving—or, come to think of it, perhaps denying, minimizing, and excusing—their sin?

She drew a row of spirals.

No mystery there. At eighteen, she hadn't had the capacity to be worried about what caused her mother stress or broke her heart. She'd had her own stress and grief to manage back then, and she had diverted all her energy into personal survival. Her mom understood that and didn't fault her for it. They'd had those conversations before.

And yet . . .

Since her mom had been so candid in confessing her own self-protection and blind spots, Sarah could do the same and acknowledge—unequivocally—not only the suffering Dad and Carol had caused, but the price her mother had paid for her own loyalty to them. Even while she had named that before, it was worth naming again. Just to be clear.

From her peripheral vision, she watched Wren lower her head in her hands. Hannah removed a tissue from her bag and offered it to her.

That was the other thing that provoked her about Wren: her fragility. Her neediness was a continual drain on Mom.

Sure, it was devastating to lose a friend. But lots of people endured just as much and more. And though her mother always insisted it was pointless to measure and compare suffering, people moved forward in their grief. They survived.

At least with whatever had upset Wren that morning, she was staying somewhere else.

Love always protects, Sarah wrote on her page. Then she drew a roof over the words, with rain beating down. Her mother had told them that was one way to interpret the Greek word Paul used. *Love provides a cover to keep the water out.* So that would be her ongoing mission: minimize the potential for Wren causing a deluge of stress, whatever that goal might entail, short or long term.

"I've been worried about your mom," several people had said to her in hushed tones in the lobby. "Half-expected her to cancel today." And who would have blamed her? But she had stubbornly insisted on persevering. Or rather, she'd insisted the Lord had given her—and would give her—what she needed to finish the race, even if crossing the finish line didn't look like what she expected. Even if being in the same space where she'd endured the panic attack triggered another one, come what may, she was saying her next yes.

Her mom glanced in Wren's direction, concern flickering across her face.

See? This was exactly what Sarah had just identified. Even from the back corner, that girl's distress was impacting her. *Take it outside,* she silently commanded Wren.

Then again, that was what had thrown Mom off last week: Wren leaving the room upset, her ego bruised by something trivial. And then she'd caused Mom even more stress by relaying what Logan had said. While she was trying to lead a retreat.

Wren could have waited to share that information. She should have waited. Or not share it at all. What had she hoped to accomplish by disclosing what she'd overheard? That decision was self-centered and stupid, and it had pushed her already exhausted mother over the brink. Mom had suffered cruelly—publicly— because of Wren's selfishness. Cluelessness.

"When we meditate on what the Lord did for us on the cross," her mother said, shifting her gaze, "we see how costly forgiveness is."

So far, Mom hadn't lost her train of thought. Good.

"And here's where our part comes in. God says, Forgive, even as I have forgiven you. Remember the enormity of your debt. Remember that your unpayable debts have been forgiven by a gracious and generous and merciful God, and then, by comparison, look at every other debt owed to you by others. The king in Jesus' story forgave that servant an unimaginable amount of money—the equivalent of two hundred thousand years of wages. He wiped the debt com- pletely clean. And yet, after receiving that kind of extravagance, could that servant not forgive his fellow servant what amounted to one hundred days' pay?

"Jesus said, 'Be merciful, just as your Father is merciful.' The mercy we extend to others flows from the astonishing mercy we ourselves have received. We can't make ourselves more loving. We can't make ourselves compassionate. But as we meditate on God's love, God's compassion, God's mercy—as we practice celebrating what God has lavished on us—we'll find ourselves being enlarged by the power of the Spirit, with compassion and love and mercy for others."

Sarah stared at the words on her page. *Love always protects.* Her mother could justifiably argue that providing shelter for Wren during the storms that assaulted her had been an expression of the love and compassion and mercy she herself had received from God. So, what were you supposed to do when your efforts to love someone with a protective love directly contradicted their efforts to do the same? What did love look like then?

Far too many variables to solve in that equation. Except . . .

She sighed softly as that other definition from Paul came to mind: love does not insist on its own way.

Yeah. Right. Guilty. The whole "yielding to others in love" thing would be her perennial challenge.

"Remember," her mother was saying, "transformation into Christ-likeness is always the Spirit's work of grace in us. But we can co-operate with that grace and practice loving others by forgiving them. This is how we practice stewarding the grace we have received."

Practice, Sarah wrote in her notebook, then underlined the word several times. Nothing in her flesh could make her more merciful to others. She knew that. No striving. No commanding herself to be better. *Enlarge my compassion,* she wrote in her notebook, and under-lined that too.

"I often hear people speak about the so-called therapeutic benefits of forgiveness," her mother said. "We're told that forgiveness is a gift we give ourselves by letting go of resentment and refusing to be controlled by the people who wounded us. In this way, forgiveness sets us free from the pain of the past. Scientific studies confirm this. There is healing power in forgiveness.

"What we need, though, is a vision beyond our own wounds to the wounds of Christ. We need a vision beyond our own needs to the sacrifice of Christ. Because if we're only focused on the personal benefits of forgiveness, we're still quite self-centered, aren't we? Jesus calls us to forgive, not because we'll feel better when we do, but be-cause forgiving others as God has forgiven us is the deepest response of gratitude for the grace we have received. We forgive for Jesus' sake, not just for our own. And in doing so, we receive healing and freedom as good and generous gifts from God."

Apart from the sound of pens scratching on paper, the room was silent.

Her mother straightened her notes. "Having said all that, God meets us where we are. If I can only be moved to forgive others for the sake of being free myself, if I can only be persuaded to forgive others because I'm tired of living in bitterness and resentment, then I will gratefully step through that gateway into freedom   not as an end but as a beginning toward understanding what it means to forgive as I've been forgiven." She smiled. "I say this from personal experience. No hypothetical situations here."

Their eyes met. No mystery who Mom was thinking about. With a nearly imperceptible raising of her eyebrows, she acknowledged not only her long, arduous journey of forgiveness, but her latest steps in extending grace to Carol. To communicate understanding and solidarity, Sarah tapped her heart.

"Don't be discouraged, friends, if a forgiveness issue comes around again and triggers anger or grief, and you think, 'But I already dealt with that! I thought I already forgave!' You did. And now there's something more to release and forgive. That takes away nothing from the work you've already done. It just means there's another layer of work to do with God, a deeper opportunity for healing.

"Remember, forgiveness can be a process—especially when trauma is involved. Some offenses are straightforward to forgive. Others are multi-layered, and we may only become aware of what we need to forgive as we grieve the losses over time. The call is to forgive whenever we become aware of our need to forgive. Bitterness, anger, self-pity, or a desire to punish or seek revenge—all these are clues that reveal our need to draw near to God for supernatural help in canceling the debts of others. And as we forgive, we ask God to restore us and meet our needs out of his abundance so that we can stop demanding from others what they cannot give."

Right, Sarah thought. She needed to remember that part too as she tried to find a good way forward with Carol, who hadn't yet replied to her text. "Give her room," Zach had said. "She'll come around." Always the optimist, that guy.

Her mother stepped away from the podium. "Forgiveness is one of the deepest ways we participate in the life and love of God," she said. "This is how we demonstrate our family resemblance and show that we are indeed beloved children of a heavenly Father who has generously given us all things in Christ. The question is, will we be stingy in extending grace to those who sin against us? Will we refuse to offer others what we ourselves have received?

"During our first retreat, I invited you to ponder Paul's words in 1 Corinthians 13 while picturing the people you find most difficult to love. I wonder, is there anyone who comes to mind when you think specifically about forgiveness? Anyone you'd like for God to punish instead of rescue and redeem? Anyone you're holding a grudge against?"

Sarah shifted in her chair.

"Think of people who have wounded you or your loved ones. Think of people who have taken from you, who owe you a debt. Are you filled with God's longing and compassion for them? Or with anger, bitterness, and hardness of heart? What conversation can you have with God about that?"

Sarah glanced toward Wren, who was staring forward with a look of utter dejection. She had seen Micah wear that expression. And her mom. And sometimes her students. If she ever glimpsed such a look on Jess or Morgan's face, she would be heartbroken.

"Be merciful," Jesus had commanded. Be kind. Tenderhearted. Compassionate. Forgiving.

With a heavy sigh, Sarah looked down at her handwriting and underlined the word *practice* again

"Need any help here?" she asked Wren as she deposited her coffee mug on the cart. With this many people standing in line to talk with her mom, she could make herself useful while she waited.

"It's okay, thanks. I've got it."

Not one to offer twice, Sarah took an oatmeal cookie from the tray. "I didn't have a chance to thank you earlier for being willing to move in with friends for a couple of days. Hope it hasn't been too much of an inconvenience for you." *Or for your friends,* she silently added.

"No, it's been okay."

"Oh. Good. Glad to hear it." She cupped her hand beneath her chin to catch stray cookie crumbs as she took a bite. "I know I can come off a little strong sometimes, especially when it comes to my mom. I've been worried about her lately."

"I know. Me too." Wren loaded more cups onto the cart. "I'm worried about the burden I've been on her this past year. I know all my struggles have taken a toll on her."

Sarah concealed her surprise with another bite of her cookie.

"I don't think I would have survived this year without her, Sarah. I don't say that to be melodramatic. It's the truth. Her support has meant everything to me, and I know I can never repay her." Her eyes brimmed with emotion. "I've apologized to your mom for the strain I've put on her. Many times. But I've never apologized to you. I know my mental health struggles have impacted you and your family too. And I'm sorry, Sarah. I truly am. Thanks for putting up with me."

Too stunned to reply, Sarah simply nodded.

"I've been trying the past few days to put together my video testimony for your mom. But there's too much for me to say. And I get too emotional trying to say it, so . . ." She flattened her lips, visibly battling to ward off tears.

Sarah tossed her napkin into the trash and brushed off her hands. "Don't worry about any of that. I'm rethinking the whole thing anyway, wondering if it's all too much to play publicly for Mom." She paused, sensing a nudge forward. "What do you think? Would it be better to show her something like that in private?"

Wren hesitated, then said, "I think she'd prefer that. Then she won't have to worry about people watching for her reactions. She can just try to receive it for herself."

"Okay. Good. We'll do it that way. Thanks."

Wren straightened a stack of unused napkins and placed those on the cart too.

"I also got to thinking"—right that very second, if Sarah was honest—"that if Mom wants a tandem bike, I'm not going to stand in her way."

The look of shock on Wren's face brought to mind occasions when intimidated students realized Mrs. Kersten wasn't the ogre they thought she was. "Did she happen to tell you what color she'd want?" Sarah asked.

"Light blue. I found a couple of options online."

"Okay. Send me a link, will you? I'll take a look."

"I'll pay for it," Wren said.

Sarah was going to suggest splitting the cost but then changed her mind. Perhaps it was more important for the gift to come entirely from Wren. With her blessing. "Go ahead, then, and choose the one you think will be best. And it's fine with me if you give it to her at the party. I think that would be fun for everyone."

"Okay," Wren said. "But I'm not good with public speaking. And I don't want everyone to know I bought it for her."

"We'll work those details out. I can present it with you if you want."

Wren looked relieved. "Okay. And I hope you'll ride it with her too."

"Thanks. I will. I might even persuade her to come to the cottage someday and ride it there."

Peering over Sarah's shoulder, Wren signaled they needed to halt their conversation. "Hey, Kit," Wren said, extending her hand, "I'll take your cup."

Sarah turned around. "All done, Mom?" A few people were still gathered near the podium.

"Almost. I wanted to catch both of you together while I could. How about if the three of us celebrate with lunch? My treat."

Wren looked as if she was going to object.

Practice, Sarah thought. "I think that's a great idea," she said. "Can you join us, Wren? Or have you got other plans?"

"I . . ." She grasped her elbows. "No. I don't have other plans."

"Good!" Mom exclaimed. "I'll just finish up my conversations."

"And I'll help with the dishes," Sarah said.

From the look on Wren's face, she wasn't sure if this was a gift or a pretext for another confrontation. They needed to find a different way forward. For Mom's sake. That was what love looked like.

She waited until her mother was out of earshot, then said, "It hasn't been all stress and strain, you know. I've never heard Mom complain about you staying with her. She's only ever expressed gratitude for the company."

Another nudge forward.

"For *your* company, Wren. And for what she's gained from you being with her."

And another.

"So, thank you for that. You've been a blessing to her."

Keep going.

"She loves you like a daughter," Sarah said, her eyes unexpectedly welling with tears.

Ah.

There it was.

Like mother, like daughter.

There it was.

As with Carol and Mom, so with Wren and her.

There it was. *Resentment.*

More than that. *Envy.*

There it was. And how could she not have seen this before now?

Because, her mother often said, *we see what we need to see when we're ready to see it.* In fact, she had recently reminded her mom of the same thing.

She looked at Wren, this young woman who had intimately shared life with Mom for the past year. They had bonded over their common suffering. Their depression. Their grief. Their losses. Even their hospitalizations and panic attacks. These were elements of her mother's life that Sarah would never be able to understand. Not like Wren had. Not like Wren could.

It wasn't just the losses, though, that had bonded them. It was their common understanding of Jesus as the Man of Sorrows, their collaboration on the Journey to the Cross, their passion for Van Gogh. Wren had introduced Mom to his work, and his work had opened her to new ways of prayer that Sarah didn't understand. Or appreciate.

Theirs was a journey Sarah could not share.

But, she could practice being grateful for the ways they had enhanced each other's lives and for the ways they had loved one another. She could practice acknowledging the mutual gift of their relationship, even as Mom had practiced acknowledging the gift of her relationship with Dad. And with Carol.

"Forgive me, Wren. I haven't loved you well." The unbidden tears cut short any further confession.

Stepping toward her, Wren offered a wordless embrace.

Sarah didn't back away.

33

"It seems to me," Sarah said to Wren as the three of them shared lunch on the restaurant patio, "that Brooke has her own issues to address about why she's drawn to men with addictions. Chris ought to be wary of being roped in as a substitute daddy."

Kit took another piece of bread from the basket and slathered it with rosemary butter. Months from now, when she thought back to her last retreat at New Hope, she knew it wouldn't be the relief of crossing the finish line or even the kind words spoken afterward that she would remember with greatest gratitude. It would be the gift of grace, enabling Sarah and Wren to move toward one another; the gift of insight, enabling Sarah to confess to both of them her resentment and envy; and the gift of forgiveness, enabling the three of them to enjoy deep and honest fellowship around a table. As family.

Not only had Wren felt comfortable enough to confide what had happened with Chris that morning, but, much to Kit's surprise, she seemed to welcome Sarah's pointed opinions and advice.

"Brooke will be telling her own version of the story to protect herself," Sarah continued, "so if I were you, I wouldn't take what she told Chris about Casey as gospel truth. We've all got our filters. We all spin. And if Brooke was accusing you of being codependent, she probably is too."

"Even so," Wren said, "I should have asked Casey more questions. I shouldn't have assumed he was telling me the truth. I was way too quick to believe his version of the story. And I'd really like an opportunity to talk with Brooke and ask for her forgiveness." Wren took another bite of her salad. "But it's like you were saying today, Kit. I don't have any control over that process. And if she won't let me ask for forgiveness, then I need to be content with God forgiving me."

"Those open loops aren't easy," Kit said.

"No," Sarah agreed, "but you also can't be held hostage by someone else's refusal to give grace. If she won't agree to see you— and if she won't accept what you told Chris then that's on her. You've done all you can do. You move on."

Easier said than done, Kit thought. Later, when the two of them were alone, she might suggest to Wren that she make another painting with ashes.

Sarah loaded risotto onto her fork. "You didn't tell your story today, Mom—the one about forgiving yourself."

"No, I guess I forgot."

"You should tell her that one. Has she told you that one already, Wren?"

"No, I don't think so."

Kit set down her piece of bread. "It's more the punchline of the story than the story itself," she said. "I had wounded someone I cared about, and I was beating myself up about it. So I talked to my spiritual director about what I had done, and Lucy heard the regret and self-condemnation in my story. She said to me, 'Did you ask your friend to forgive you?' I told her I had. 'And you asked God to forgive you?' I told her I had. 'But you won't forgive yourself?' I told her I couldn't. Then she looked at me and said, 'Are you bigger than God?'"

Wren's eyes grew wide.

"I repented right then and there," Kit said. "I had never considered that refusing to let myself off the hook of my own disappointment and shame was a manifestation of pride. But if I claim my standards are higher than God's, then that's what it is. Pride."

Sarah took another bite. "Lucy knew how to cut right through."

"Yes, she did. She had no problem being direct. Reminds me of somebody else I know and love."

Sarah laughed. "Moi? Direct?"

Kit held up her fingers, half an inch apart. "Just a little bit."

"Well, life's too short to be vague," Sarah replied. "So, I'll take another page out of Lucy's playbook and say this, Wren. All his addiction and mental health issues aside, your friend Casey treated you like dirt."

Wren stiffened, then slouched forward, elbows planted on the table and hands steepled to her lips. "I know," she said softly.

"I'm sorry for that," Sarah said. "It can be hard to forgive the dead."

Wren nodded. "I thought I had already forgiven him. But there's more." She looked at Kit. "Another letter to write and bury. Lots of letters, probably."

Even if Sarah didn't understand the reference, she didn't ask questions.

"It's all part of the process," Kit said. "We just need to be patient with it." From inside her purse, her windchime ringtone sounded.

When she made no move to answer the call, Sarah said, "That might be Bill or one of the other trustees."

"They can wait."

"I can't," Sarah said with a smile. "At least check and see."

Kit reached into her bag and eyed her phone. "You're right. It's Bill."

"Take it!" Sarah and Wren chorused.

At this point, confidentiality seemed unnecessary. Turning slightly away from the table, she said, "Hey, Bill. Everything okay?"

"I'm hoping it will be," he said. "Rick couldn't move past his own concerns about hiring Logan, so he's resigned from the board. We'll likely lose the donor too, but the rest of us are confident that Logan is the one God has called to lead us into the next chapter. So we'll need to trust the Lord to provide everything we need."

"Just like we always have," Kit said. "And he always has."

"Right."

Wren and Sarah were both watching her, waiting.

"Listen, Katherine, I'm wondering if you can help us out. Logan was understandably troubled by all this, and he's asked for more time to think and pray about whether he should take the job. I've done as much as I can to reassure him of our commitment to him and his vision, but we wondered if you'd be willing to talk with him again. He said he would appreciate that opportunity."

She wasn't sure what she could offer Logan beyond the questions she'd already answered, but if he wanted to speak with her, she wouldn't refuse. "I'm at lunch with family right now, but I'd be happy for him to call me later."

Bill thanked her. After she put away her phone, she relayed the news.

"Bet the board is freaking out," Sarah said. "And that's not your problem, by the way."

"I know. I'm just glad they have an opportunity to work through this now instead of later. The timing was good."

"Love the way you reframe things, Mom. It's your superpower."

Kit chuckled. "I don't know about that. I just know light is always a gift, even when it's disruptive."

"Sometimes especially when it is," Sarah replied, and Wren agreed. They all had fresh evidence of that.

"Speaking of things being brought to the light," Kit said to Wren, "how did you leave it with Chris?"

Wren shrugged. "He said he would try to talk with Brooke, but no promises. I asked him to call or text and let me know how it goes. I hope he will. But I know I don't have any control over that either." She opened her hands on the table. "Like you've taught me, Kit. Release and receive."

"No shortage of opportunities to practice that," Kit said.

"No. But it feels like I have to do it constantly."

Kit smiled at her. "Then you're doing it well."

Not long after she arrived home from the restaurant, her phone buzzed with a text from Logan: *Is it a good time to talk?*

She poured herself a glass of iced tea and stepped onto her patio, where she slid a chair into a patch of shade and then typed, *Sure.*

"I'm grateful for your time," he said after they exchanged pleasantries a few minutes later. "I'm assuming Bill has told you everything."

"Yes. He filled me in." She heard Logan take a deep breath.

"Nikki told me I shouldn't post my views publicly. She was worried something like this might happen. But I spent so many years being blind about racism, and then once I started seeing the truth about it, I kept silent. I tried to be so careful not to post anything controversial on social media, nothing that could be viewed as divisive or political. But if trying to be faithful to what God has been showing me means making some people angry, I'm going to have to live with that." He paused. "I guess it didn't occur to me, though, that a board member would read my post and react that way. I thought after our interview process that we were all on the same page in terms of moving forward with a commitment to diversity and promoting racial justice. Now I'm not sure."

The donor who found the link won't be the only one upset, Sarah had commented after reading Logan's post to them at lunch. *But I hope he won't back down.* Wren had agreed.

"Here's what I'm concerned about," Logan said. "I don't want the board to make significant changes just because they want to hire me. I don't need to be placated. This isn't about me. This is about discerning what God has in mind for the future of New Hope. And if they're panicking because they want to fill a position—if they're trying to do whatever it takes just so I'll take the job—that isn't going to serve anyone well."

No, Kit thought. It wouldn't. "Is that the impression they're giving you? That they're making these decisions only because they want to appease you?"

"You know them far better than I do," he said, "but I got the sense from Bill that they're not eager to start the search process from scratch. And he seemed surprised when I didn't immediately leap at the news that Rick had resigned. I guess he thought that would seal the deal, once and for all. But as far as I'm concerned, it's not about who's left the board or why. It's about the ones who remain and the ones who will join."

Names and faces of board members long gone flashed across her mind, some of them more memorable than others. In both good and bad ways.

"I get the impression they haven't been active ministry partners with you, Katherine, that they've been good support for prayer but haven't really participated in anything else, apart from financial oversight."

"I think that's fair," she said. "But that's more about my style and what I asked for rather than their negligence." In fact, the deference of the current board had been far easier for her to manage than some of the more opinionated and aggressive leadership in the past.

"I'm not sure they truly understand the commitment I'll need from them," he said. "I'm not interested in being hired to do a job and then left alone to do it."

"Have you told them that?"

"Multiple times. And Bill keeps saying the same thing: 'You have our full-fledged support.'"

As she'd had. That was all she had ever sought from them. "It sounds like you're not hearing something you need to hear from them in order to move forward. What's missing?"

He sighed. "You know what word comes to mind? Initiative. I shouldn't have to state the obvious: if God is calling us to engage in this kind of ministry, it starts with the board. After all our conversations— and especially after what happened with my blog post—I would have thought one of them would have said, 'Since we've got an opening now, we'll seek a person of color who can help lead us forward in the vision.' Not as a token presence for appearances' sake either. But when I asked them what their process is for replacing a board member, Bill talked about trying to find someone who has Rick's networking skills and rapport with donors."

She leaned back in her chair. Evidently, Bill was more nervous about the financial future than he had indicated with his "trusting the Lord to provide" comment.

"You might need to provide the leadership with regard to that," she said. "I don't think any of the board members would object to making diversity a priority. But they'll need help recognizing blind spots. Like you helped me." She paused. "I think their determination to pursue you is a good sign of how open they are. When the donor discovered your blog post and reacted that way, it could have shut everything down. The Lord could have used it to redirect all of you. Instead, it sounds like they're reaffirming support for you, even at a financial cost."

Relational too, she thought. Bill and Rick were good friends.

"As far as whether they're panicking about filling the position," she went on, "from what I can see, they could function without any director in place for at least the next few months. The fall retreats and workshops are already lined up. Not that there isn't room to add new events—just that there isn't any pressure from the programming side of things. And the facilitators of those groups are so experienced, they don't need much input or administrative support. Gayle has worked with all of them. In fact, I'm sure she would be happy to continue in her job."

Those last words carried an edge she hadn't intended. Oh, well. Let him respond if he wanted. She took a slow sip from her glass.

"Sounds like maybe you blame me for that," he said quietly.

"I'm not casting blame, Logan, just stating fact. Gayle has relied on that income to make ends meet. But you wouldn't have had any way of knowing that when you and the board negotiated the terms of your contract."

"No, but maybe I should have asked more questions before I jumped to accept a solution that met our needs." There was a moment of silence. "Is that true for Wren too?"

"Wren has some other options she's exploring."

"Oh. That's good. A blessing in disguise, maybe."

She decided not to comment. Whatever blessing might emerge for Wren was for her to name, not him.

"Anyway," he said, "thanks for being willing to share your perspective on things. It helps to hear that I'm not necessary to God's plans going forward."

Her eyebrows shot up. "I didn't mean to imply that you aren't part of what God's doing with—"

"No, it's good, Katherine. It's good to be reminded it's not about me. And maybe this was exactly the freedom I needed. Like what Mordecai said to Esther: if you don't step forward, help will come from somewhere else." He paused. "I need to keep remembering that the future of New Hope doesn't depend on me. It depends on God. So if I know I'm free to walk away, I also know I'm free to remain and dig in and do the work. With a good dose of humility."

What a good place to begin, she thought. And remain. "It seems to me the board is confident you're the 'for such a time as this' servant God has called, Logan. They haven't chosen you just to fill a slot. They recognize your gifts. I recognize your gifts. And I look forward to watching what the Lord will do in you and for you and through you as you continue to offer your next yes."

After they finished their call, she stretched out her legs and reclined in her chair. As for her next yes, a nap in the shade seemed the perfect way to embrace endings and beginnings. With a gentle breeze grazing her cheeks and a Carolina wren trilling from the uppermost branches of the honey locust tree, she opened her hands and closed her eyes.

"I woke you up, didn't I?" Sarah asked when her mother drowsily answered the phone. "I'll call you back later."

"No, no, it's okay. I'm awake."

Sarah lifted out a mixing bowl from the cabinet. "I won't keep you. Just wanted to thank you for the advice you gave me about Carol. We were able to talk a little while ago."

"Oh! I'm so glad to hear that!" Mom sounded sincerely pleased. "Did she apologize?"

"No, and I decided not to rehash anything with her. It's pointless, trying to hold someone who doesn't share my faith to my own expectations of integrity. Like you said this morning, I was demanding something from her that she isn't capable of giving. I need to let it go." If she could keep trying to listen to Carol with patience and compassion, that would be enough for now. "She's going through a stressful time"—no need to share any of those details with her mom—"and just needs someone to vent to. It might as well be me. I can at least be praying for her." And for herself as she listened to all the complaining. Forty-six minutes of it.

Love is patient. Long-suffering. Kind. Carol would provide ample opportunities for practice.

She went to the stove and lowered the heat for the pot of red potatoes, then removed celery and an onion from the fridge. "I know it cost you, Mom, encouraging me to reach out to her and try to move forward."

"Oh, I don't know about cost. It was more like an invitation to see things more clearly than I'd seen before. And to try to respond faithfully."

"Seems like that's the theme for a lot of us lately," Sarah said.

Morgan came into the kitchen and mouthed, *Who are you talking to?*

Gram, Sarah mouthed back.

"Hey, Gram!" she called.

"Morgan just came in, Mom. I'm going to put you on speaker so you can say hi." She set her phone on the counter.

"Hey, my sweet Morgan!"

"Hey! When are you coming to hang out with us?"

"Soon, now that I'm a retired lady."

"Are you? Cool!"

"Your mom says movie night and a sleepover."

Morgan raised her eyebrows. "You should spend the night here before your party. That would be way fun."

"I think that sounds way fun too," her mother said.

Sarah poked a potato with a fork. Ready. The skins ought to come right off. She emptied the pot into a colander in the sink, the steam rising. "Did I tell you Linda still makes your potato salad recipe?"

"Does she? I haven't made that in years."

"Zach fell in love with it, so I'm making it now."

"Micah used to like it too," her mother said.

"Did he?"

"Yes. He liked being in the kitchen. I didn't do much cooking, but he loved helping Linda with her pies."

Sarah shimmied the colander. "Linda told me that. She actually sent me home with some photos. I meant to bring those to show you, but I keep forgetting."

There was a slight catch in her mother's voice when she replied, "I'd love to see them."

"I've seen them," Morgan said as she poured herself a glass of lemonade. "I think I look a lot like Uncle Micah."

Sarah stared at her.

Morgan stared back. "What? Don't I?"

"Yes, you do, hon. I can see that."

Her mom added, "You've got your Uncle Micah's nose and mouth and your mom's pretty smile."

In reply, Morgan gave Sarah a cheesy grin. Sarah mimicked her, then lightly pinched her cheek.

"So, next weekend, Gram, right?"

"It's a date. I'll even make cookies."

"Ooh, Mom, now that's commitment!" Sarah couldn't remember the last time she had mentioned baking anything. "I'll make the potato salad," she said as she started peeling off skins.

"What's this about cookies and potato salad?" Zach asked when he entered the kitchen.

"We're planning a party, Zach," her mom said. "You're invited."

"Cool! Thanks, Kit!"

Sarah pointed to his chest. "Did you drive home like that?"

He glanced down. "Yep."

"He's wearing his stethoscope, Mom."

"Just in case there are any medical emergencies anywhere," he said. "Saves me time hunting for it." He wrapped an arm around Morgan and kissed the top of her head before putting the tips in his ears and extending the chest piece toward Sarah. She played along by taking a deep breath. "Normal," he said, then leaned in for a kiss.

"Don't let that daughter of mine hassle you, Doc. You do what you need to do to keep us all safe."

"He saluted you, Mom," Sarah said as Zach sauntered to their room.

Morgan rested her elbows on the counter. "Think about what movie you want to watch, okay, Gram?"

"Oh, I'll leave that up to you and Jess. Anything is fine with me."

"Then pray for the two of them to agree on something," Sarah said.

"Or we can make it a double feature," Morgan suggested, "and we'll each choose one."

"That'll work too," her mom said. "I'll be like water. I'll go with the flow."

Morgan laughed. "Okay. Love you, Gram! See you soon."

"Love you too, honey."

Sarah waited until her daughter retreated upstairs with her lemonade, then said, "You should see Morgan's face. She's so excited. She'll probably ask you to come to the lake next."

"Well, I think I'm long overdue on that too."

Surprise after surprise, Sarah thought. With a little bit of rearranging and the framing of a few family photos, the cottage would be ready for her visit. "I look forward to sharing that space with you again, Mom."

"So do I."

Upstairs, Jess was tuning her cello. Sarah hoped she would start with scales rather than diving straight into practicing the retirement party surprise. She turned off the speaker and picked up the phone. Best to avoid any potential spoilers.

"I'll let you get back to resting," Sarah said. "Let me know if you need anything, okay? I've got meetings all week at school, but we can work it out if anything comes up." Then again, Wren would be returning from Mara's sometime tomorrow. If her mother needed anything, Wren would be able to help. "Hope you're able to rest well tonight, Mom."

With an audible yawn, she replied, "I don't think I'll have any trouble at all."

They said their goodbyes just as Jess began playing the opening phrase of "Gabriel's Oboe." Sarah slid out a knife from the cutting block and started dicing the onion.

When Zach emerged from their room a few minutes later, wearing shorts and his "Don't Worry, I'm the Doctor" T-shirt, she gestured toward the ceiling.

He listened for a while, then said, "Your mom is going to love that."

"Yeah. She will." She pictured their daughter, her head gently swaying with the movement of her bow. "Don't film Mom's reaction when she's listening, though, okay? Just film Jess. And we're not going to show the testimony video at the party. Jess can edit all the clips together, and then we can just watch it here with Mom." That way, they could share in the beauty of the love and affirmation with her.

She swiped a few onion tears from her cheeks. "I told Wren she could go ahead and get Mom a tandem bike. I figure if Ed and Linda can have one, she'll be okay riding with Wren or one of us."

Zach grinned. "Way to let go, hon."

He didn't know the half of it. She would tell him everything while they drank their wine on the deck. As the last melodic strain from Jess's cello faded away, she pictured herself and her mom at the cottage, riding a bicycle built for two around the lake, and wiped her eyes again.

34

I can't thank you enough for putting me up the past few days," Wren said as they drove to Mara's church Sunday morning.

"It's been fun having you. You're welcome anytime the room is free."

Welcome. That was one of the many gifts Wren had experienced the past year, first from Kit and now from Mara and the neighbors who had welcomed her into their shared life. She had needed the quiet peace of Kit's home to recover and regain her sense of equilibrium. But the past few days at Mara's house had presented her with a vision of new possibilities. "Someday I'd love to live in a neighborhood like yours."

"My neighborhood would love to have you. Yasmin and Bibi will miss doing art with you."

"I'll come back. Maybe you'll look outside your window sometime and see me sitting at your table, coloring."

Mara laughed. "The girls will come running the second they see you." She glanced into her rearview mirror. "The neighborhood's pretty transient. If you want, I can let you know whenever I hear about any rentals opening up."

"Thanks, but I couldn't afford that."

"Not on your own, maybe. But with a roommate."

"I don't know. Casey and I had enough trouble trying to find someone to live with."

"Yeah, but you never know what opportunities will come your way. You just gotta stay open." At the traffic light, Mara rested her forearm on the steering wheel and turned toward her. "You hear back from your friend yet about being a reference?"

"Yep. She's okay with it." Just last night Allie had texted to say she wasn't working at Bethel House anymore—she had gotten married and moved to Lansing—but she wished Wren well and hoped the job would be a good match for her passions and gifts.

"Good," Mara said. "Get your application in, then."

Wren smiled. Ever since hearing about the job prospect, her mom had texted her the same reminder. Several times. "I submitted it this morning."

"Excellent."

Wren waved at the green light just as the driver of the car behind them honked his horn.

"Ah, cool it, buddy," Mara spoke into her rearview mirror. "You'll survive." When he sped around her in the right lane, she returned his middle finger with a wave. "You know 'em by their fruit, right? You drive like a jerk, chances are you're a jerk."

The other driver cut in front of them with a parting gesture.

"Nice," Mara said. "Class act, eh? Reminds me of my ex." She tapped the steering wheel in a jaunty rhythm. "Where were we? Oh, yeah. Job stuff." She tapped the wheel again. "I'd love for you to do art with our residents. Especially with the kids. I know there's no money in it for you, though."

"That doesn't matter. I'd love to do it."

"All right, good. Before you head back to Katherine's, let's get a date on the calendar when you can come to the shelter and meet some people."

"That sounds great."

They drove the next few blocks in silence, Mara seemingly lost in thought. "I know you've got a lot going on," she finally said, "and I haven't wanted to burden you with my own crap, but say a prayer for my son Jeremy, okay? He's been going through a rough time lately, and I've been worried about him."

Wren studied her profile. "Of course. I'm sorry to hear that."

"Thanks." Mara kept her gaze forward. "He got laid off work in July and started drinking again. Abby's had to give him ultimatums before, and he's always managed to turn it around with AA and help from his sponsor. But this time, he's not pulling out of it, so Abby took the kids and moved in with her parents a couple of weeks ago."

"Oh, Mara. I'm so sorry."

"I don't blame her," Mara said. "She's worried about the kids' safety around him—not that he's violent or anything. But he can hide it so well, she can't trust him to take care of them when she's working." She blew out a slow sigh. "Abby's parents moved down there after her father retired. Thank God. I don't know what she'd do without their help."

Wren pictured the women who sought refuge at Bethel House because they didn't have any other safe place to go after leaving alcoholic partners. She was glad Abby did. "Could Jeremy come and stay with you while he tries to regroup?"

Mara sighed. "That's what I was talking to Dawn about this week. Not sure it's a good idea. I've got my own codependent issues. I need to find a way to love and support him without trying to interfere and rescue. But boy, it's hard. You know about that. You went through it with Casey."

"Yeah. But this is your son. Your grandkids. I can only imagine what that feels like." She rested her hand on Mara's shoulder. "I'm so sorry." She didn't know what else to say.

"Thanks." They turned left into a parking lot filled with cars. "I learned a long time ago that Jesus does some of his best work right in the middle of the mess. I just need to keep watching for him to show up. And let him do his stuff. It's hard to wait, though. Especially when he and I never seem to be on the same schedule."

"I know what you mean," Wren said. "Hannah did a great preaching series a few months ago about all the waiting in Scripture and how God shapes us while we wait."

"Sounds like I should go online and listen to that one. Does she know you're coming to my church today?"

"No, I forgot to mention it to her."

Mara unbuckled her seatbelt. "Well, get ready for lively. Never know how the Spirit is gonna move when we're all together."

"Do you want a ribbon?" a little girl in a wheelchair asked Wren as she waited near the auditorium doors for Mara to finish a conversation. On her lap was a basket filled with streamers attached to short wands.

"What color do you think I should have?" Wren asked.

The little girl cocked her head, closed one eye, and sized Wren up and down. Then she reached into her basket. "How about yellow?"

"I love yellow!" Smiling, she accepted the wand from the child. "But I think I might need you to show me how to use it."

"Okay. It's easy." She chose a pink ribbon from the basket, then directed Wren to take a few steps back. "You have to hold this plastic part tight so you don't poke anyone with it, and then you wave it like this." She rhythmically swished the wand above her head, the ribbon gliding like a graceful kite tail. "But you can only march around during the songs. Not when Pastor's talking."

"Got it," Wren said.

"You can practice." The girl folded her hands in her lap and waited.

Wren held the wand near her chest and wagged her hand back and forth.

"No, do it higher. Like this." She raised her arm again to demonstrate.

Mara sidled up next to them. "Rosie, are you helping my friend?"

"Yep. She's new."

"Yes, she is, and it was very nice of you to welcome her."

Rosie reached into her basket again. "Here's your purple one, Miss Nana."

Mara leaned forward and kissed the top of her head. "Thank you, Miss Rosie."

Rosie giggled.

"Don't feel like you need to use that," Mara whispered as they entered the auditorium. "Then again, one of the kids might grab your hand and pull you into a procession. Or one of the grownups."

Wren grinned. "I'll go with the flow."

"It started out being just for Easter a few years ago, but the kids loved it so much we kept doing it every week."

Normally, Wren preferred the hiddenness of a back corner, but Mara led the way to the third row. As she slid into her chair, Wren eyed the worship team, relieved to see she wouldn't be subjected to the noise of a full drum set. Instead, a young man in dreadlocks and sandals sat on a cajón, drumming quietly as an older musician played a keyboard. At the other side of the stage, a small group huddled in prayer.

Given what Mara had described about the racial diversity of her church, Wren wasn't surprised to see the beauty of the kingdom on display as all different colors worshiped together. But what she also noticed was diversity in age and appearance and ability and culture: the muscular, tattooed man in a white undershirt who pushed Rosie in her wheelchair as she led the procession of ribbon-waving worshipers through the aisles; the well-dressed middle-aged woman who signed the whole service from the front, her facial expressions animated; the teen with Down syndrome who read Scripture and pumped his fist when he finished, shouting Jesus' name with such joy that Wren cried.

As she listened to people share prayer requests about unemployment and addictions and broken relationships, she thought about Casey. This was the sort of unpretentious worshiping community he might have found a home in. This was the sort of community that knew how to lament, weep, hope, and cry out together for the kingdom of God to be revealed. They knew how to celebrate together too. As Pastor Lamar preached in a rhythmic, musical cadence about new and old wineskins, the auditorium echoed with shouts of "Amen," "Well?," and "Hallelujah." Sometimes people jumped to their feet, hands raised or ribbons waving, and from somewhere a few rows behind them, someone expressed joy with the jangling of a tambourine.

"Told you it could be lively," Mara said after the pastor gave the closing blessing. As the band erupted into a musical response, some people knelt in prayer, others stood with arms lifted.

"It was beautiful," Wren said. "Every bit of it." She looked up at the overhead screen, where event announcements scrolled by on slides: prison ministry, prayer groups, Bible studies, literacy programs, AA meetings, a support group for people battling mental illness.

"I'm glad you came, Wren. Come again anytime. I mean, I know you're connected at Wayfarer and everything."

Wren ran her fingers along the ribbon, then wound it around her wrist. "I'm connected to Hannah, not so much to the church. But that isn't their fault. I haven't had energy to get involved. Lots of weeks it felt way too hard even to get dressed and go anywhere to worship."

"Lots of people here would understand that," Mara said. "You come as you are. No judgment."

As soon as the music faded, children carrying baskets raced up and down the aisles, collecting abandoned wands from chairs and the floor. "Are you done with yours?" a little boy asked Wren as Mara placed her wand in his basket.

"Oh, sorry. Yes." She quickly unwound the ribbon from her wrist and handed it to him before he raced off again.

"Rosie!" he called. "I got eleven!"

"Sixteen!" another yelled as all around the room children shouted out numbers.

Near the exit doors Rosie sat regally in her wheelchair, waiting. Wren smiled. Evidently, she was the arbiter of the competition.

"You want coffee or cookies or anything?" Mara asked as she retrieved her bag from beneath a chair.

"No, it's okay. I need to get going to the nursing home soon."

"Ah, right. I forgot all about the big party." Mara mimed a hula dance with her hands.

Wren laughed. "I'm happy to get an Uber. I don't want to rush you."

"Nah, it's fine. We can go whenever you're ready."

As Wren bent forward for her bag, her gaze landed on the stage, where musicians were putting away their instruments and a man wearing a backward ballcap was gathering wireless microphones.

She froze.

"Thanks, bro," the guitarist said as he handed him a mic.

She spun toward Mara, her back to the stage. "It's Chris."

"Chris who?"

"Chris-Chris. Casey's friend. The one with Brooke."

Mara craned her neck. "Here? Where?"

Wren gestured over her shoulder.

"That Chris is your Chris? The sound guy?"

Wren nodded.

"So, go say hi to him. I'll wait for you."

No, she didn't understand. "I can't, Mara. He'll think I'm stalking him."

"You're not."

"I know that. But he won't believe me."

"I'll vouch for you."

"No, it's okay. I'll just sneak out with you." Her hands trembling, she picked up her bag and hoisted it onto her shoulder just as—

God, no. Her knees buckled. She was going to be sick.

Brooke was shuffling down the aisle behind Estelle, gripping both her hands as she toddled forward on tiptoes, mother and daughter each grinning broadly. As soon as Chris saw them, he set aside the microphones and knelt, arms extended, waiting for Estelle to reach him.

Wren caught her breath. The scene was straight out of Vincent's *First Steps* painting, the man in his hat, setting aside his work to kneel with outstretched arms while the mother, stooping over her little one, urged the baby forward.

Mesmerized, she couldn't pull her gaze away.

"Wait," Mara whispered, "is that . . . ?"

Wren stood rooted to the spot, unable to reply. It should have been Casey kneeling there, waiting to embrace his daughter. She wished it could have been Casey.

A sixth sense must have alerted Chris he was being watched, because at that instant, his attention drifted and he spotted Wren, the wide-eyed confusion quickly morphing to furrowed brows. Brooke must have seen it too. Still clutching Estelle's hands, she half-turned, searching for whatever had distracted him.

Their eyes met.

No need to wonder if Brooke recognized her from photos. Face flushing with rage, she scooped up Estelle as Chris bounded to his feet and grasped her forearm. She shooed him away, then marched up the aisle with Estelle on her hip, an accusing finger pointed at Wren. "I swear to God if you—"

Mara quickly intervened, stepping around Wren into the aisle. "Hey," she said, lifting her hand. "It's okay. Wren's here with me. She had no idea Chris worked here, all right? She's as surprised as you are."

Brooke stopped in her tracks, her eyes narrow slits.

"I promise I didn't know," Wren spluttered.

"I didn't tell her I worked here, hon," Chris said when he approached. "The whole thing's just a weird coincidence."

"Or not," said Mara. She planted her hand on Wren's shoulder.

Chris did the same on Brooke's.

"Could be a God thing," Mara said. "Everybody just take a deep breath."

Estelle's eyes were fixed on her mother's face. Brooke pulled her closer, covering her head as if shielding her from the contamination of Wren's gaze.

"I'm so sorry, Brooke," Wren said, her heart pounding in her ears. "I'm so sorry for everything. I never meant to hurt you. I promise. I didn't know what Casey had done. He didn't tell me the truth. If I had known about Estelle . . ."

At the sound of her name, the baby squirmed and looked at Wren with such innocent curiosity, she almost burst into tears. Inches separated her from Casey's daughter. Let Brooke shout at her for the next two minutes. It would be two minutes of proximity to Estelle, two minutes being face to face with the little girl who carried his life forward into the world. She wished she could smile at his baby, wished she could reach forward and stroke her cheek or the little red curl dangling onto her forehead. Instead, she pinned her arms to her body, afraid they would defy her silent commands.

"I told Brooke about our conversation," Chris said. "It's a lot to process."

"I know, and I'm not asking for anything from you, Brooke. Just your forgiveness. If you can't manage that right now, I understand. It's okay. But maybe someday."

Brooke fastened her forehead to Estelle's.

Wren could feel Mara's thumb rubbing her shoulder, back and forth in silent solidarity, just as Kit or her mom might have done. "I'm so sorry Casey hurt you," Wren said.

Brooke slowly lifted her gaze.

Wren saw. Beyond her own desire for closure and forgiveness, her heart ached. Here was a companion in sorrow. In misfortune. In betrayal. "I can only imagine the pain he caused you. I think he saw it. I hope he did."

Brooke pressed her lips to Estelle's cheek. "I loved him," she said after a while. "But I couldn't help him."

Neither could I, Wren silently replied. She would leave their common grief and regret unspoken.

"That can hurt like hell," Mara commented.

Brooke nodded, her eyes welling with tears.

"Awww, give that woman a hug," Mara commanded Chris, "or I will."

Brooke's shoulders heaved with a combination of a laugh and a sob as Chris enfolded both her and Estelle.

Wren squeezed her lips together, determined not to cry. This wasn't about her. If she made this about her own need for help or comfort, she might sever the tenuous connection with Brooke. And then what?

"I've seen you here before, haven't I?" Mara asked Brooke after Chris released her from their embrace.

Brooke wiped her eyes with the back of her hand. "I've visited a couple of times since Chris started working here."

"Thought so. I recognize your baby. I had redheads too. She's gorgeous." Mara leaned closer to Estelle. "You're a little punkin, aren't you?" The baby studied her face before her lips broke into a wide grin. "Ah, look at you! What a smiley girl! Her name's Estelle?"

"Yes."

"Ooh, love that. I'm Mara, by the way."

Whether Mara was simply being her usual warm, chatty self or whether her friendliness was a calculated part of a de-escalation strategy, it was impossible to tell. But Wren wasn't going to interfere. While Hannah might have encouraged all of them to sit down for a moderated conversation, Mara was doing things her own way, and it was working. Brooke seemed to have nearly forgotten Wren was still standing there.

Mara reached out and stroked Estelle's chubby knee. Such an ordinary gesture. How deeply Wren wished she could do the same. "How old is she?" Mara asked.

Brooke smoothed Estelle's hair. "Eight and a half months."

"Get ready, she'll be cruising soon."

"Yeah, she's already started that."

Mara tickled Estelle's shin. The child beamed. "I work in the nursery here sometimes. Gives me my baby fix. Maybe I'll see you again."

No, keep going, Wren silently pleaded as Mara picked up her bag. *Don't end the conversation there.*

Brooke shifted Estelle to her other hip.

Don't go. Please. Wren searched in vain for something she could say that wouldn't freak Brooke out. She looked at Chris, hoping he might jump in and help, but he was staring at the floor.

Again, Mara placed her hand on Wren's shoulder. "Listen, Brooke, I know things are complicated here, and you don't know me from

Adam. You've got no reason to trust me or my word. But I actually met Casey when he came to town last year because he stayed at the homeless shelter where I work."

At this, Brooke's eyes widened.

"He told me his name was Kevin. I remember that because my son Kevin is a redhead too. I felt sorry for him. He said his wife had just died, and he needed a place to stay while he regrouped."

Chris's head shot up, his gaze now riveted on Mara. Brooke seemed too stunned to reply.

"We believed his story and let him stay a few days. Seemed like a nice enough guy. Far as I know, he never told Wren any of that." She looked at Wren for confirmation.

"No, he never did. When he called me, he claimed he had only just arrived at his parents' house but that he couldn't stay there. He wanted to crash at my apartment instead, but I didn't have one anymore. I had moved in with my great-aunt." She hesitated, trying to figure out how to phrase the next part without inflaming Brooke. "He told me he had to flee Reno because he was being physically abused"—at this, Brooke scoffed—"and I bought his story about needing help. All of it. Never questioned him." All her work at Bethel House had predisposed her to believe any story about abuse. Casey probably knew that. "When Mara told me what he'd said, I panicked. That's why I tried to contact you after he left, Brooke. When I discovered everything he'd been lying about, I was worried he might try to harm you. Or that he already had."

There was silence. The musicians had finished packing up their instruments and had left the auditorium. The children had long ago finished collecting their ribbons. From the lobby floated the mingled sound of chatter and laughter.

"Here's the deal," Mara said. "I work with lots of people with addictions and mental illness. I know how messy it is. And there's never just one victim. Casey suffered. No doubt about it. And everybody who loved him—still loves him—has suffered too. Maybe you can find some common ground in that." She gripped Wren's shoulder.

"Not to guilt any of you into anything, but I bet Casey would want his wife and the friend who was like a sister to him to move forward. You don't have to be friends. Just close out the past. Make peace. Life's too short for holding grudges. Believe me, I've held my share of them. Not worth it."

Brooke regarded the top of her daughter's head. Chris shifted his weight from one leg to the other. Wren silently prayed.

And Estelle puckered her baby lips and blew a raspberry.

Without missing a beat, Mara set her hands on her hips, tilted her head, and blew one too.

Estelle stared at her, buzzed her lips again, and then burst into such a hearty baby laugh, Wren couldn't suppress a chuckle. Brooke smiled too. Then she lifted Estelle's floral-print top and blew a raspberry on her tummy. Squealing with laughter, Estelle leaned back, her head upside down, and grinned at Wren. Without thinking, Wren extended her fingers and gently stroked Estelle's silky hair.

Immediately, Brooke shoved out her hand, scooped her daughter upright, and covered her head.

"Hey," Chris said quietly. "It's okay. Wren's good people, Brooke."

Squirming free, Estelle leaned back, her arms extended. Casey's daughter was reaching for her.

Wren swallowed hard. "I'm so sorry," she said, commanding herself not to cry. "I shouldn't have."

Mara looped an arm around her. "No harm done," she said, looking pointedly at Brooke. "Babies know. They just know."

When Brooke pulled her upright again, Estelle began to fuss. "We need to go," she said to Chris.

He turned his back toward Mara and Wren and whispered something to Brooke, who slowly inhaled and exhaled. Still clutching Estelle, she frowned at Wren. "I've hated you."

"I know. I understand."

Brooke combed her fingers through Estelle's hair. "I don't know if I can trust you, but I'm tired of hating you. And I don't want to

walk around Kingsbury every time I visit, worried I'll run into you.
I can't live that way."

"I understand."

Brooke took another long, deep breath. "She's getting fussy. She
needs her lunch. But if she'll let you, you can hold her a sec."

Wren was so startled, she didn't respond.

"Hold your arms out," Mara directed her.

It was all happening too fast. No chance to prepare emotionally
or mentally for a moment she had dreamed of ever since she first
discovered Casey had a daughter. All the prayers she had said for
this little girl, all the hopes she had cherished of someday, somehow
meeting her—everything merged into this single opportunity and
hinged on the willingness of an infant to be embraced by a stranger
who loved her with every fiber of her being.

Wren's lips trembled, and the tears streamed down her cheeks.

Brooke watched. And as she watched, her expression softened.
"It's okay. Just hold out your hands."

Wren extended them. Open. Waiting.

"That's your daddy's friend," Brooke said to her daughter before
kissing her cheek and offering her to Wren.

"Can I hold you, Estelle?" she asked quietly, her hands still extended. "Would that be okay?"

How long was that moment when the baby gazed into her eyes
with an impossible knowing? Then, with a tiny twitch of her head,
she thrust out her arms to meet Wren's and did not cry when Wren
drew her close and pressed her lips to her red hair.

35

As soon as she got home from worship, Kit changed out of her skirt and blouse, put on her lounge pants and a T-shirt, and made herself a peanut butter sandwich. With a few hours before Wren returned from Mara's, she wanted to read the cards she had been too tired to open after the retreat yesterday. "With everything else you've had going on," Russell had told her during their spiritual direction session on Friday, "you'll need to be deliberate about taking to heart the good words spoken over you." Yes, she'd had her blind spots, he said, but it was important not to let any regrets about oversights or missed opportunities eclipse the good work God had done through her

She murmured a prayer. "For all I've done well, thank you for your grace. For all I've done poorly, thank you for your grace."

As she ate her lunch and drank her tea on her patio, she savored the words of thanks and encouragement.

"You've helped me travel more deeply into the love of God."

"You've helped me see I can rest in his grace. Without condemnation."

"I'm saying yes to pouring out my sorrow and anger to God without being afraid he'll reject or punish me."

"Dear Katherine," the last note began, "I'm the one who knelt beside you on the floor while you were having your panic attack."

Kit immediately glanced down at the signature. *Barb.* A companion in affliction. No wonder she had known how to help.

"That was the first time in my life when I've seen someone else struggle like I do," Barb wrote, "so it was the first time in my life when I was able to offer help out of my own experience. I was able to 'steward my affliction,' just like you said in your talk. It was one thing to hear you talk about your mental health struggles during the retreat last spring. But it was another to see your struggles in person and to watch how you didn't express any shame afterward. You just pressed forward with this final retreat, without needing to apologize. I wanted you to know how that's given me courage. I've been praying about how God's strength is made perfect in my weakness, even in the weaknesses I'm ashamed of. Thanks for demonstrating how that's true. I hope someday you'll come to our church and speak about this type of affliction and how God meets us in it, and how we can boast about him in it, and how we can steward the comfort and hope we've received. Well done, good and faithful servant. Rest well."

Setting the cards on the patio table, she pictured Vincent's sower flinging seeds to the wind, not knowing where they would land or what kind of fruit they might bear. The harvest was grace, with all its surprises. Sheer grace.

"You're looking good, friends!" Kayla called out from the front of the activity room. She swished gracefully in a grass skirt while Don Ho crooned "Lovely Hula Hands" from a speaker. "Wave your hands. That's it!"

Wren watched as residents lifted and waved their hands as best they could while grandchildren—some more seriously than others—swayed their hips and tried to copy Kayla's movements. Near the speaker, a white-haired volunteer wearing a Hawaiian shirt and a red plastic lei strummed on a ukulele, his tongue sticking out of the corner of his mouth as he attempted to keep time with the recording.

"Move those fingers, everyone!" Peyton chimed in. "Good job! Lovely hula hands. Keep watching Kayla!"

Wren stepped closer to Mr. Kennedy's wheelchair as he tried to stretch out his trembling arms. Taking his hand in hers, she helped him make the gentle movement. When the song faded, he kept ahold of her hand, his tremor vibrating her arm.

"Give yourselves a good round of applause," Kayla said, clapping. "That was great!"

Wren lifted his hand in a victory grip as a familiar drumbeat sounded and a saxophone purred.

"Okay now," Peyton shouted above the music, "this is one of our favorites. C'mon, everybody, let's twist! Get those shoulders going. You know how we do it. That's it, Dorothy, show 'em how it's done!"

Teri, who was sitting beside her mother with a plastered smile, visibly fought tears as Mrs. Whitlock jiggled her arms.

Molting. So much molting.

With a silent prayer for both mother and daughter, Wren turned again toward Peyton, who was cueing the kids on when to freeze and when to start twisting again, lower and lower to the ground. Near the front of the room, one of the security guards twirled Audrey. Several of the residents clapped in time with the beat and looked as if they wished they could jump out of their chairs and show the kids how it was truly done.

"Take me by my little hand," Chubby Checker sang.

As if in response to the words, Mr. Kennedy squeezed her hand. Wren leaned closer to him. "Shall we twist a little in your chair?"

He swallowed before saying, "Sure."

"Okay, I'm going to take the brake off." He released her hand as she checked to make sure his shoes were securely planted on the foot plates. Then she backed him away from the group and gently began to weave the chair to the left, to the right, and around. Against his chest the tissue-paper lei she had helped him make swayed back and forth.

"And go like this," he said, and smiled.

He didn't want to come to a party, Mr. Page had told her when she arrived. Why would he want to be surrounded by reminders of everything he had lost? Or never had? "And the noise!" he'd said. "It'll be bad enough having to listen to it from my room."

Wren waited until all the residents and their family members were enjoying ice cream sundaes before she loaded vanilla scoops into two different bowls and smothered one with hot fudge, the other with pineapple sauce.

"Hungry?" Kayla teased as she sidled up beside her.

Wren grinned. "I'm taking them to Mr. Page. He can choose which one to eat."

"Don't let Greta see you, then. She told him he wasn't allowed to have any if he didn't come to the party for a little while."

Wren rolled her eyes. "That's pretty harsh, isn't it? I'll play stupid if I run into her. Or tell her I couldn't decide which kind I wanted."

Kayla laughed. "Good luck."

Wren wasn't sure whether she meant with Greta or Mr. Page. Maybe both.

His door was ajar when she arrived—probably at Greta's insistence. "Knock knock," she said as she observed his paintings hanging beside his shadow box. Either he hadn't noticed them in all his comings and goings, or he had decided not to object.

She pushed the door open with her elbow. He was dressed and sitting in his armchair, staring at closed blinds. "I've brought contraband, Mr. Page."

At this, he turned his face slowly toward her. "Ah. Not the kind I was thinking. Pity."

She set the bowls on his tray table. "I'm not eating both. Which one would you like?" When he didn't bother to look at either, she said, "Hot fudge or pineapple? You get to choose."

"You forget," he said. "I get to choose nothing."

Since cajoling never seemed to work with him, she decided to ignore the "Never talk back to a teacher" command inside her head. "It would be rude of you to make me eat by myself, Mr. Page. Choose not to be rude."

"Ah," he said with what appeared to be an effort to smile, "appealing to my long-lost gentlemanly self. Clever. Go ahead, then, ladies first."

"Do you like pineapple?"

"No."

She scooted the bowl with hot fudge closer to him. "I can tuck a towel into your shirt if you'd like."

"Fine."

As she stepped toward the closet, her gaze happened to land upon the wastepaper basket near his tray table, where a partially crumpled paper napkin displayed intentional pen strokes. Similar to what a very young child might draw, a few wavy horizontal and vertical lines nearly connected in the shape of a house. Or a covered bridge.

Her eyes blurred with tears. Even if he had discarded it, the effort was an inconspicuous, monumental victory. The first of many attempts, she hoped.

Pretending her shoe had come untied, she knelt near the basket, her back turned toward him, and swept his triumph into her pocket before rising to fetch a towel. Someday, she might present it to him in a frame. To remind him where he had begun again.

"You missed all the fun at the party," she said as she tucked the towel under his freshly shaved chin.

"Thank God," he replied.

She handed him a spoon, then sat down on the edge of his bed. "I sketched some of the kids. The ones that would hold still long enough, anyway." She had also sketched Teri with her mother, both wearing leis. Teri had thanked her. Profusely.

"No problem finding stationary models in a place like this," he said. "Even the ones who are trying to move."

She laughed. "Guess you're right about that. Plenty of opportunity for practice." Come to think of it, Vincent had done a lot of his early sketches at an almshouse for elderly residents in The Netherlands, including the *Worn Out* sketch Kit was so fond of. The residents were obliging helpers, willing to be dressed in a variety of costumes to suit Vincent's settings and themes.

She swirled the pineapple topping into her ice cream, then loaded her spoon. With painstaking slowness, he managed the same task in his bowl. The sundae would likely melt into a soupy mess before he finished, but she didn't want to embarrass him by offering help. After a couple of tries, he successfully maneuvered a first bite into his mouth, then licked the hot fudge from the spoon, his expression of satisfaction so subtle, he might not even have been aware he'd divulged his pleasure.

She wouldn't call attention to it.

"You're not wearing your uniform."

She glanced down at her blouse and tissue-paper lei. "I'm not working today."

"Then, why come?"

"Because, hard as it might be for you to understand, I like being here."

He scoffed. "Free to choose, and you choose this."

"Yes."

"Are you hiding from something?"

"Sorry?"

"Are you hiding from someone or something, Wren? Is that why you're here?"

She loaded her spoon again. "When I first started working here, yes. I guess that was true." She took her bite, then set her spoon down. Since he had asked a specific question, she decided to give a specific answer. "My best friend died. Casey Wilson. Do you remember him? He was in art class with me, and you persuaded him to help out with a school play once. *The Outsiders.*"

He appeared to be concentrating.

"Red hair," she went on, "skinny, freckles. Kind of a class clown."

"Casey," he repeated. "Yes. I remember." He stared at her. "He died?"

"Last December. Suicide, we think, but we're not sure."

"I'm sorry to hear that."

Before she could reconsider, she was telling Mr. Page everything: her long battle with depression and anxiety, her aborted career as a social worker, her stint in a psychiatric hospital, her life with Kit, her grief over Casey, her slog at recovery, her gratitude for Vincent and art. She didn't mention her time with Estelle, though. That was too fresh. Too precious to mention to anyone yet.

As she spoke, he listened without interrupting, his focused concentration on his bowl and spoon making it easier for her to confide in him.

"Age has no monopoly on suffering or losses or fear," he said quietly when she had finished pouring out her story. "Quote by Wren Crawford."

She was astonished he had been paying close enough attention to remember, let alone quote from their conversation about the mouse poem. "Vincent wrote about companions in misfortune," she said, "and Kit has helped me see that even though solidarity doesn't take away the pain, it makes it easier to bear." Someday, perhaps, she would tell him what she had discovered about Jesus' solidarity in the pain. But not today.

He set aside his spoon and lifted the bowl to his lips, the remaining liquid dribbling down his chin.

"Can you keep a secret?" she asked.

One half of his mouth curled into a slight smile as he lowered his empty bowl to the tray. "Who would I tell?"

She gently wiped off his chin, then untucked his towel and set it beside the bowl. "I applied for the volunteer coordinator job here. Audrey says I have a good chance of getting it."

"I would think you'd be overqualified."

"Maybe, but that didn't stop me from getting the cleaning job." She crossed her ankles and folded her hands in her lap. "I guess all of this has been a very long answer to your question about whether I've been hiding here. But with the other job possibility, it feels like I could start using some of my gifts again."

He looked at her a long time. "You didn't stop using them," he finally said. "Dig it?"

She cupped her hand over his on the tray table. "Yes," she said. "Dug."

When Wren opened the front door shortly after five o'clock, Kit was transferring cookies from a baking tray to a cooling rack.

"Smells good in here," she called as she set down her duffel bag and slipped off her shoes. She couldn't remember Kit making cookies before. "What's the occasion?"

"A welcome back gift for you. And a practice run on a promise I made to Morgan."

Wren kissed her on the cheek. "Peanut butter blossoms! Yum."

"Wait and see first." Kit peered out the front window toward the driveway. "Did Mara bring you home?"

"Yeah. She said to say hi and that she's looking forward to your party."

Kit gestured to the lei, which Wren had forgotten to take off. "How did yours go?"

"Good. Most of the residents enjoyed it, I think. Hard on some of the family members, though."

"I can imagine. It's hard to be reminded of everything you've lost when you can't see what you've gained." She put the spatula in the sink and turned off the oven. "What we miss, what we mourn—all of it speaks deeply to who and what we've loved."

In the quiet, Wren savored again her embrace of Estelle, feeling the weight of the baby's head upon her shoulder and the softness of her little hand touching her cheek before she grasped and tugged on a strand of Wren's hair. "Don't pull hair, Estelle," Brooke had commanded, and Wren had been afraid she might snatch her away. But Brooke let her remain. "She likes you," Mara said as Estelle gazed into Wren's eyes, and Brooke didn't disagree. When Estelle reached out and touched her lips, Wren kissed her fingers, then reluctantly handed her back to her mother. Better to give Estelle up than have her taken away.

Kit inspected the cookies. "Feel free to try one after they cool a bit. Micah was always my tester whenever I baked—which wasn't too often, but he liked these."

"I was always my grandmother's tester," Wren said. "I used to love being in the kitchen with her." She pictured Gran removing madeleines from the oven. *You have to eat them while they're hot,* Gran would say. They wouldn't even bother to sit down at the table first. As soon as Gran extracted the delicate cakes from the scalloped shell mold and sprinkled them with powdered sugar, they would stand at the kitchen counter and take that first bite, the steam emerging like a satisfied sigh.

"Bet you ate well at Mara's. She's quite a baker."

"Yeah. She's got a reputation in her neighborhood. She's Nana to all the kids."

"She landed in such a good place for her gifts," Kit said, and Wren agreed.

"Hope I'll see you again," Mara had said to Brooke before they left the sanctuary. Not "we." *I.* Wren wasn't sure if it was a deliberate choice, making that hope singular. But Brooke had seemed comfortable when she replied, "I'm sure you will." Singular "you," probably. But if Mara formed a relationship with Brooke . . .

No, Wren thought. Stop. No more stalking. No more trying to get information that wasn't freely offered. That would need to be a new spiritual practice going forward. With supernatural help. For now, it would need to be enough of a gift to have shared that singular, irreplaceable embrace.

"I'm hoping my friend Wren here will come worship with me again," Mara had said to Brooke and Chris in a "heads up, just so you know" sort of way. Chris had said, "Yeah. Sure." And Brooke hadn't disagreed. So maybe—

Or maybe not. It wasn't hers to manipulate or control. She just needed to keep moving forward in as much freedom as possible. And keep saying her next yes to God, whatever that next yes might be.

"You look like you're deep in thought," Kit said.

She pulled herself back to the present moment. "I have lots to tell you. Would it be weird to light the Christ candle and eat cookies?"

Kit laughed. "Recognizing the presence of God while we feast sounds perfect to me."

36

No point taking the day off, Kit thought as she drove to New Hope on Monday. The sooner she finished packing up her office, the sooner Wren could thoroughly clean and ready the space for Logan. Early that morning he had emailed to thank her for their conversation and to say he had taken the job and looked forward to introducing her to Nikki and the kids after they arrived in town.

Gayle was already at her desk when she entered the office. "You prayed, Katherine, didn't you?"

Kit shrugged out of her lightweight cardigan and draped it over her arm. "You were able to enjoy the wedding?"

"The wedding was gorgeous. All of us had a wonderful time." Gayle swiveled in her chair. "I'm talking about the job."

"You already got a new job?"

"No! The job here."

Kit looked at her, confused.

Gayle said, "You don't know, do you? Bill called me this morning. Logan's wife isn't going to be able to do the admin after all, so he asked if I'd be willing to stay. He said I've done good work and that it would help them out if I'd keep going."

"Gayle, that's wonder—"

"I know, right? I figured you had prayed for a miracle or something."

"I asked God to provide everything you need," Kit said with a smile, "but I didn't get specific with him." Well done to Logan, she thought. Well done to Nikki and Logan. And well done to the board. "I'm thrilled for you, Gayle."

"Thanks. I can't tell you how relieved I feel. I know it won't be the same, working for him, though. He might not be as patient as you."

Kit patted her shoulder. "Just be honest with him. Tell him what you need and see what he does." Only after she started down the hallway did she realize those words could be spoken of God too.

Slowly, she made her way past Vincent's paintings of sowers, reapers, wheatfields, and sheaves—each of them visual parables. She could email Logan and ask whether he wanted the prints to remain and assure him she wouldn't be offended if he didn't. She just wanted them to have a good home.

She stopped in front of a painting of a man and woman stretched out for a midday nap against a haystack, their sickles laid aside, their cattle grazing contentedly beside their wagon. If Logan could come to appreciate Vincent's work, she might suggest he take this one, *The Siesta*, to heart. In the midst of the planting, rest. In the midst of the reaping, rest. Don't wait until you're exhausted, she would remind him. Rest. And rest together.

Her phone buzzed with a text from Wren. *Bill's offering me my job back.*

Kit punched her number. "Really? What did you say?"

"I told him I'd think about it. But I feel like it's time for me to move on. Like I'm ready to move on. If I get the coordinator job, I couldn't keep going at New Hope anyway." She paused. "I'm going to tell him thanks, but no thanks. It doesn't sound like they're desperate for me to keep it, just that they didn't want me to be stranded without work."

Well done, Logan. Again.

When they finished their call, Kit walked over to the painting of the sower she had meditated on a few weeks ago, her attention drawn first to his open hand and then to the seeds falling on ground streaked with color. Pink. Lavender. Periwinkle and navy blue. Tan— or was it gold? She leaned in for a closer look. The seeds were dark— blue or maybe black, some of them marked with the same gold that streaked the ground. And—was this too much to imagine?—a few of them resembled tears. Lines from a favorite psalm came to mind, and she whispered them as prayer. "May those who sow in tears reap with shouts of joy. Those who go out weeping, bearing the seed for sowing, shall come home with shouts of joy, carrying their sheaves."

When she closed her eyes, she could picture the saints gathered at her childhood church, joyfully singing an old hymn she hadn't heard or thought about in years. "Going forth with weeping, sowing for the Master, though the loss sustained our spirit often grieves; when our weeping's over, He will bid us welcome. We shall come rejoicing, bringing in the sheaves."

Rest, beloved, she heard the Spirit whisper, *and come home rejoicing. Your work here is done.*

Slinging her sweater over her shoulder, she strode to the chapel, humming.

The lyrics were fine, Sarah decided, but the tune was totally cheesy. She finished playing the first stanza on the piano and groaned.

Zach looked up from the couch, where he was reading. "What's wrong? Sounds good to me."

"It's straight out of old *Little House on the Prairie* episodes. And now Mom wants us all to sing it at her party." She banged out the chorus melody, exaggerating the jaunty bounce of it.

He smiled. "Toe-tapping stuff right there."

"You can lead the marching around the room, then."

"She wants us to march?"

"No. I'm kidding. She just wants us to sing. And since it's the only thing she's requested for the entire party, I'm not going to say no." She would need to warn Jess and Morgan ahead of time, though. Enthusiastic participation, no eye rolling. "Mom said she has happy memories of singing it with her grandmother, and the sowing and reaping theme fits. The celebrating part too. I just wish there were a different tune."

"Yeah, but I bet a lot of the older people there will know it, and you don't go messing with the classics."

No, she thought. But it amused her to think of all the complaints she had heard over the years about contemporary praise choruses being repetitive when all this chorus said was, "Bringing in the sheaves, bringing in the sheaves, we shall come rejoicing, bringing in the sheaves." And then—repeat.

She studied the page she had printed from an online hymn site. She had to admit, the lyrics described well the work her mother had done: sowing in daytime and evening, in summer and winter, in sunshine and shadows. She had sown seeds of kindness. She had sown for her Master. And now it was time to celebrate the harvest and the end of this particular labor.

She played the verse again, then set it aside. "I think that's it," she said. "Everything else is ready." Wren had already set up tables and chairs in the chapel and buffet tables in the lounge. Gayle had decorated the space with fairy lights and silk floral arrangements from her son's wedding. The tandem bicycle, along with two helmets Sarah had purchased, was hidden away in a storage closet, ready to be presented.

She stared at the piano keys. Now that they weren't showing the tribute video at the party, there would be time for more singing. If her mom had requested one hymn, why not sing others? That would be the perfect way to honor her, not only in her love for music but in her desire to divert attention away from herself.

Good. Decided. She would ask Mom to pick two more favorites.

"Gram's here!" Morgan called as she bounded down the stairs to the front door. She must have spotted the car from her bedroom window.

Sarah rose from the bench and followed Morgan outside to greet her.

"Hey, my sweet girl!" she said as she embraced her granddaughter in the driveway. "I think you've gotten taller since your birthday party."

Morgan stood up straighter and tugged on the hem of her tank top. "Maybe a little."

"Hey, Mom." Sarah embraced her too. "So glad you're here."

"I'm glad to be here." She reached into the car and removed a round cookie tin with a snow-covered lane and a horse-drawn sleigh.

Sarah laughed. "I remember that! Save much?"

"It was either this one or the poinsettias. Seemed more festive than plain Tupperware. Especially for a slumber party." She handed the tin to Morgan, then opened the rear door.

"I'll get it, Mom." Sarah unloaded a small carry-on case and a garment bag. "Is this all you've got?"

"It's plenty for one night, don't you think? I couldn't decide what to wear for the party, so I brought options. Figured the girls could help me choose."

"Jess is the one who's good with fashion stuff," Morgan said.

Mom chuckled. "Not much fashion to choose from, sweetie. I just don't want to look silly."

"You never do, Gram." Morgan looped her arm through hers as they strolled to the house.

"Anything I can help you with, Sarah?" she asked after hugging Zach and Jess on the front porch.

"No, just come in and put your feet up, Mom. This is your time to relax and receive."

Smiling, she replied, "I can do that."

Zach reached for the bags. "I'll carry those upstairs. And how about if I fire up the grill in half an hour?"

"Perfect," Sarah said.

"Come and look at these pictures, Gram," Morgan called from the couch.

"Let her sit and relax first," Jess said. "You don't need to bombard her with stuff the second she walks in the door."

"It's fine, Jess. I've come to be bombarded with any stuff you want to show me." She set down her purse and made her way to Morgan, who had spread out the family photos Linda had found.

"I told you I look like Uncle Micah."

Sarah watched her mother's eyes fill with emotion as she bent forward to see them. "You do, honey. You sure do." She picked one up. "Ahh, there's Micah with his rocks." She ran her finger slowly across the photo, a tender and wistful expression on her face. "He loved collecting them. Your grandpa and I used to tell him he

couldn't bring the whole beach home. But he brought some of it."
She glanced over her shoulder at Sarah. "I probably still have some
of his polished stones in a basement box. I should find a way to use
them in my garden."

Sarah had forgotten about Micah's rock tumbler. Often, when
she'd gone into the garage to get her bike, he would be sitting at
Dad's workbench, reading his comic books while the metal cylinder
spun, the chemicals slowly working their magic. She had never paid
much attention to the finished product, which he had spent countless
hours organizing and inspecting.

"I've got Petoskey stones," Morgan said, "but I haven't polished
them. I just soak them in vinegar. I can show them to you later, Gram."

"Sure, I'd like to see them." They sat down on the couch to view
more photos. "Oh, goodness! Look at my kerchiefs. I forgot about
those. Maybe I should go back to wearing them. Save time fussing
with my hair."

"Head scarves are cool," Jess said as she poured herself a glass of
water. "I've got some if you want to try them again."

Mom grinned. "They must be an updated version if they're cool."

During their dinner of burgers, potato salad, and watermelon,
the storytelling continued, with tales about Micah and Dad and
Carol flowing just as freely and comfortably as ones about Mom or
Zach or herself or the girls. Hearing her mother laugh so heartily
was a gift. Sometimes their eyes welled up as they reminisced about
Micah, and this, too, was communion.

After the table was cleared and the dishes were loaded into the
dishwasher, Sarah said, "There's something we want to show you,
Mom, something Jess edited together for you. I had planned to show
it at the party but decided it was better to do it here."

Once the five of them were gathered in front of the television,
with Mom nestled on the couch between the girls, Sarah clutched
the remote control and, with a silent prayer, hit play.

Lucy. Her dear beloved mentor.

Kit leaned forward on the couch, eyes fixed on the screen. "The Lord bless you and keep you."

As tears splattered onto her lap, she mouthed the rest of the blessing along with her. How she ached to reach out and grasp Lucy's trembling hand.

And how grateful she was that Sarah had given her this beautiful gift in the intimacy of this setting rather than in a public space. Here she could gasp with uninhibited surprise and delight as each beloved face appeared on the screen. Here she could laugh and cry and remember with gratitude the life and wisdom and joys and losses shared. Face after beloved face. Here she could savor each good word spoken and give God thanks.

Who was she to have been the recipient of so much kindness? All of it offered with so much love.

"Did you like it, Gram?" Morgan asked after the last face faded from view.

She tapped her heart and blew a kiss to Sarah. Then she wrapped an arm around each granddaughter and kissed their cheeks.

So much love.

🐦🐦🐦

Wren had never been to a retirement party and wasn't sure what to expect until she saw a copy of the program. Words of welcome from Sarah. An opening prayer from Russell. Expression of thanks from Bill. A few testimonies. Singing "Great Is Thy Faithfulness," "Bringing In the Sheaves," and "Amazing Grace." A cello solo from Jess. The presentation of gifts. And a closing prayer from Hannah.

Though Wren had planned to sit at a table with Hannah, Nate, Mara, and their friend Charissa, Sarah insisted that she join them at the family table near the front. From her seat between Zach and Morgan, she had a good view of Kit's response to each part: her surprise and wonder, her laughter and tears, and her occasional shifting in her seat when people effusively expressed their praise and appreciation. Frequently, Kit tapped her chest to express heartfelt, wordless gratitude, and when Jess returned to the table after playing a stirring rendition of "Gabriel's Oboe," Kit stood and embraced her with unmistakable pride.

"Want me to help you wheel it in?" Zach whispered to Wren as the applause faded.

She had been so caught up in the music, she had forgotten about the presentation of the bicycle. Sarah was standing near the piano, looking in her direction. Wren jumped up from her seat. "It's okay," she told him. "I've got it."

As soon as Wren reached the front, Sarah stepped up to the microphone. "Sometimes we learn things about our moms that we never knew before," she told the crowd. "For instance, I learned this week that one of the songs we sang today—'Bringing In the Sheaves'—is a song Mom remembers her grandmother singing with her, not just at church but at home too. Mom told me they used to march around the yard, singing the words to old hymns, and this was one of their favorites. I told her we could sing it on one condition—that we not have to march—and Mom agreed."

Kit laughed with the rest of the room. When Zach leaned across the table to say something to her, she laughed again and nodded.

"The other thing I learned about Mom a few weeks ago is that ever since she was a little girl, she's wanted a particular gift."

Wren caught Kit's eye. With a questioning eyebrow and a "You didn't, did you?" look on her face, Kit steepled her fingers to her smiling mouth.

"A gift she never got," Sarah went on. "Until now."

That was Wren's cue. As Sarah hit the play button on the "Daisy, Daisy" song, Wren retrieved the bike, which had been concealed behind a row of chairs, and wheeled it to the front. Kit rose, grinning and shaking her head and pointing her finger at Wren in a playfully accusatory way.

"We won't ask you to give it a spin yet, Mom," Sarah said above the music. "But when we've finished eating the delicious feast Mara has prepared for us, we're all going out to the parking lot to watch you take your inaugural ride with Wren."

This was news to her. Wren had pictured the first ride belonging to mother and daughter. She stared at Sarah, who smiled and nodded and pressed her hand to her chest, just like her mom.

Still gripping the handlebar, Wren tucked her head to her shoulder and wiped her eyes.

"Good job with that one, Wren," Zach said after she embraced Kit and returned to her seat.

Morgan added, "That's way fun."

Casey, she knew, would have agreed.

After Kit received a gift envelope from the board, Hannah stepped forward and asked her to remain near the podium as she offered a blessing and a closing prayer. "Katherine," Hannah said, "we rejoice in all the good work our God has enabled you to do. We celebrate your faithful stewardship of all he has entrusted to you. Our words of appreciation and affirmation today are only a small portion of our gratitude, and we share in a much larger community who bear witness to the difference your love and generosity have made in our lives. Paraphrasing Paul's words to Philemon, 'We have received much joy and encouragement from your love, Katherine, because the hearts of the saints have been refreshed through you.'"

Kit swallowed hard.

"Even as we celebrate the good work God gave you to do and your faithful completion of that work, we remember that we are not defined by our work or our usefulness in the kingdom. Our worth and significance are not based on what we do for God but in who we are to him and in what he has done for us. You are God's beloved, Katherine. You are the one Jesus loves. In his love and by his grace and through his power, you enter a new season of life. Even as we mark this significant change, though, we also mark all that has not changed. May you continue to know the lavishness and faithfulness of God's steadfast, enduring love for you. And may you continue to enjoy the love of dear and trustworthy traveling companions on your journey."

Hannah stretched out her hand to the gathered community. "If you're able, please rise and extend your arms toward Katherine as we commit her to God's care and pray his blessing upon her."

Kit cast a tearful, grateful look around the room, as people who had shared the journey with her stood and reached out in love. Then, bowing her head, she opened her hands to receive.

Early Monday morning, before she started her final cleaning shift at New Hope, Wren stood with Kit in the lobby, listening to Bill tell Logan and Nikki the story of watching them ride off into the neighborhood on the tandem bike.

Logan gently pushed Eli's stroller back and forth, rocking the weary toddler to sleep. "I sure hope someone got video."

Kit laughed. "I'm told that multiple versions have already been shared."

"From all different angles," Wren added. She had already sent Zach's party footage to her mom, who had been delighted by all of it.

"Sounds a bit like riding off into the sunset," Nikki said, her green eyes crinkling in a smile. Savannah, who was a little younger than Phoebe, looked up at her mother, then ducked behind her long white skirt and pulled back the ruffled hem, revealing a cross tattoo on Nikki's ankle, just above her strappy sandals. Her turquoise toenails matched her Batik print blouse.

"A perfect ending," Bill said. "Tell Sarah again what a great job she did, planning everything. Mara too. If we ever have any other events that need catering, we know where to go." He looked at his watch, then at Logan. "I need to get to the office. All right if I check in with you later?"

"Sure. Sounds good. We're just going to do a quick tour before Gayle gets here. I promised Savannah she could see the courtyard garden."

"Do you like flowers, Savannah?" Kit asked as Bill waved goodbye.

Savannah peeked out from around her mother's skirt and nodded, her long blonde curls bobbing.

"Ever seen sunflowers? The really tall yellow ones?"

She emerged from hiding. "I like to pick the seeds out."

Kit and Wren exchanged looks. "That's exactly what we need to do," Wren said. She bent forward so she could be eye-level with her. "We need to pick the seeds out so we can plant more sunflowers. Would you like to help?"

Nikki placed a hand on her daughter's head. "What do you say, Savannah?"

"Thank you."

"How about 'yes, please'?"

Savannah parroted the words, then clutched her mother's hand.

"Why don't we head there now?" Kit said.

Logan motioned for them to walk ahead of him, then followed with the stroller. As soon as they turned the corner, Nikki gasped. "You didn't tell me!" she called to him over her shoulder.

"Tell you what?"

"All the Van Gogh prints!"

"Sorry, hon. Didn't know that's what they were."

She scoffed. "I've been trying for years to convert him, but he just won't budge."

"You like Vincent?" Wren asked.

"Like him? I love him!" She stopped in front of one of his sowers. "Who put these up?"

Kit said, "Wren's the artist."

"Oh, we'll have so much to talk about." Nikki viewed a few more along the hall. "You did a great job curating. I guess I'll let my husband off the hook. These aren't the well-known ones."

"Nikki paints too," Logan said.

"*Used* to paint," she corrected him. "Before we had kids."

So, Logan was married to an artist. Interesting. She might have guessed from Nikki's clothes and pendant jewelry and colorful threaded charm bracelets, which adorned both her and her daughter's wrists.

Guess he wasn't anti-artist after all. The guy was full of surprises.

"Wren's kept her studio here this year," Kit said. "She's done beautiful paintings for us."

"I'd love to see your work," Nikki said. Savannah tugged on her hand. "After we see the garden. First things first." But as they walked past the open door to Wren's studio, the room cluttered with empty cardboard boxes, Nikki stopped again. "Are you moving out?"

Wren was so taken aback by her question, she wasn't sure how to reply.

"I guess we both just assumed," Kit said, "since she won't be working here anymore."

Logan leaned over the stroller to reposition Eli's teddy bear. "I'm sorry, Wren. I never even thought about that. Let me talk with the board. If you'd like to keep your space here, it's fine with me. I can't imagine we'll need the room right away. Down the track, maybe, but not yet."

Again, full of surprises.

Nikki refashioned her long curly hair into another loose ponytail, a few unruly tendrils escaping the quick and casual sweep. "You might decide you need an artist in residence down the track too, hon." She turned toward Wren. "I keep telling him, he'll need to make use of every bit of creative energy and vision the community has to offer. And art reaches across barriers. All kinds of barriers. As an artist, you know that."

I'm not a real artist, Wren was going to object. But, meeting Kit's eyes, she changed her mind and said, "Yes. I do."

When they arrived at the courtyard, Savannah took off skipping toward the row of bowed sunflower heads, their petals lining the ground. Beneath the towering stalks, the child stooped and picked up something from the dirt. "Look!" She waved a gray feather above her head, then tucked it behind her ear. "Daddy! Come pick me up!"

Logan parked the stroller in the shade and checked to make sure Eli was asleep. Then he clasped Nikki's hand, and together, they joined their daughter to harvest the seeds.

Kit smiled at Wren. "I'm no artist, but it seems to me that all those fallen petals look a bit like feathers that have molted. Might make a nice painting someday."

In her imagination Wren could already see the composition, how the cast-off golden petals of the sunflowers would intermingle with the cast-off crimson feathers of a cardinal, like flames engulfing the soil. There on that holy ground, she would paint a bird stripped of its visible glory, picking at the scattered seeds. And if you looked carefully, you might just glimpse tiny stubs piercing through the tender skin. Like feathers of hope, waiting to unfurl.

ACKNOWLEDGMENTS

My beloved son, David, was my coauthor in every way, from the conception to the completion of this book. I can't overstate the impact he had on the development of the characters and the arc of their stories, and it was my greatest joy to spend 2020 writing *Feathers of Hope* with him. Words can't adequately express my love and gratitude for you, David, and I couldn't be prouder of who you are. Thank you for sharing the journey with me. I hope we have many more writing adventures together.

Like Katherine, I'm on a journey of confronting my own blindness and sin regarding issues of racial justice and reconciliation. I'm deeply grateful to Sharon Ramsay, who gently accommodated my first tentative steps in exploring these themes in this book. Sharon graciously received my ignorance, asked perspective-shifting questions, and helped me see what I hadn't yet seen. Thank you, friend.

I'm also deeply grateful to Gloria Curry, Tiffany Sturdivant, Claudia Guillaume, and Kaitlin Murphy, who served as sensitivity readers. Each of you offered significant insights and suggestions that shaped the content of this book. Your voices matter, and your encouragement is a gift to me. Thank you.

Heartfelt thanks to friends who read early drafts and gave generous feedback: Krisha, Jeff, Rachel, Elizabeth, Debra, Cathline, Amy, Tamera, Rosie, Maureen, Nancy, and Shalini. Thanks, too, to Hugh Cook, for editing the first draft with the gifts of a skilled and compassionate teacher. And to readers who sent me personal accounts about life in nursing homes from the perspective of staff, residents, and family members, thank you. I was honored to receive your tender stories.

Rebecca Konyndyk DeYoung shared with me the spiritual practice of keeping an anger journal. Gail Ramesh answered all my questions about middle school math teachers. Sean and Amy Nemecek taught me about pinfeathers. And Shirley Moerdyk introduced me to Socrates. Thank you, friends.

To my ministry partners at InterVarsity Press. Thank you for every generous yes you have said to me along the way. Special thanks to Cindy Bunch, my trustworthy editor. I mean "trustworthy" in every sense of the word. You are a gift.

To Mom, my very first proofreader. Thank you for sharing your wisdom and holding me in love and prayer. All my work has been better because of you. I love you.

To Dad, who cheers me onward from his place in the communion of saints. I miss you. I love you.

To Beth, the best kind of sister and friend. Thanks for always telling me the truth and sharing the journey with me. I love you.

To Jack, who lays down his life in love, enabling me to say each next yes. I love you and thank God for you.

To my readers who take these books and characters to heart and who encourage me to press forward. I'm so grateful for you. Let's continue to learn and grow and say yes to all of God's invitations. And may we glimpse his presence in all the prickly places of discomfort and change.

And finally, to Jesus, in whom all God's promises find their yes. "For this reason it is through him that we say the 'Amen,' to the glory of God" (2 Corinthians 1:20). I love you, Lord. *Hineni.*

RESOURCES

For Mental Health

- National Suicide Prevention Lifeline: 800-273-8255. This is a 24/7 line. If you or someone you love is in crisis, please call this confidential number for immediate care. You can also text HOME to the Crisis Text Line at 741741 or go to www.suicidepreventionlifeline.org.

- National Alliance on Mental Illness (www.nami.org) works to raise awareness and provide support for those afflicted with and impacted by mental illness through advocacy, local support groups, and education.

- Grace Alliance (www.mentalhealthgracealliance.org) provides Christian mental health resources and programs for individuals and families, as well as leadership tools for developing active community support.

- Fresh Hope for Mental Health (www.freshhope.us) provides Christian mental health resources through support groups, an award-winning blog, podcasts, and webinars.

- InterVarsity Press publishes many excellent nonfiction books about mental and emotional health. Here are a few that may be helpful:

- *Grace for the Afflicted: A Clinical and Biblical Perspective on Mental Illness*, Matthew S. Stanford
- *Troubled Minds: Mental Illness and the Church's Mission*, Amy Simpson
- *Grieving a Suicide: A Loved One's Search for Comfort, Answers, and Hope*, Albert Y. Hsu

FOR GRIEF AND SPIRITUAL FORMATION

- *A Grace Disguised: How the Soul Grows Through Loss*, Jerry Sittser
- *A Sacred Sorrow: Reaching Out to God in the Lost Language of Lament*, Michael Card
- *When Heaven Is Silent: Trusting God When Life Hurts*, Ron Dunn
- *Broken Hallelujahs: Learning to Grieve the Big and Small Losses of Life*, Beth Allen Slevcove

FOR ART AND SPIRITUAL FORMATION

- *Contemplative Vision: A Guide to Christian Art and Prayer*, Juliet Benner
- *Spiritual Formation: Following the Movements of the Spirit*, Henri Nouwen with Michael J. Christensen and Rebecca J. Laird

FOR VINCENT VAN GOGH

- All his letters are available to read online: vangoghletters.org.
- *Learning from Henri Nouwen & Vincent van Gogh: A Portrait of the Compassionate Life*, Carol A. Berry
- *Vincent van Gogh: His Spiritual Vision in Life and Art*, Carol A. Berry
- *At Eternity's Gate: The Spiritual Vision of Vincent van Gogh*, Kathleen Powers Erickson
- *The Shoes of Van Gogh: A Spiritual and Artistic Journey to the Ordinary*, Cliff Edwards

FOR RACIAL JUSTICE AND RECONCILIATION MINISTRY

- *Be the Bridge: Pursuing God's Heart for Racial Reconciliation*, Latasha Morrison
- *Mother to Son: Letters to a Black Boy on Identity and Hope*, Jasmine L. Holmes
- *White Awake: An Honest Look at What It Means to Be White*, Daniel Hill
- *Birmingham Revolution: Martin Luther King Jr.'s Epic Challenge to the Church*, Edward Gilbreath
- For more resources, see books on racial justice at InterVarsity Press, ivpress.com

ALSO BY
SHARON GARLOUGH BROWN

Feathers of Hope Study Guide
978-1-5140-0064-9

Remember Me
978-0-8308-4670-2

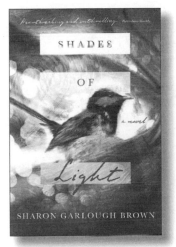

Shades of Light
978-0-8308-4658-0

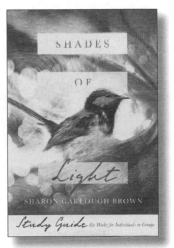

Shades of Light Study Guide
978-0-8308-4664-1

Visit sharongarloughbrown.com for book club resources

The Sensible Shoes Series

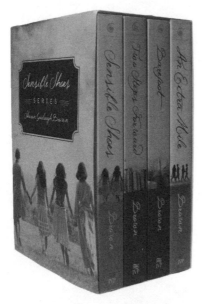

Sensible Shoes

Two Steps Forward

Barefoot

An Extra Mile

STUDY GUIDES

For more information about the Sensible Shoes series,
visit ivpress.com/sensibleshoesseries.
To learn more from Sharon Garlough Brown or to sign up for her newsletter,
go to ivpress.com/sharon-news.